WATCHLIST

WATCHLIST

32 STORIES BY PERSONS OF INTEREST

EDITED BY BRYAN HURT

CATAPULT  NEW YORK

Published by Catapult
catapult.co

Anthology selection copyright © 2015 by Bryan Hurt
All rights reserved
First published in the US by OR Books

ISBN: 978-1-936787-41-8

Catapult titles are distributed to the trade by
Publishers Group West, a division of the Perseus Book Group
Phone: 800-788-3123
Library of Congress Control Number: 2015951166

Printed in the United States of America

9 8 7 6 5 4 3 2 1

To Kate and Bonnie

Contents

Contents

Contents

Introduction

It began with the baby monitor. Months before I'd conceived of this book, my wife and I bought an Internet-connected camera to watch over our infant son as he slept. With a swipe of our fingers we could call him up on any of our iDevices—on our phones while we were out to dinner at our favorite Thai restaurant, or on our tablets while we watched TV on our couch—and there he'd be, butt lifted cartoonishly into the air, breathing softly but visibly, in grainy green-and-black. We could swivel the camera 180 degrees, taking in all corners of his room, or zoom in on his face, and then past his face, filling our screens with two giant, dilating nostrils, an open mouth. Then we could go back to eating our vegetarian spring rolls, or watching whatever it was we were watching on TV. Seeing him was a comfort. Watching him meant we knew that he was safe.

When I told my neighbor—novelist and contributor to this very anthology Alexis Landau—about the camera, she asked if he could see it. Did he know that he was being watched?

We were at the park, pushing our kids on the swings.

I told her that the camera was on a table next to the crib, a few inches away from his face. "It's not like we're spying on him," I said.

But her question lingered. Were we spying on him? Was my son aware of the camera we had trained on him while he was sleeping? At the time he was six months old and the only direction he'd figured out to crawl was backward. I doubted that he was aware of the camera, and even if he was, so what?

I shrugged and went back to pushing.

Get used to it, little dude. Being watched is part of life.

WE ARE BEING watched. That this statement probably no longer shocks is itself somewhat shocking. But ever since Edward Snowden revealed the NSA's massive, clandestine surveillance program in June 2013, we've been inundated with news—seemingly every week—about yet another aspect of our once-thought-private lives that is now subject to some kind of scrutiny. We've learned that the U.S. government or one of its allies has been reading our e-mail, listening to our phone calls, and watching nearly everything we do on the Internet—Facebook posts, Google searches, instant messages, World of Warcraft gaming sessions. In early 2016 Apple was called before Congress to testify about its refusal to obey a court order to unlock an iPhone that was used by one of the terrorists who murdered fourteen people in San Bernardino, California, in December 2015. Privacy experts said that the stakes couldn't be higher. If Apple were forced to comply with the court, it would be required to build custom software for the FBI that would create a so-called backdoor into the San Bernardino iPhone, and other devices like it, that would allow law enforcement to access everything on it, from location to e-mail and text messages. Worse, it would set a larger precedent. "If a court can ask us to write this piece of software, think about what else they could ask us to write," said Apple's CEO, Tim Cook, in a recent interview. "Maybe it's an operating system for surveillance, maybe the ability for law enforcement to turn on the camera. I don't know where it stops. But I do know that this is not what should be happening in our country."

Yet so far we've responded to news of this surveillance with . . .

. . . a burp of indignation . . .

. . . some outrage in the op-eds . . .

. . . by and large, a collective shrug.

Perhaps we're largely untroubled by this news because it doesn't register as anything new to us. Every private thing that's been taken, we've already been giving away for free. Facebook, Twitter, Instagram—since the advent of social media, and long before it, we watch ourselves more closely, keep tabs on each other better than any government agency ever could.

The technology certainly helps. Pew Research estimates that collectively we now spend seven hundred billion minutes on Facebook each month. But in the eighteenth and nineteenth centuries, aristocrats would also invest lots of time *and* money to pose for intimate portraits that they would put on public display. There's value in being seen—always has been—and so it's funny but not coincidental that the word *status* is linked so integrally with today's social networking: the more you see me, the more I'm worth.

WATCH SOMETHING AND you change it. This is something that we all know pretty intuitively, and something that's been explored by philosophy and science. Photons change from waves to particles when they're observed under electron microscopes. There's the paradox of Schrödinger's cat.

We act differently, perform differently, when we know we're being watched. Or even when we think we are. That's the logic of the panopticon, the circular prison in which the inmates can't escape the watchman's eyes.

The question that inspired this book is how we are affected by this constant surveillance. Does a camera trained on a sleeping child change him? How does an ever-present, faceless audience alter who we are? One way to interpret the Delphic maxim "Know thyself" is to take it as a warning to ignore the masses, their judgment and opinions. But what does it mean when our notion of self is tied so inextricably with our notion of audience? In a world without privacy, what becomes of the private self?

I decided to explore these questions through fiction not because fiction gives us good or definitive answers—good fiction is very bad at that—but because fiction allows for the widest range of inquiry. Through stories we can document, verify, speculate, scrutinize, judge, and watch. Stories help us put human perspectives and particularities on otherwise faraway topics and distant news headlines, drawing us closer because of fiction's powerful empathic lens. Fiction, then, is another kind of surveillance technology. We read to better see and understand the world around us—other places, other people, other lives. But the best stories inevitably do much more than that. They help us see ourselves by revealing the unacknowledged and undiscovered parts within us, the parts of ourselves that we had not uncovered, that we had not yet known. We read stories to see the world and to see ourselves.

When I approached the contributors for stories about surveillance, the only guideline I gave them was that the book's scope would be broad and imaginative. I'd take stories that were "ripped from the headlines," that were set in far-flung and not-so-distant futures, or that took place one hundred years in the past. What surprised me about the stories they gave me was not how uniformly excellent they are or how thoroughly they explore the topic—I expected that all of the stories would be excellent and that they'd leave no stone unturned. There are stories collected in *Watchlist* that are political, apolitical, ethical, cautionary, realistic, experimental, "genre" stories—science fiction, historical, noir. Stories by authors who are well known and stories by authors whom you'll know well soon enough, authors who should be on your own personal "watchlist." What surprised me was that despite their breadth, each of the thirty-two stories in *Watchlist* suggests that the real price of surveillance is intimacy. The more we know about each other, the less we actually know.

For what it's worth, I hope they're wrong, even though I know they're not.

Still, stories are powerful not because they let us see the world as it is—fallen, flawed, full of loss—but because they show us the world as it can be. The most powerful stories help us recuperate loss, transform it, and turn it into something beautiful, a work of art. So here's an alternative surveillance story I propose, a fantasy, I know:

Watching is close attention. Close attention is an act of love.

So get used to it, little dude. Being watched is part of life.

—*Bryan Hurt*

Nighttime of the City

by Robert Coover

She drifts through the bleak nighttime of the city like an image loosely astir in a sleeping head, disturbing its rest, destined for the violent surreality of dreams. She wears a belted black trench coat, a black silk scarf around her throat, a black felt hat with a wide pliable brim shadowing her face. Streetlamps mark her isolate passage, drawing her out of the velvety dark and casting her back into it, until, under one where she is expected to appear, she does not. Nor is the clocking of heels on wet pavement now heard. There are echoey calls and whistles, as from hungry men, but none are seen, nor is she. As if by a conjuring, a man wearing a black narrow-brimmed fedora now appears under the streetlamp that had been awaiting her arrival, his belted black trench coat not unlike hers, black silk tie and white collar at the throat. Somewhere there is a menacing rumble as of a train passing underfoot or overhead. As it fades away, the man withdraws a pack of cigarettes, taps one out, fits it between his lips, drops the pack back in his pocket, lights the cigarette inside cupped black-gloved hands. His sharp cruel features are briefly illuminated. Then, hands in pockets, cigarette dangling in the shadows beneath his hat brim, he slips into the dark space she was last seen entering. Distantly, a siren can be heard, rising, falling. She reappears, stepping into the damp light, then continues on into darkness, into the light of the next streetlamp, into darkness, light, gone again. A second man appears under the streetlamp toward which she had last been moving, dressed like the first. The soft muffled rumble, ominously coming and going. He cups his gloved hands, lights a cigarette, disappears into the shadowed space she last entered. Faint wail of a distant siren. After it fades to silence, she reappears, moving from streetlamp to streetlamp as before. The two men, thought dismissed, if they be they, have also returned, cigarettes burning beneath their hat brims, and they follow her at the distance of a lamp, visible, then lost to sight, as she is visible, lost to sight. She pauses under a lamp. They pause. There is a third man already standing under the next one, his face in shadows. He cups his gloved hands, lights a cigarette. The wings of his white collar gleam at the margins of his black silk tie like place markers. She turns back: the other two are silently watching her. She steps into the darkness. Hat brims lowered, they follow. There is something like a sighing wind, rising, falling, and the streetlamps brighten, dim again. Behind them in the darkness, nothing can be seen or heard, but for what might be the scurrying of vermin, the icy clicking of knife blades opening. But then a bottle shatters explosively against a brick wall, and there is suddenly a blazing light, revealing an alleyway heaped with headless corpses clothed in black. Not far away, tires are screeching, cars crashing, and something like screams that are not screams rip past and fade again. She rises impassively from the pile of bodies, and as the headless men also slowly rise, she reaches up as if to pull down a window blind. As her hand descends, darkness does as well. Silence.

She enters an elegant white marble bar filled with men, some headless, some not, those with heads wearing black fedoras, lit cigarettes in the shadows beneath their brims. There are mutterings, the scratch of matches, clinking glasses, chairs scraping, all fading as she enters, a glacial silence falling. She crosses the white room under her broad-brimmed black hat, hands in trench coat pockets, black heels ticktocking on the marble floor, toward a black leather door at the other side. The men, those headless, those not, their white shirt collars crisp and gleaming, rise to follow her. She pauses at the door as the men gather menacingly around her; then she opens the door and steps into the next room, the men pushing through behind her. But only she arrives on the other side, a severe and solitary figure as before. It is a glossy white marble bar much like the other one, with motionless men scattered about, some with heads, some without, faint barroom sounds fading away to a taut silence. Her measured tread on the marble floor fills the silence the way a heartbeat might resound in a hollow stone breast. A headless man rises to block her passage, two men with heads and hats, cigarettes aglow beneath the brims, a second headless man, a third. She passes through them as though they were not there to the black leather door at the other side, where she pauses. The men crowd up around her, threateningly as before. She steps through to the next room; they step through. But only the men arrive on the other side. They stumble about in seeing and unseeing confusion, knocking over tables, chairs, each other. They turn back toward the door. She is standing there, just beyond the threshold in the room that they have left, scarved and hatted. She closes the door. They press against it, pounding on it silently or on each other as darkness descends.

She moves down a dark street lined by parked cars, her way lit only by the occasional streetlamp, each dropping a small puddle of wet light for her to step through. As she passes, headless men and others with heads in black fedoras step out of the parked cars and follow her in and out of the light of the lamps. She turns down an unlit alleyway, heels clocking hollowly, now little more than the shadow of a moving shadow, the men behind her jostling one another between the dark brick walls, their shirt collars eerily luminous. Where the alley opens out onto the lamplit street, she pauses. Behind her, the walls of the alley, grating harshly, slam together on her pursuers. She crosses the empty night street (distantly, sirens cry and fade away) to the next alley, followed by another lot of men in belted black with and without heads and hats, many emerging from parked cars, streaming in from all directions. This time, at the far end, she turns to watch impassively from under her wide soft hat brim as the brick walls crash shut. In the docklands, they follow her out to the end of the pier, her heels thudding on the wet wood to guide them in the dark. Some of them are now pressed flat, looking like paper cutouts of men in belted trench coats, some of these with heads and hats, some also without. She steps silently aside. The headless ones, unseeing, both flat and full, tumble off the end of the pier, and those with heads, pushed along by the confused headless ones, tumble in, too. The water is soon filled with drowned men. The flat ones float on top along with bobbing fedoras, their bodies rippling rhythmically as the waves roll under them and softly lap the pier.

In the rail yard, she crosses the tracks in total silence, the hatted and headless men following, the flat ones wrinkled and waterlogged, the full ones bloated, and they are crushed by a train roaring suddenly out of the night.

She stands in pale light against a brick wall as if pinned there, her face shadowed by the wide soft brim of her black hat, hands in her black trench coat pockets. Somewhere, hungry men are growling and muttering. Her shadow darkens in contrast to the rapidly brightening wall. She steps out of the dazzling light as the men pursuing her step into it, and a large truck, horn blasting, tires screeching, crashes explosively into the wall, its own headlights extinguished by the impact, dark descending amid an invisible rain of falling brick and felt fedoras.

Everywhere there are men under streetlamps, stepping out of parked cars, those with heads lighting cigarettes, all of them roaming the docklands, moving in and out of bars, patrolling the rail yards, and scurrying—seeing and unseeing—through the bleak labyrinthine streets of the night city. There is an occasional ominous rumble, underfoot or overhead, and the distant wail of sirens can be heard, the crumpling of crashing cars, the muffled *kerwhumps* of dull explosions. Also, from time to time, never far away, the echoey hammering of heels on pavement, which causes the men to pull up short, cock their ears if they have them, turn toward the clocking heels, then continue, redirected, when they stop. The men are headless or else they wear black fedoras, brims pulled down over lit cigarettes; they are wet and ripply if flat like cutout men or bloated if not, and all now carry silvery handguns in their black-gloved hands. Remotely, shots can be heard, the whine of ricocheting bullets. Sometimes a man falls clutching his chest, but after a moment rises again to continue his mazy pursuit. Drawn by the pulsating footsteps, the men converge upon a small barren lot from which lamped streets radiate damply in all directions. She appears out of the ubiquitous shadows, first in one of the wet streets, then another, the men firing upon her wherever and whenever she is seen. She appears in two streets at once, dually approaching the men in the empty lot, then three, five, eight, all of them. There is a rattle of gunfire in all directions, the glittery shattering of glass, the dull thuck of bullets striking bodies; she is fragmenting, disintegrating in all the streets, while the men—flat, full, hatted, headless—topple, one after another, surrendering their small measure of dignity to the black city streets. She walks, whole again, among their sad crumpled bodies, glass crunching underfoot; then, as the streetlamps brighten briefly, only to fade again, she disappears into the descending night. The men are all dead. No, they are not. They rise once more, step under streetlamps, light cigarettes in cupped black-gloved hands, tug their hat brims down if they have them, adjust their black silk ties in their gleaming shirt collars, cock their ears. In the silence, the clocking heels resume.

Sleeping Where Jean Seberg Slept

by Katherine Karlin

My school librarian was first to tell me about Jean Seberg. Miss Breedlove, her cat-eye specs suggesting a whiff of counter-cultural recalcitrance, recognized in me a sullen fellow soul, and she pulled a book from the shelf to show me: here was Jean on *The Ed Sullivan Show*, and here were Jean's bewildered parents; here was Jean arriving in Paris; here was Jean burned at the stake. Jean was from Marshalltown, a Saturday morning bike ride from our town of Edna, the prettiest girl in Iowa, and of all the pretty girls in America she was chosen to play Joan of Arc. She lived in Paris and she married a famous writer. She was a movie star. And you can't blame Miss Breedlove for withholding the rest—the dead child; the wicked COINTELPRO harassment; Jean's own boozy, blub-bery decline; the death in a white Renault, obstructively parked in a Paris alleyway, her body in such an advanced state of decrepitude it had to be scooped, not lifted, into the gendarmes' body bag. The librarian wanted to show me there was life beyond Edna.

And I was hooked. Unbelievable that the same late fifties Paris that produced Brigitte Bardot—that portable mattress, who spent her days curled up and waiting—also gave us Jean Seberg, darting around the arrondissements in her beep-beep Citroën, leaving her lover at the curb, lightly adjusting the rearview mirror with a "Sorry, darling," and a revealing flick of the wrist. Lithe and slightly androgynous. She was as much a product of Iowa as of Paris. Here from the humus with the corn and soy and swine she grew, her Nordic blood the same as mine.

I left Edna the day after I graduated from high school and today I am back, twenty years older. Early mornings I hear from across town the hoarse shriek of pigs about to be gutted. Sometimes I wake up terrified that I will die in Iowa, although I'm only thirty-eight. Jean Seberg died at forty, and when I was a teenager that seemed like a good long life—who wouldn't want to die upon finding herself forty? Now I'm close enough to smell the blood. I lie in bed and listen to the hogs, and I count all the bad choices that forced me back to Edna.

On the night of the Iowa caucuses, Edna seemed like a good idea. I was living in Russian Hill and had been handed my eviction notice, and calculated how far east I'd have to go to find a place my proofreader's wages could afford. There on the TV was our mayor; there was our town, and our state that put Obama into play. I left California in the afterstink of Proposition 8, heading for something brighter, same as I'd once left Iowa for San Francisco. Someplace spacious, quiet, a chance to write the book on Jean Seberg I'd always wanted to, the unburdening of her legacy.

This morning in May I turned on my computer and struggled with Jean's story, getting hung up in the place I always got hung up. Her friendship with Hakim Jamal, such an itchy self-promoter even the Black Panthers ejected him. Jean met him on a plane. Now, to most people, the very fact that he was flying first class would be enough to trigger a note of caution. Or later, when he accepted her offer of a ride in Sammy Davis Jr.'s Learjet, or when he lounged in Davis's Lake Tahoe retreat, claiming it as his safe house, hectoring Jean about his several enemies.

Yikes, Jean. Try (and I do) to see this misstep in its historical context, the heady lure of Black Power, this is the moment she betrays herself. I just can't channel her intentions. What I channel is a powerful thirst for a caramel macchiato. Lucky for me, one of Edna's new acquisitions is a Starbucks. Not an actual Starbucks, but a Starbucks kiosk in the supermarket, with a couple of the trademark burgundy comfy chairs adding authenticity. I wouldn't have been caught in a Starbucks in San Francisco, but I'm grateful there's one in Edna. When I was in high school the only place to get "gourmet coffee" was a Christian tchotchke shop that kept a thermos of lukewarm hazelnut and a sleeve of Styrofoam cups amid the doilies and angels.

At one time elms and oaks lined the streets of Edna, but they have been dismantled by disease and by guys in orange vests, bobbing overhead in cherry pickers. Trash trees—hackberries, locusts, Arizona ash—have replaced them; the sidewalk is littered with spongy green pods and the yolky innards of cardinal eggs. I moved into a cottage five blocks from downtown; walking, and maybe someday bicycling, was part of the vision of my small-town repatriation. I'd forgotten how clammy and cold a Midwestern spring could be, crystallized fog bearing down hard. Already the cherry pickers were out, amputating limbs still in bud. The thrum of a bass came from somewhere, it got louder and louder, and then, there was a tattoo of horns.

I turned the corner of Decatur Street and ran into a parade, led by three brown-skinned girls in white spangled leotards, chubby girls with sincere smiles. A few dozen people, old people and little kids, stood about the sidewalk, waving. Rows of trumpeters, twelve or thirteen years old, marched while they followed the music on their lyres. A few trombones, a lone girl in a French braid blowing a tuba, and then, five men in dark shirts with embroidered yokes playing mandolins.

I had forgotten. It was Cinco de Mayo.

Then came the floats, a truck from Mama Rosita's, a ragtop Caddy from Esquivel's, the fire engine and a couple of squad cars, strobes flashing. At last, in a white Ford pickup, our mayor, Charlie Burt, waved both arms, wildly, as if he were drowning, followed only by a couple of farm tractors dragging Porta-Johnnies.

Charlie Burt was not your typical small-town mayor. Anyway, not what I thought of as a mayor. He wasn't a guy in a cheap suit and a comb-over, some petty-level bureaucrat who went into public service to work off a bankruptcy. Charlie didn't own a suit, and if he had hair I never saw it. He always wrapped his skull in a bandana, biker style, changing the bandana as the mood suited him, and today he wore a Snoopy and Woodstock pattern. He had on his usual Lee jeans with a watch fob, denim jacket, and a John Cougar Mellencamp T that dated back to *Scarecrow*.

"Whoa, whoa," he said, staggering as the Ford halted. "If it isn't Odile Dahlquist."

I came up alongside the truck and shook his hand. The door to a Porta-Johnny flung open and a boy in a striped shirt hopped out with a trombone in his hand.

"You all right there, Javi?" the mayor asked.

"I got stuck in there when the parade started," Javi mumbled, trotting past us.

"Happy Cinco de Mayo," Charlie Burt said to me. "You know, I heard you were in town, what was it, I think Florence Rasmussen over there on Lombard said she had run into your mother, at the Lutheran church I guess it was."

"If it was church, it wasn't my mother." Why did I argue? Iowans could go on all day about the minutiae of hearsay.

"Well then it was some such, I guess the potluck they had for the crisis shelter."

"That's possible."

"I'll tell you what," the mayor said, "we're only going to be parading for another two blocks, what do you say I buy you a corunda and an agua fresca at the fairgrounds."

With a lurch, he was off. The parade headed up to the fairgrounds and I followed, like a stray hound. That corunda sounded good but I really wanted that macchiato.

What if Jean Seberg's passions had been allowed to flare up and die, as a man's would be? Maybe there would be no infant buried under the Marshalltown willows, no abandoned Renault. Jean herself, in her seventies and thick with brie, would be wearing muumuus in a Parisian apartment and granting the occasional interview to the perseverant Godard fan or Belmondo biographer. It pleases me to think that the baby, Nina Gary, would have grown like other second-generation Euramericans, dour like her father, plucky like her mother, maybe an actress, choosing roles in communally made Danish films or playing heroin-addicted bounty hunters in gritty indie flicks.

But Jean was a woman. A woman who had ideas. An *attractive* woman who had ideas, and this is why she had to be neutralized. Hoover chose her as his mission. While she was busy creating art, or raising money for Watts preschools, Hoover and his band of sweaty gnomes studied her phone calls, letters, meetings transcribed by some poor junkie who ducked jail time by offering Jean Seberg. And the feds, spittle at the corner of their lips, their suspenders strained, their lentil brains taxed, could bend the evidence into a single narrative, the only narrative they could understand: the blonde from Iowa liked dick, and lots of it. In particular, black dick.

THE BOY AT the Edna supermarket Starbucks took a lot of pride in his product. He was talking to a woman in a leopard-skin top, thinner than most of the women I saw in Edna, thinner than me.

"This has two shots," the boy said.

"Two shots?"

"You usually have one so I don't want to jolt you."

"Oh, what the hell!" The woman slapped the counter and turned to me conspiratorially. "Jolt me!"

She was middle-aged and wouldn't know me.

"Odile Dahlquist, as I live and breathe. I heard you were back in town. I think it was Faye Eckhardt at yoga told me she spoke to Cindy Franck at the Golden Cup."

The espresso machine squealed.

"You don't remember me," she intuited. "Megan McKibbee. I *used* to be Megan Sondergaard."

The name swam toward me: the smell of Obsession and overcooked peas, and something about a broken zipper. Whoever she was, she triggered unpleasant associations.

"You've been living in California, right? I always said you were meant for big things. You with that haircut, that cocktail hat with the birdcage veil." I did have a hat. And a haircut. "So why *did* you come back?"

I was not about to mention Jean Seberg. I did not want to dangle my pearl before this particular sow. When she was handed her latte with a whipped cream dome she reared like a pony, pointed her phone, and snapped a picture of it.

I let the Starbucks boy sell me a muffin with my macchiato, and I ate it quickly, wiping my finger grease on a tiny cocktail napkin. I carried my macchiato to Swensen Park, named for the enterprising brothers, pig farmers, who came up with the idea of disemboweling the swine right here in Edna, carving them for good parts, grinding the rest for baseball franks and hosing the blood into a cistern so it could be siphoned for headcheese. The Swensens could not have guessed their eponymous park would be the roaming grounds for a Cinco de Mayo party, ranchera music blaring from the cars, the pickups dressed in bunting, the children from the band, relieved of their duties, wandering in groups of three or four with their instruments in one hand and ices in the other, babbling with the rush of accomplishment. Everything about this party—the refreshments, the clothes, the classic convertibles—had been planned for a much warmer day.

Our mayor was now in a striped serape and a sombrero, spread-armed like a prophet, blessing the subjects who approached him with a goose in the ribs or a jocular half nelson. I was in high school during the last strike, the big strike, when Charlie Burt was the union president, leading a very different parade of angry meat workers down Decatur and toward the gates of the abattoir from which they'd been locked out. The slaughterhouse employees were Anglo then, the grandsons of the Germans and Swedes who busted this sod a century ago: my dad and my uncle, Charlie Burt, almost everyone we knew. They never got back into the plant; my father works at the jail now, and comes home in the morning to sit still for an hour or two. The tendons of his hands were so often serrated, his fingers curve in a permanent cup-shaped craw.

My parents hold a lot of goodwill toward Charlie Burt. Everybody does. That's why he's been mayor so long. He spent his political capital smoothing Edna's transition. In my weekly phone calls from California I heard my father's voice ebb in bewilderment. Charlie Burt says don't blame the Mexicans, they're just workers same as us, except they get paid half as much. Charlie Burt says it's a good thing, brings business to town: the taqueria, the money-transfer agency, the furniture rental. My father would be looking out the window, watching the tree surgeons bobbing in their baskets.

I have to credit the mayor, with his biker clothes and horse teeth. Edna never turned into one of those news-making towns like our Iowa neighbors, busting landlords for housing immigrants, jailing Mexicans for traffic violations, threatening the schoolteachers who refused to turn over lists of Hispanic-surnamed children. Edna had soccer games and harmony dinners, and when the one priest in town refused to perform Spanish mass, Charlie Burt persuaded the Lutheran minister to donate church space to a Spanish-speaking circuit priest who rode into town once a week. Even the mild Lutherans put down their collective foot when Charlie Burt suggested hanging a crucifix at the altar.

Charlie spotted me and cuffed the top of my spine in his enormous scarred hand. "Look here, everybody," he said. "This here is Odile, and she went off to California for a few years but now she's back. Odile, I bet you never thought we'd have a true-to-life Cinco de Mayo right here in Edna, did you?"

"I guess not."

"A lot's changed here in Edna. A lot's changed. For the better! Let me buy you something. A corunda, Mexican wedding cookies." He enunciated coo-roon-dah. "You can't get those in San Francisco, can you?"

"Actually—"

"You know what mistake they made out there? Putting everything in the dot-com bubble. Here in Edna we never had a bubble.

That's why we're still thriving. We're going to be thriving, too. As long as people eat bacon we will be okay."

His boosterism exhausted me. The hand on the neck felt good, though. It hit me how many weeks it had been since a man's fingers had been wrapped around my neck.

To be honest, I'd had a girlhood crush on Charlie Burt. Who didn't? Charlie talked slow but clever circles around management, Charlie faced down the cops, Charlie chatted on the phone with Bruce Springsteen. I've been tainted by San Francisco, though, where a guy as ungroomed as Charlie would be mistaken for an old roadie who would pin you to a barstool with his tedious tales about touring with the Dead.

Still I went out for coffee with Charlie Burt, for a drink at the Lion's Den. For dinner. Jean Seberg had instilled in me early the thirst to go out with a variety of men: young/old, cute/ugly, married or not. I wanted to be that girl in the Citroën pulling away from the curb.

I guess I am not the best person in the world to tell Jean's story. But what the fuck, nobody else is doing it. Her evaporation from the landscape depresses me; there are mornings I don't want to inhabit a world that fails to imagine Jean Seberg. Before I left San Francisco I had a long talk with a girl who made me believe, fleetingly, the city still could be young and hip: she was a collagist who procured police reports of rapes, scissored them up, and reassembled them as poetry. I thought she would be interested in Jean Seberg, and I rambled, the way my mother used to ramble to my friends about having once seen Patricia McBride dance (her fondest moment!), ignoring the polite, indifferent coughs. I heard myself tell the girl all about Hakim and his wife, about the Panthers, about J. Edgar Hoover's vow to neutralize her, and when I paused the girl said, "I hate it when people racialize everything. I just don't see people in terms of skin color." Which made me want to go to bed. Forever.

But instead of honoring Jean's story, weaving the threads that resist any pattern, I ordered a floral dress and T-strapped sandals. I got a thrill when the UPS box arrived, and I ordered more: a book about the FBI, an espresso maker, garnet earrings. I dedicated a corner of my kitchen to flattened cartons. I picked a fight on Facebook with a Bay Area friend about how the anti–Prop 8 campaign went wrong. I saw in my newsfeed a group of women celebrating a birthday and I was haunted, throughout the day, by the certainty that, even if I had been in California, I wouldn't have been invited. I came to think of Edna as a deeply earned jail term.

"That's why I try not to get involved with the so-called social media," Charlie Burt said, as we sat in a booth at Esquivel's. "Now, don't get me wrong: I tweet. But only in the name of the city of Edna."

"You tweet?" I helped myself to the tomatillo salsa.

"Only as the city of Edna. I sing its praises. Of course, people know it's me behind the avatar, judging from the comments I get. Not all of them kind, mind you."

"How could anyone not be kind to you?" I asked. I wasn't flattering. Charlie created a circle of calm around him, a fortress. I had been trying to be unkind for days to no avail.

"Oh, well, you'd be surprised." He sliced his enchiladas with his knife. "Now, usually, what they have to say is not very original. But sometimes people can get very creative, particularly with anatomical improbabilities and commands of incestuous actions and some such and so forth. But, like I say, that's not the usual."

"What's the usual?" I asked.

"Oh, you know. Nigger lover, spic lover, faggot lover, badabadonk, badabadink." His do-rag had a *Finding Nemo* motif. Charlie's daughter was a pediatric nurse in Iowa City and every week she drove out to Edna to sponge down his countertops and bring him a box of old scrubs he could scavenge for kerchiefs. She was a blond, jolly girl, strong round arms; she friended me after we met and filled her page with pictures of her and her girlfriends hoisting martinis and affecting gang signs.

"Still?" I asked.

"Every day."

"Every *day*?"

A boy of twelve appeared from the kitchen with a broom and long-handled dustpan. He started sweeping in brisk strokes, as if he were raking leaves.

"I'd say about every day. You would be amazed what people can say from the veil of anonymity. You would be amazed."

Guillermo Esquivel, the owner, a man with a comically alarmed mien, brought a plate of flautas we hadn't ordered.

"Now look at that," Charlie Burt said. "How much do I owe you, Guillermo?"

Guillermo wagged a finger at him.

"You are too good to us," the mayor said. "Now this right here is the upside to being mayor."

Charlie's daughter told me when the Mexicans began to appear—first by carload, to be housed in trailers off State Road 24, then by van and bus—Charlie did more than welcome them. "He totally went native." She had a raucous laugh; she seemed to inherit all of Charlie's equanimity and was uncursed by his powers of reflection. "That's the reason my mom left," she said. "Two years of a lockout? Hey, no problem. Black union janitors from Chicago sleeping on the living room floor? That's cool. But once he jacked the pickup on hydraulics she hauled outta there."

I said to Charlie, "That's what fucked up Jean Seberg. Anonymity. The rumors about her getting pregnant by a Black Panther. She got so upset, her baby died a few hours after birth."

"Oh, well, sure. But that was the FBI." Charlie threw one arm across the back of the banquette and rubbed his belly with the other hand. "That was a sophisticated operation." One thing I liked about Charlie was that I never had to explain to him about Jean Seberg. He knew all about her, as he knew about all the famous people from this part of Iowa—an astronaut, an opera singer, a gay novelist from the fifties. A mass murderer, too.

"The net result is the same, isn't it," I said darkly.

"Neutralizing? Well, only if you allow it to be. Of course I don't attract the interest of the FBI. Not anymore. No, I just attract a bunch of cowards with too much time on their hands. Now that poor girl there, she never had a chance."

The sweeping boy came to our booth and gestured impatiently at my feet. I lifted them and he swept beneath me, knocking my soles with his broom handle. The front window admitted the milky haze of the Iowa afternoon. The streets were damp and empty; hard to believe we once crowded them, shoulder to shoulder, meatpackers with their wives and kids, hollering for an end to the lockout.

"I wonder what happened to all those strikers," I said.

Charlie stared where I was staring. "Oh, they're still around. They just all went indoors."

AFTER I HAD Googled Barack Obama a couple times I started getting pop-up ads for chocolate singles. Every morning at the same time I craved a macchiato, went to the supermarket Starbucks, and ran into Megan McKibbee, who was now concerned that the Iowa Supreme Court had legalized same-sex marriage. "I'm *concerned*," she said, photographing her beverage. "I am not a homophobe. But I do believe in freedom of religion." The oftener I saw Megan the more I remembered her from high school, sitting in the front of

English class, waving her hand, declaiming that Jane Austen was so *relatable*.

I drew deeply on my iced macchiato, trying to induce brain freeze.

Jean Seberg's baby, Nina Gary, was buried in Marshalltown, not far from the rest of the Seberg family (except for Nina's parents, both suicides, both laid to rest in Paris). The Riverside Cemetery was inclusive, but segregated: the Catholics lay across the footpath from the Lutherans, the Germans cordoned from the Swedes, with a small but special spot for the blacks; the veterans mingled in death as in life. It was a gorgeous old graveyard, shaded by sycamores. There was Jean's father, Ed the pharmacist; her mother Dorothy; her brother David, who celebrated his high school graduation gunning the dusty road to Edna and was killed when his car skidded and ignited a dry patch of grass; Jean's beloved grandmother, a frontierswoman with a creative streak, the only member of Jean's family who adored meeting the likes of Bobby Short and Burl Ives. The graveyard was tended but not manicured, bouquets here and there in various stages of desiccation, one freshly dug grave awaiting its coffin, the black Iowa clay piled alongside it. The tombstones straight or leaning. I considered buying a little bunch of forget-me-nots at the cemetery shop to place on Nina's grave, but what was the point, really? Who would see? Instead, I took a picture.

I ordered a black cocktail dress that was supposed to be straight out of *Mad Men*. I had no idea where I would wear it, and by the time it arrived I'd gotten too fat.

Charlie Burt asked me to ride with him outside of town. There was something he wanted me to see. I fiddled with the door release of his pickup and listened to him go on, something about the family farm. During the strike the farmers surrounding Edna crawled into town on their tractors and threshers, parading in support, blocking the access of the Iowa Guard. They had their own troubles, deep in debt, looking down the barrel of foreclosure.

"Oh, they kept their farms all right," Charlie explained. He talked so slow I wanted to stuff my hand down his throat to unthrottle his words. "If you can call it that. But they gotta *buy* everything from Monsanto and they gotta *sell* everything to Monsanto. The family farmer is no better off than a sharecropper." I began to think Charlie Burt might be insane. How would I know? He was the only person I regularly talked to; I had no frame of reference.

As we drove by the slaughterhouse Charlie fell silent—from nostalgia or rage, maybe both. I thought about the packages of madeleines they had at Starbucks, whether I'd want that or a biscotto when we got back to town. Charlie had a Mexican station on the radio, a cheery accordion.

"See, look there," he said. We had just crossed the Edna limits. I strained to see what he was pointing out, a filament on the horizon. Then another, then another, taller than telephone poles, white and slender. I hoped whatever Charlie wanted to show me we could see from the pickup; laziness drained me.

Windmills, they were. Three blades apiece, at any moment two blades lifted 120 degrees, like raised arms in a glyph of despair. The more I looked, the more of them emerged, scare quotes on the horizon, ahead of us and behind us, blotting out Edna, and the hogs and crops.

"It's a wind farm, Odile!" Charlie Burt had to shout so I could hear him over the hum. He pulled to the side and hopped out. Luckily the shoulder was banked so I had only to roll out of my side of the cab. The noise was everywhere but, like the polyphonic buzz of an air conditioner, so constant as to be hardly perceptible. This was a good spot, all right—the wind, which we hadn't noticed in the middle of Edna, was wild here: Charlie had to tighten the knot on his *Little Mermaid* bandana. "What do you think?"

"It's nice," I yelled, unconvincingly.

"It's the future!" His left eye watered; condensation collected on his cheeks. "Green energy." His voice rose and fell with the turning of rotors. "Don't matter if Obama wins or Hillary, they're both committed. And Iowa is going to be right here at the heart of it."

And then Charlie Burt, the mayor of Edna, released a cowboy whoop, as if the energy carried through the cables beneath us thrummed through the soles of his boots.

"You can't outsource energy," he said. And he took off running, toward the windmills, which seemed too far away to touch. I think he clicked his heels. As he trotted away he looked back at me, like a dog, and the farther he ran the more I wanted to lie down on the moist ground, the dead May grass on my cheek, the soil enriched by ancient glaciers, acid wind, and waves of newcomers, the flat earth absorbing every desecration of our ancestors. Here was the blood of the shoats born for slaughter, here were the severed tongues of our grandmothers, here were the amnia they buried, here lay the stillborn imagination, here are the intestines and the shit, here are seeds of corn. And the snakes slithering from the creek beds, the farms and towns that rose and subsided, the punishment for the girl who transgressed, the atrophy for the rest of us. Here grew a girl who wanted to leave a mark in the dirt, and for that she was eviscerated, in body or in spirit, whichever put up the least resistance.

Testimony of Malik, Israeli Agent, Prisoner #287690

by Randa Jarrar

I'm waiting for the Turks to x-ray me. They placed me under arrest two nights ago, after the bloody fight in Karaköy. I am flightless, stuck in a small metal cage. They assigned a guard to me. The guard is very alert. Whenever I stretch out or move my neck, he turns to observe me. They think I'm a spy. Me. A kestrel. A very small falcon.

I would never be a spy. As a child, I saw the bodies of collaborators hung from the lines my kin and I used to hunt from. Their bodies swayed. The punishment for spying was always death. And death never appealed to me.

My name is Malik Hassan Kareem El-Hajj Aamer Ahmed Kan'oun. Yes; my great-grandfather Aamer performed the pilgrimage to Mecca. He flew there from our village of Aqraba, over Jerusalem, past the Dead Sea and the ruins of Petra, along the Red Sea, and over Umluj and Jeddah, eating grasshoppers and moths, which he hunted on the wing, all along the way. Once he arrived in Mecca, he performed the seven rounds around the holy rock, drank from the water of Zamzam, and flew between Safa and Marwa. When he came home, my father and his father were relieved to see him—he had been missing for weeks and they worried hunters had captured and killed him—but they were suspicious of his story, and asked if he could prove that he had truly gone on the pilgrimage. My great-grandfather, expecting his children and their children to be unbelievers, brought out a rock from his mouth, a pebble the likes of which his caste had never seen. This was one of the pebbles he had gathered to throw at the walls of the devil. From then on, all the falcons called him El-Hajj Aamer.

I was born eight years ago, and my father would take me on flights to the Mediterranean, flights that he said were dangerous because the people living to the west of our village, Israelis, carried large guns and monitored their airspace vigilantly. I never questioned why this was, but followed closely behind my father's tail. We are small birds of prey, which sometimes works to our advantage: we can go on long-distance flights without arousing too much suspicion. At the Mediterranean, I saw humans without feathers swimming in the sea, and humans in large black feathers playing in the sand. My father explained that the featherless ones were in Tel Aviv, and the feathered ones were in Gaza.

The best prey was in Gaza. My favorite meal is cicadas—followed by voles, butterflies, and grasshoppers. I'll eat a mouse if I have to. But I prefer songbirds and shrews. Gaza had plenty of my favorites. After Father passed, I would go on solo trips to the coast for the cicadas.

One day, while I was en route to the sea, I saw the bigger birds, the warplanes, hovering far above me. I knew trouble was coming, and it did. The white phosphorous that the plane urinated clouded the air I flew in, and soon, I was in the sea. A group of children found me and nursed me to health on the balcony of their apartment.

Father always said to stay away from humans; they had roasted and eaten some of my sisters and brothers. But the children were kind, and bored, since they were under curfew. They released me when I was healed.

On my flight back to Aqraba, I was captured by university students in Tel Aviv. They took me into their white labs, recorded information about my feathers, beak, feet, and clipped a metal bracelet on my leg. They wanted to study my and my family's migration patterns. No matter what I did in the months afterward, I could not remove the metal bracelet, which had etchings on it in their language.

IN AQRABA, EVERYONE was angry with me for being captured by the Israelis. My wife at the time shat all over our nest, a common message to prey, husbands, and humans to stay away. I respected her wishes, even though I missed my children. My mother was elderly and would allow me visits in the early mornings. I asked her if she was afraid of death, and she said she wasn't. She told me that she had heard that at death, no one suffers, because each of us has a pleasant, short hallucination before we let go forever. This brought me comfort, as I'm sure it did for her. I hunted voles to nourish her, finding them at night by tracking their urine lines, which I can find in the pitch dark because I am able to see ultraviolet light.

Mother died in winter. We all buried her, my kin making peace with me for the day. The children pecked at my bracelet, trying to break me free of it. After Mother's death, I left to the sea in Gaza. There was nothing left for me in Aqraba anymore.

It had been almost two years since my injury there. And again, as soon as I arrived, I knew I had come at the wrong time. The large bird warplanes dropped bombs on balconies, bridges, and beaches. I could not recognize the building of the children who had nursed me. It was rubble. I could not find the children. I could not find cicadas. There were no fishermen to accompany at the sea.

So I flew east. I didn't know where I was going, only wanted to leave everything I had known. I flew past Aqraba on my way east and it was difficult for me not to land as I always had. I kept flying; lucky for me, I can fly even in stationary, fixed air. I flew north, toward Cyprus. When I arrived there, I found a quarry and had my fill of toads, shrews, and snakes. I kept traveling north, arriving in the Aegean Sea. There, I stayed on islands and hunted from clotheslines and high telephone wires. The local birds paid me no mind, neither welcoming nor shunning me. Every morning on the island I liked best, a round, elderly widow sat outside her white rock house and watched me through binoculars. She believed I belonged to her, and I enjoyed her sense of ownership over me—it was the closest thing to love.

Come winter, the woman left, and the island's white houses became covered in snow. I wanted to fly homeward, but decided to go west to Athens until it got warmer. In Athens, I lived in Exarchia, with anarchist birds who accepted me so long as I helped them find and share prey. About my metal bracelet they said nothing, only that they respected me for escaping the confines of whatever hell the Israelis had made me live in. They smelled awful, refusing to groom themselves, and had long, tedious conversations about the 1800s, when anarchism was alive and well in the region. I flew with them to the Acropolis at sunset, and they shat against the Parthenon's walls. In the evenings we watched hippies dance in Syntagma Square, and we ate the kebabs they left in their wake.

At the first sign of spring, the anarchist birds got feisty. One in particular cautiously declared that she was unsure about anarchism as a functional social system. The other birds laughed and told her that that was the point. Becoming braver, she said she had observed a group of bees that afternoon who had voted on which place to settle and live in. She described their dance, the way the rest of the bees grew convinced by their bodies' votes. The birds viciously attacked her when she said this, pecking at her feathers until she relented. I flew northeast in the morning.

IN WESTERN TURKEY I survived by remembering a story about my cousins: they had become famous one spring and summer by hanging on poles under the floodlights of a soccer stadium, hunting moths and other insects. They'd been recorded doing this and the footage had aired around the world. So, from the air, I looked for stadiums. And I found them; in their floodlights I hunted and ate to my heart's content, watching teenage boys chase soccer balls into nets. I kept flying west.

That's when I found Istanbul, and the seagulls of Istanbul. Over the Bosphorus, chasing ferries and being fed by humans, I became a cliché: I fell in love. She wasn't anything special, and to the human eye, there was no difference between her and any of the other gulls. But I flew near her every early evening, the sunset athaan being garbled by the Turkish muatthin, his Arabic awful and funny. I told her so, made her laugh. She said we could never breed, because I was not one of them. I said that was part of my attraction. We were friends through the summer. In early fall, she moved to the island of Burgazada, and I asked if I could join.

Her pack did not allow me to. In Karaköy, by the fish market, they zoomed at me from all angles, which reminded me of the anti-anarchist bird in Athens, her blood, her stand. They taunted me for my bracelet. They asked where my pack was; said I had been left behind on purpose. She did not come to my defense.

I lay bleeding on the rocks near the river. A policeman found me, and, reading my bracelet, instantly called his commander. The commander and a special terrorism unit came and collected me in a cage, ran tests on me all day. Tomorrow, as I said, they will x-ray me.

IT IS NOW morning and I am sedated. They place me in the belly of a machine. They capture an image of my insides. They shout. They whisper. There is nothing inside me—no microphones, no chips. The room empties. I am placed back in the cage. Three men in uniform take down notes. An important man enters the room. He stands in front of me, looks into my eyes.

We are not afraid of you, he says. I think he is talking to me, but then realize he is speaking in case I really am a spy, in case I am recording. Then, he takes me out into the sun, and releases me.

I am too elderly to fly home now. I want to return to Aqraba, to say good-bye, not to those who have shunned me but to my land; to the olive trees, the earth, and the cicadas. Instead, I live out the rest of my days on the grounds of a garden in Topkapi, a beautiful once-palace.

When death comes, I take comfort in what my mother once said.

But Mother lied, because a bitterness fills me, and then, the black light.

The Relive Box

by T. Coraghessan Boyle

Katie wanted to relive Katie at nine, before her mother left, and I could appreciate that, but we had only one console at the time, and I really didn't want to go there. It was coming up on the holidays, absolutely grim outside, nine thirty at night—on a school night— and she had to be up at six to catch the bus in the dark. She'd already missed too much school, staying home on any pretext and reliving all day, while I was at work, so there really were no limits, and who was being a bad father here? A single father unable to discipline his fifteen-year-old daughter, let alone inculcate a work ethic in her?

Me. I was. And I felt bad about it. I wanted to put my foot down and at the same time give her something, make a concession, a peace offering. But, even more, I wanted the box myself, wanted it so baldly it was showing in my face, I'm sure, and she needed to get ready for school, needed sleep, needed to stop reliving and worry about the now, the now and the future. "Why don't you wait till the weekend?" I said.

She was wearing those tights which all the girls wear like painted-on skin, standing in the doorway to the living room, perching on one foot the way she did when she was doing her dance exercises. Her face belonged to her mother, my ex, Christine, who hadn't been there for her for six years and counting. "I want to relive now," she said, diminishing her voice to a shaky, hesitant plaint that was calculated to make me give in to whatever she wanted, but it wasn't going to work this time, no way. She was going to bed, and I was going back to a rainy February night in 1982, a sold-out show at the Roxy, a band I loved then, and the girl I was mad crazy for before she broke my heart and Christine came along to break it all over again.

"Why don't you go upstairs and text your friends or something?" I said.

"I don't want to text my friends. I want to be with my mom."

This was a plaint, too, and it cut even deeper. She was deprived, that was the theme here, and my behavior, as any impartial observer could have seen in a heartbeat, verged on child abuse. "I know, honey, I know. But it's not healthy. You're spending too much time there."

"You're just selfish, that's all," she said, and here was the shift to a new tone, a tone of animus and opposition, the subtext being that I never thought of anybody but myself. "You want to, what, relive when you were, like, my age or something? Let me guess: You're going to go back and relive yourself doing homework, right? As an example for your daughter?"

The room was a mess. The next day was the day the maid came, so I was standing amid the debris of the past week, a healthy percentage of it—abandoned sweat socks, energy-drink cans, crumpled foil pouches that had once contained biscotti, popcorn, or Salami Bites—generated by the child standing there before me. "I don't like your sarcasm," I said.

Her face was pinched so that her lips were reduced to the smallest little O-ring of disgust. "What *do* you like?"

"A clean house. A little peace and quiet. Some privacy, for Christ's sake—is that too much to ask?"

"I want to be with Mom."

"Go text your friends."

"I don't have any friends."

"Make some."

And this, thrown over her shoulder, preparatory to the furious pounding retreat up the stairs and the slamming of her bedroom door: "You're a pig!"

And my response, which had been ritualized ever since I'd sprung for the five-thousand-dollar, second-generation Halcom X1520 Relive Box with the In-Flesh Retinal Projection Stream and altered forever the dynamic between me and my only child: "I know."

MOST PEOPLE, WHEN they got their first Relive Box, went straight for sex, which was only natural. In fact, it was a selling point in the TV ads, which featured shimmering adolescents walking hand in hand along a generic strip of beach or leaning in for a tender kiss over the ball return at the bowling alley. Who wouldn't want to go back there? Who wouldn't want to relive innocence, the nascent stirrings of love and desire, or the first time you removed her clothes and she removed yours? What of girlfriends (or boyfriends, as the case may be), wives, ex-wives, one-night stands, the casual encounter that got you halfway there, then flitted out of reach on the wings of an unfulfilled promise? I was no different. The sex part of it obsessed me through those first couple of months, and if I drifted into work each morning feeling drained (and not just figuratively) at least I knew that it was a problem, that it was adversely affecting my job performance, and, if I didn't cut back, threatening my job itself. Still, to relive Christine when we first met, to relive her in bed, in candlelight, clinging fast to me and whispering my name in the throes of her passion, was too great a temptation. Or even just sitting there across from me in the Moroccan restaurant where I took her for our first date, her eyes like portals, as she leaned into the table and drank up every word and witticism that came out of my mouth. Or to go farther back, before my wife entered the picture, to Rennie Porter, the girl I took to the senior prom and spent two delicious hours rubbing up against in the back seat of my father's Buick Regal—every second of which I'd relived six or seven times now. And to Lisa, Lisa Denardo, the girl I met that night at the Roxy, hoping I was going to score.

I started coming in late to work. Giving everybody, even my boss, the zombie stare. I got my first warning. Then my second. And my boss—Kevin Moos, a decent enough guy, five years younger than me, who didn't have an X1520, or not that he was letting on— sat me down in his office and told me, in no uncertain terms, that there wouldn't be a third.

But it was a miserable night, and I was depressed. And bored. So bored you could have drilled holes in the back of my head and taken core samples and I wouldn't have known the difference. I'd already denied my daughter, who was thumping around upstairs with the cumulative weight of ten daughters, and the next day was Friday, TGIF, end of the week, the slimmest of workdays, when just about everybody alive thinks about slipping out early. I figured that even if I did relive for more than the two hours I was going to strictly limit myself to, even if I woke up exhausted, I could always find a way to make it to lunch and just let things coast after that. So I went into the kitchen and fixed myself a gin and tonic, because that was what I'd been drinking that night at the Roxy, and carried it into the room at the end of the hall that had once been a bedroom and was now (Katie's joke, not mine) the reliving room.

The console sat squarely on the low table that was the only piece of furniture in the room, aside from the straight-backed chair I'd set in front of it the day I brought the thing home. It wasn't much bigger than the gaming consoles I'd had to make do with in the old days, a slick black metal cube with a single recessed glass slit running across the face of it from one side to the other. It activated the minute I took my seat. "Hello, Wes," it said, in the voice I'd selected, male, with the slightest bump of an accent to make it seem less synthetic. "Welcome back."

I lifted the drink to my lips to steady myself—think of a conductor raising his baton—and cleared my throat. "February 28, 1982," I said. "9:45 p.m. Play."

The box flashed the date and time and then suddenly I was there, the club exploding into life like a comet touching down, light and noise and movement obliterating the now, the house gone, my daughter gone, the world of getting and doing and bosses and work vanished in an instant. I was standing at the bar with my best friend, Zach Ronalds, who turned up his shirt collars and wore his hair in a Joe Strummer pompadour just like me, only his hair was black and mine choirboy blond (I'd dye it within the week), and I was trying to get the bartender's attention so I could order us G and Ts with my fake ID. The band, more New Wave than punk, hadn't started yet, and the only thing to look at onstage was the opening band, whose members were packing up their equipment while hypervigilant girls in vampire makeup and torn fishnet stockings washed around them in a human tide that ebbed and flowed on the waves of music crashing through the speakers. It was bliss. Bliss because I knew now that this night alone, out of all the long succession of dull, nugatory nights building up to it, would be special, that this was the night I'd meet Lisa and take her home with me. To my parents' house in Pasadena, where I had a room of my own above the detached garage and could come and go as I pleased. My room. The place where I greased up my hair and stared at myself in the mirror and waited for something to happen, something like this, like what was coming in seven and a half real-time minutes.

Zach said what sounded like "Look at that skank," but since he had his face turned away from me and the music was cranked to the sonic level of a rocket launch (give credit to the X1520's parametric speaker/audiobeam technology, which is infinitely more refined than the first generation's), I wasn't quite sure, though I must have heard him that night, my ears younger then, less damaged by scenes like this one, because I took hold of his arm and said, "Who? Her?"

What I said now, though, was "Reset, reverse ten seconds," and everything stalled, vanished, and started up once more, and here I was trying all over again to get the bartender's attention and listening hard when Zach, leaning casually against the bar on two splayed elbows, opened his mouth to speak. "Look at that skank," he said, undeniably, and there it was, coloring everything in the moment, because he was snap-judging Lisa, with her coathanger shoulders, Kabuki makeup, and shining black lips, and I said, "Who? Her?" already attracted, because in my eyes she wasn't a skank at all, or, if she was, she was a skank from some other realm altogether, and I couldn't from that moment on think of anything but getting her to talk to me.

Now, the frustrating thing about the current relive technology is that you can't be an actor in the scene, only an observer, like Scrooge reliving his boarding school agonies with the Ghost of Christmas Past at his elbow, so whatever howlers your adolescent self might have uttered are right there, hanging in the air, unedited. You can fast-forward, and I suppose most people do—skip the chatter; get to the sex—but, personally, after going straight to the carnal moments the first five or six times I relived a scene, I liked to go back and hear what I'd had to say, what she'd had to say, no matter how banal it might sound now. What I did that night—and I'd already relived this moment twice that week— was catch hold of the bartender and order not two but three G and Ts, though I only had something like eighteen dollars in my wallet, set one on the bar for Zach, and cross the floor to where she was standing, just beneath the stage, in what would be the mosh pit half an hour later. She saw me coming, saw the drinks—two drinks—and looked away, covering herself, because she was sure I was toting that extra drink for somebody else, a girlfriend or a best bud, lurking in the drift of shadow that the stage lights drew up out of the murky walls.

I tapped her shoulder. She turned her face to me. "Pause," I said.

Everything stopped. I was in a 3-D painting now, and so was she, and for the longest time I just kept things there, studying her face. She was eighteen years old, like me, beautiful enough underneath the paint and gel and eyeliner and all the rest to make me feel faint even now, and her eyes weren't wary, weren't *used*, but candid, ready, rich with expectation. I held my drink just under my nose, inhaling the smell of juniper berries to tweak the memory, and said, "Play."

"You look thirsty," I said.

The music boomed. Behind me, at the bar, Zach was giving me a look of disbelief, like *What the?*, because this was a violation of our club-going protocol. We didn't talk to the girls, and especially not the skanks, because we were there for the *music*, at least that was what we told ourselves. (Second time around I did pause this part, just for the expression on his face—Zach, poor Zach, who never did find himself a girlfriend, as far as I know, and who's probably some-place reliving every club he's ever been in and every date he's ever had, just to feel sorry for himself.)

She leveled her eyes on me, gave it a beat, then took the cold glass from my hand. "How did you guess?" she said.

What followed was the usual exchange of information about bands, books, neighborhood, high school, college, and then I was bragging about the bands I'd seen lately and she was countering with the band members she knew personally—like John Doe and the drummer for the Germs—and letting her eyes reveal just how personal that was, which only managed to inflame me till I wanted nothing more on this earth than to pin her in a corner and kiss the black lipstick right off her. What I said then, unaware that my care-fully sculpted pompadour was collapsing across my brow in some-thing very much like a bowl cut (or worse—*anathema*—a Beatles shag), was "You want to dance?"

She gave me a look. Shot her eyes to the stage and back, then around the room. A few people were dancing to the canned music, most of them jerking and gyrating to their own drugged-out beat, and there was no sign—yet—of the band we'd come to hear. "To this?"

"Yeah," I said, and I looked so—what was it?—*needy*, though at the time I must have thought I was chiseled out of a block of pure cool. "Come on," I said, and I reached out a hand to her.

I watched the decision firm up in her eyes, deep in this moment which would give rise to all the rest, to the part I was about to fast-forward to because I had to get up in the morning. For work. And no excuses. But watch, watch what comes next . . .

She took my hand, the soft friction of her touch alive still somewhere in my cell memory, and then she was leading me out onto the dance floor.

She was leading. And I was following.

*

WILL IT SURPRISE you to know that I exceeded my self-imposed two-hour limit? That after the sex I fast-forwarded to our first date, which was really just an agreed-upon meeting at Tower Records (March 2, 1982, 4:30 p.m.), and then up to Barney's Beanery for cheeseburgers and beers and shots of peppermint schnapps (!), which she paid for, because her father was a rich executive at Warner Bros.? Or that that made me feel so good I couldn't resist skipping ahead three months, to when she was as integral to my life as the Black Flag T-shirt that never left my back except in the shower? Lisa. Lisa Denardo. With her cat's tongue and her tight, torquing body that was a girl's and a woman's at the same time and her perfect, evenly spaced set of glistening white teeth (perfect, that is, but for the incisor she'd had a dentist in Tijuana remove, in the spirit of punk solidarity). The scene I hit on was early the following summer, summer break of my sophomore year in college, when I gave up on my parents' garage and Lisa and I moved into an off-campus apartment on Vermont and decided to paint the walls, ceiling, and floors the color of midnight in the Carlsbad Caverns. June 6, 1982, 2:44 p.m. The glisten of black paint, a too bright sun caught in the windows, and Lisa saying, "Think we should paint the glass, too?" I was oblivious of anything but her and me and the way I looked and the way she looked, a streak of paint on her left forearm and another, scimitar-shaped, just over one eyebrow, when suddenly everything went neutral and I was back in the reliving room, staring into the furious face of my daughter.

But let me explain the technology here a moment, for those of you who don't already know. This isn't a computer screen or a TV or a hologram or anything anybody else can see—we're talking retinal projection, two laser beams fixed on two eyeballs. Anybody coming into the room (daughter, wife, boss) will simply see you sitting there silently in a chair with your retinas lit like furnaces. Step in front of the projector—as my daughter had done now—and the image vanishes.

"Stop," I said, and I wasn't talking to her.

But there she was, her hair brushed out for school and her jaw clenched, looking hate at me. "I can't believe you," she said. "Do you have any idea what time it is?"

Bleary, depleted—and guilty, deeply guilty—I just gawked at her, the light she'd flicked on when she came into the room transfixing me in the chair. I shook my head.

"It's 6:45 a.m. In the morning. The *morning*, Dad."

I started to say something, but the words were tangled up inside me, because Lisa was saying—had just said—"You're not going to make me stay here and watch the paint dry, are you? Because I'm thinking maybe we could drive out to the beach or something, just to cool down," and I said, or was going to say, "There's, like, maybe half a pint of gas in the car."

"What?" Katie demanded. "Were you with Mom again? Is that it? Like you can be with her and I can't?"

"No," I said, "no, that wasn't it. It wasn't your mom at all . . ."

A tremor ran through her. "Yeah, right. So what was it, then? Some girlfriend, somebody you were gaga over when you were in college? Or high school? Or, what, *junior* high?"

"I must have fallen asleep," I said. "Really. I just zoned out."

She knew I was lying. She'd come looking for me, dutiful child, motherless child, and found me not up and about and bustling around the kitchen, preparing to fuss over her and see her off to school, the way I used to, but pinned here in this chair, like an exhibit in a museum, blind to anything but the past, my past and nobody else's, not hers or her mother's, or the country's or the world's, just mine.

I heard the door slam. Heard the thump of her angry feet in the hallway, the distant muffled crash of the front door, and then the house was quiet. I looked at the slit in the box. "Play," I said.

BY THE TIME I got to work, I was an hour and a half late, but on this day—miracle of miracles—Kevin was even later, and when he did show up I was ensconced in my cubicle, dutifully rattling keys on my keyboard. He didn't say anything, just brushed by me and buried himself in his office, but I could see that he was wearing the same vacant pre-now look I was, and it didn't take much of an intuitive leap to guess the reason. In fact, since the new model had come on the market, I'd noticed that randy, faraway gaze in the eyes of half a dozen of my fellow employees, including Linda Blanco, the receptionist, who'd stopped buttoning the top three buttons of her blouse and wore shorter and shorter skirts every day. Instead of breathing "Moos and Associates, how may I help you?" into the receiver, now she just said, "Reset."

Was this a recipe for disaster? Was our whole society on the verge of breaking down? Was the NSA going to step in? Were they going to pass laws? Ban the box? I didn't know. I didn't care. I had a daughter to worry about. Thing was, all I could think of was getting home to relive, straight home, and if the image of a carton of milk or a loaf of bread flitted into my head I batted it away. Takeout. We could always get takeout. I was in a crucial phase with Lisa, heading inexorably for the grimmer scenes, the disagreements—petty at first, then monumental, unbridgeable, like the day I got home from my makeup class in calculus and found her sitting at the kitchen table with a stoner whose name I never did catch and didn't want to know, not then or now—and I needed to get through it, not to analyze whether it hurt or not but because it was there and I had to relive it. I couldn't help myself. I just kept picking at it like a scab.

Ultimately, this was all about Christine, of course, about when I began to fail instead of succeed, to lose instead of win. I needed Lisa to remind me of a time before that, to help me trace my missteps and assign blame, because, as intoxicating as it was to relive the birds-atwitter moments with Christine, there was always something nagging at me in any given scene, some twitch of her face or a comment she threw out that should have raised flags at the time but never did. All right. Fine. I was going to go there, I was, and relive the minutiae of our relationship, the ecstasy and the agony both, the moments of mindless contentment and the swelling tide of antipathy that drove us apart, but first things first, and, as I fought my way home on the freeway that afternoon, all I could think about was Lisa.

In the old days, before we got the box, my daughter and I had a Friday afternoon ritual whereby I would stop in at the Italian place down the street from the house, have a drink and chat up whoever was there, then call Katie and have her come join me for a father-daughter dinner, so that I could have some face time with her, read into her, and suss out her thoughts and feelings as she grew into a young woman herself, but we didn't do that anymore. There wasn't time. The best I could offer—lately, especially—was takeout or a microwave pizza and a limp salad, choked down in the cold confines of the kitchen, while we separately calculated how long we had to put up with the pretense before slipping off to relive.

There were no lights on in the house as I pulled into the driveway, and that was odd, because Katie should have been home from school by now—and she hadn't texted me or phoned to say she'd be staying late. I climbed out of the car feeling stiff all over—I needed to get more exercise, I knew that, and I resolved to do it, too, as soon as I got my head above water—and as I came up the walk I saw the sad, frosted artificial wreath hanging crookedly there in the center panel of the front door. Katie must have dug it out of the box of ornaments in the garage on her own initiative, to do something by way of Christmas, and that gave me pause, that stopped me right there, the thought of it, of my daughter having to make the effort all by herself. That crushed me. It did. And as I put the key in the lock and pushed the door open I knew things were going to have to change. Dinner. I'd take her out to dinner and forget about Lisa. At least for now.

"Katie?" I called. "You home?"

No response. I shrugged out of my coat and went on into the kitchen, thinking to make myself a drink. There were traces of her there, her backpack flung down on the floor, an open bag of Doritos spilling across the counter, a Diet Sprite, half full, on the breadboard. I called her name again, standing stock-still in the middle of the room and listening for the slightest hint of sound or movement as my voice echoed through the house. I was about to pull out my phone and call her when I thought of the reliving room, and it was a sinking thought, not a selfish one, because if she was in there, reliving—and she was, I knew she was—what did that say about her social life? Didn't teenage girls go out anymore? Didn't they gather in packs at the mall or go to movies or post things on Facebook, or, forgive me, go out on dates? Group dates, even? How else were they going to experience the inchoate beginnings of what the Relive Box people were pushing in the first place?

I shoved into the room, which was dark but for the lights of her eyes, and just stood there watching her for a long moment as I adjusted to the gloom. She sat riveted, her body present but her mind elsewhere, and if I was embarrassed—for her, and for me, too, her father, invading her privacy when she was most vulnerable—the embarrassment gave way to a sorrow so oceanic I thought I would drown in it. I studied her face. Watched her smile and grimace and go cold and smile again. What could she possibly be reliving when she'd lived so little? Family vacations? Christmases past? Her biannual trips to Hong Kong to be with her mother and stepfather? I couldn't fathom it. I didn't like it. It had to stop. I turned on the overhead light and stepped in front of the projector.

She blinked at me and she didn't recognize me, didn't know me at all, because I was in the now and she was in the past. "Katie," I said, "that's enough, now. Come on." I held out my arms to her, even as recognition came back into her eyes and she made a vague gesture of irritation, of pushing away.

"Katie," I said, "let's go out to dinner. Just the two of us. Like we used to."

"I'm not hungry," she said. "And it's not fair. You can use it all you want, like, day and night, but whenever I want it—" And she broke off, tears starting in her eyes.

"Come on," I said. "It'll be fun."

The look she gave me was unsparing. I was trying to deflect it, trying to think of something to say, when she got up out of the chair so suddenly it startled me, and, though I tried to take hold of her arm, she was too quick. Before I could react, she was at the door, pausing only to scorch me with another glare. "I don't believe you," she spat, before vanishing down the hall.

I should have followed her, should have tried to make things right—or better, anyway—but I didn't. The box was right there. It had shut down when she leaped up from the chair, and whatever she'd been reliving was buried back inside it, accessible to no one, though you can bet there are hackers out there right now trying to subvert the retinal-recognition feature. For a long moment, I stared at the open door, fighting myself, then I went over and softly shut it. I realized I didn't need a drink or dinner, either. I sat down in the chair. "Hello, Wes," the box said. "Welcome back."

WE DIDN'T HAVE a Christmas tree that year, and neither of us really cared all that much, I think—if we wanted to look at spangle-draped trees, we could relive holidays past, happier ones, or, in my case, I could go back to my childhood and relive my father's whiskey in a glass and my mother's long-suffering face blossoming over the greedy joy of her golden boy, her only child, tearing open his presents as a weak, bleached-out California sun haunted the windows and the turkey crackled in the oven. Katie went off (reluctantly, I thought) on a skiing vacation to Mammoth with the family of her best friend, Allison, whom she hardly saw anymore, not outside of school, not in the now, and I went back to Lisa, because if I was going to get to Christine in any serious way—beyond the sex, that is, beyond the holiday greetings and picture-postcard moments— Lisa was my bridge.

As soon as I'd dropped Katie at Allison's house and exchanged a few previously scripted salutations with Allison's grinning parents and her grinning twin brothers, I stopped at a convenience store for a case of eight-ounce bottles of spring water and the biggest box of PowerBars I could find and went straight home to the reliving room. The night before, I'd been close to the crucial scene with Lisa, one that was as fixed in my memory as the blowup with Christine a quarter century later, but elusive as to the date and time. I'd been up all night—again—fast-forwarding, reversing, jumping locales and facial expressions, Lisa's first piercing, the evolution of my haircut, but I hadn't been able to pinpoint the exact moment, not yet. I set the water on the floor on my left side, the PowerBars on my right. "May 9, 1983," I said. "4:00 a.m."

The numbers flashed and then I was in darkness, zero visibility, confused as to where I was until the illuminated dial of a clock radio began to bleed through and I could make out the dim outline of myself lying in bed in the back room of that apartment with the black walls and the black ceiling and the black floor. Lisa was there beside me, an irregular hump in the darkness, snoring with a harsh gag and stutter. She was stoned. And drunk. Half an hour earlier, she'd been in the bathroom, heaving over the toilet, and I realized I'd come too far. "Reset," I said. "Reverse ninety minutes."

Sudden light, blinding after the darkness, and I was alone in the living room of the apartment, studying, or trying to. My hair hung limp, my muscles were barely there, but I was young and reasonably good-looking, even excusing any bias. I saw that my Black Flag T-shirt had faded to gray from too much sun and too many washings, and the book in my lap looked as familiar as something I might have been buried with in a previous life, but then this was my previous life. I watched myself turn a page, crane my neck toward the door, get up to flip over the album that was providing the soundtrack. "Reset," I said. "Fast-forward ten minutes." And here it was, what I'd been searching for: a sudden crash, the front door flinging back, Lisa and the stoner whose name I didn't want to know fumbling their way in, both of them as slow as syrup with the cumulative effect of downers and alcohol, and though the box didn't have an olfactory feature, I swear I could smell the tequila on them. I jumped up out of my chair, spilling the book, and shouted something I couldn't quite make out, so I said, "Reset, reverse five seconds."

"You fucker!" was what I'd shouted, and now I shouted it again, prior to slapping something out of the guy's hand, a beer bottle, and all at once I had him in a hammerlock and Lisa was beating at my back with her bird-claw fists and I was wrestling the guy out the door, cursing over the soundtrack ("Should I Stay or Should I Go"—one of those flatline ironies which almost make you believe everything in this life's been programmed). I saw now that he was bigger than I was, probably stronger, too, but the drugs had taken the volition out of him, and in the next moment he was outside the door and the three bolts were hammered home. By me. Who now turned in a rage to Lisa.

"Stop," I said. "Freeze." Lisa hung there, defiant and guilty at the same time, pretty, breathtakingly pretty, despite the slack mouth and the drugged-out eyes. I should have left it there and gone on to those first cornucopian weeks and months and even years with Christine, but I couldn't help myself. "Play," I said, and Lisa raised a hand to swat at me, but she was too unsteady and knocked the lamp over instead.

"Did you fuck him?" I demanded.

There was a long pause, so long I almost fast-forwarded, and then she said, "Yeah. Yeah, I fucked him. And I'll tell you something"—her words glutinous, the syllables coalescing on her tongue—"you're no punk. And he is. He's the real deal. And you? You're, you're—"

I should have stopped it right there.

"—you're *prissy*."

"Prissy?" I couldn't believe it. Not then and not now.

She made a broad stoned gesture, weaving on her feet. "Anal-retentive. Like, who left the dishes in the sink or who didn't take out the garbage or what about the cockroaches—"

"Stop," I said. "Reset. June 19, 1994, 11:02 p.m."

I was in another bedroom now, one with walls the color of cream, and I was in another bed, this time with Christine, and I'd timed the memory to the very minute, postcoital, in the after-glow, and Christine, with her soft aspirated whisper of a voice, was saying, "I love you, Wes, you know that, don't you?"

"Stop," I said. "Reverse five seconds."

She said it again. And I stopped again. And reversed again. And she said it again. And again.

TIME HAS NO meaning when you're reliving. I don't know how long I kept it up, how long I kept surfing through those moments with Christine—not the sexual ones but the loving ones, the companionable ones, the ordinary day-to-day moments when I could see in her eyes that she loved me more than anybody alive and was never going to stop loving me, never. Dinner at the kitchen table, any dinner, any night. Just to be there. My wife. My daughter. The way the light poured liquid gold over the hardwood floors of our starter house, in Canoga Park. Katie's first birthday. Her first word ("Cake!"). The look on Christine's face as she curled up with Katie in bed and read her *Where the Wild Things Are*. Her voice as she hoarsened it for Max: "I'll eat you up!"

Enough analysis, enough hurt. I was no masochist.

At some point, I had to get up from that chair in the now and evacuate a living bladder, the house silent, spectral, unreal. I didn't live here. I didn't live in the now with its deadening nine-to-five job I was in danger of losing and the daughter I was failing and a wife who'd left me—and her own daughter—for Winston Chen, a choreographer of martial-arts movies in Hong Kong, who was loving and kind and funny and not the control freak I was. (*Prissy*, anyone? *Anal-retentive*?) The house echoed with my footsteps, a stage set and nothing more. I went to the kitchen and dug the biggest pot I could find out from under the sink, brought it back to the reliving room, and set it on the floor between my legs to save me the trouble of getting up next time around.

Time passed. Relived time and lived time, too. There were two windows in the room, shades drawn so as not to interfere with the business of the moment, and sometimes a faint glow appeared around the margins of them, an effect I noticed when I was searching for a particular scene and couldn't quite pin it down. Sometimes the glow was gone. Sometimes it wasn't. What happened then, and I may have been two days in or three or five, I couldn't really say, was that things began to cloy. I'd relived an exclusive diet of the transcendent, the joyful, the insouciant, the best of Christine, the best of Lisa, and all the key moments of the women who came between and after, and I'd gone back to the Intermediate Algebra test, the very instant, pencil to paper, when I knew I'd scored a perfect 100 percent, and to the time I'd squirted a ball to right field with two outs, two strikes, ninth inning and my Little League team (the Condors, yellow Ts, white lettering) down by three, and watched it rise majestically over the glove of the spastic red-haired kid sucking back allergic snot and roll all the way to the wall. Triumph after triumph, goodness abounding—till it stuck in my throat.

"Reset," I said. "January 2, 2009, 4:30 p.m."

I found myself in the kitchen of our second house, this house, the one we'd moved to because it was outside the LA city limits and had schools we felt comfortable sending Katie to. That was what mattered: the schools. And, if it lengthened our commutes, so be it. This house. The one I was reliving in now. Everything gleamed around me, counters polished, the glass of the cabinets as transparent as air, because details mattered then, everything in its place whether Christine was there or not—especially if she wasn't there, and where was she? Or where had she been? To China. With her boss. On film business. Her bags were just inside the front door, where she'd dropped them forty-five minutes ago, after I'd picked her up at the airport and we'd had our talk in the car, the talk I was going to relive when I got done here, because it was all about pain now, about reality, and this scene was the capper, the coup de grâce. You want wounds? You want to take a razor blade to the meat of your inner thigh just to see if you can still feel? Well, here it was.

Christine entered the scene now, coming down the stairs from Katie's room, her eyes wet, or damp, anyway, and her face composed. I pushed myself up from the table, my beginner's bald spot a glint of exposed flesh under the glare of the overhead light. I spoke first. "You tell her?"

Christine was dressed in her business attire, black stockings, heels, skirt to the knee, tailored jacket. She looked exhausted, and not simply from the fifteen-hour flight but from what she'd had to tell me. And our daughter. (How I'd like to be able to relive *that*, to hear how she'd even broached the subject, let alone how she'd smoke-screened her own selfishness and betrayal with some specious concern for Katie's well-being—let's not rock the boat and you'll be better off here with your father and your school and your teachers and it's not the end but just the beginning, buck up, you'll see.)

Christine's voice was barely audible. "I don't like this any better than you do."

"Then why do it?"

A long pause. Too long. "Stop," I said.

I couldn't do this. My heart was hammering. My eyes felt as if they were being squeezed in a vise. I could barely swallow. I reached down for a bottle of water and a PowerBar, drank, chewed. She was going to say, "This isn't working," and I was going to say, "*Working?* What the fuck are you talking about? What does work have to do with it? I thought this was about love. I thought it was about commitment." I knew I wasn't going to get violent, though I should have, should have chased her out to the cab that was even then waiting at the curb and slammed my way in and flown all the way to Hong Kong to confront Winston Chen, the martial-arts genius, who could have crippled me with his bare feet.

"Reset," I said. "August, 1975, any day, any time."

There was a hum from the box. "Incomplete command. Please select date and time."

I was twelve years old, the summer we went to Vermont, to a lake there, where the mist came up off the water like the fumes of a dream and deer mice lived under the refrigerator, and I didn't have a date or time fixed in my mind—I just needed to get away from Christine, that was all. I picked the first thing that came into my head.

"August 19," I said. "11:30 a.m. Play."

A blacktop road. Sun like a nuclear blast. A kid, running. I recognized myself—I'd been to this summer before, one I remembered as idyllic, messing around in boats, fishing, swimming, wandering the woods with one of the local kids, Billy Scharf, everything neutral, copacetic. But why was I running? And why did I have that look on my face, a look that fused determination and helplessness both? Up the drive now, up the steps to the house, shouting for my parents: "Mom! Dad!"

I began to have a bad feeling.

I saw my father get up off the wicker sofa on the porch, my vigorous young father, who was dressed in a T-shirt and jeans and didn't have even a trace of gray in his hair, my father, who always made everything right. But not this time. "What's the matter?" he said. "What is it?"

And my mother coming through the screen door to the porch, a towel in one hand and her hair snarled wet from the lake. And me. I was fighting back tears, my legs and arms like sticks, striped polo shirt, faded shorts. "It's," I said, "it's—"

"Stop," I said. "Reset." It was my dog, Queenie, that was what it was, dead on the road that morning, and who'd left the gate ajar so she could get out in the first place? Even though he'd been warned about it a hundred times?

I was in a dark room. There was a pot between my legs, and it was giving off a fierce odor. I needed to go deeper, needed out of this. I spouted random dates, saw myself driving to work, stuck in traffic with ten thousand other fools who could only wish they had a fast-forward app, saw myself in my thirties, post-Lisa, pre-Christine, obsessing over Halo, and I stayed there through all the toppling hours, reliving myself in the game, boxes within boxes, until finally I thought of God, or what passes for God in my life, the mystery beyond words, beyond lasers and silicon chips. I gave a date nine months before I was born, "December 30, 1962, 6:00 a.m.," when I was, what—a zygote?—but the box gave me nothing, neither visual nor audio. And that was wrong, deeply wrong. There should have been a heartbeat. My mother's heartbeat, the first thing we hear—or feel, feel before we even have ears.

"Stop," I said. "Reset." A wave of rising exhilaration swept over me even as the words came to my lips, "September 30, 1963, 2:35 a.m.," and the drumbeat started up, *ba-boom, ba-boom*, but no visual, not yet, the minutes ticking by, *ba-boom, ba-boom*, and then I was there, in the light of this world, and my mother in her stained hospital gown and the man with the monobrow and the flashing glasses, the stranger, the doctor, saying what he was going to say by way of congratulations and relief. A boy. It's a boy.

Then it all went dead, and there was somebody standing in front of me, and I didn't recognize her, not at first, how could I? "Dad," she was saying. "Dad, are you there?"

I blinked. Tried to focus.

"No," I said finally, shaking my head in slow .emphasis, the word itself, the denial, heavy as a stone in my mouth. "I'm not here. I'm not. I'm not."

Scroogled

by Cory Doctorow

> Give me six lines written by the most honorable of
> men, and I will find an excuse in them to hang him.
> > —Cardinal Richelieu

> We don't know enough about you.
> > —Google CEO Eric Schmidt

Greg landed at San Francisco International Airport at 8:00 p.m., but by the time he'd made it to the front of the customs line, it was after midnight. He'd emerged from first class, brown as a nut, unshaven, and loose-limbed after a month on the beach in Cabo (scuba diving three days a week, seducing French college girls the rest of the time). When he'd left the city a month before, he'd been a stoop-shouldered, potbellied wreck.

Now he was a bronze god, drawing admiring glances from the stews at the front of the cabin.

Four hours later in the customs line, he'd slid from god back to man. His slight buzz had worn off, sweat ran down the crack of his ass, and his shoulders and neck were so tense his upper back felt like a tennis racket. The batteries on his iPod had long since died, leaving him with nothing to do except eavesdrop on the middle-aged couple ahead of him.

"The marvels of modern technology," said the woman, shrugging at a nearby sign: IMMIGRATION—POWERED BY GOOGLE.

"I thought that didn't start until next month?" The man was alternately wearing and holding a large sombrero.

Googling at the border. Christ. Greg had vested out of Google six months before, cashing in his options and "taking some me time," which turned out to be less rewarding than he'd expected. What he mostly did over the five months that followed was fix his friends' PCs, watch daytime TV, and gain ten pounds, which he blamed on being at home instead of in the Googleplex, with its well-appointed twenty-four-hour gym.

He should have seen it coming, of course. The US government had lavished $15 billion on a program to fingerprint and photograph visitors at the border, and hadn't caught a single terrorist. Clearly, the public sector was not equipped to Do Search Right.

The DHS officer had bags under his eyes and squinted at his screen, prodding at his keyboard with sausage fingers. No wonder it was taking four hours to get out of the goddamned airport.

"Evening," Greg said, handing the man his sweaty passport. The officer grunted and swiped it, then stared at his screen, tapping. A lot. He had a little bit of dried food at the corner of his mouth and his tongue crept out and licked at it.

"Want to tell me about June 1998?"

Greg looked up from his *Departures*. "I'm sorry?"

"You posted a message to alt.burningman on June 17, 1998, about your plan to attend a festival. You asked, 'Are shrooms really such a bad idea?'"

The interrogator in the secondary screening room was an older man, so skinny he looked like he'd been carved out of wood. His questions went a lot deeper than shrooms.

"Tell me about your hobbies. Are you into model rocketry?"

"What?"

"Model rocketry."

"No," Greg said. "No, I'm not." He sensed where this was going.

The man made a note, did some clicking. "You see, I ask because I see a heavy spike in ads for rocketry supplies showing up alongside your search results and Google mail."

Greg felt a spasm in his guts. "You're looking at my searches and email?" He hadn't touched a keyboard in a month, but he knew what he put into that search bar was likely more revealing than what he told his shrink.

"Sir, calm down, please. No, I'm not looking at your searches," the man said in a mocking whine. "That would be unconstitutional. We see only the ads that show up when you read your mail and do your searching. I have a brochure explaining it. I'll give it to you when we're through here."

"But the ads don't mean anything," Greg sputtered. "I get ads for Ann Coulter ringtones whenever I get email from my friend in Coulter, Iowa!"

The man nodded. "I understand, sir. And that's just why I'm here talking to you. Why do you suppose model rocket ads show up so frequently?"

Greg racked his brain. "Okay, just do this. Search for 'coffee fanatics.'" He'd been very active in the group, helping them build out the site for their coffee-of-the-month subscription service. The blend they were going to launch with was called Jet Fuel. "Jet Fuel" and "launch"—that would probably make Google barf up some model rocket ads.

They were in the home stretch when the carved man found the Halloween photos. They were buried three screens deep in the search results for "Greg Lupinski."

"It was a Gulf War–themed party," he said. "In the Castro."

"And you're dressed as . . . ?"

"A suicide bomber," he replied sheepishly. Just saying the words made him wince.

"Come with me, Mr. Lupinski," the man said.

By the time he was released, it was past 3:00 a.m. His suitcases stood forlornly by the baggage carousel. He picked them up and saw they had been opened and carelessly closed. Clothes stuck out from around the edges.

WHEN HE RETURNED home, he discovered that all of his fake pre-Columbian statues had been broken, and his brand-new white cotton Mexican shirt had an ominous boot print in the middle of it. His clothes no longer smelled of Mexico. They smelled like airport.

He wasn't going to sleep. No way. He needed to talk about this. There was only one person who would get it. Luckily, she was usually awake around this hour.

Maya had started working at Google two years after Greg had. It was she who'd convinced him to go to Mexico after he cashed out: anywhere, she'd said, that he could reboot his existence.

Maya had two giant chocolate labs and a very, very patient girlfriend named Laurie who'd put up with anything except being dragged around Dolores Park at 6:00 a.m. by 350 pounds of drooling canine.

Maya reached for her Mace as Greg jogged toward her, then did a double take and threw her arms open, dropping the leashes and trapping them under her sneaker. "Where's the rest of you? Dude, you look hot!"

He hugged her back, suddenly conscious of the way he smelled after a night of invasive Googling. "Maya," he said, "what do you know about Google and the DHS?"

She stiffened as soon as he asked the question. One of the dogs began to whine. She looked around, then nodded up at the tennis courts. "Top of the light pole there; don't look," she said. "That's one of our muni Wi-Fi access points. Wide-angle webcam. Face away from it when you talk."

In the grand scheme of things, it hadn't cost Google much to wire the city with webcams. Especially when measured against the ability to serve ads to people based on where they were sitting. Greg hadn't paid much attention when the cameras on all those access points went public; there'd been a day's worth of blogstorm while people played with the new all-seeing toy, zooming in on various prostitute cruising areas, but after a while the excitement blew over.

Feeling silly, Greg mumbled, "You're joking."

"Come with me," she said, turning away from the pole.

The dogs weren't happy about cutting their walk short, and expressed their displeasure in the kitchen as Maya made coffee.

"We brokered a compromise with the DHS," she said, reaching for the milk. "They agreed to stop fishing through our search records, and we agreed to let them see what ads got displayed for users."

Greg felt sick. "Why? Don't tell me Yahoo was doing it already..."

"No, no. Well, yes. Sure. Yahoo was doing it. But that wasn't the reason Google went along. You know, Republicans hate Google. We're overwhelmingly registered Democratic, so we're doing what we can to make peace with them before they clobber us. This isn't PII." Personally Identifying Information, the toxic smog of the information age. "It's just metadata. So it's only slightly evil."

"Why all the intrigue, then?"

Maya sighed and hugged the lab that was butting her knee with its huge head. "The spooks are like lice. They get everywhere. They show up at our meetings. It's like being in some Soviet ministry. And at the security clearance we're divided into these two camps: the cleared and the suspect. We all know who isn't cleared, but no one knows why. I'm cleared. Lucky for me, being a dyke no longer disqualifies you. No cleared person would deign to eat lunch with an unclearable."

Greg felt very tired. "So I guess I'm lucky I got out of the airport alive. I might have ended up 'disappeared' if it had gone badly, huh?"

Maya stared at him intently. He waited for an answer.

"What?"

"I'm about to tell you something, but you can't ever repeat it, okay?"

"Um . . . you're not in a terrorist cell, are you?"

"Nothing so simple. Here's the deal: airport DHS scrutiny is a gating function. It lets the spooks narrow down their search criteria. Once you get pulled aside for secondary at the border, you become a 'person of interest' and they never, ever let up. They'll scan webcams for your face and gait. Read your mail. Monitor your searches."

"I thought you said the courts wouldn't let them . . ."

"The courts won't let them indiscriminately Google you. But after you're in the system, it becomes a selective search. All legal. And once they start Googling you, they always find something. All your data is fed into a big hopper that checks for 'suspicious patterns,' using deviation from statistical norms to nail you."

Greg felt like he was going to throw up. "How the hell did this happen? Google was a good place. 'Don't be evil,' right?" That was the corporate motto, and for Greg, it had been a huge part of why he'd taken his computer science PhD from Stanford directly to Mountain View.

Maya replied with a hard-edged laugh. "'Don't be evil'? Come on, Greg. Our lobbying group is that same bunch of crypto-fascists that tried to swift-boat Kerry. We popped our evil cherry a long time ago."

They were quiet for a minute.

"It started in China," she went on, finally. "Once we moved our servers onto the mainland, they went under Chinese jurisdiction."

Greg sighed. He knew Google's reach all too well: every time you visited a page with Google ads on it, or used Google Maps or Google mail, even if you sent mail to a Gmail account, the company diligently collected your info. Recently, the site's search-optimization software had begun using the data to tailor Web searches to individual users. It proved to be a revolutionary tool for advertisers. An authoritarian government would have other purposes in mind.

"They were using us to build profiles of people," she went on. "When they had someone they wanted to arrest, they'd come to us and find a reason to bust them. There's hardly anything you can do on the Net that isn't illegal in China."

Greg shook his head. "Why did they have to put the servers in China?"

"The government said they'd block us otherwise. And Yahoo was there." They both made faces. Somewhere along the way, employees at Google had become obsessed with Yahoo, more concerned with what the competition was doing than how their own company was performing. "So we did it. But a lot of us didn't like the idea."

Maya sipped her coffee and lowered her voice. One of her dogs sniffed insistently under Greg's chair.

"Almost immediately, the Chinese asked us to start censoring search results," Maya said. "Google agreed. The company line was hilarious: 'We're not doing evil, we're giving consumers access to a better search tool! If we showed them search results they couldn't get to, that would just frustrate them. It would be a *bad user experience.*'"

"Now what?" Greg pushed a dog away from him. Maya looked hurt.

"Now you're a person of interest, Greg. You're Googlestalked. Now you live your life with someone constantly looking over your shoulder. You know the mission statement, right? 'Organize the world's information.' Everything. Give it five years, we'll know how many turds were in the bowl before you flushed. Combine that with automated suspicion of anyone who matches a statistical picture of a bad guy and you're—"

"Scroogled."

"Totally." She nodded.

Maya took both labs down the hall to the bedroom. He heard a muffled argument with her girlfriend, and she came back alone.

"I can fix this," she said in an urgent whisper. "After the Chinese started rounding up people, my podmates and I made it our 20 percent project to fuck with them." (Among Google's business innovations was a rule that required every employee to devote 20 percent of his or her time to high-minded pet projects.) "We call it the Googlecleaner. It goes deep into the database and statistically normalizes you. Your searches, your Gmail histograms, your browsing patterns. All of it. Greg, I can Googleclean you. It's the only way."

"I don't want you to get into trouble."

She shook her head. "I'm already doomed. Every day since I built the damn thing has been borrowed time. Now it's just a matter of waiting for someone to point out my expertise and history to the DHS and, oh, I don't know. Whatever it is they do to people like me in the war on abstract nouns."

Greg remembered the airport. The search. His shirt, the boot print in the middle of it.

"Do it," he said.

THE GOOGLECLEANER WORKED wonders. Greg could tell by the ads that popped up alongside his searches, ads clearly meant for someone else: "Intelligent Design Facts," "Online Seminary Degree," "Terror Free Tomorrow," "Porn Blocker Software," "The Homosexual Agenda," "Cheap Toby Keith Tickets." This was Maya's program at work. Clearly Google's new personalized search had him pegged as someone else entirely, a God-fearing right-winger with a thing for hat acts.

Which was fine by him.

Then he clicked on his address book, and found that half of his contacts were missing. His Gmail in-box was hollowed out like a termite-ridden stump. His Orkut profile, normalized. His calendar, family photos, bookmarks: all empty. He hadn't quite realized before how much of him had migrated onto the Web and worked its way into Google's server farms. His entire online identity. Maya had scrubbed him to a high gloss; he'd become the invisible man.

Greg sleepily mashed the keys on the laptop next to his bed, bringing the screen to life. He squinted at the flashing toolbar clock: 4:13 a.m.! Christ, who was pounding on his door at this hour?

He shouted, "Coming!" in a muzzy voice and pulled on a robe and slippers. He shuffled down the hallway, turning on lights as he went. At the door, he squinted through the peephole to find Maya staring glumly back at him.

He undid the chains and dead bolt and yanked the door open. Maya rushed in past him, followed by the dogs and her girlfriend.

She was sheened in sweat, her usually combed hair clinging in clumps to her forehead. She rubbed at her eyes, which were red and lined. "Pack a bag," she croaked hoarsely.

"What?"

She took him by the shoulders. "Do it," she said.

"Where do you want to . . . ?"

"Mexico, probably. Don't know yet. Pack, dammit." She pushed past him into his bedroom and started yanking open drawers.

"Maya," he said sharply, "I'm not going anywhere until you tell me what's going on."

She glared at him and pushed her hair away from her face. "The Googlecleaner lives. After I cleaned you, I shut it down and walked away. It was too dangerous to use anymore. But it's still set to send me email confirmations whenever it runs. Someone's used it six times to scrub three very specific accounts all of which happen to belong to members of the Senate Commerce Committee up for reelection."

"Googlers are blackwashing senators?"

"Not Googlers. This is coming from off-site. The IP block is registered in DC. And the IPs are all used by Gmail users. Guess who the accounts belong to?"

"You spied on Gmail accounts?"

"Okay. Yes. I did look through their email. Everyone does it, now and again, and for a lot worse reasons than I did. But check it out. Turns out all this activity is being directed by our lobbying firm. Just doing their job, defending the company's interests."

Greg felt his pulse beating in his temples. "We should tell someone."

"It won't do any good. They know everything about us. They can see every search. Every email. Every time we've been caught on the webcams. Who is in our social network . . . did you know if you have fifteen Orkut buddies, it's statistically certain that you're no more than three steps to someone who's contributed money to a 'terrorist' cause? Remember the airport? You'll be in for a lot more of that."

"Maya," Greg said, getting his bearings. "Isn't heading to Mexico overreacting? Just quit. We can do a start-up or something. This is crazy."

"They came to see me today," she said. "Two of the political officers from DHS. They didn't leave for hours. And they asked me a lot of very heavy questions."

"About the Googlecleaner?"

"About my friends and family. My search history. My personal history."

"Jesus."

"They were sending a message to me. They're watching every click and every search. It's time to go. Time to get out of range."

"There's a Google office in Mexico, you know."

"We've got to go," she said, firmly.

"Laurie, what do you think of this?" Greg asked.

Laurie thumped the dogs between the shoulders. "My parents left East Germany in '65. They used to tell me about the Stasi. The secret police would put everything about you in your file, if you told an unpatriotic joke, whatever. Whether they meant it or not, what Google has created is no different."

"Greg, are you coming?"

He looked at the dogs and shook his head. "I've got some pesos left over," he said. "You take them. Be careful, okay?"

Maya looked like she was going to slug him. Softening, she gave him a ferocious hug.

"Be careful, yourself," she whispered in his ear.

*

THEY CAME FOR him a week later. At home, in the middle of the night, just as he'd imagined they would.

Two men arrived on his doorstep shortly after 2:00 a.m. One stood silently by the door. The other was a smiler, short and rumpled, in a sport coat with a stain on one lapel and an American flag on the other. "Greg Lupinski, we have reason to believe you're in violation of the Computer Fraud and Abuse Act," he said, by way of introduction. "Specifically, exceeding authorized access, and by means of such conduct having obtained information. Ten years for a first offense. Turns out that what you and your friend did to your Google records qualifies as a felony. And oh, what will come out in the trial . . . all the stuff you whitewashed out of your profile, for starters."

Greg had played this scene in his head for a week. He'd planned all kinds of brave things to say. It had given him something to do while he waited to hear from Maya. She never called.

"I'd like to get in touch with a lawyer," was all he mustered.

"You can do that," the small man said. "But maybe we can come to a better arrangement."

Greg found his voice. "I'd like to see your badge," he stammered. The man's basset-hound face lit up as he let out a bemused chuckle.

"Buddy, I'm not a cop," he replied. "I'm a consultant. Google hired me; my firm represents their interests in Washington to build relationships. Of course, we wouldn't get the police involved without talking to you first. You're part of the family. Actually, there's an offer I'd like to make."

Greg turned to the coffeemaker, dumped the old filter. "I'll go to the press," he said.

The man nodded as if thinking it over. "Well, sure. You could walk into the *Chronicle*'s office in the morning and spill everything. They'd look for a confirming source. They won't find one. And when they try searching for it, we'll find them. So, buddy, why don't you hear me out, okay? I'm in the win-win business. I'm very good at it." He paused. "By the way, those are excellent beans, but you want to give them a little rinse first? Takes some of the bitterness out and brings up the oils. Here, pass me a colander?"

Greg watched as the man silently took off his jacket and hung it over a kitchen chair, then undid his cuffs and carefully rolled them up, slipping a cheap digital watch into his pocket. He poured the beans out of the grinder and into Greg's colander, and rinsed them in the sink.

He was a little pudgy and very pale, with the social grace of an electrical engineer. He seemed like a real Googler, actually, obsessed with the minutiae. He knew his way around a coffee grinder, too.

"We're drafting a team for Building 49 . . ."

"There is no Building 49," Greg said automatically.

"Of course," the guy said, flashing a tight smile. "There's no Building 49. But we're putting together a team to revamp the Googlecleaner. Maya's code wasn't very efficient, you know. It's full of bugs. We need an upgrade. You'd be the right guy, and it wouldn't matter what you knew if you were back inside."

"Unbelievable," Greg said, laughing. "If you think I'm going to help you smear political candidates in exchange for favors, you're crazier than I thought."

"Greg," the man said, "we're not smearing anyone. We're just going to clean things up a bit. For some select people. You know what I mean? Everyone's Google profile is a little scary under close inspection. Close inspection is the order of the day in politics.

Standing for office is like a public colonoscopy." He loaded the cafetière and depressed the plunger, his face screwed up in solemn concentration.

Greg retrieved two coffee cups, Google mugs, of course, and passed them over.

"We're going to do for our friends what Maya did for you. Just a little cleanup. All we want to do is preserve their privacy. That's all."

Greg sipped his coffee. "What happens to the candidates you don't clean?"

"Yeah," the guy said, flashing Greg a weak grin. "Yeah, you're right. It'll be kind of tough for them." He searched the inside pocket of his jacket and produced several folded sheets of paper. He smoothed out the pages and put them on the table. "Here's one of the good guys who needs our help." It was a printout of a search history belonging to a candidate whose campaign Greg had contributed to in the past three elections.

"Fella gets back to his hotel room after a brutal day of campaigning door to door, fires up his laptop, and types 'hot asses' into his search bar. Big deal, right? The way we see it, for that to disqualify a good man from continuing to serve his country is just un-American."

Greg nodded slowly.

"So you'll help the guy out?" the man asked.

"Yes."

"Good. There's one more thing. We need you to help us find Maya. She didn't understand our goals at all, and now she seems to have flown the coop. Once she hears us out, I have no doubt she'll come around."

Greg glanced at the candidate's search history. "I guess she might," he replied.

*

THE NEW CONGRESS took eleven working days to pass the Securing and Enumerating America's Communications and Hypertext Act, which authorized the DHS and NSA to outsource up to 80 percent of intelligence and analysis work to private contractors. Theoretically, the contracts were open to competitive bidding, but within the secure confines of Google's Building 49, there was no question of who would win. If Google had spent $15 billion on a program to catch bad guys at the border, you can bet they would have caught them. Governments just aren't equipped to Do Search Right.

The next morning Greg scrutinized himself carefully as he shaved (the security minders didn't like hacker stubble and weren't shy about telling him so), realizing that today was his first day as a de facto intelligence agent for the US government. How bad would it be? Wasn't it better to have Google doing this stuff than some ham-fisted DHS desk jockey?

By the time he parked at the Googleplex, among the hybrid cars and bulging bike racks, he had convinced himself. He was mulling over which organic smoothie to order at the canteen when his key card failed to open the door to Building 49. The red LED flashed dumbly every time he swiped his card. Any other building, and there'd be someone to tailgate on, people trickling in and out all day. But the Googlers in 49 emerged only for meals, and sometimes not even that.

Swipe, swipe, swipe. Suddenly he heard a voice at his side.

"Greg, can I see you, please?"

The rumpled man put an arm around his shoulders, and Greg smelled his citrusy aftershave. It smelled like what his divemaster in Baja had worn when they went out to the bars in the evening. Greg couldn't remember his name. Juan Carlos? Juan Luis?

The man's arm around his shoulders was firm, steering him away from the door, out onto the immaculate lawn, past the herb garden outside the kitchen. "We're giving you a couple of days off," he said.

Greg felt a sudden stab of anxiety. "Why?" Had he done something wrong? Was he going to jail?

"It's Maya." The man turned him around, met his eyes with his bottomless gaze. "She killed herself. In Guatemala. I'm sorry, Greg."

Greg seemed to hurtle away, to a place miles above, a Google Earth view of the Googleplex, where he looked down on himself and the rumpled man as a pair of dots, two pixels, tiny and insignificant. He willed himself to tear at his hair, to drop to his knees and weep.

From a long way away, he heard himself say, "I don't need any time off. I'm okay."

From a long way away, he heard the rumpled man insist.

The argument persisted for a long time, and then the two pixels moved into Building 49, and the door swung shut behind them.

California

by Sean Bernard

Summer evenings we gather in newly restored Craftsmans, extended ranch houses, post-and-lintels built in the sixties, these are our homes, we have money and mortgages now, children who swim in carefully fenced backyard pools, we grill chicken and fish, corn on the cob. We sip wine and eat cheese and grapes and speak of life and weather, sometimes we bring out the guitar, strum a few chords and laugh, waiting for the air to cool, the sun to set, the kids to bed down.

Then we look at each other, wondering if it's time, if we're ready. Always, we are.

We go with slick refilled glasses of wine into the living room, we sit on sofas and chairs, on the floor like children. The lights dim. A screen is pulled. Tape flaps, a fan whirs, a soundtrack clears its throat, and we watch film from an old projector. The projector reminds us of moments we've seen in movies, a nostalgia for a time we never knew.

None of the clips we watch have made the Internet. At work, when we vaguely mention their existence to colleagues, we draw blank stares. No one else knows of them. The clips pull us here—partially—because they are so rare, they are private, only ours. And it's also that our lives are so ordinary, we're not disappointed in this exactly, just cheerfully resigned.

The clips are something else entirely, new, unexpected. Nothing about them has been explained. They are mailed to us intermittently. No return address. We recognize people in them we don't know personally. We feel they are moving us somewhere, propelling to a climax we cannot guess. And we sit forward in our seats, hungrily, waiting for the next clip to begin.

THE FOOTAGE IS especially grainy in #4, the sound cluttered, immediately we hear the whine of the diesel VW Westfalia. The public television show host is on the road again, we see, precisely what the voice-over says as the clip begins, *The public television show host is on the road again, ho-hum, always on the road, hum of engine, hum of road, rectilinear agricultural fields, irrigation canals, mountains, deserts, etc., etc., look at him, the host, so solemn, so distracted.*

The camera zooms in on his face. His chin and jaw are strong. His white flattop seems gray in the footage. There are wrinkles deep around his eyes, like an old surfer from quieter days.

He stares out a window, chin on fist. The voice says, *The host ruminates over a recurrent nightmare: empty deserts, the vast Central Valley with nothing but oil derricks and bones and him standing alone in denim shorts and boots and a white muslin shirt, sunglasses missing and microphone in hand, but not a soul to speak to. It's a nightmare a mind could get lost in.*

On the screen, audibly, the host sighs.

What could it all mean? asks the voice. *Does emptiness forespeak of great miseries?*

The host laughs shortly, "Ha!" and turns from the window. He looks directly at the camera, at us, and it is this moment that always disarms us—that he knows he's being filmed.

He smiles. What does he see? Who is behind the handheld camera?

Why is he smiling?

The camera pulls away as he looks down and taps his hiking-booted feet against the bus's floorboards. The host smiles, the voice exclaims, *Floorboards, he thinks! Such an antiquated word! Were cars truly once fitted with floorboards, actual pieces of wood that somehow did not cause fires? Combustion? Is there an auto museum in this state with an auto museum docent who can say if once cars had floorboards? Do auto museums have docents? Attendants? A pit crew? There is the Internet of course, but we don't use the Internet, we use real people, That Is Who I Am, thinks the host happily, He Who Speaks to Folks, this is how we learn about the world thinks the host how we experience life here in the western Americas, here on the road, and yes! there is indeed one of course the auto museum on Museum Row in downtown Los Angeles, what a fool,*

The film flaps, the clip is over.

EARLY ON WE choose favorites, usually the purer ones lacking voice-over. #10 for example is amusing, behind the scenes, the host and his cameraman in a bright studio, sitting at an older PC, editing segments from their television show. They speak in the monosyllables of men who know each other well. "Too long." "Yep." "Cut here?" "Cut here." "Chatty Cathy, isn't he?" "They all are." #5, too, is enjoyable, the host standing outside an office building (in Studio City, we all agree, though we're only guessing) paying for a delivery of gyros. "Are the fries in there?" he asks in his soft drawl. "I gotta have my fries, delivery man!" He laughs and clearly tips well—the delivery man thanks him twice. The office door shuts, the clip ends, warm, lighthearted.

The majority of us prefer #6. It is long and simply shows the host making coffee. He seems aware of the camera but not distracted. He glances up, nods at us, doesn't speak. He is deliberate: he opens his refrigerator, removes a bottle of water, pours it into an electric kettle, flips a switch. He opens his freezer, removes four bags. He smells each, shutting his eyes tenderly with each sniff. He lingers over one bag, nods. Measures three scoops into a black grinder. Seals and returns the bags to the freezer. He presses a button and grinds the coffee. The kettle begins to steam. He flips a switch. The steam recedes. Onto the counter he sets a coffee mug fitted in what looks like a wet suit; on this, he sets a perfectly fitted filter. Spoons grounds into the filter. Last he pours the steaming water slowly, incrementally, everything precise, just so.

He removes the filter, blows steam from the lip, sips, smiles. And so the clip ends,

WE LAUGH OVER the phone, over email, over text—simultaneously we've realized that we've each been reconsidering our coffee habits, how much we tip, our interactions with coworkers.

After the laughter dies down, we start to wonder if this is no accident.

#23 BEGINS WITH the host sitting forward on a brown leather sofa. On the wall behind him hangs a mirror. There is reflection of neither camera nor crew, a crack in logic that disturbs us.

"But *how* was it done? An F/X program? How much money was spent on this, really?"

This is what Don always wants to know. The strangeness worries him greatly.

Hush, we tell Don. He sighs, sits back, sighs again, frustrated.

In the clip, the host leans over a clear glass coffee table set upon iron claw feet.

On one side of the table is an enormous mound of walnuts, still in shell.

The host pilfers the pile. Eventually he thumbs a single nut into his palm, shuts his eyes, and squeezes. The cracking of the shell is audible. He opens his eyes, his palm, and reaches in for the meat, which he sets on the opposite side of the table. The shell bits he wipes to the floor.

The voice-over says, *The host cracks walnuts just like the Godfather or more to the point, Brando. He never tells anyone of this ability though it is a source of great pride. He cherishes the strength of his hands. It makes him feel of the land. Self-reliant. He could have been an arm-wrestler, he thinks sometimes, and is surprised at his regret in not having been an arm-wrestler.*

The host is wincing, eyes squeezed, two hands around a nut.

He looks at his palm, frowning, and suddenly throws the shelled nut across the room.

He is six feet, four inches, strong as most any man, even at sixty, and when his cameraman of eighteen years (whom he still calls "cameraman") cuts off his feet or hair in close shots, the host cries, "Least you got my guns, cameraman!" flexing his biceps.

The host, reaching over, begins cracking walnuts again, one nut at a time.

From the start we recognized the host, of course. We have all lived in this state longer than expected—some of us born here—and so we all know the public television show, the ebullient host interviewing this person and that, exploring the magnificent wonders of California. The first clip, marked #2, we thought mailed mistakenly: it shows the host washing his hands in an anonymous white bathroom. The clip is shot through a stall in the bathroom. It is barely twenty seconds long. We watched it and wondered what it meant, ignored it, laughed.

Two days and the second clip, #3, arrived: the host in a Ralphs grocery store, considering maple syrups, seemingly unaware of the camera, again the clip short, a minute at most.

Then the third, the fourth, and so on. Sometimes two, even three, four in a week.

We don't yet know what they mean.

After each ends, we go outside and it is cool, even in summer, the ocean breeze only half warmed by the breath of millions between us and the seas; we sip the harder drinks we've moved on to, the gins and scotches, or those of us still driving home our simple glasses of tap water. The kids sigh in sleep through screen windows. We stand barefoot in grass. Something like stars resound above the city skies. Wonderings about the host. Does he know? Is he part of it all? The more modern of us imagine that the clips have been found by an enterprising PBS intern, a film student with a taste for the avant-garde, amused by the potential in these odd and casual outtakes.

This is our early innocent theory, when all the clips seem that way, innocent.

"What if he *doesn't* know?" Don says. He always worries. "What if it's a threat?"

We laugh Don off—certainly the clips are a prank by someone's distant cousin at the public television station. A joke with us. It's all simple fun, and one of these early nights, when we're drunk, enjoying ourselves, someone brightens and suggests, "Let's call him! See what he knows!" We applaud the concept. Quick research is done and we find an extension at the television station attributed to the host. Maybe he's in! It is decided we'll use a pay phone—Don insists, no cell phones, no home numbers. We think this very hip, very noir. Cynthia, our only smoker, recalls once using a pay phone at a nearby convenience mart. Being a water drinker, I'm sent as driver.

We don't speak on the drive, not at first, those balmy winds blowing through my window.

I have the air-conditioning on but she doesn't seem to care.

Finally I ask if she's lived in California long, if she's from Los Angeles.

"No one's from here, everyone knows that." She seems bored. Smokes without asking.

I ask if she's excited about making the call.

She shrugs.

I stay in the car while she puts in quarters, dials the number. She speaks into the phone. I lean forward to eavesdrop. She cups the mouthpiece and turns away. Her face, first smiling, shifts to alarm—and I, so late in the night, so excited, imagine that she's paled in fear. I step from the car, worried, but she's hanging up, saying into the phone, "Good-bye," almost breathlessly.

She looks at me steadily. "Wrong number," she says. She tells everyone else the same.

I'm too nervous to contradict her story, to describe the faces she made.

We all go home disheartened. All week I worry, what has happened, what it means.

Late Thursday the call comes. Another clip. We must gather.

We sit with unusual anxiety, sundown, curtained windows, breath held. We lean forward as the lights dim.

This clip doesn't show the host. It's me. I'm in my car, staring anxiously from a window.

A female voice-over says, *He doesn't know what to do with all his learning, is paralyzed by education, by the choices before him. Does he go to her? Does he sit quietly? Does he—?*

I gape, confused, worried. What will happen next? What will happen to me?

Then I realize everyone in the living room is watching me, holding in laughs, exploding.

It's a pretty good prank, I agree, but it upsets me all the same.

That's the night, you'll remember, we go home early and I refuse to speak to you.

SOME OF US think clip #27 has been unjustly overlooked. It is the briefest of all, a photograph of the host pinned to corkboard. The camera trembles as it zooms in. In the photograph he wears a tuxedo and holds a microphone, addressing an audience we cannot see. One arm swings wide in storytelling grandeur. The voice-over tells us, *At gatherings he says, "How about ol' Marlon Brando? Cracking those walnuts? Ever seen anything so amazing?"*

No one has seen anything so amazing.

He feels overjoyed by this.

AND THEN SOMETIMES you call, which must cost you effort, pride. I appreciate that, I do.

"We haven't seen you," you say. "They miss you."

Sometimes the patience in your voice irritates me.

"I haven't been by," I agree. "You're very perceptive. You should be a private detective."

"You've been drinking." You always sound more tired than angry.

"I don't have to be drunk to be angry," I say.

"Are you ever going to explain it all to me?" Now your voice is sad.

"I saw her in Whole Foods today," you say. Sadder.

Maybe I should explain it all, the *her*, the *they*, the *you*, the *me*. But does any of it matter anymore? All that remains from these stupid pronouns is your voice and its many shades, sad, angry, distant, forlorn, calm, pensive, brusque, bitter, small, and hurt. And hurt.

#9 CONFIRMS OUR unspoken suspicions. No more can we pretend it's all simply a prank.

The clip begins with the host inside a ranch-style home—certainly in the foothills, we agree, above Pasadena, we can tell by the plant life, the yard, the architecture, the curve of earth, sun. The host sits at a kitchen island. Newspaper spread before him. The wet-suited coffee mug.

This time the camera is outside the house, looking in.

Inside, a phone rings very lightly, muted. The host picks it up, we hear and read his lips as he gives a (muted) booming "Hello." *Hello!* cries the voice-over.

We see the host's lips repeat, "Hello!" We see his mouth form the words, "Who's this?"

The host! says the voice.

In his kitchen, the host frowns, pushes a button, sets the phone down. He looks annoyed.

The phone rings again. He checks the number, sets it back down. Now he is worried.

After a moment, though, he answers it.

Hello? whispers the voice-over. *Hello? Hello? Hello?*

And we can see, quite clearly, the speaker's breath against the kitchen window.

THEN WE STAND out on the porch, itchy, it is summer, allergies, invisible pollens swell the air.

"We having fun yet?" Cynthia says to no one, to everyone, lit cigarette wanding the air.

#15 IS ONE of the longest and most unsettling clips. It begins with a black screen and that ever-present voice-over: *The host has always felt restless, he is a jittery man, he understands that all his life he's been waiting for a grand moment. That most people bore him is the great irony of his work. All he wants is what all of us want, a shift, an opportunity to prove himself.*

The screen lights up, is blurry, comes slowly into focus. The host and his cameraman sit in a booth in a diner. Plates of half-eaten eggs and toast. A jar of dark syrup that looks black. Glasses of either milk or orange juice. The two men eat without speaking.

The voice-over explains, *Today they film an Indian and his old oak tree.*

"They don't smile!" the host says suddenly. "They totally creep me out, cameraman!"

The host quietly distrusts Indians, explains the voice-over.

The cameraman looks worried. "You can't say that!" he whispers. "People will hear!"

The host waves at the empty diner. "Hello, everyone! I'm racist!"

The camera pulls away from the men and zooms in on the front door. After a moment a shadow appears. The door opens. (Did the camera know this would happen? It seems so.) A man in brown uniform walks to the table. "Sir?" he says to the host. He holds out a sealed envelope. The host takes the envelope, and tosses it aside. The man walks away.

The cameraman watches this all but says nothing.

The host pokes at the liquid yolk with a crust but does not eat.

The clip goes dark—but after a moment it is light again, we've moved outdoors, time has passed. The host and another man stand beneath what the camera reveals to be a remarkable oak tree, a canopy almost fifty yards in diameter and so thick with branches that it is nearly pitch-black beneath. "Remarkable!" exclaims the host. "What significance has this for your people?"

The Native American is wearing jeans, an ironed polo shirt. His hair is combed neatly.

The voice-over says, *The host can see that this man before him has crazy eyes.*

The Native American talks a little about how his people were persecuted and some even hanged here beneath this sacred ancestral tree, and the host mumbles sadly. The Native American says, "There will be a turning point, of this we are certain. A day of reckoning in this land. There is too much history of violence. Old angers are bone-deep. All the blood has not yet bled."

The voice-over says, *The host is worried. Does this madman think this will make an actual episode? Does he care? This is a wasted trip, the host thinks. But let the man keep talking.*

The Native American calms down and speaks more about the tree, the host asking questions, smiling. Their voices are muted as the voice-over says, *Think about his words, host. A day of reckoning. Interesting, isn't it? After all your hands are strong, you'd be fine, if the world tilted crazy couldn't you lead us into alpine valleys where we will thrive in the climates as once we were meant to in peace and harmony? Couldn't you be the one to save us all?*

In the clip the two men walk away from the tree. The cameraman follows.

The image lingers on the tree. Slowly it zooms to the base of the oak.

We see a torn envelope—one we all agree is the same delivered in the diner.

Beside it, a sheet of paper. The camera zooms in and we read in block letters,

I NEED YOUR HELP. I WILL CALL WITH INSTRUCTIONS.

WE SIT ON the porch in the cool air. Was the man in the delivery uniform part of the plot?

Every time we watch the clip his face is lowered, obscured by the bill of a cap.

How could the host, the cameraman, *not* know they were being watched?

How could they *not* see a second camera filming their every step?

Why the talk of destruction? Of blood?

It's a treasure hunt. We're Hansels and Gretels picking crumbs off the forest floor.

That's what Cynthia says, softly, before she leaves.

She means it lightly but her words don't reassure.

YOU SEEM DISTRACTED. Somewhere else.

Where am I? I'm on a cell phone. You don't know where I am.

You say that as if you're angry, like you need to win a fight. *You* hurt *me*, remember?

No, that's not it at all. You think I did the damage but it's always the other way around. Don't you know that when a person is angry it's only because they were hurt first? Who in this world gets angry without being hurt first? No one. No one. Certainly not me. I'm not crazy.

You don't make sense anymore.

Nothing does and it never did. Who thinks it should? Who came up with such a theory?

Certainly not a person with open eyes. Living in this world. Not him. Not her.

#24 BEGINS IN a darkened house, a camera stepping through fluttering curtains and an open sliding door. The footsteps of the invisible cameraman are barely audible, a faint shuffling on wood floors. The camera enters a room and there's a lump shape in a bed.

A digital clock says it's 3:00 a.m.

The phone rings, the camera pulls back.

A hand reaches from the bed, hits a button. The host speaks softly to the phone. "Hello?"

The voice-over says, *Go to Silver Lake, swim to the fountain, find the next clue.*

And then, as always, darkness.

Our theory is that clip #8 follows #24, at least chronologically. #8 is a long and quiet night sequence, filmed from a car we cannot see. We are following taillights—presumably the host's—and that is the only visual. The voice-over speaks softly. *Los Angeles at night, the 110 freeway, always puts the host in a pensive mood. This is the hidden freeway, curving through hills, past homes where men once raised cows, planted corn and squash, didn't care about the gleam of Dodger Stadium, Chavez Ravine, a canyon named for a hacendado from the nineteenth century, an old husband of a daughter of a son-in-law of a conquistador who killed Indians with muskets and put plow to land and lived by that one word all men in this land once lived by: build. The host knows this, reflects on this now, during his late-night drive. He knows that the landowners died, that the land was parceled, the ranch house fell into disrepair, was razed, the land scooped up by speculators, Broad and Bren, Kaufmann and Argyros, Emmerson, Roski, great place for a ballpark! The history as it always is in this state—vanished. Gone. Amazing.*

Amazing. Amazing. The word is his now. Several years ago he interviewed an etymologist who explained the word's origin. It was unsurprising, after all—maze, labyrinth, to be confused, confounded, caught in a world of unseen connections . . . but still there is a logic to mazes, isn't there? The spool of thread in the first labyrinth, Ariadne, spider's web. Amazed.

Night brings back memory, how he was taunted once as a child back home in Tennessee squalid Tennessee where to dream to delight to awe was not correct. Smoky Mountains sunset, sad, evocative. He had an old Pentax Q10 rigged to a fencepost as tripod and took time-elapsed photos of dying light. He showed the pictures at school. Isn't it amazing? he whispered.

The teacher and the older kids beat him after class. He has admitted this to no one.

The voice quiets but the taillights keep moving, pulling farther away, until the clip's end.

"WHAT IT IS is a meditation on the nature of television, of film," Don suggests one night. We've all had too much to drink. Now we're frustrated—this week's clip, #62, is blank. Nothing. Angrily we blame the creators of this absurd virtual chase that never leaves our living rooms. We assign petty motives. "Bored rich kids," we agree. "Avant-garde assholes," we say.

But Don has a larger and more complex point; he's an academic. "Isn't television after all the great medium of our time? Our country? This state? We live fifteen minutes from Hollywood. We *are* the image, not the thing itself. We are the gaze *and* the object. Why trust these clips as real? They are *film*! Two-dimensional!" Don spills his drink and swears loudly. He's under pressure. Up for tenure in the fall, struggling to complete his book, to find a publisher. Normally we cut him off but tonight we let him ramble.

"What do we know about the host? He is like us—like us, he loves television. He remembers moments—moon landing, Watergate, Ali-Frazier, Munich, those transcendent moments offered only by television. Television is one-way immersion without obligation. You sit, you flip a button, you look away, you read the paper, you look up, you mute, you change channel, take piss, heat pizza, wander house, push-up, sit-up, phone call, text. The Internet? You can't wander from it, it's too needy. Only television is so accommodating!"

He's almost shouting. "It wouldn't work on the Internet! This is film, this is community! Here we are in other worlds—real ones, real people! The world used to be parks! Then it was benches! Then it was sofas at home!" He stares at us, desperate. "I've seen gaming chairs in Target, speakers built in and wires for kids to sit in for hours!" He looks madly. "Quick! I need to write!" Someone passes him a pen and napkin, he grasps them, begins jotting furiously.

We pity and loathe Don. I hold Cynthia's elbow as we walk to our cars. She smiles sadly.

"Now calm down, that was an ocean of gin you drank, cowboy."

She blows me an air kiss, is gone.

In August I take to night-driving, Mulholland, very quick, very romantic, clichéd, stupid.

You know how it goes, of course—the strange things that matter don't go on forever.

First we get a call: there is a new clip, yes, but we will not be watching it.

Why? The police have been contacted. The host has been notified. Much grave concern.

We move harried through the week. Worried at each police car, flinching at each phone ring. Don dutifully sends panicked emails at the top of each hour. The police call some of us in, those who've hosted screenings. One, at the police station, being led to an interrogation room, sees the host. "Of course I'm concerned!" the host is yelling at a detective. "Who wouldn't be?"

Enraged, he looks at our passing friend. The host's face is red, wild, incensed.

A few of us meet in a bar Friday night, sitters for the kids, those with kids. Cynthia can't make it. I tell you as much later. You don't believe me. Another goddamn fight. Over drinks we murmur, booth-cramped. What we know—thanks, police—the clips aren't old. They're made each week. The host has recognized several—he knew where he was, what he was doing. The detectives want answers but the consensus is they don't suspect us. As if that reassures us.

"Why *should* they suspect us?" we protest. "We're not suspect!"

We drink our drinks and agree that police are fools. Someone else is the guilty party.

Or maybe we just can't bear suspecting each other—your cruel theory all along.

YOU TELL ME they like monkeys so Saturday, monkeys. Of course a gorilla escapes its cage.

Really. I need to piss so I leave them in the cotton candy line. Too much water in me, it's too hot in this city, this state. Thirty-five million people roasting three months a year. Madness.

I wash my hands and outside lean over the water fountain. I hear a snorting, a snuffling.

I turn. A gorilla is staring at me. He's much larger than me. Wider. Firmer base. His eyes are dilated, he looks stressed. His muscles are enormous and shagged with coarse hair. Such fingers. He could destroy me. We turn at a siren coming through trees. He grunts, scoots along.

They are at a picnic table, lips coated in pink puffed sugar, and what do I say to them to explain the police swarming the zoo? That those peaceful gorillas can get loose and maybe if you're lucky you won't get hurt? Is that the lesson here? Instead I tell them a story about a father who invents magical glass boxes for his children, all they have to do is push a button and whoosh, glass walls all around, safe and sound. They say what about air? Food? Xbox? I reassure them. These are advanced glass boxes! Totally decked out! They exchange skeptical looks.

I drop them off and you say to me, "Hear the one about the escaped gorilla?"

I tell you the gorilla was me and you don't understand how such a thing could be true.

ON MONDAY NIGHT, in my mailbox, a large yellow envelope. No return address.

I open it inside, lights out, feeling nauseous.

A film canister.

CLIP #49 BEGINS as many do—nothing but darkness. Then a voice from the void.

"Like Genesis," murmurs Cynthia, fanning herself with the business section.

I ask for quiet and listen to the words.

He has seen and touched every part of this state literally traveled every paved road, been to every county seat, every damn landmark and boy there are a few thousand, aren't there, has spoken to professors and town folk to historical society ladies and blue-collar workers to illegals and Border Patrol to vigilantes and human rights crusaders has sat with mayors and senators and oh so many civil engineers, dam builders bridge builders highway designers public transportation consultants architects and other assorted madmen, the oldest living woman in the state, and when she died the next one, and the next, and the next, plucked fruit with original fruit pickers packed crates with original crate packers flipped patties with original burger makers made fries with the sad McDonald brothers and once talked with Ray Kroc himself before that rich and sleazy salesman kicked the bucket has surfed with surfers dived with anemone divers flown with kite fliers sand volleyball players racecar drivers rock climbers artists of every color ate donuts with Sonny Barger Sonny Bono a very young Arnold and so many cultural representatives schnitzel tabbouleh pupusas cricket tacos Oaxacans Basques Guatemalans Romanians Filipinos even Tasmanians all here in this Popeye-arm-shaped state

At this point the darkness recedes. Light enters the frame. It reveals a swastika.

"Holy shit," says Cynthia.

The camera pulls back farther. The swastika resides on the face of a deranged man.

"Whitman?" wonders Cynthia.

The voice continues, *and still the most famous, the one above them all, the firmament over this state is and always has been him, the single most unsettling person the host has ever spoken to, and the host believes that there is something of this man in us all, in the water, in the air, we are all this man, a derangement not as the rest of the country thinks, not Californians as hippies and crystals and free love but anger to the bone that anchor on Popeye's arm swinging round and round the chain digging into the skin of the palm that pressure that needs burst.*

Staring at us steadily is Charles Manson.

That's it. That's the last of the clips.

*

YOU LEAVE VOICE messages via can-and-string, say they're worried about me, you are, too.

Stop working. Take a break. Come inside. Dinner's ready.

But mustn't we believe that if we can unravel just one thing the maze will come undone?

I dream of walking at night in the dark.

I see a large man ahead of me, saying, *Who are you? Why are you following me?*

Carter Sullivan and Jack Benny, oh Jack, *Your money or your wallet* . . . golden silence.

California gold? Television! That clever image, those flashing lights! We are all moths!

I lie awake tonight, thinking of mankind fleeing darkness, flapping at bright screens.

It's not a lightly thought thought.

The state of California. Been there. Not sure I made it back.

Cynthia blocks my number. Don gets tenure. Everyone sort of tolerates me but they don't hide it well. I move out of the city, to an apartment in Eagle Rock. We don't see each other anymore, them, me, you, us. We were part of the group of smart people, so smart, our group of smart clever smart people, and then you and me baby we split and sure we tried to make up, but we split again and they all chose you. No, no, that's not exactly what happened but it's close. I call Don late the way I used to, drunkenly smoking on our porches, but he's married now, has to sleep, notes for tomorrow's lecture. "Those were some strange days," I tell him, my voice thick, I can't help it. He's polite. "Yes, indeed. Strange days. Like in that the Doors song," he says. *That the.* Always smart, Don. "Gotta tuck up, bud," he tells me. "We'll get together soon."

Some days I sit watching reruns of the host's television show. How cheery he is! How sated! I know that TV-him isn't real-him, that he's a different man with his own fears, his own struggles, I know I need to stop need to let go of Cynthia/her the kids/them you/you so I/me can move on but the words trip me up every time, move on, isn't moving on just moving back? Yielding? A surrender? I've never liked this state, it's always felt uneasy to me, trembly, on the verge of explode, it's the air, the winds, the fires, tides under ocean, deserts, I don't know, such foreboding, just a sense is all. You can come to the West what you can do is you can come to this land of grand scale and learn to think in shadows, in shadows men will pan for gold backroom deals buy all the land steal the water forces align, it's obvious, look around, such tremendous forces after all. Look, that dome, that volcano, that geyser. That beach. That bear. Eagle. Whale. Ronald Reagan. Woolly mammoth. Joshua tree. Death Valley. Donner Party. Neverland Ranch. John Muir. Manson. To think no forces are conspiring would be to be a fool! Sometimes I think I could learn a bit by reading up on Manson but what good would that do? It'd only make me obsessive and it's bad to obsess over crazies. Obsess over normal things. It's healthier.

UNPACKING BOXES THIS week, I find these words in an old notepad:

Go to Silver Lake, swim to the fountain, find the next clue.

I laugh about it. So silly, all that, the days of magical mysterious clips, when everything was so cosmic and fraught. Nostalgic, I take a drive to the area. I walk the path that loops the reservoir. There's live music from a bar. Young people laughing. Couples walking past, smiling.

I consider swimming to the fountain. Instead I sit on a bench in sight of the fountain.

A man walks past me. He pauses. Of course I know who it is—of course it's the host.

We stare at each other.

"You're the one," he says. "I dream about you. You're always following me."

I shake my head in denial.

"Why are you here?" he asks. "Who are you?"

"I'm no one," I say.

His voice is soft. He sounds tired. I feel bad for him. He's old. "You did all this," he says.

"All what?"

He sighs. He's confused. Exhausted. Something falls from his hand. I pick it up. A photo. On the back is written #1. It's a Polaroid of a chalked word on a blackboard:

CALIFORNIA

I rise and hand it to him. He nods thanks. For a minute we stand there together. Looking at the photo, then around us, at everything. "What is this?" the host asks softly.

"All this time I thought you'd know," I admit.

We stare out. It's dark but we know what's out in the darkness. The valleys below us. The seas. Hills and roads. People. Silence. Trees. I'm pretty sure we can hear waves crashing in the bay.

Adela[*]

primarily known as The Black Voyage, later reprinted as Red Casket of the Heart, by Anon.

by Chanelle Benz

We did not understand how she came to be alone. We wished to know more, the more that she alone could tell us. It was well understood in our village that Adela was a beauty, albeit a beauty past her heyday. But this was of little consequence to us, no?[†]

We came not to spy and discover if indeed her bloom had faded; we came because Mother did not nod to Adela in the street when so rarely she passed, under a parasol despite there being no sun; we came because we knew that on occasion Adela had a guest of queer character who alighted in her courtyard well past the witching hour; we came because Father fumbled to attention when we dared mention "Adela" at supper, piping her syllables into the linen of our diminutive napkins; and finally, we came because

---

[*] Appears in the French translation as "Alela."

[†] The earliest edition attests to a far more implicit positivism, arguably a glass-half-full tone, emphasized in the substitution of "yes?" for "no?"

Adela alone welcomed us: we, the unconsidered, the uninvited, the under five feet high.

Uncountable afternoons that year, after we had gotten our gruel*—some of us trammeled up with the governess, others, the tutor—we raced en bloc to the back of beyond, letting ourselves into the bedimmed foyer of Adela's ivy-shrouded, crumbling house. She who was alone could not wish to be, yet she alone had made it so, and we altogether wished to know why. Fittingly, we slid in our tender, immature fingers to try and pry Adela open. Perchance she felt this to be a merciless naïveté; as if we, Edenic formlings, did not yet have the knowledge of our collective strength.

What is it, the youngest of us ventured to ask, that has caused you to cloister yourself all through your youth? A thwarted wish to be a nun or a monk?

It was child's play for us to envision Adela pacing down a windowless hall, needlework dragging over stone, her nun's habit askew.

Her stockinged toes working their way into the topmost corner of the divan, Adela fluttered in her crinoline. She pressed the back of her hand to a crimson'd cheek, laughing, Oh dearest children, why it has been years since I have blushed! I suppose I must confess that it was as lamentable a story as any of you could wish . . .

One with pirates, we asked, one of dead Love and dashed Hope? Then we all at once paused, for her eyes summoned a darkling look as if she had drifted somewhere parlous, somewhere damned.

Pirates? Adela? Pirates?

No, she cried with a toss of her head. The lamp dimmed and the window rattled, lashed by a burst of sudden rain.

---

* Here, punishment. There is yet another edition, likely from the turn of the century, which, as such, establishes that upon meeting the children, Adela applies a poultice to their wounds, thereby tinging her kindness with practices of the occult.

Adela, we did chorus, Adela?

Her silhouette bolted upright. Children? The lamplight returned restoring Adela's dusky radiance. You curious cherubs, why it's a foolish tale of romantic woe. I was in love and my love turned out to be quite mad, and well we know, no candle can compare to fire. And so I have chosen to remain alone. Mystery solved.

But for us the mystery had only begun. Who was this Unnamed Love? Was he of our acquaintance? Had he wed another? Was his corpse buried in the village graveyard? Was he locked in a madhouse wherein he paced the floors, dribbling "Adela" into the folds of his bloodstained cravat? We wished to know and demanded that she tell us.

Oh, he is quite alive, murmured Adela languidly, pouring herself a glass of Madeira, *meio doce*, to the brim, stirring, spilling it with her little finger, passing the glass around when we begged for a driblet.

Is he married? we asked, our lips stained with wine.

He is not. Though I have heard it said that he is betrothed . . . to a lovely heiress of a small but respectable estate in North Carolina.

We choked on our commutual sip. Won't you stop him if indeed you love him? You will, won't you? Tell us you will, Adela, do!

No indeed. I wish them happy, she said with a deep violet tongue.

We did not think she could mean what she did say. We pressed her as we refilled her glass, Do you love him still? Was it not a lasting attachment?

Oh yes. I'll love him forever. But what of it? she asked.

How was it possible, we mulled aloud, that Love did not rescue the day? Was this not what she had read to us from these very volumes by which we were surrounded? What of *The Mysteries of Udolpho*? Lord Byron's *Beppo*?

Adela nodded in affirmation yet was quick to forewarn, Do not forget the lessons of *Glenarvon*!*

But should not Love and Truth strive against aught else, ergo it is better to Perish Alone in Exile? Adela, you must be mistaken, we assured her, the oldest patting the top of her bejeweled hand, for if your Love knew you loved him in perpetuum, he would return and return in a pig's whisper!

That would be ill-judged, nor would I permit such a thing, she snapped. As I said, he is quite mad and impossible to abide. Please, let us not speak of it, it was all too too long ago.

Adela, we wheedled, won't you at least tell us the name of your lost love? Don't you trust us, Adela? Why there is nothing you do not know of us! Nothing we have not gotten down on our knees to confess! You know that we borrowed Father's gun and we shot it; that we broke Mother's vase and we buried it; that we contemplated our governess and tutor in the long grass giving off strange grunts and divers groans till their caterwauling ceased in a cascade of competing whimpers.

Now hush! Didn't I tell you not to speak of that? Very well. His name is Percival Rutherford, she yawned, entreating us to close the blinds.

*

IT WAS A bad plan. A wicked plan. We did not know if it came from us or the Devil so full was it of deceit. At home, milling in

---

* A Gothic novel by Byron's jilted lover, Lady Caroline Lamb, that Byron himself reviled as a "Fuck and Publish" in which the innocent, Calantha (the avatar for Lamb), is seduced by the evil antihero, Glenarvon (a thinly veiled portrayal of Byron). Both Calantha and Lamb were subsequently ruined.

the library, in perusal of our aim, we selected a volume of Shakespeare's Comedies since they all ended in marriage and marriage was by and large our end. The Bard, we suspected, had a number of strategies upon the matter.

We set about with quill and ink and put our nib to paper. Sitting cross-legged on the dais of a desk whilst we huddled below in consternation, the oldest clapped us to attention to declaim, feather aloft:

~ Dressing as boys or the boys of us dressing as girls!

We were uncertain as to what this would achieve and thus struck it off.

~ Dressing Adela in disguise so that she can visit Percival and get high-bellied!

We were equally uncertain as to whether Adela was past the fecundating age.

~ Have Adela rescue her love from a lioness thereby making him everlastingly indebted to her!

While there was no doubt in our collective hearts that Adela could, if put to the test, best a lion—was she not the owner of a mighty sword that hung on her wall belonging to her long-deceased father?—we did doubt we could procure a lioness in this part of the country. The second oldest elbowed their way up to the desk, chastising the oldest for bothering to scribble down a strategy that was so abominably foolhardy. The oldest sneered back that the second was the one with no veritable sense of Byronic ideals. To which the second scoffed, Airmonger! But the oldest merely chose to employ a snub and concluded:

~ Fake Adela's death and give Percival report of it? Or! Send a false missive to each, swearing that one loves the other!

Enough, barked the second oldest, crossly claiming that no remedy to our ails could be hit upon in the Comedies. Thus, we began undividedly to search elsewhere in the Canon and quickly fell upon our consensual favorite, *Othello*.* We conferred, then confirmed by a show of hands: we must find Adela a beau to make her lost love jealous; Percival, in turn, would wrestle with the arrogance of his tortured soul until goaded into a violent show of love which would cure him of his madness, whereupon they would be wed, us serving as the bridal party.

Our unanimous impetus was thus: one day, someday, one by one, we would leave this village and behind us, Adela: a tawny, companionless outcast. This we found insupportable.

IT HAD COME to our attention that the ladies of the village were increasingly fond of the new architect, Mr. Quilby, who had taken a lodging above the apothecary. Our aunts were made prostrate admiring his finely wrought neckties and excellent leg. He is not quite Brummell,† the second oldest of us had quipped, not thoroughly convinced of Quilby's suitability let alone his foil status. However, the oldest had been quick to counter that Adela was a spinster by most everyone's calculations—though no lamb dressed in ewe's clothes, with a countenance that was beyond pleasing to the eye—still most of the unattached gentlemen would think her

---

* See Mamney, "In works such as Shakespeare's *Othello*, the female character is a canvas onto which the male character ejaculates his fears of emasculation and desire for dominance."

† The reference to Beau Brummell (1778–1840), the innovator of the modern man's suit and inspiration of the Dandy movement, many scholars believe, infers that Quilby will not suffer Brummell's profligate fate of dying penniless and mad.

a Tabby. However, Mr. Quilby, the oldest had gone on to expostulate, has streaks of silver in his sideburns plainly visible. A man of his years will be less concerned by Adela's being a Thornback.*

THE FOLLOWING AFTERNOON we tromped through the fields and into the village square where we found Mr. Quilby at his drafting table, his sleeves rolled high. Under our arms we had baskets of fresh-baked bread and preserves, for we knew how to be satisfactorily winning children, to lisp and wreath smiles when such a display was demanded.

Mr. Quilby was intrigued by our description of the enchanting recluse with whom all men dangled and yet no man had ever snared. He quizzed us as to why we thought him the one to win such an elusive prize? Though Quilby admitted he well understood that as the village's newest bachelor, matchmaking mamas would be upon him, he owned he was surprised to find that they would recruit their children to employ such endeavors.

We said in one breath that we believed Adela to be lonely and thought perhaps it would cheer her to have a worthy friend near to her age in whom she could confide. Quilby, breaking off a chunk of bread said, betwixt his chews, that he was not averse to such a meeting. The second oldest of us deplored the profusion of Quilby's crumbs, hissing that Quilby was not capable of being the understudy's understudy let alone the rival. But Quilby, unmindful of this sally, inquired, How do you think you could lure such a confirmed hermit?

---

* Nineteenth-century audiences suspected that Adela suffered from syphilis. This disease was thought to result in hardened lesions on the trunk, which serves to give a double resonance to "thornback."

But we were there well before him. The next evening, the youngest of us was meant to take part in a glee at the chapel, a recital to which Adela had long been promised to attend. In this fashion was Quilby gulled and the first act of our accursed cabal complete.

ON THE DAY in question, we were trembling in our boots and slippers, shaking in our corsets and caps, when at long last Adela slipped in at the back of the church. She was a trifle hagged, but we conjectured that if our star was noticeably dimmed, Quilby would only be made less shy on his approach. In the final applause, the oldest of us mimed to Quilby that he should come make her acquaintance, which Quilby did with a genteel air, bowing and being so courtly as to bestow a light kiss atop Adela's hand. The second of us was obliged to yield an approving nod. That blush which we ourselves had beheld only the other day returned and we pursued it down Adela's throat and across her breasts. Bobbing a sketch of a curtsey, Adela made to turn, fretful for her carriage, but Quilby was quick to inquire, Ma'am, is it you that lives in the old Nelson place?

Why yes, sir, I am a Nelson. My father passed it on to me when he died.

Ah, I am an architect. I had thought it quite a rare specimen of local architecture.

Very likely, sir, she mumbled.

Ma'am, I do wonder if I might take it upon myself to intrude upon you, and pay a visit to view the interior?

Feeling the weight of the eyes of the village bearing down upon her, Adela flung out her consent and fled.

Mother appeared at our sides, peeved we'd been seen speaking to Adela, though she would not show her displeasure before Mr. Quilby, with whom she became something of a coquette.[*]

But we, with the newly acquired address of Percival Rutherford in our combined grasp, sent our hero an invitation for Adela's forthcoming, fictive nuptials to Quilby, thus setting the stage for a disastrous second act.

HE WAS NOT what we expected. No, he, who burst into Adela's parlor inarticulate and unannounced, in a mode of dress which was slightly outmoded. He, who had not even donned a white, frilled poet's shirt to our thronged disappointment. On first perusal, his chin flapped, his considerable belly paunched and his forehead accordioned. It was a Rum go,[†] his hasty shuffling to the pianoforte, where moments before we had been in concert, ranging from soprano to falsetto, the boys of us having dropped neither balls nor voices, while Adela played and Quilby turned pages with gusto.

Adela got to her feet, crying out in wonderment, Percy? But this, too, was a disappointment: an unsatisfactory sobriquet. It would have been better had he been named Orlando or Ferdinand or Rhett, even calling him Rutherford we thought would have more than sufficed.

I apologize for coming without so much as sending my card, but I find I must speak with you, his breaking voice inviting despite the want of delicacy in his manner.

Adela flushed, confirming that we had made no synchronized misstep. Pray Percy, this is—you, sir, are unexpected. I have guests.

---

[*] This negation of their mother's sexuality is an example of the male policing the children engage in to mediate any potentially disruptive female power.

[†] An oblique reference to Percy as a dissolute alcoholic.

We sensed it was not us to whom she was referring and used this vexed pause to reexamine our attempt at a retrieved Gallant. Percy did have a thin black mustache of which the second oldest was mightily pleased, and waves of disheveled black hair of which the oldest suspected the application of curl papers, but we contemporaneously disregarded this for Percy displayed the requisite lock clutching. His skin was appropriately pale, a near silky iridescence and we could forgo, on this occasion, to note the plump shadows beneath both his eyes. Lips ruby, chin cleft, sadly brown not blue eyes—yet he was the owner of a fine aquiline nose that any Antony might have had.[*] We would have continued to be encouraged by our mustered précis as we concomitantly plumbed our imaginations in order to restore the bloom of his cankered youth, had not Percy abruptly swooned, causing Adela to bid us: Fetch me the smelling salts!

To this very day, we are haunted by the image of Percy splayed unceremoniously across the divan, his black curls crushed in Adela's lap whilst she wafted him awake. Mr. Quilby, mumpish, hovered, desperate to comment on the impropriety of Percy's head resting so near Adela's nether region. But Quilby bit back his tongue, bided his time and played his part, inquiring, Should a doctor be fetched?

Adela brushed back Percy's hair as he blinked awake and struggled to sit. I do apologize. Percy blenched. I am not altogether well.

Ashley Quilby, declared Quilby coming forth to shake hands. How do you do?

---

[*] Yet another veiled barb as to Adela's sexual depravity, for since the success of Emperor Augustus's propaganda machine, Cleopatra has long been portrayed as oversexed.

This is Percy Rutherford, said Adela, then looking down meaningfully, Percy, no doubt you are fatigued. Why don't you retire to the guest bedroom while you are thus indisposed?

Percy staggered up, nodding vaguely, his greatcoat slipping to the carpet, his stare fixed but not seeing, a rolling intensity in that mad, reckless eye.

Percy having taken his leave, Quilby signaled to us. We affected to be admiring the parlor's wood paneling. He then asked Adela with the utmost civility, I take it that he is known to you? Does this gentleman come unannounced often?

Percy is—we were, you see, childhood friends, wavered Adela.

Friends, repeated Quilby.

Well to own the truth, when I was very young and very silly, we almost eloped.

Good God, ejaculated Quilby, laughing.

Adela's smile did not reach her eyes. Yes, well never fear, we were caught by Percy's mother, and we outgrew such . . . pranks.

Quilby asked Adela to take a turn in the garden. She put out her hand. That does sound agreeable. Will you excuse us, my angels?

Of course, we curtsied and bowed. But as the joint benefactors of her fortune, we naturally followed, concealing our youthful limbs in the bramble.

Once in the garden, Mr. Quilby pumped her palm, saying, Adela, my darling girl—I mean to say, dear madam—I am compelled to confess that since making your acquaintance, I have felt myself enraptured in your presence. This has not happened, nor did I imagine it ever would, since a mild case of calf-love in Virginia almost thirty years ago!

Adela looked pained but primly amused. I thank you. I expect at our age it does seem that it is past all hope.

I suppose it is all too soon but I feel the expediency of—Mr. Quilby dropped to one knee crushing the toes of her slipper and she yelped. Oh sweet heart, forgive me! I am all nerves. Ahem, Quilby cleared his throat, Adela, my pet, I would like permission to pay my addresses to you.

We shuddered in the shrubbery. We had not expected this hasty realization of our fiction. Adela's expression remained bland, as if Quilby had merely inquired about the weather. Eventually, she made a movement, lifting her chin, looking up at what seemed to be the heavens, but what we side by side saw to be the guest bedroom window, and with a gleam in her eye, she said: Why, yes.

AFTER MR. QUILBY had departed, we stationed ourselves at the parlor windows which looked out onto the garden. Ensemble'd, we watched Adela while she read, or rather tried in vain to read, flinging down novel after novel. Hearing a heavy tread on the stairs, she paused and we shrank to the sill, pushing the windows open an inch. Percy came striding through the parlor doors, promptly accosting her, So he's the man you are going to marry? Foisting himself upon her where she lay curled on the divan, he lifted up her skirts to administer some tutor-like touching, from which Adela, no governess, tore away.

You're being a dead bore. She cuffed him.

I find myself unable to resist, came his protest.

You hypocrite, Adela said. What would your betrothed have to say to this vulgarity?

Percy began to turn wildly about the parlor. I don't care! I got the invitation!

Adela watched him from beneath heavy lids. What invitation?

You haven't changed. Do I not have a right to happiness after all this time? I'm not a girl in the first blush of youth.

But I am meant to be the one, Percy sobbed, tearing at his corkscrews.

We, Adela included, were similarly disconcerted; we did not expect that our Gallant should blub.

Pray Percy, don't be vexed. How did you get here? she asked, leading that sad romp back to the divan.[*]

Putting his head on her shoulder, the ramshackle Percy wiped his nose against her sleeve. I suppose you'll think it ill-judged of me, but I borrowed my mother's carriage, he said.

Your dibs out of tune again?[†] she asked.

Percy shrugged, tracing the plunging neckline of Adela's gown. I'm at a stand save for Mother's coin. She leaned back languidly, watching the movement of his fingers. Percy slipped a hand between cloth and flesh. Is that it, Adela? He groped, pinching. You're marrying that man for his money?

Adela was rueful with an air of recklessness we had never witnessed. Pooh, I'm not going to keep correcting you. Though Quilby is a kind, most obliging man. One could not wish for more. In a husband.

Percy kissed her down the side of her neck. I may not have Quilby's annuity, Adela, but you shall always be She and I am He.

Adela seemed to collect herself and fobbed him off. Oh, fetch me a drink.

---

[*] This trope was frequently used to denote a "wild child," however in the context of the Byronic hero discourse, the children are referring to the acute chronic melancholy of Percy's ruttish dissipation.

[†] Adela is revealing that, by bringing his agenda of disharmony upon her, Percy is threatening to dismantle her authenticity with his financial cacophony.

He spied the Madeira. Your father's brand? You think me a fool but I will not let you get away with this, he growled, pouring.

Behind the window, our mouths were watering.

Whatever do you mean? She stood and we ducked.

I won't, he said and polished off the Madeira, holding out an emptied glass. If your precious Quilby knew what you really are, do you think he would still countenance the nuptial?

Nuptial? Stop it. You wouldn't. Adela filled his glass and handed it to him but not before dipping in her little finger.

But I would, he countered. Depend upon it. Percy took that finger in his mouth and suckled. Adela tried to pull away.

She frowned. Your mother would not permit us to be together now as she did not permit it then.

Percy threw her hand from him: O blast your secret! tossing his glass in the fire, almost rousing us to burst into collaborative applause. He shall not have you! our summoned Gallant roared and flew up the stairs, leaving Adela with the arduous task of picking up hundreds of shards of glass.

This too was not what we had expected. Adela had a secret. And this secret was spoiling our plot. We bunched under a marble cherub to consider a concurrent abandoning of ship. But the second oldest leapt up on the angel's knee, a hand round its marble neck and holding a penknife high, condemned us roundly as traitors to the cause, rasping, We must needs rally! Each of us must take a blood vow to help Adela no matter what the twist!

Hand in hand, we solemnly rose to the penknife and were poked, suckling our little fingers as hard as any Percy. In line unbroken, we marched and orbited Adela who was still kneeling in the shards.

Weep no more, we have come! But before we tell you the wrongs we wish to undo, you must tell us, Adela, what is your secret? What are you?

Adela brushed her mussed dress with shaky fingers. Oh no. Oh my dears . . . You see, my father was not a gentleman but a pirate, and he saved Percy's father's life. His sole request was that Percy's father keep watch over me, his motherless daughter born on the wrong side of the blanket. Yes. That Merry-begot was myself.*

Till then we had never met a Two-legged Tympany!† We inspected her anew for signs. Why did your father jilt your mother? Was it at the altar, we asked, our eyes filling with the image.

Adela turned to gaze into the fire, muttering, It is abominable that this should happen now. I thought I should be safe! Oh but why did I ever hope to escape?

Will you toss Quilby aside, Adela? we asked rubbing our hands together. You must! The second oldest averred, Quilby will certain not want you, Adela, if you are a base-born.

But Mr. Quilby has been all tenderness. Dear children, please be kind, please endeavor to understand what you cannot possibly . . .

We moved as one to tug her skirts but exchanged this tactic for a rough shake. Percy knows your secret and still loves you, Adela! We will go and fetch him and he will whisk you away!

No, she cried, you will not! I will not!

Is there something more that you are not telling us? we inquired.

No, don't be silly, little ones, she said.

---

* Such vernacular as "merry"-ness suggests that Adela's "merry" sexual misconduct has been enjoyed since birth.

† Note the children's conception of Adela's bastardy approaches deformity.

You would unburden all to us, wouldn't you? You wouldn't want to wound us by keeping more secrets. Mother might ask what we've been up to all day and why we look so blue-deviled. It makes us ever so sad that you do not trust us as we thought. Why, we are positively sick! we choked. We're about to have spasms! On cue, the youngest of us started sobbing. Oh won't Mother wonder why all our eyes are so red, why our complexion is so wan? Shall we unburden ourselves to her, Adela, shall we?

Adela stared at us as if we she hardly knew. I am so tired, she said in a strangled voice not quite her own. No. Don't, please. I will tell you. I will have done.

We lay on our fronts, our chins on our fists, rapt to receive!

My father was a tawny-moor of the West Indies and because of it, Percy's mother would not allow us to be married.[*] He is badly dipped and lives practically on her purse strings.

We will here divulge that we were jointly taken aback. We had never seen the daughter of a tawny-moor before, let alone stood in the daughter of a tawny-moor's library. We did not desire to think of Adela differently, but we could not deny that she had become someone quite Other.

You have been unfaithful to us, Adela, we quavered and asked if we could touch the hair of a black base-born.

She lowered her head, saying, But you must believe that I had no intention of breaking your trust.

The oldest of us traced her cheek as if a slight swarth should

---

[*]*Adela*, lighting the way for *Wuthering Heights*, is known to have thoroughly inspired Charlotte Brontë to pay homage in the creation of Heathcliff, the construction of Moor as man, allowing Brontë to position the subaltern as the vessel of violent agency.

rub off.* Our fingers fingering her, the second oldest speculated, Her moorness merely lends her character—the secret was only an error in judgment. And she does not look yellow-pined, the oldest approvingly replied. No indeed, she is perfectly fair, the second urged and concluded, Why the curtain is not down, but we are in another tale entirely!

All the while Adela stood, unmoving, watching us from far back in her eyes.

However, we all must agree she is metamorphose'd and that for this she must suffer, the oldest said feverishly kissing her hand in the manner of a Percy.[†]

Adela flushed, snatching it away rigidly. How dare you! Do not touch me! You are but still in the Nursery!

The oldest climbed on Adela's desk, clapping us to attention, declaiming, quill aloft:

~ Suiciding by poison or suiciding by knife!

We were dubious as to what this would achieve and thus we struck it off.

~ Bake her children in a pie, then invite her to the feast!

Not only did Adela not have children, but we were equally uncertain as to whether we wanted to be in a Revenge Tragedy.

~ Be strangled, be drowned, have her eyes gouged out?

---

* This fluidity in their conception of race typically predates the nineteenth century and is most often found in the eighteenth century where skin color was a less fixed secondary identity marker. For a charming and oft incisive exploration of this, see Roxann Wheeler's *The Complexion of Race: Categories of Difference in Eighteenth-Century British Culture.*

† A Creole female, which Adela has now claimed as her identity, was commonly depicted in the discourse of white colonial domination as lascivious and unstable due to the West Indian heat.

While there was no doubt in our collective minds that Adela could, if put to the test, achieve a nobly gory end, we did not know how to go about it.

The youngest of us tripped forward, opening *Troilus and Cressida*. Zounds! cried the oldest, Adela'd make a beautiful prisoner of war. We can sell her and our early idyllic notion of the ownership of love will remain ours evermore. False as Cressid, concurred the second.

Just then Percy, the Percy whom we ourselves had procured, whom we had selected as the hero of our hobby-horse,* leaned in the door with a pistol cocked. You naughty children, he smiled yet snarled. Now since you are so anxious to be a part of Adela's fate, I will prevail upon you all to tie up my darling girl with the curtain cord.

We shall not, we sputtered. We haven't sold the Negress so she is not yet yours!

The Devil she isn't! he shrieked, lifting the pistol.

Percy, you fool, they are but children! Adela exclaimed.

Yet Percy pointed his gun at us. I suspect it is these brats who have entrapped you. I wouldn't have taken you for such a milksop, Adela. O my sweet martyr, Percy cackled. My little devils, shall you help your bit of ebony to her cross?

We did not want to do it but we all together did; the sum of us helped the villain. Adela offered us no violence, not even when some of us, being fascinated by her whimper, tightened the cord so that it bit into her breast.

So my underlings, how would you choose this story to end? Love or Death? Percy pointed the barrel at the oldest: You, choose.

---

* This carries the connotation of Percy's animalistic virility astride Adela's noble savagery. See Dowd, whose *Barbarous Beasts, White Toys, and Hybrid Paternities: Considerations on Race and Sexuality in the Caribbean* examines these tensions.

The oldest of us looked to the rest of us, but we shook our heads, having come to no unanimous answer. We had not had the time to parley.

Come child, let me see how well Adela has magicked you, he said.*

L-l-love? stuttered our oldest and the rest of us, knowing it necessary, absolutely necessary, to preserve an absolutely unified front, followed suit: Love! Love! Love!

Percy crowed. Well I do believe Love has conquered all. Adela, my sweet, Percy congratulated her wryly, you have taught them so well.

Not I, replied Adela. For I would have chosen Death.

Don't be such a ninnyhammer, spat Percy, shaken.

No, she corrected, you cannot think me so chicken-hearted. All these years I have done without you, what makes you suppose I should want your uneven tyranny now?

All plus Percy were silent. Then he intoned: It would be best to gag her mouth, she's ruining my arc. We, wrenching down more curtain rope, pushed it into the wetness of her mouth.

However, Quilby, unheralded, unexpected, taking us by unawares, burst into the parlor, bellowing in horrified accents, Adela, my poor girl! Damme, what has this blackguard done?

She's a black base-born and she wants Death! we shouted.

Quilby's eyes fairly started out of his head. She is God's creature, he said, throwing off his coat then loosening his cravat. And you shall not harm her.

The two men, prodigiously embroiled in fisticuffs, grappled at each other, vying for the pistol. Adela worked furiously to extricate

---

* This accusation hearkens to the seemingly fixed, misogynist association between West Indian women and black magic which was stereotypical during the period in which *Adela* was composed.

her wrists and, once free, pulled down her gag, crying, No you shall not! rushing toward Percy. And we, en masse, ran as one toward Death, wedding our wee bodies with hers, until her, our, their fingers wrapped about the pistol.

O Adela, though we now know the Why, that How is known solely by those individual fingers which pulled the lone trigger. We only know presently, and indeed knew then, that he looked more elegant in death than we ever knew him to be in life, or even when we first had collaboratively imagined entangling him.[*]

We, no longer the children we have been, have never forgotten that, no matter what shade the skin, the blood is always red. And for this denouement, we beg you, Adela, to forgive.

Finis.

---

[*] In the first German translations, it is curious to note that "she" rather than "he" dies.

Ladykiller

by Miracle Jones

Tre took the entire weekend to change his profile status from "IN A COMPLICATED RELATIONSHIP WITH THE DEVIL" to "ENGAGED TO JESSICA TRAPPER."

He almost waited too long. Jess's hurtness was seeping out of the walls like ectoplasm, almost manifesting physically in the apartment they shared.

"It doesn't matter what it says on Facebook," he lied casually, when she asked him. "This is about us: not all those assholes on Facebook."

"I changed it in the bathroom literally ten minutes after I said yes," she said, squeezing one of his thighs as she curled up against him, trying to be more amused by her own response to her own joy than upset by his willful rejection of this extremely clear and obvious new rule w/r/t love.

"We are gonna talk about Facebook in the future like our parents talk about cocaine," he said. "Man, I can't even remember that decade. I was on Facebook the whole time. I met your mother on Facebook. I did so much Facebook that my balls went numb and I could only fuck on Facebook. You want to see pictures? They are on Facebook."

"You sure you aren't having second thoughts about being relationshipped?" she asked him.

"You make it sound nonconsensual," he said.

"Nine times out of ten it's somebody you already know," she said.

"The real problem is relationship culture," he said.

Eventually, she decided he was merely being dumb and not having "secret thoughts." She drifted off to sleep beside him.

But Tre lay awake all night, watching who liked the post and responding to the comments.

At Buzzfeed the next day, Tre felt doomed. He coasted through work, trying to get as much done as possible. Everyone kept sarcastically congratulating him, which didn't help. He figured out thirteen things that only people born in 1990 would know, found proper .gifs for them, and then he left early.

Jess had her Pilates class on Mondays so they usually both fended for themselves when it came to dinner. He wasn't sure what to do.

He drove over to a strip center where they sometimes went for Appalachian food. There was a Chili's there. He would go to Chili's. Chili's was the right place. It was a place you went when your life was over and you were ready to die.

He got a glass of wine and a plate of fried cheese at the bar.

He took a long gulp of the bad wine, feeling cursed, and opened Facebook on his phone.

He started looking through the profiles of old girlfriends, trying to figure out what qualities they had in common, besides dating him. Maybe if he could determine some essential quality they shared he would find out something useful about himself, something he could use as a wedge or weapon.

He resisted the temptation to like anything they posted or to make any comments. Surely doing so now, post-engagement, would seem hostile.

"Drone over there just bought you a drink," said the bartender. "What do you want?"

"The fuck?" said Tre.

"Are you Tre?" said the bartender. "Drone said your name was Tre. You want another glass of wine or like top-shelf scotch or what?"

Tre craned his neck over his shoulder. He had never seen a drone in person before.

"Over there," said the bartender. "By the bathroom."

The drone slumped along one side of a vinyl booth, smiling at him with high-definition red lips and big soft cartoon eyes. It was female-shaped. It was wearing a tight black dress and was sitting over a fizzy cocktail that had been purchased purely for decoration. The drone's proportions were disorienting and hallucinogenic: the six-tone skin rippled in metallic tones, showcasing abstract animated tattoos that seemed to change hue and texture based on the amount of indirect light it absorbed from the stained glass bar fluorescents.

"I've never seen one in real life before," said the bartender. "Somebody you know?"

"I really doubt it," said Tre.

As he stared, the drone stood up and arched its back. Everyone in the restaurant was watching the machine seduce him. They were laughing at him and pointing, or else gawking and taking pictures.

Tre found himself slipping off of his barstool and walking over, his head swimming, his heart filling with quiet murder. He had to talk to the drone or it would keep trying to get his attention. He slid into the booth and sipped his drink.

"Hello," said the drone in its digitally altered machine register. There was a human being on the other end of that voice typing words to him. Some hidden secret subjectivity. It was entirely possible that people didn't have any kind of external soul that mattered and might survive death, but this drone definitely did.

"Do I know you?" asked Tre.

"Sure," said the drone. "Sure you do."

"Then do you mind if I inquire as to who is piloting this magnificent machine that is buying me drinks?"

"I am Anonymous, lol," said the drone in the same throaty but uninflected half-tone voice. "Does Anonymous get you hard? Does Anonymous make you feel sex feelings lol?"

Tre set his drink down carefully on a Chili's coaster. The drone immediately slid around so that it was sitting right next to him. It leaned in so that it was touching his thigh. There was a warm hum coming from inside the drone that he could feel through the plastic seat. He could feel it vibrating his prostate; pulling at his testicles. The smell coming from the drone was simultaneously musky and artificial, like a werewolf that had just fucked a rack of fashion magazines.

"No seriously," he asked. "Who is in there?"

"I hear you are getting married," said the drone. "That must be exciting. Such a change lol."

"Do you know me for real or are you just learning stuff about me right now on the Internet?"

"Come on now Tre," said the drone. "Relax a little bit. Talking to us is like praying. We only want to help you and we have the power to do it."

The drone reached over and put one firm flexiflesh hand on his thigh.

"Do you want to see a picture?" asked the drone. "Something exciting?"

"I need to go," said Tre. His phone vibrated and he looked down. He had a message. He opened it. It was a picture of the drone all tied up with a ball gag. There was semen, or some kind of semen substitute, trickling down its haunches and it was looking trustingly at the camera. There was a poster on the wall behind the drone for *Finding Nemo*.

"Do you like that?" asked the drone. "Does it excite you?"

The image was sudden and shocking. It was an exact replica from a series of photos he had taken of his college girlfriend in her dorm room, back long ago before people realized that everything digital was permanent. It was a perfect replica in every detail.

The picture was still on one of his old hard drives. His forehead broke out in a cold sweat. That's where it had to have come from. When was the last time he had connected that hard drive to a computer?

"Where did you get this?" he asked.

"Do you want to see more?" asked the drone. "We just want to make you happy lol. We can make more, if you like. Tonight. Right now. We can have all the sex! LOL!"

"I'm not going anywhere," said Tre.

"I thought you were leaving?" said the drone, bemused. "Well, if you are going to stay, we should talk about interesting subjects."

"What do you want to talk about?" asked Tre. He was stalling. He needed to think. This could be an old friend; an old enemy. Someone he had hurt in the past. Some thirteen-year-old kid. Why today? Did it have something to do with changing his relationship status? Had somebody been watching him all along, waiting for him to finally decide to "settle down" before striking?

They didn't have to live anywhere close to him. They could be on the other side of the world.

It didn't have to be someone alone, either. It could be a team of people. A bunch of his friends could have all chipped in together and rented the drone for the evening, and they were now fucking with him, all sitting around with beers laughing and debating what to type next. One person at the controls, another busily hacking his laptop, another person figuring out what to say next to make him sweat. They didn't even have to be American. They could be feeding everything through a language filter.

He had no power here.

He realized all of a sudden that he was very turned on. He needed to focus; to keep his mind away from the very real creature in front of him made out of silicon and rubber and firm warm plastic, he tried to imagine a bald and overweight middle-aged man chain-smoking in front of a bank of computers, pacing back and forth, barking out orders to acne-faced teenagers who were pulling levers and cackling, all wearing Babymetal T-shirts.

"Relax," said the drone. "We can talk about your fiancée if you like. She seems nice lol. How long have you known her?"

"Four years or so," said Tre.

"You seem nervous," said the drone. "Don't be nervous. How did you guys meet?"

Tre paused. He needed to ascertain what the drone knew about him in order to figure out who it was. Anybody could find out facts about him. They were everywhere; nothing was private anymore. He needed to know the color and shape and taste of these facts in order to triangulate the drone's likely pilot.

"We met at a little crab restaurant," said Tre. "I was there with a buddy and we sat at the bar. She wasn't ordinarily a bartender there, she was normally a server, but she was filling in for the night and we got to talking."

"Did you go home with her right away?" asked the drone. "Are you a player? LOL."

"What does it matter? Don't you already know the answer?"

"Does she know how you met?" asked the drone.

"What do you mean?" said Tre.

"I mean, if I asked her how you met, would she tell the same story?"

"Yes," said Tre. "Of course."

"So you haven't told her."

"Told her what?"

"About your buddy the doctor," said the drone. "And the program the two of you made to have a good time in bars. About Ladykiller lol."

Tre's mouth went dry. The drone leaned in close, seeming to taste the aroma of his panic. He and Peter had sworn each other to secrecy about that. In fact, his shame and revulsion were so complete that he had mostly managed to convince himself it had never happened. Where was Peter now? He was practicing medicine in Florida. He was happy. This couldn't be Peter. But what if Peter had a secret LiveJournal or something?

He wanted to run away, but the drone was too dangerous. It knew everything about him, and he didn't know what it wanted or who it was yet. It was as precise as a cat with a beetle, flipping him over onto his back and watching him scramble to his feet before flipping him over again, staring at him, watching him struggle, trying to learn something about the nature of struggle itself.

"You should tell the truth when people ask," said the drone. "It's a much better story lol. One night your friend the doctor was drunk on tequila after passing one of his big doctor exams. He had recently dissected a cadaver that had died from a self-inflicted drug overdose and he was having an existential crisis because the cadaver had such glorious and stirring breast implants. He Facebook-messaged you about it. He had been worried about his sexual response to a dead woman, and you tried to cheer him up by going as far as you could along with him, talking about breast implants and how they all had to have RFID tags embedded inside them so that they could be tracked for insurance and emergency purposes. And then you said: maybe we could track those RFIDs in living people. With the right open data algorithm, you could find all the people with breast implants in a three-hundred-yard radius and match them up to their Facebook profiles. You both spent the next month coding it up. It was good code lol! And even though you found a few people with plates in their knees and artificial limbs, it worked like a goddamn charm, yo. You became a sex wizard! You had weird confidence, knowing things about people before you even said hello. You got so laid. You got ten thousand times laid. And *that's* how you met your fiancée. It was good and smart. We salute you."

"How do you know all that?"

"Because we care about you," said the drone. "We are Anonymous. We are legion. Sometimes we are benevolent lol and reward those who serve the world. It was a brilliant program. Did you know that people still use it to this very day? You are almost a hero in certain circles. In other circles you are not a hero at all. There are many circles."

"I didn't know that," said Tre.

"Ladykiller," said the drone. "Was that your title or your friend Peter's?"

"That was me," he said weakly.

Tre realized now that it didn't matter who was piloting the drone. He was in an extremely precarious situation and he needed to get away.

"What do you want from me?"

"We don't want anything," said the drone. "We are giving ourselves to you as a wedding present, like a fruit basket. You can do whatever you want to us. We are yours to keep. We thought about hacking a power user on FetLife and sending some willing slave from the bottom of a leather family to you as a gift, but this is more clean. We will both keep our secrets: you won't tell anyone what happened, and we won't tell you who we really are. It will be so fun for both of us. This whole body is artificial. Have you ever wanted to fuck the Internet? LOL."

The drone reached into its purse and pulled out a Band-Aid-colored pill bottle. The drone shook the bottle, rattling the contents.

"What are those?" asked Tre. "Now you want to drug me?"

"They are harmless," said the drone. "Just sugar. But they are password pills. For the suite."

"I can't stay with you," said Tre. "I have to get home. You are trying to hurt me somehow."

"You don't have to stay the night," said the drone. "You can leave whenever you like. But you should really come with us. So we can be alone together. I bet you aren't really honest with your . . . desires . . . until you are alone with someone lol."

A shadow fell across his face.

There was somebody standing over them.

The bartender was standing at their table, grinning knowingly.

"Your car is ready," said the bartender.

Tre followed the drone out of the restaurant, unsure of how to get away. Could he run? He found himself getting into the back seat of the car beside the drone. The car didn't have a driver. It navigated the streets carefully and persistently, tinted windows concealing this terrifying vacuity from other drivers on the road.

The drone slipped its hands down Tre's pants and encouraged him to feel the warmth of its perfect mouth, the wetness of its breath.

"You have to take one of the pills whenever you want to come up," said the drone. "Your stomach acids will dissolve the coating and prime the transmitter. It is temporary; a bit like a glow stick. By the time it stops working, you have to be gone, or otherwise security will be called. You can take another pill if you want to come see us again. We are a present to you. For all you have done. From Anonymous. For the lulz."

Tre dryswallowed one of the pills and put the rest in his pocket.

The lobby of the building they stopped in front of was also empty. The elevator snapped open. There were no buttons in the elevator, just smooth metal on every side.

"It is scanning the pill inside you," said the drone.

The elevator opened on the top-floor suite.

"This is nice, isn't it," said the drone. "Facebook tells us whose birthday it is and who is in a relationship and who is having kids. We like these things. We say: 'Happy birthday.' Facebook measures how responsive we are to our peers, and to ads, and how much money we make based on the trips we take and the wonderful things we buy and the exciting jobs we have. And when we want to fuck somebody with a drone as a present, Facebook makes it so easy, doesn't it? Everything is so nice now lol."

Tre waited for the drone to turn its head to walk deeper into the suite.

And then he slammed into it from behind, tackling it to the ground. The drone was not made for combat or battle. Its responses were silky and catlike as he straddled it and got his knees onto its shoulder blades. He put his boot on its neck.

"Lol," said the drone. "You mad?"

His phone beeped at him. Alerts. Hadn't he turned his ringer off?

There was a marble side table by the foyer. With his boot still on the drone's neck, he swept a ficus and an antique clock from the tabletop and then picked up the table by the base. He swung the table around and broke the legs off. He just wanted the slab of marble.

The drone writhed beneath him, stroking his ankle seductively. He slammed the piece of marble into the drone's head, cracking it. He heaved and sweated, bringing the slab of marble down again and again. His phone kept bleeping at him. The alerts streamed from his pants pocket, a nearly constant irritating whine.

"Shut up," he said.

Any piece of the drone that moved, he bashed it with the slab of marble. He was precise and consistent. The fingers twitched; he bashed them. An eyelid fluttered; he smashed it as hard as he could, making sparks, sending chips of marble flying.

Eventually, the drone lay completely still on the soft rug beneath him. He was sweating and kept burping up stomach acid, though he felt nothing but cold inside.

It's the equivalent of breaking a camera, he thought to himself. The fact that it feels like murder is part of the camera's new defense mechanism.

He leaned against the door of the suite and finally checked his phone. The alerts were all from Facebook. There were thousands of them and they were still coming in.

He scrolled over to his Facebook wall. It was filled with pictures of him from every angle smashing the drone. The only text accompanying the pictures was a frowny face. There were thousands of them; each moment captured in beautiful three-tone sepia. Too many to delete.

He looked for the camera taking the pictures. Was it in the ceiling tiles? Was it embedded in the doorframe?

He was up on a chair using his phone to look at Facebook with one hand and searching the ceiling tiles with the other when a security guard unlocked the door.

"I had to smash it," said Tre. "It was hacking my computer."

"The cops are on their way," she said. "Just so you know."

"Man," he said. "Why did you call the cops? It's a fucking *robot!*"

"It calls the cops automatically, dude," said the security guard. "Do you know how much these things cost? You basically just crashed somebody's yacht, dude."

"Whose apartment is this?" asked Tre.

"You mean you don't even know where you are?" asked the security guard, laughing.

His phone was ringing. It was Jessica. He put his phone on the ground and started smashing it with the slab of marble, gritting his teeth so hard that they squeaked, while the security guard just shook her head and laughed, not getting too close, quietly taking video with her phone just in case the cops had questions.

The Transparency Project

by Alissa Nutting

After college, Cora found it hard to get a well-paying job. Amidst stints as a waitress, a bartender, a barista, she came across a few medical testing gigs at a local research facility. Usually, these paid a few hundred dollars and required her to put a cream onto her skin that sometimes caused a rash and sometimes didn't, or to put drops into her ears that caused variable levels of itching and/or burning and then required her to rank the intensity of itching and/or burning on a numerical scale.

There were many things in life that Cora found difficult, like choosing which scent and brand of dishwashing soap to purchase. If all bottles of dish soap cost the same amount of money, were all the same size and color and merely differed in fragrance, it would still, she felt, be a very hard decision, because there were many fragrances and they weren't even in the same fragrance category: there was citrus, floral. There were atmospheric titles like Ocean Breeze that inspired their own line of thought and questioning altogether (for example, which ocean? How strong a breeze?). But other tasks, such as being at a given place at least fifteen minutes prior to the time when she actually needed to be there, had never proved to be a struggle for Cora. The researchers noted and appreciated this, and it led to her being offered The Transparency Project.

The Transparency Project was not a one-day test but a hired, permanent job that would last until her natural death. When the leader of the research team said the word "natural" in the phrase "natural death," he emphasized it in a very unnatural way. Each year, her paid salary would be the previous year's average salary for all full-time workers in the city where she lived, in addition to a generous benefits package. All she had to do in order to receive this money every year until her *natural* death was come into the facility for monitoring and testing two days a week, eight hours per day. And have the operation. She could travel up to six weeks of the year, provided she allowed a monitor to meet her at a nearby hotel room for monitoring twice a week during each week of travel. If she were ever injured, comatose, or unable to come to the facility for any reason despite being alive, she would allow them to come to her for the monitoring. There would be legal documents outlining this permission. She would sign them.

The operation would remove all existing skin and fat from a front section of her torso, starting at the top of her ribs and ending at the top of her pelvis. Her blood and muscles would be infused with a harmless solution that would allow them to become transparent under select wavelengths of light, including daylight and fluorescent lighting, allowing researchers to easily see through to her internal organs. Her skin in this region would be replaced with a clear, waterproof polymer film; when she wasn't at the facility, she could wear a flesh-colored silicone panel that would easily snap onto a sternum-mounted fastener. When they showed her the panel plate, she rubbed her hand across its surface carefully, like it was asleep and she didn't wish to wake it up. "What's this?" she asked them. It was a small brown nub in the sternum's center that had been designed to look like a protruding mole. It was the panel's release button.

The first few months after the surgery, she never released the panel on her own, and on observation days at the facility when the panel was removed, she felt very cold despite the fact that there was no drop in her temperature readings. She began bringing a blanket that she'd put around her shoulders when the panel came off. She avoided looking down at her own organs when the panel was off, mindful to keep her posture straight and her head directed forward or looking up at the ceiling. In order to do this, she pretended she was standing on the ledge of a very tall building, because she was very afraid of heights. Dropping her eyes would not provide a welcome view.

But gradually, this changed. The panel didn't feel like her own skin so much as a bodice or a giant waistband; she always wore the panel beneath her clothes in public, but when she got home she found she liked removing it and walking around her house in an open robe. The panel wasn't capable of sweating, but it often felt that way—despite being dry and even slightly cold to the touch, it felt like a tight shirt that was collecting her body's warm moisture; when she snapped it off and set it on her nightstand, always balancing it upright on its edge against a reading lamp, she swore her organs felt a pleasant rush of air. This wasn't possible, of course; the plastic layer that coated them wasn't porous or permeable. But the psychological feeling was a pleasant one that she enjoyed. At first she only caught sight of her organs in accidental peripheral glances—the mirror, the reflective surface of the new chrome kitchen appliances she'd bought with her new salary. Then, day by day, the coils and twines of her insides became familiar geography with patterns and symmetry that didn't threaten her sense of order but instead increased it.

The only sight that continued to give her discomfort was her beating heart. Not its image but its constant movement when she was at rest. Its pulsing reminded her of the way a digital alarm clock's numbers would flash repeatedly when the power went out and made her feel like an essential part of her needed to be reset. During each session at the research facility, a therapist came into the room at some point and spoke with her and sometimes Cora would talk about the sight of her beating heart with the therapist. Usually the therapist had her speak directly to her heart, saying affirming sentences such as, "Heart, I appreciate you keeping me alive. Heart, I am grateful for your service." Other times, the therapist asked her to report any unpleasant dreams. Early on, she had a dream that she was at the beach in a bikini, and upon seeing her internal organs a flock of gulls swarmed around her and tried to peck them out. Later she had a dream where she thought she'd woken up only to find herself standing at the foot of her bed watching herself sleeping. Her dreams were being projected on the skin panel resting on her nightstand, playing upon it like a video. It was the dream where seagulls attacked her at the beach.

Recently the therapist asked Cora to consider starting to date again. Cora replied that she'd never enjoyed dating, but that prior to the operation, it had been her habit to seek out companions for one-night sexual encounters. That she'd done this a few times a year prior to the operation, but had not done it since. "Then try finding someone and having sex," the therapist said.

So she joined an online service and tried. The first man declined to meet after hearing about the operation she'd had. The next said it was okay but changed his mind when she took her shirt off and he ran his fingers along the edges of the panel's thin seams. "I work on computers all day," he explained, "taking their cases off. Sometimes I get repair calls because the cases come loose and fall off by accident, all on their own." She assured him that it wouldn't, declining to admit this was possible if he pressed the release mole firmly enough by accident, or if she pressed it firmly enough on purpose. The third was fine with the operation and the panel's seams and even asked her to take the panel off and leave the bedroom light on. He wanted to watch her organs during intercourse.

They began having sex, but soon he stopped. "Sorry," he explained. "I feel like I'm watching a surgery in progress or something," he said. Cora was annoyed but thought it was better to pretend to be confused. She got ready to say, "There's no surgery," or tell him she'd had the operation over a year ago, except she got distracted by her dresser's mirror. She watched her heart beating again and again like an unanswered question, like a phone in her chest that would not stop ringing. "Hello?" Cora said. In the mirror's reflection, she could see that the man was no longer next to her in bed. Maybe he'd gone to the bathroom, or maybe he'd quietly left.

The Gift

by Mark Irwin

He was about the size of a wooden match and floated—arms spread out—like a skydiver in a small jar his wife had given him, perhaps because they were childless and he was always traveling.

She gave it to him on their twenty-fifth wedding anniversary, in October, while they were on a retreat at a monastery in northern New Mexico. They were having dinner at Francisco's, just north of Tres Piedras, sitting by the fire when she said—more tenderly than he'd ever known—"Here Mark, I'd like you to have this."

At first he thought it was a small salamander, for they used to catch those in mountain ponds, but upon looking in astonishment he could see that this tiny figure swimming about in a thick fluid appeared to be a man—perhaps because of its short black hair. He could see no sexual organs, and the body tight he thought it was wearing appeared to be its own skin.

"Claire, what a wild gift," he said. "Thank you. Where'd you get it?"—then from her solemn, penetrating, and almost religious stare, he knew it was real.

Sliding, sometimes somersaulting, while at other times resting on its side, the tiny figure always seemed buoyant.

"Well," he said, as if to bolster his own disbelief, "*he* must have cost a fortune!"

"Nothing," she said.

"Where'd you get it? Some lab in California?" he said in jest, half mockingly, but she only smiled, as she did when he'd asked her to marry.

Smiling again, she added, "He'll keep you company on your trip, since I have the cats, but don't open the jar. His food source is infused in the liquid and all the waste is absorbed."

Too good to be true, he thought—a pet man—and nodded in disbelief. He was driving to Los Angeles on Friday and would be there for a month, doing some research on language divinely inspired, more specifically on "speaking in tongues," and the Pentecostal Church had its American origin around there in the early 1900s.

THE DAY BEFORE he left, Claire explained once more why they could no longer live together—how they wanted different things. "Books are your family," she said. A phrase that haunted him, but he finally agreed. It was something they'd both long sensed—talked about—and she was going to move in with her elderly mother.

"Take care of your little man," she said.

They both felt terrible, but in one sense he was glad to be leaving. En route he stopped in northern Arizona at a rural B&B called La Rose des Vents, run by a French couple. After a long and wonderful meal, which included salmon pâté and bouillabaisse, he retired to his room where he read and watched the tiny creature glide effortlessly about the jar on the end table. Later he placed the jar on his chest, in order to get a better look as he lay in bed, feeling guilty that he hadn't given it a name, perhaps because he was still a bit spooked by the recent course of events, and how at times that homunculus would push its tiny face against the glass like a child peeking into a house full of other, hidden children.

Later that evening as he stared, mesmerized by its movements, it appeared to be writing something on the inside of the jar, writing furiously with all its will—some word over and over. Slowly he unscrewed the jar and with his finger reached toward its outstretched hand, but when he tried to pull it up the inside of the glass, the arm detached and the wound, like a slow red spill into a greater stain, suffused first the body, then the entire liquid to an incandescent pink.

WAKING, STARING INTO the desert sunrise, he wondered if it was his own name or perhaps Claire's that it had tried so willfully to trace on the glass, and he saw how large and red everything became there, forgetting who he was, as he reached toward the open window.

What He Was Like

by Alexis Landau

Nadia works at the convenience store a block away from my house. They sell anything from Vaseline to saltines, bruised apples, and floss. I mostly go there for stamps, quarters, and Cascade. Nadia is from North India and she has two teenage sons and one daughter, away at college. She praises the daughter and curses the sons. She says her sons are slow. Her daughter, on the other hand, is studious and diligent and always tries to please. "Similar to you," she adds.

I stop by the store maybe once a week, sometimes twice. Nadia has taken a liking to me. She usually comments on my appearance, which at first made me uncomfortable but now I have gotten used to it and I realize it's just something she does. Scrutinizing my face, she will say that I look tired, or that I have lost weight. I tell her that I always look tired. Once she asked me about my eyebrows because she liked the shape. Another time she wondered about the small blond hairs on my upper lip. "How do you get rid of them?" she asked from behind the counter. Yesterday when I ran into the store for a bottle of water, dressed in black jeans and a white button-down shirt for teaching, Nadia raised her eyebrows, impressed, and told me I should wear makeup more often. "You look better today," she said, pinching her cheeks. "More color."

Oftentimes it seems as if she is squinting into the sun, her own long shapely eyebrows drawn together. Her skin reminds me of how tea looks when clouded with milk. A few gray strands glint in her light brown hair, which she has recently cut because she says it's easier this way. I ask if her husband liked her long hair better, but she laughs bitterly and says he doesn't care at all. I ask this only because my husband prefers long hair to short and was disappointed when I cut it off last summer. Since then, my hair has grown back, longer than it ever was, past my shoulder blades.

Nadia's husband sporadically appears in a gray BMW with tinted windows. He owns the store. On an odd Tuesday morning or late Friday afternoon, he'll pull up to the curb and check things out. He has salt-and-pepper hair and a beard trimmed close to his face. She will argue with him about not having enough inventory. He will cajole her into covering another shift. I imagine they also fight behind closed doors because Nadia has said that she hates her life. She tells me this casually, ripping off a neat line of ten stamps from the roll. The coiled-up little American flags are released into my open palm. Her sons are stupid and she must help them with their homework every night after working here all day. If not, they will never get into college. Behind her, miniature bottles of Purell gleam on the shelf, along with new toothbrushes and disposable razors. Her sons are twins and I have seen one of them riding his bicycle down Lincoln Boulevard, dangerously weaving in and out of traffic, his T-shirt billowing in the wind. She constantly tells me not to have children because children will ruin my life. "No more movies, no more vacations, no more anything. All your freedom, gone! I work here day and night to send my daughter to college in Canada. It costs fifty thousand dollars a year." I nod, wondering why her daughter is in Canada. The cash register opens, signaled by that high-pitched ring. Instead, she advises, a dog is better than a child. She allows my dog into the store even though dogs aren't allowed. My dog sniffs at all the candy bars and packaged nuts, leaving a slight trail of saliva on the plastic wrappings.

WHEN I GOT pregnant I felt nervous about going into her store. Especially since I knew I was having a son. But I finally forced myself to go there because we were in dire need of milk and paper towels one morning, and when she saw my protruding stomach she was solicitous and asked if my hair had grown thicker, if my skin had stayed clear, if I felt sluggish? When I answered each question, I wondered if she secretly thought that my life was ending. Nonetheless she pressed a special ginger drink from Australia into my palm for nausea. The dark brown bottle felt cool to the touch.

Walking home, I ran my palm along the honeysuckle hedges, the white flowers nestled in the green, giving off a sweet puckered scent. It was the height of summer and the jacaranda trees were shedding their lavender petals, crying violet. Bougainvillea sprouted erratically over walls and fences, bursts of magenta and faded orange. I walked up the hill, noticing my shortness of breath, which I had also noticed a few days ago in ballet class during the barre exercises. I placed a hand on my stomach, and felt the heaviness there.

I could see my next-door neighbor standing outside on her porch, fussing with her potted plants, all succulents, her white hair in a wispy bun. She never leaves her house and on rainy days the smell of cat piss emanates through her screen door. She has lived on this street for forty years with her husband who has gray skin and gray hair and does not speak. He is eternally busy in their garage tinkering with a vintage car that seems irreparable. When we first moved here three years ago, she used to stare at us through her living room window. When we ate dinner, and I passed the salad, I'd catch a glimpse of her ghostly face peering through the darkened window. Once she took a photograph of us, the flash reflecting off the glass and I screamed, which my husband thought unnecessarily dramatic. When my husband confronted her, she explained in a lilting little girl's voice that she was only taking a Polaroid of her cat. After that we hung curtains in the living room and planted more ficus trees along the border of our property.

As I approached my house, she turned around and the sight of her high forehead, a great expanse of white papery skin, startled me. She fixed her eyes on my face and dropped her rake. The clang of it against the cement sent my heart into a frantic throb, as if someone could see it beating under my shirt. I hurried inside, closing the front gate behind me, relieved to find myself safe in our sequestered front yard, enclosed by thick ficus trees. But I was sweating, and in an instant, I remembered a dream from last night. I looked into the old woman's attic, as if the roof of her house had been lifted off. An empty baby crib stood in the middle of the room with faded newspapers scattered on the floor. The crib was old and made of dark wood, cushioned with a few dirty blankets, and bats flew in and out of a broken window. A mobile hung lopsided from the ceiling, circling over the crib. The dreamscape was bathed in monochromatic light; all muted sepia hues as if I were examining an ancient photograph. I wondered where the baby was, and even now, the dream hung in the air as I tried to calm down and reassure myself that this was real life, here in the garden with our nice garden furniture made of weathered teak. The lone table and two chairs planted on the far side of the yard was where my husband and I sometimes drank coffee. Yesterday, sitting there, we'd shared raspberries straight from the carton. This was real. The dream wasn't.

A WEEK LATER we found an enormous spider hanging from the carport, dangling from its web as nimble as an acrobat. The spider was light brown and furry and as large as my outstretched hand. Standing in front of it with our arms crossed over our chests, we debated what to do. I worried that the spider would make its way into the house and hide in some dark corner, and when the baby was born, the spider might creep into his crib, and kill him.

"What do you think?" my husband asked.

"Kill it."

But I knew he felt bad about killing insects. He always let spiders and bees go free, ferrying them carefully out of the house in a wad of toilet paper, depositing them into the potted aloe plants.

He looked at the spider wistfully, his hands deep into his pockets. The spider slowly began to lower itself down and then stopped at eye level.

"If it's poisonous then it'll be loose, running around," I said, convincing him to get a can of Raid. He sprayed the spider until it became weak and fell from its web. Then he smashed the spider with a large rock from our garden, to make sure it was dead.

That day, while I was explaining the Russian scorched earth policy to my class, I stopped feeling him move. It must be the heat, I thought, and he's probably just resting. I pictured him with his little baby legs crossed, hands behind his head, as if he were at the beach taking a break. After dinner I thought I felt him moving again while we watched TV in bed, a stupid romantic comedy about a house sitter and her search for the owner's standard poodle. Of course the woman finds the poodle and in the process, falls in love with a landscape architect.

Early the next morning, I went to the doctor. "Just to make sure everything's fine," my husband said, kissing me lightly on the mouth. "Because I'm sure it is," he added.

"Yes," I said, buoyed by his optimism, "of course."

I lay on the examining table. The nurse had already tried to find a heartbeat, but she seemed unfamiliar with the Doppler machine and I internally criticized her lack of skill, for the way she nervously fumbled around my abdomen, moving the Doppler from one side of the stomach, and then to the other. *She just doesn't know what she's doing*, I thought. Then my doctor walked in and she looked concerned, impatiently taking the Doppler from the nurse. She said, "You should have come earlier." Earlier than what? I wanted to say, but didn't, cowed by her voice. I remember staring at her silk wrap dress, a paisley print against navy blue. I almost said I liked her dress but for some reason decided against it because by that time she too was fumbling with the Doppler and it didn't seem appropriate to compliment her dress. I remember thinking that she wasn't wearing her white coat because she had just come into the office, and her hair, freshly washed, was slightly wet. I remember the ghostly sound of the swish of my blood coming through the Doppler and nothing else. It sounded as if someone were whistling through the skeletal shells of bombed-out buildings. And then she quickly said she would do a sonogram. I nodded, feeling reassured by the word sonogram, as if this would all be cleared up in a minute. I remember wondering why she wasn't saying anything, and why her unwavering eyes, a light blue, kept staring at the screen in front of her where she had the image of the baby up. The screen was behind my right shoulder. I remember thinking that I didn't even have to ask her what was wrong. I already knew from her face, a face stripped down to its bare elements as if blinded by the sun, rendering her mute. After a pause, she looked away and said, "I'm so sorry, I'm so sorry, I cannot imagine, I'm sorry." I heard myself say, "Is he gone?" She nodded. Then she left the room, saying she'd be right back, and before the door closed I heard her curse, "Jesus fucking Christ." I sat there, my legs dangling off the examining table, the white thin paper crinkled under my thighs, and I couldn't believe this was really real but I knew it was real and I knew that I would have to call my husband very soon, the cell phone was in my hand, and I would tell him what happened and then it would be real for him too and the more people who knew the more real this would be and the less real everything that came before this would become.

Afterward, I avoided going to Nadia's store because she would be another person I'd have to explain it to. Some people cried when they saw me. Some people acted as if nothing had changed. My close friend Laura brought me muffins and peaches and jam all in carefully wrapped parcels and listened to me tell the story of how I'd lost him, of how kind the nurses had been on the labor delivery floor, of how we were planning to scatter his ashes off Point Dume in Malibu but we couldn't bring ourselves to let him go yet, as if keeping him in a little box in the bedroom bookcase that also housed *The Trial* and *Civilization and Its Discontents* was a comfort. When I was strong enough to return to ballet class, one woman congratulated me on having my baby, unaware that I'd lost him. Another woman commented that at least I'd lost the weight quickly. I wanted to punch her in the face.

When I finally walked into Nadia's store, she immediately knew what had happened, and so she wasn't shocked, and I was grateful for this. The last time Nadia had seen me I was twenty-seven weeks, just a few days before. I thought about her two sons, and how they displeased her but at least she knew them as living breathing creatures, as entities outside of herself. Before she said anything, I blurted out, "The doctors don't know what happened.

They're doing tests." I didn't feel like telling her the details: that the autopsy results came back inconclusive and all the usual reasons, such as a cord accident, chromosomal or genetic abnormalities, an undetected infection or a lack of amniotic fluid, did not happen. The doctors kept saying that finding nothing was better than something, because if they found something then there would be an issue to treat, a complication next time around. And I kept correcting them, saying *if* there's a next time because we don't know if there will be. Nobody knows that. Nobody knows anything.

Nadia pursed her lips, nodding sadly. And then she rang me up for toothpaste and stamps, stamps I needed for all the thank you cards, thanking people for the white lilies and orchids and roses they had sent in elaborate displays, which had filled our living room. Giving me change, she carefully asked, "Are you okay?" Through her fingers, pennies and dimes slid into my hand.

I don't know why I told her this next thing, which I'd been turning over in my mind for weeks. I'd been thinking about that dream, my neighbor's attic with the empty crib. "I think my neighbor gave me the evil eye. She stared at me right before this happened and maybe she willed it."

Nadia smiled wanly. "You are an educated woman. You shouldn't think such things. It is not your kind of thinking. In my country, we believe this, but not here." She shook her head, somewhat amazed. "In my country, if something goes wrong with the pregnancy it is always the woman's fault. They blame her for going out too late, for not wearing warm enough clothes, for sleeping too little, for not taking all the precautions. Even for attracting the evil eye, they say she should have stayed inside more, at home."

She paused, considering what to say next. Her face looked as pale and full as the moon. "You think the way they do in India. Backwards."

I considered this. Recently, I'd hung a ceramic turquoise eye from Turkey on our front door to ward off evil spirits, and I tried to purify the house with white sage, the thin blue smoke filling every room until the smoke detector went off. And now I wanted to move to a different house, to get away from the old neighbors because sometimes I really believed they took him from me, like in a fairy tale. My husband keeps repeating that the neighbors have nothing to do with it, and that I shouldn't nurture such unhealthy thoughts. He speaks to me as if I am a small child, or someone who is quietly losing her mind.

"Meet me for tea?" Nadia called out as I was leaving the store.

I only ever saw her here, the cash register a familiar and comforting fixture, which seemed to facilitate our conversations. I couldn't imagine her anywhere else. "Okay," I managed.

She smiled. "Tomorrow, one o'clock. Come to my house. It's just around the corner. With the green gate on Marine."

A BLACK-AND-WHITE CAT treaded silently through her front yard, jumping gracefully onto the green gate and then off again, disappearing into the birds of paradise, the flame-like beaks beckoning. As I opened the gate, I wondered if he was Nadia's cat, but the cat was collarless and Nadia seemed too conscientious to let a pet roam free. The gray BMW wasn't in the driveway and the house seemed quiet. Standing in front of the door, I felt strangely nervous, and I wondered if she could already see me, through the peephole. Before I knocked, the door opened and Nadia stepped out of the darkened entryway wearing something around her head, almost like a bandage. As the door opened wider I realized it was a belt usually attached to a terry cloth robe. It was tied around her head, resting there like a laurel wreath. "So glad you came," she said, and I followed her into the hallway. I expected to smell cumin or coriander or some other spice but instead the house carried a musty scent. She had all the windows open to generate a cross breeze, but it was still stifling and leading me into the living room, she complained about the heat and pointed to her head, explaining that was why she was wearing the terry cloth sash, because it was cooling, which seemed entirely implausible but I didn't have the energy to ask more about this.

We sat down on the leather couch and she closed her eyes for a minute, pressing her knuckles into her temples. "Pressure points," she said with her eyes still closed. I nodded, taking in the blue-skinned Vishnu caught in a graceful pose, his four arms fanning out from his body. She had placed him next to a potted plant, an angel ivy ring topiary, its foliage trimmed into a tidy green orb. A tepid breeze blew in and she opened her eyes, gazing at me intently for a second before pouring us some iced green tea that had been placed on the coffee table. Fresh mint leaves floated among the ice chunks. When the tea was poured she settled back into the couch and I fingered the tassel of an oversized pillow.

"I know these are very personal things to speak of." She paused. "But it is much worse to be alone in these matters."

Her house was so quiet and still, I thought I heard the red numerals of the digital clock change from 1:07 to 1:08. I swallowed, feeling a tough lump gathering in my throat, and to stop my eyes from watering, I focused on the long beaded earring dangling from her ear. The beads were dark red, maybe coral.

"I lost my first son too. I was nine months pregnant—it happened on my due date—when they took my vitals at the hospital, and checked for the baby's heartbeat, there was nothing." She glanced at me and then quickly looked down into her tea, studying a floating mint leaf.

"Oh," I said, "I'm so sorry." I stared at my nails, which were torn and bitten down, and realized why I'd been invited to tea, because now I was part of this universal worldwide group, the childless mothers' group.

She touched the terry cloth band around her head and feeling that it was in place, she continued, "And like you, they never found out what happened. I remember his lips—so red—but otherwise he looked perfect."

"Do you ever feel him—around?" I asked this because I've heard of people feeling the presence of loved ones after they've died. I have not felt my son around at all and it makes me think that he is too far away, or that I was a poor mother to him, even in death. Possibly if I had been a better mother, with a keener sense of intuition, I would know it if he came to visit. The other thought is that nothing follows after death but a great yawning darkness.

Nadia's eyes lit up and she leaned forward, pressing the tips of her fingers together. "Oh, yes. He gives me little signs. Yesterday I started a novel." She told me the title and asked if I knew it.

I shook my head.

"Guess what the main character's name is? Aanand. Same name as my son. A sign, you see. And in the book he was just as playful and mischievous as my son, because my son was always moving around like a fish, poking my ribs with his toes, making me laugh in the middle of serious conversations."

"Aanand," I said, and this made Nadia smile. My husband and I cannot say the name of our son. It is too painful even to say "him" or "he" let alone the name we'd picked. Instead we say, "When the accident happened" or "When September came."

"So." Nadia's voice dropped. "Tell me. What was he like?"

I couldn't speak because there was so much pressure in my mouth, in the place where words form; a blankness funneled down my throat like sand. I turned up my palms, as if to say: I only knew what I thought he might be like, a blurry forecast of a boy.

I swallowed hard, the sand thickening, and looked up at her. Her eyes were liquid and malleable, as if she yearned to enter into the fantasy realm where dead sons were suddenly alive enough to speak of in material terms.

"Well," I said, trying to catch my breath but feeling as if someone had shoveled even more sand down my throat, burying me. I thought about telling her how I had played Brahms for him and how I had always stood close to the piano in ballet class so he could hear the Russian pianist play Chopin nocturnes as I *demi-pliéd* and *élevéd*, and how I had often imagined him as fluid and strong as Nureyev but I had hoped he would play basketball.

"I," I caught myself. She wanted to know about him, not me.

"He," I tried again. I didn't know how I could ever explain him to me.

The Entire Predicament

by Lucy Corin

My head hovers over the floor, and my hair dangles, and my foot teeters near my ear, and my backside is exposed. I'm separated. I'm gagged and behind my gag I can't feel my voice. Homebound, on my very own threshold, I am of two minds or more about most things. I am of no mind about the rest, suspended, here in the doorway, within a network of ropes. I'm dangling upside down, one foot bound to the doorframe, an arm bending somewhere behind my back, another hip rotated, thigh stretching toward my ear, knee bent, a foot hovering somewhere above it. I have never felt so asymmetrical.

A bird yaks from a tree in the yard behind me. Bright air moves like a thousand singing bees as I breathe. I can release my head and look at the floor or I can raise it and gaze across my house. I can see beyond the living room, past the breakfast bar, into the shining kitchen, and beyond that, through the glass doors to my pool fuming with chemicals. Expensive house, cheaply made. Inside, the doors are hollow, the knobs brass-plated. Nick a wall and it crumbles.

I've lost the education I worked so hard for, or at least, it turns out I know nothing. My money is down the drain; I can see my last dollar from here, where I swing in the doorway, shifting my weight enough to revolve; I can see it blooming in the kitchen sink. My dog caught two rabbits in the backyard, finally, after years of failure. He slung them in a bundle over his shoulder and went packing.

My country's at war, and I don't mean venereal disease.

I swing here, hung, dumb, limb after limb, by hook and crook, bound, naked, open. I'm also turning. I moon every direction I don't face as I turn. I moon the blank world out my front door, and then I moon the desirable open floor plan inside. I moon my living room and its seven broad windows, and I moon the kitchen beyond it, mirrored deep in the appliances. I moon the patio set beyond the sliding glass doors. Sunshine hums in the windows and gushes along the walls, bounces and lolls on the flanks of my overturned furniture, the coffee table warming its belly, the sofa slashed, stuffing bulging, books like fallen moths, bits of china and glass from the buffet doors fairy-dusting my Pergo floors and tasseled throw pillows. How many hours has it been since my sunny eggs winked from their squares of toast? Since the tongue of my dog splashed in his water dish, since I sprinkled confetti for the fish, since my daughter donned her red boots and tromped to the school bus with bows in her hair and my husband, the dumb lug, backed over the roses on his way into town for the bacon? Enough hours for my hands to grow rubbery in their rope cuffs, for blood to fill my ears to bursting, my eyes rolling in their humble sockets, my brain rocking in its everlasting bath. How many hours since my dear withdrew himself from my cozy body and flopped onto his back in the moonlight, his grin sliding about his face, the silhouetted dots on the dotted bedroom curtains swaying in the breeze as I am swaying now, the motion moving them like a galaxy in a planetarium, night insects cruising and making their soft landings on the sill and on the branches of the tree that drags its nails across our shingles—

And before that the sleeping in feathers—

And before that the dog curled with the daughter in the wooden bed—

And before that the peace of nothing happening that I even thought to know of—

And before that the lives I could have led, and the cells that made me.

ANYONE COULD SEE I can do nothing, nothing, but there's nobody that I can see to see me. As I turn I can look across the planks of my porch and if I tuck my chin I can see my lawn above me and the broad black band of the street with no cars parked along it because everyone's taken all their cars to work, and on errands and vacation. Or else the neighbors are cowering in their houses, cars tucked into garages with the doors squeezed shut, or else they're peeking through their windows and they *can* see me and I make them afraid to come out. All I can see through my windows as I pass one and then the next are boiled reflections of the ideas of the colors of things like flowers, like hedges, like lampposts, like a cloud here and then there, and that's all.

My vertebrae push at the skin of my back. My whole skeleton is apparent to me as it has never been before. It's as if I don't have the fat I have. It's as if I'm stripped of more than clothes. What's left of my breasts slides near my armpit on one side and under my chin on the other. When I turn, backside out, craned neck bulging, I feel my home and my body as intricate and intricately connected contraptions, a Rube Goldberg that produces the drip of my mere and continuing life. The ropes that stretch and support me are like the wires and pipes in the walls. My cavities are rooms, my organs are furniture, my blood, transporting air, is air. Now, truly for the first time since my babyhood, there is nothing I can do. I can cry or I can not cry. As a baby I cried, but now if I know anything I know better. I can hold my breath. I can open or I can close my eyes.

I close my eyes. Here, upside down and overbalanced, the thing that happens is not what I make happen, it's what I am within the definition of suspense. First, my shoulders ache, and next they ache more. They ache in relation to how much my neck aches which aches in relation to my ankles which ache unlike each other because of how simultaneously bent and splayed I'm hung. The only other thing that happens in the time I can witness by the wall clock in the kitchen with the rooster on its face as I pass is the ticking of my mind as it tracks the shifting pulse of my body and maneuvers around the ideas lodged in its coils. My mind is a lost snake stuffed in a bowl and pressed. My mind is a snake too crushed to strike.

I open my eyes. I am turning, upside down and tangled, as if on a vertical spit, such that window after window passes in a rhythm, and then, as I let my eyes blur, I can begin to see the walls of my square house ease into curves and soon my windows make one watery strip of blue-green world. All this motion, and I am almost used to it, time passing and nothing happening outside my body's placement within everything, in fact I am almost used to this level of pain, almost content to spin within it, when peeping into the windows I see bobbing mounds of heads of hair, and one has doffed a cap, and one has pigtails like ears on her head, and another has a Blow Pop in her mouth, and another has a backpack that bounces up behind him as he bounces, and another must be holding an enormous toy giraffe because the giraffe's head bobs above his head and hops with him, and nods as the boy hits the ground below the sill, and bends as the boy is rising or falling each time I pass. Children are bouncing in no particular rhythm; they're like Whack-A-Moles at a county fair.

I unblur my eyes a little and I can see mountains creeping up behind them, green and brown, and then the children rise in slow motion and stop, framed in groups of twos and threes in the windows, as if secreted in my shrubbery, looking into my house and at my family's things, looking at me in my doorway, backdropped by the empty street. They wiggle but are almost still, as if making every effort at a dinner table.

Are these children I know? Are they from my daughter's school? Is it a field trip? Is my daughter one of them? I just can't tell—their faces and affectations, their clothing and hairdos—all aspects I recognize but aspects arbitrarily distributed to one being and then another. As individuals, not one child rings one hollow bell.

Then I remember to unblur my eyes entirely and the mountains in the background materialize into soldiers with camouflage outfits, their faces as stiff and suspicious as pioneers' in photographs, lifting the children so that they can see. The children's faces go slack, taking me in as I sparkle in my house. Some of the windows are open, with screens, and I can hear a child suck and swallow. I can hear the Blow Pop shift across her teeth. Then the children start squirming, because their armpits are uncomfortable and they're bored. So here and then there the soldiers put them down and I can hear shoes and voices in the shrubbery. For a few moments the soldiers talk to one another on their walkie-talkies, looking across my living room at one another, window to window, nodding and shrugging, hatching ideas, making plans. They seem to come to a decision. The giraffe's head is still in its window but I have no idea if there's anyone down there supporting it. The soldier standing framed with it does not seem to know it's there. The giraffe looks directly at me, and the soldier is in profile, with his walkie-talkie, and every burst of static has the rhythm of affirmation—roger that, ten-four—

But I'm still turning. Some of the children appear in the background, in the hilly yard of my neighbor next door. They are tossing a ball. They are jumping a jump rope. They are writing with chalk on the walkway. A soldier shifts from his window and shouts an order at them. Bark, spit, he says. One of the children comes to him, but the others ignore him. What can I do? Atrocities are imminent.

Outside another window a soldier is examining my barbecue.

Outside another a soldier is tying his boot.

Outside another a soldier continues to look at me each time I pass, because I am still turning, and turning as if the opening and closing of my eyes propels the turn, as if time itself is what turns me, as if my turning makes time move. He continues to look at me and I know everything he might do; I can see everything he might do move across his eyes in scenarios I remember from news and movies. Then he walks around the house. I can see him pass by window after window. I am following him as I turn, or my turning is pushing him along in a dance of magnets. He collects the giraffe as he passes. He hands the giraffe to the soldier who is standing with my barbecue. He's rounding the porch and I'm turning to meet him as he approaches the threshold, removing his flak helmet. His face is at my crotch. He is wiping his boots on my welcome mat.

Then I do, I cry. I try to control my breath enough so that I can do it with the duct tape gag. It's all I can do.

MY HOUSE IS like the world. The furniture is islands and continents now, in sun and shadow, its inhabitants the bugs, the mice, the dust, and the knickknacks we collected on our travels. Air is water, and sky hangs, as always, above the roof, though here the roof is ozone, leaks intact. How did I get here? Sleepwalking? Sleephanging? Sleepbinding and sleepgagging? Sleepransacking of my home? Or did soldiers do this in the night?

He stops my spinning. He turns me and turns with me as if I'm a bookcase to a secret room and I can feel a shaft of sunlight settle onto my ass. He takes a poker from my fireplace and pokes me carefully so that I swing a little. Who do you think you are? Poke. What do you think you're doing? Poke. He tucks it under his arm like an umbrella and goes into the kitchen and starts opening and closing drawers. Why don't you have any pancake mix in this kitchen? (I do, but it's in the cabinet and he's still looking in drawers.) Don't you have any decent snacks?

Outside, the soldiers are directing the children to do something, to ready something, and they're scurrying about with their accessories. I am suddenly unsure if the soldiers are directing the children, or if the children are directing the soldiers, as if it's simply their toys that have grown life-size. I spot the giraffe standing near the barbecue. It's large for a toy, but it is not nearly life-size. And the soldier in my kitchen has opened his fly and let his penis flop out. This, I recognize, is nothing a grown doll could do.

Then my husband comes home. There's no sign of the car, but he comes in the back gate, stands at the patio doors, kicks his boots off, and then, as if remembering my instructions, he retrieves and sets them tidily next to the geranium pot. I have no idea why he's home so early, but the soldier has scooted back around me, taking the porch steps in one stride, setting me spinning again. He's somewhere in the yard with the rest of them, and he must have zipped up because now I cannot tell him apart from the rest of the soldiers, some of whom have found fold-out lawn chairs and are setting them up around the grill. Others are primping the coals.

My husband comes inside and makes a peanut butter sandwich. Behind my gag I am trying to regulate my breath enough to make a noise, but then he pulls a stool from the breakfast bar over to where I'm hanging and stops my spinning so we can both look the same way, out the window to the grassy side yard where they have dragged the barbecue. It's good to be still. It is so good to be still that I hardly wonder why my husband remains unalarmed. We watch as first they barbecue the giraffe and then they barbecue each other. A soldier, sitting lotus on the grill, salutes, and next it's the boy with the backpack, grinning like wax, and like wax, his face moves from comedy to tragedy mask. One and then another disappears into smoke and flames, another soldier and then the child with lollies, everyone nodding appreciatively at everyone's sacrifice.

I know there is blood, but I cannot see blood. There is a way that I want to see the blood because I feel it's my responsibility to see the blood, and it must be there, given the circumstances, but I cannot see it. I sniff but all I can smell is my own salty fluids. I focus my mind on my ears and I hear bubbles, and I hear myself swallow saliva, and beyond that I hear only what could be the ambient liquid tune of a washer or of a toilet awry.

I hear my husband chewing. Then he rests the sandwich in his lap for a moment and unties one of the ropes around my wrists and I realize that I can feel his fingers on the rope as if it is a part of my body. I think about it, and I am not making this up. The rope is part of my body. It occurs to me that when I dream I almost never have a body, let alone a face, and then it occurs to me that this phenomenon is not one exclusively of sleep. If I am as I dream, as they say, then I am a blur to myself. Unless I am looking at my reflection I never look like anything.

In this suspense, what of myself can I see? The hand my husband released has fallen out of my vision, but the bound one has shifted such that I can see my wrist as if I am checking the time, but it's ropes that I see there. They say you can tell a person's age on her hands more clearly than on her face. You can see a person's history in her hands. I'm facing the back of my hand. I know it like the back of my hand, I think, but it turns out I don't know the back of my hand at all. There's not much to my hand, now that I'm finally looking. This is not, for example, a farmer's hand. And this is a hand that has been kept clean, that has washed itself of almost everything. Skin's a little looser than it has been, the map or lake top made up by lines more pronounced than I might have guessed. On the other side of my hand, hidden on my palm, is my future.

Now I feel the rope dangling like a phantom limb. Now I remember how I came to this. I remember in slow motion that by midmorning—in the open space after "bye-bye sweet-ums," "have a lovely, sugar," and that final wag from my dog's behind—in that open space the world had slipped two degrees farther in a direction it must have been shifting for a long time, like water from an eye-dropper that heaps above the rim of a glass and then one more drop and it just spills. In such a way the substance of the air had suddenly thickened, becoming almost gelatinous, I remember now. I was elbow-deep in dishes and the water in the sink began to feel the same as the air, and soap bubbles felt like rubber pellets, and then I was moving through it like a deep-sea diver in all that gear, or not moving through it so much as moving with it, it guiding me as much as anything, no leading or following, just me shifting with the breath of the earth, and then these ropes growing from inside my body like extensions of my tendons as my clothes fell away, the gag rising like a scar across my face. I was moving toward the door because I wanted to get out—

I wanted to do something—

I wanted to change, and I wanted to change the world—

I opened the front door, but I couldn't move through; the planks of the porch and the wide lawn yawned before me and gravity seemed to tip and I walked on up the space where the door had been as my furniture tumbled about the room, the chandelier catching on a sofa cushion and stuffing bulging from where it tore, coffee table cracking its back over the arm of a wingback armchair. I just walked on along where the door no longer hung and my ropes coiled around me and fastened to the doorframe, merged there with house; I remember the crumbling feeling of the popcorn texture of the ceiling; and I could feel the guts of the house, the pipes, the ducts, the wires, the stretching and sagging two-by-fours clinging to the drywall, and then I could feel myself stretch into warm roads coursing across town and then the country, and then I could feel myself as the jet stream and the gulf stream, planetary currents of air and water. I felt it hard, and fully. It wore me out and perhaps I slept because when I woke the world seemed as loose as ever and there I hung as if I'd been abducted by my own home.

There is simply no end to the suspense when one becomes one's own psychic landscape. Here, my unbound hand flops in the sunshine. My husband holds the dangling end of my rope in one hand, and I can feel the warmth of his hand, which is so familiar, as he resumes eating his sandwich with the other. I remember, and now I know. I am my home, and I am the world I live in. I am the ropes that bind me and the silver tape that stops my voice, hanging here, in this predicament. It did it to me, I did it to myself, I did it to it, all the same. My husband and I look out the window, head to head, although mine remains upside down, and outside, children are running about with soldiers. Some are helping each other onto the barbecue. They're all squirting one another with sauce.

Coyote

by Charles Yu

Today is your first day here in the Division. You have been assigned a cubicle next to Henry. Henry is your boss. He hands you a file, tells you to wait until you're alone to open it. Good luck, Henry says, and he goes to get a cup of coffee. You hear his soft footfalls on the sound-eating carpet, as he pads away in his patent-leather dress shoes. You are mildly surprised about his choice in footwear. When you can't hear him anymore, you open the file to find a security envelope, complete with an official Division-logo-embossed thermal seal. You press your thumb to it and hold it there until the sticker turns from green to red. You slide the letter opener under and against the sticker, break it open with the edge, and slide out an ultra-thin sheet of silverish chemical paper. There's a circle in the middle and you inhale and breathe on it. Markers in your DNA attach to bioactive receptors in the paper, developing the photographic image, which fades into and out of view within seven seconds. Which is just long enough for you to see the face in the picture, the subject of your investigation: Henry.

You go to lunch with Henry. Henry invites along Carol. Henry has a prepackaged chicken salad from Whole Foods. You wonder if Henry and Carol have ever had sex. Henry has a higher security clearance than you, which you know because it is in your file, but which you would have assumed anyway, because Henry is your boss. Carol has a higher security clearance than you as well, something you know only because that fact is in your file on Henry. What is interesting, however, is the fact that Carol has a higher security clearance than Henry, which Henry does not know. Which is not surprising, because as between any two people, the one with the lower security clearance does not usually know the security clearance of the person with the higher level. What is surprising, however, is that Carol does not know that she has a higher security clearance than Henry. You know, though. You try to figure out what it is you know, and this is what you come up with: what you know is the fact that Carol knows things that Henry does not know, and also that Carol does not know that she knows things that Henry does not know. Carol laughs at Henry's jokes too much and too loud for this to be a just-friends thing. She touches his forearm three times during lunch, the last time leaving it there for maybe two seconds before lifting it off and brushing the hair behind her ear. Carol has an egg salad sandwich in wax paper for her lunch. Between small bites, she sips from a can of diet root beer.

Henry's clearance level is Five. Carol's is Seven. Yours is Three, so in general, you know a fair amount less than Henry does about security matters, and much, much less than Carol does. But you know things about each of them individually, and about both of them in relation to each other. You know things about what they know. So in that sense, you aren't purely a Three. You are something else. You're a Three Plus. If you were all animals, Henry would be an ox. Carol a bear. And you, you are a lowly canine. Smaller, weaker, less fearsome. Except to larger, slower animals. You aren't a wolf. More like a coyote.

Henry asks you how your investigation is coming along. You say just fine. He says he has heard good things about the work you are doing. He hopes that you'll succeed in your objective. You make a mental note to yourself to recheck the file because you were pretty sure you didn't see any objective in there. You and Henry and Carol go out to lunch at Olive Garden. It was not your choice. It was no one's choice, really. Olive Garden is the only walkable place for lunch, and the three of you only get an hour. The soup of the day is vegetable minestrone. You order a cup and have the bottomless breadsticks and salad. Carol orders a glass of the house red. Halfway through the meal, Henry and Carol excuse themselves at the same time. They head off toward the restrooms, but a minute later you see them outside talking to each other. Henry is nodding a lot and looking over in your general direction. Carol has a look on her face which you have a hard time interpreting. You consult your handbook of unintentional facial expressions. This book has a chart that shows how people intend to convey Emotion A but unintentionally convey their real feeling about someone, call it Emotion B. If you can properly identify the intended Emotion A, and then identify certain indicators of stressors in their voice and demeanor, you should be able to zero in on the real Emotion B. The difference between A and B is called leakage. Leakage is a bad thing if you have a security clearance, especially if it is as high as Five or even Seven. You have previously noted in your daily reports that Carol is leaking pretty bad. She wants to convey benevolent apathy toward you, given that you are significantly lower than she is on the totem pole. But instead what Carol unintentionally conveys is that she hates your stupid face, or something of that approximate nature. You eat your salad and breadsticks and expertly convey naive unawareness of all of this. When the waitress comes by to ask if your absent dining companions want free refills, you lie to her and say that they don't, even though Carol specifically mentioned that if someone came by she'd like another Arnold Palmer.

When you get back from lunch, there is another envelope on your desk. You do the whole thing with the thumb, and the breath and the breaking of the seal and all of that, and you slide the picture out. It's Carol. The note at the bottom explains that you are not to investigate Carol (except to the extent necessary or unavoidable in connection with your investigation of Henry). This communication is merely to inform you that Carol is investigating you. You quickly reassess the division of knowledge. Carol, if she is looking into your file, knows you are investigating Henry. And therefore investigating her, albeit indirectly. And now you know that she knows that. And you also know that she doesn't know that you know she knows. You need to figure that out, or you might be fired. Or killed. You are thinking of getting a snack from the vending machine. Either the one-hundred-calorie snack package of Wheat Thins or a package of Lorna Doones. Carol pops her head into the cubicle. What's up, rook? she says. That's what her mouth says, anyway. Again with the leakage. You look at your desk, but the image of her has already faded to white. Now you're no longer sure whether she knows you know she knows. This uncertainty about the exact epistemological environment could mean big trouble for you down the road. How you handle this could lead to a major breakthrough in your investigation, or to your downfall at the Division. You choose the Lorna Doones, because why not. Life's too short to count calories all the time.

You're in an elevator with Henry. You think about saying something to him. What would you say, though? I know things about you. That's not true. You don't. You know things about what he does and does not know about Carol. What would that accomplish? You just like the fact that you are on one side of a wall, and he is on the other, and he doesn't know there is a wall there. Everyone in the Division initially enjoys this part of the job, and then eventually comes to feel conflicted about it. On the one hand, the human condition is already so isolating, to celebrate the systematized compartmentalization of knowledge and awareness among a large group of people for the purpose of maximizing control and informational leakage seems, at best, insensitive. On the other hand, Henry kind of deserves it. Carol steps onto the elevator, along with another woman, whom you have not yet met. Henry nods to Carol and the other woman and steps off. You stand there silently, as the elevator goes from the seventeenth floor to the forty-seventh, staring at the back of Carol's head.

The new woman's name is Donna. She has just transferred to the Division. You see Donna in the lobby sometimes, or rather, right outside it, near the ashtray, smoking a cigarette. Previously, she was an operative in the field. You know this because Henry has been assigned to investigate Donna, and what he learns about her makes its way into your file on Henry. You are now a Four, and Henry is now a Six. Carol has progressed above the number clearances and is now into the Greek letters. There are five levels of those clearances, Epsilon, Delta, Gamma, Beta, and Alpha. After Alpha there are more levels but your level of clearance doesn't allow you to even know the names of clearances above Alpha. Needless to say, Alpha is pretty high. Carol is at Epsilon, which is not as high, but still way higher than you are likely to ever get. You start to feel resentful about your situation. Low on the totem pole, and yet, by virtue of this odd circumstance, functionally much higher than your clearance. You don't know anything. All you know is what the people above you don't know. It's as if everyone who works at the Division is standing in front of a huge viewing window, looking out into some kind of vista. You can imagine what Henry and Carol and Donna are looking at. The grandeur, the absolute incontrovertibility of the brute fact of nature. They can see out the window. And all you can see is the backs of their heads. You are trapped behind them, for some reason, or maybe no reason. And yet despite the wide gulf of disparity between your point of view and theirs, you know something about each of them that none of them can ever experience in the same way that you do. You know what they look like from the back. Donna's preferred cigarettes are Parliaments, although she'll accept almost anything if she's bumming off of someone else. Sometimes, you have noticed, Donna smokes two in a row, especially if she is talking to Henry.

Terro(tour)istas

by Juan Pablo Villalobos

translated by Annie McDermott

This story begins when João sees a photo of the K2 mountain on Facebook. We'll call him João instead of using his real name in order to respect, at the very least, that minuscule detail of his privacy. Next to the photo is the phrase: "Mountains are not fair or unfair, they're just dangerous." Both the photo and the phrase were posted by Paulo, who, by the looks of things, is a fan of mountains but not of intellectual property: he doesn't say who the author of the phrase is. Some of his Facebook "friends," especially the ones who don't know him in "real life," could even come to believe that Paulo himself is the author of the phrase, that Paulo himself has scaled the K2 in "real life," and that, as he stood on the summit, his face lashed by the icy Himalayan winds, the mountain muses whispered that profoundest of thoughts into his ear. A thought of a profundity inversely proportional to the height of the K2. And yet, Paulo is a sedentary character. Paulo has not scaled the K2, and neither has he left his city in the past three years. To tell the truth, he has hardly even left his house. Indeed, the K2 mountain is located more than fifteen thousand kilometers away from where Paulo is currently resting his behind, his eyes on his computer screen. *That* sets alarm bells going in **Some Place in the Empire**. *That* and the fact that João, who really did like the photo and the phrase, has clicked "like." And take note: João is the only person who has liked the photo. A photo that beautiful and a phrase that profound, of a profundity inversely proportional to the height of the K2, and only one like? Very suspicious. Tremendously suspicious. Or rather: terrifyingly suspicious. For one thing, because João and Pablo live in different cities and, according to the records kept by **The System** in **Some Place in the Empire**, they haven't seen each other for ten years, not since João was nineteen years old and Paulo was eighteen.

The System sets its algorithms running and detects three terribly serious issues that could result in a **Threat to National Security**. To the **National Security of the Empire**, that is, which is the only kind that matters.

Firstly, that João and Paulo met in Porto Alegre (they're Brazilian), at the World Social Forum: that hotbed of revolutionaries of various kinds, including communists, eco-warriors, cannabis smokers, landless farmers, defenders-of-Fidel-Castro-and-Hugo-Chávez, greens, pro-Palestinians, vegans, union members, peasants, university students, and so on and so forth.

Secondly, that the K2 is located on the border of Pakistan, Kashmir, and China. In the so-called Northern Regions of Pakistan, also known as Gilgit-Baltistan, a gunpowder barrel crowned by snowcapped mountains. There are only two things there: terrorists and tourists.

The third problem is rhetorical: the use of the adjectives "fair" and "unfair," which refer to the fairness/unfairness dichotomy. Classic anti-imperialist rhetoric.

Three coinciding factors: alarms sound in **Some Place in the Empire**. Are João and Paulo potential tourists or actual terrorists?

Whatever the answer to that might be, something must be done urgently. One of two things: either detaining and torturing them immediately to extract the information about their terrifying terrorist plans, or unleashing a spam attack of all-inclusive travel packages to the Himalayas.

Who will take responsibility for deciding? An analyst from **The System**, whom we'll call Anyone.

João and Paulo are Latin American, and *that* puts Anyone on the defensive: he knows only too well the kind of third-world anti-imperialist resentment that can build up in countries like that. Resentment that could easily fill the Pacific and Atlantic Oceans to overflowing. Resentment that so often turns into anger, anger that is then channeled in just the same way as the anger of terrorists.

Anyone is a specialist in Latin American resentment and anger, which is why the alert was assigned to him and not to any of the other thousands of Anyones who manage **The System**. He's just the man for the job: on September 11, 2001, when he was an exchange student in a Latin American country, he saw on television how the twin towers collapsed amid the applause and cheers of no small number of students and, worse, teachers. The union of Latin American resentment and anger with terrorist resentment and anger seems quite plausible to him. What's more, he's been expecting it for years. So Anyone postpones what he's doing (following the trail of a girl in Guatemala who has been obsessively visiting Nepalese handicraft websites, among them the website of an NGO funded by a shady Qatari emir, and combing the biography of an old man in Venezuela—oh, *Venezuela*!—who just this morning, moments after waking up, tweeted something that Yasser Arafat said in 1963), and makes a start on the new investigation.

There are no emails between João and Paulo. João uses Twitter and Paulo does not. Paulo uses Google+ and João does not. Trawling through the other **Subsystems** (YouTube, Flickr, Instagram, Candy Crush, Match.com, Ashley Madison, Gaydar, etc.) doesn't reveal anything interesting. For the time being, the only link between the two of them is Facebook. Anyone thinks once again, as he always thinks, that **The System** could not have invented anything more perfect than the **Subsystem** Facebook: information that agents of **The System** would once have had to kill themselves to get hold of, people now distribute quite contentedly of their own accord.

Anyone builds up a profile of João using the **Multi-Platform Method**: that is, with the information gleaned from all the **Subsystems** that João uses. João is twenty-nine years old, mixed-race, heterosexual, married, with a two-year-old son, a degree in communications, and a job in an advertising agency . . . Then comes all his contact information, followed by his favorite brands of chocolate and shampoo. Et cetera.

Paulo's profile: twenty-eight years old, white, homosexual (alert!), single, no children, a degree in journalism, a doctorate in social anthropology (alert!), has lived in five different cities on two continents (alert!), works freelance for various magazines and newspapers (alert!), et cetera. **The System** also informs him that over the past ten years, Paulo has spent an average of fourteen hours a day connected to the Internet. That is to say, he moves between cities and countries only to remain shut up in his bedroom. He belongs to a tribe that postmodernity has named "sedentary nomads" (alert!).

João and Paulo have been Facebook friends for just eleven months. Why? Why did they get back in touch only now if they've known each other for ten years? This is very interesting indeed: if something's going on, some terrorific and terrifying plan in which both João and Paulo are to play a part, this plan is already in progress. This plan has been in progress for at least eleven months.

Let's see. Friends in common . . .

Bingo!

A certain "W.H." appears on the scene, a Tunisian who lives in . . . Mexico!

In a city on the border!

Questions shoot into Anyone's mind: What on earth is a Tunisian doing in Mexico? How many Tunisians can there possibly be in Mexico for conventional reasons?

Anyone upgrades the alert to the next level. It's all too much for him, this Tunisian who lives on the border of Mexico with the United States, connected to two left-wing Brazilians who are "interested" in Pakistan. But let's not forget the really crucial information: Anyone has just won a bonus for finding a case involving sufficient coincidences for it to be analyzed by the next-level analysts. The bonus, of course, is paid in delicious dollars.

The alert reaches a more highly qualified and terribly perspicacious analyst, let's say he's called Somebody. Somebody immediately stops what he is doing (infecting the computer of a Jamaican singer with spyware) and directs his attention to W.H. (last night, at a show in a little bar in Amsterdam, the Jamaican singer performed a cover of a song that is, without question, an apologia for revolutionary violence).

And oh, oh! The analysis of W.H.'s Facebook wall reveals that he took a contradictory attitude to the Arab Spring. Sometimes he was in favor of it and sometimes he was against; at points he was moderate, at others conservative, at others radical . . . It was as if he were trying to come across as a normal person! Tremendously suspicious. Or rather: terrifyingly suspicious. And what had he gone to Mexico for? How on earth had a Tunisian guy ended up in Mexico? Facebook knows this as well: W.H. wants to live out his sexual preferences in peace. W.H. has a Mexican boyfriend whom he met in Barcelona.

The big question now is: How do João, Paulo, and W.H. know each other?

Somebody fires up the **Historic Location-Mapping Cross-Referencer Program**. It takes a while to display the results, so Somebody has a quick look to see if there are any new selfies from that twenty-one-year-old Swedish girl. The Swedish girl takes photos of herself in the bathroom mirror and sends them to her boyfriend via WhatsApp—so bold! But there's nothing. Bullshit. And then the alarm sounds.

Aha!

Paulo and W.H. took the Memory and Holocaust seminar together in the Autonomous University of Barcelona seven years ago. Somebody is unsure that this is enough to justify calling his contact in the Mossad (it would get him a few pennies more, but shhhh, keep it under your hat). By the looks of things, João and W.H. don't know each other in person, and are Facebook friends through Paulo, their friend in common.

Well then, who is W.H.? Somebody reads the profile that Anyone has prepared for him: twenty-nine years old, Maghrebi (alert!), homosexual (alert!) . . . and so on. Then he sees: W.H. was in Pakistan a year ago!

It's a Maghrebi-Latin-American-gay-terrorist conspiracy!

This isn't a matter for Somebody: more than two oppressed minorities at once, as a source of anger and resentment and a motive for a conspiracy, is high-grade stuff. This must go to the next level, where another analyst, let's say Someone, will take charge of analyzing it.

Somebody, by the way, has also just received a bonus. A bonus paid, as you can guess, with money from **The Empire**'s taxpayers.

At the moment when Someone receives the dossier, which is headed GAY-TERRORIST-LATIN-AMERICAN-MAGHREBI CONSPIRACY THREATENS NATIONAL SECURITY, things start to snowball. Now it's João who's posting a photo of a mountain in Pakistan on Facebook. The photo isn't accompanied by a phrase this time: João just posts the image of the snowy mountain. Pretty, isn't it? Someone waits, holding his breath, for a sign that will reveal to him the meaning of this activity, and he doesn't have to wait long, in fact he has to wait only seven minutes, before Paulo clicks "like" and, two minutes later, so does W.H.!

Someone puts together a file containing all the information, compresses it, encrypts it, and sends it to the very **Director** of **The System** himself, from where it goes zooming to the **Agency Director**, the **Defense Secretary**, and, the next day, to the **President of the Empire**!

There's a supernatural agitation, as if they had all seen a ghost—and not the ghost of communism but rather the much-feared alliance of third-world anger with Arab terrorism and a gay revenge plot! The code breakers do not rest for a moment as they work to unravel the nefarious scheme behind that fiendishly complex strategy of photos and likes.

The **Defense Secretary** knows exactly what they have to do and the **President of the Empire** authorizes it: three drones are sent immediately to fly above the heads of the terrorists, three drones that follow the GPS signals from the three iPhones of the three unfortunates.

Now it all depends on the **President of the Empire**: if he says the word, João, Paulo, and W.H. will all be liquidated.

The **President of the Empire** thinks about the diplomatic consequences. He would rather not use his beloved drones in allied countries. How he loves his drones, by the way; how fond he is of those little flying beasties! But in this case he still isn't sure: the Brazilian president goes in pretty hard in her UN speeches, and he'd give anything not to have to talk on the phone to the Mexican president, who makes him uneasy with his incomprehensible chattering. And that hair packed full of gel! The last time the **President of the Empire** saw him, his palm was left sticky after they shook hands.

An urgent meeting is called in **The System**'s **Control Room** so a decision can be made.

"Mr. President? We have a five-minute window," the **Defense Secretary** says to the **President of the Empire**, as if they were inside an episode of *Homeland* rather than reality.

The **President of the Empire** opens his mouth and is about to say, "Go."

"G—" says the **President of the Empire**.

"Stop!" shouts a Whoever. "Stop!" he repeats.

There is significant activity in the network. Paulo has just entered the website of a travel agency that specializes in expeditions to the Himalayas. Facebook announces that Paulo is visiting that site, and immediately João contacts him via chat: "Are you thinking of going?" he asks. "Me too! I've been saving up for years. Let's do it—I need some fresh air, things at home are unbearable." W.H. posts a message on Paulo's wall: "I went last year, totally unmissable."

These men aren't terrorists, they're tourists!

The **President of the Empire** orders his drones to come home (he's been missing them, the little darlings). The **Defense Secretary** looks at the **Agency Director** as if they'd just had coitus interruptus.

Before leaving **The System**'s **Control Room**, the **President of the Empire** inquires about the status of the PUIICP (Protocol on the Use of Irrelevant Information for Commercial Purposes). "It's functioning at one hundred percent, Mr. President," replies the

System Director. "Prove it," says the **President of the Empire**. "Don't let those individuals get away." The **President of the Empire** leaves, but then comes back and adds, "I don't like that Tunisian being in Mexico. Poor little guy, if he really wants to live in freedom bring him here." "As you wish, Mr. President," the **Agency Director** answers.

To their astonishment and joy, over the following days João and Paulo start to see banners strewn all over the websites they visit, offering unbeatable deals on trips to the Himalayas. They receive personalized emails from travel agencies and airlines. The bank telephones to inform them that it has increased the limit on their credit cards.

Weeks later, João and Paulo go on holiday to Pakistan (spied on by Mossad agents). At the top of a modest mountain (not the K2, of course), João decides to leave his wife and Paulo feels happy in the knowledge that such an exotic trip gives him the right to twenty more years of sedentary life.

W.H. is offered a job in San Francisco.

Anyone, Somebody, and Someone receive their bonuses in delicious dollars.

The budget for **The System**, **The Agency**, and **The Defense Department** is increased as a result of the magnificent results of the PUIICP.

The **President of the Empire** orders the purchase of more drones, including one to deliver pizza to the Presidential Manor.

And they all lived happily ever after.

Safety Tips for Living Alone

by Jim Shepard

Twenty-five years before Texas Tower No. 4 became one of the Air Force's most unlikely achievements and most lethal peacetime disasters, marooning each of nineteen Air Force wives including Ellie Phelan, Betty Bakke, Edna Kovarick, and Jeannette Laino in their own little stewpots of grief and recrimination, the six-year-old Ellie thought of herself as forever stuck in Kansas: someone who would probably never see Chicago, never mind the Atlantic Ocean. Her grandfather wore his old brown duster whatever the weather, and when he rode in her father's convertible always insisted on sitting dead center in the back seat with a hand on each side of the top to maintain the car's balance on the road. This was back when the army was running the Civilian Conservation Corps, the navy exploring the Pole with Admiral Byrd, and the air corps still flying the mail in open-cockpit biplanes. Gordon had reminded her of her grandfather, in a way that stirred her up and set her teeth on edge—she'd first noticed him when he'd stood up on the Ferris wheel before the ride had begun to make sure another family's toddlers had been adequately strapped in—and her first words to him when they'd been introduced had been "Who made *you* the Ferris wheel monitor?" And when he'd answered with a grin, "Isn't it amazing how much guys like me *pretend* we know what we're doing?" she'd been shocked by how exhilarating it had been to catch a glimpse of *someone* who saw the world the way she did.

She'd always been moved and appalled by the confidence that men like her grandfather and Gordon projected when it came to getting a handle on their situations. But like her grandfather he'd had a way of responding to her as if she would come around to the advantages of his caretaking, and she'd surprised herself by not saying no when after a few months of dating he'd asked her to marry him. That night she'd stood in her parents' room in the dark, annoyed at her turmoil, and had switched on their bedside lamp and told them the news. And when they'd reacted with some of the same dismay that she felt, she'd found herself more and not less resolved to go ahead with the thing.

Her father had pointed out that as a service wife she'd see exotic places and her share of excitement, but she'd also never be able to put down roots or buy a house and year after year she'd get settled in one place and have to disrupt her life and move to another. Her children would be dragged from school to school. Her husband would never earn what he could outside of the service. And most of all, the Air Force would always come first, and if that seemed too hard for her, then she should back out now.

When her mother came into her bedroom a few nights later and asked if she really did know what she was getting herself into, Ellie said that she did. And when her mother scoffed at the idea that her Ellie would ever know why she did anything, Ellie said, "At least I *understand* that about myself," and her mother answered, "Well, what does *that* mean?" and Ellie said she didn't want to talk about it anymore.

"Now that we see that you're not going to change your mind, we give up," her father announced a few days later, and she didn't respond to that, either. His final word on the subject was that he hoped that this Gordon understood just how selfish she could be. She lived with her parents for two more months before the wedding and it felt like they exchanged maybe ten words in total. Her mother's mother came for a visit and didn't congratulate Ellie on her news but did mention that the military was no place for a woman because the men drank too much and their wives had to raise their children in the unhealthiest climates. She offered as an example the Philippines, that sinkhole of malaria and vice.

They were married by a justice of the peace in Gordon's childhood home in Pasadena, and her parents came all the way out for the ceremony and left before the reception. They left behind as a wedding present a card that read *Take care and all best wishes. Mom.* The following week Gordon was posted to a base in Upstate New York and Ellie spent a baffled month alone with his parents and then took the Air Force Wives' Special across the country: Los Angeles to Boston for $140, with stops everywhere from Fresno to Providence and seats as hard as benches and twenty infants and children in her compartment alone. The women traveling solo helped the mothers who were the most overwhelmed. Ellie spent the trip crawling under seats to retrieve crayons and shushing babies whose bottles were never the right temperature.

In Upstate New York the place Gordon found for her while they waited for quarters on the base was the kind of rooming house that had ropes coiled beneath the bedroom windows instead of fire escapes. She had only her room to herself, with kitchen privileges. "At least it's quiet," he told her when he first saw it, and then asked a few days later if her nightly headaches were related to what he'd said about her room.

She was at least relieved that he mostly served his time on the base. Larry was born, and Gordon worked his way up to captain, and when in 1957 he was offered the command of some kind of new offshore platform, he wanted to request another assignment—since what Air Force officer wanted to squat in a box over the ocean?—but he told Ellie that it was her decision, too. "You have a family, now," she said. "I just want anything that keeps you closer." "I wouldn't get home any more often," he told her. "And safer," she said. So after sleeping on it he told her he'd take the command, though afterward he was so disappointed that he wasn't himself for weeks.

By 1950 the Department of Defense had determined that the radars carried on navy picket ships and Air Force aircraft on station were not powerful enough to detect incoming Russian bombers sufficiently far offshore to enable fighter interception. The radar stations comprising the Distant Early Warning system arcing across the far north of the continent provided some security in that direction, but given that nearly all of America's highest-priority targets were situated inside its northeastern metropolitan corridor, protection from an attack launched across the Atlantic seemed both essential and entirely absent. The Air Defense Command in response urgently ordered the Priority One construction of five platforms along the northeast coast in a line from Bangor to Atlantic City. The platforms were called Texas Towers because of their resemblance to the oil rigs, numbered from north to south, and cost $11 million apiece.

They faced engineering problems as unprecedented as the space program's. Tower No. 4 in particular had presented a much greater challenge than the other towers since its footings would stand in 185 feet of water, more than three times as deep as the others. In 1955 the maximum depth at which anyone had built a structure under the sea was sixty feet, and that had been in the Gulf of Mexico. Because of that, the Air Force had decided that Tower 4 would require bold new thinking in its conception, and had hired a firm known for its bridge design. The firm had had no experience at all in the area of ocean engineering for marine structures.

Tower No. 4 stood on three hollow legs nearly three hundred feet long. The legs were only twelve feet in diameter and braced by three submarine tiers of thirty-inch steel struts. The main structure was a triangular triple-leveled platform that stood seventy feet above the waves. From its concrete footings on the seafloor to the top of its radomes it was the equivalent of a thirty-story building out in the ocean.

Oil-drilling platforms had weathered for the most part the storms and seas of the Gulf, but the Gulf at its worst was nothing like the North Atlantic.

And something was already wrong with Tower No. 4. Unlike the others it moved so much in heavy weather or even in a good strong wind that everyone who worked on it called it Old Shaky or the Tiltin' Hilton.

The first time Gordon had set foot on it he'd stood at the edge of the platform hanging on to the rope railings designed to catch those blown off their feet by wind gusts or prop wash and had looked down into the waves so far below and out at the horizon empty in all directions and had said to the officer he was relieving, "What the hell am I doing here?"

The tower housed seventy men. Besides its crew and officer quarters and workstations it had a ward room, bakery, galley, mess, recreation area, and a sick bay. Seven locomotive-sized diesel engines provided electricity, and ionizing machines converted salt water to drinking water on the lower level. Fuel was stored in the hollow legs.

The crew was half Air Force personnel and half civilian welders or electricians or technicians. For every thirty days on you got thirty days off. The military guys liked it because they got more time than they were used to with their families, but the civilians hated the isolation, and complained they were always away for the big holidays. Everyone seemed to be stuck out on the platform for New Year's and home for Groundhog Day.

But the tower shuddered and flexed so much in bad weather that whoever had painted *Old Shaky* over the door in the mess hall hadn't even been able to paint it straight, and the floors moved so much in the winter that everyone was too seasick to eat. Ellie had heard from Gordon in his first phone call that the medic who'd flown out with him hadn't served out his first day. When he'd seen how much the platform was pitching he'd refused to get off the helicopter and had taken the next flight out. Once he'd left, Gordon had found a crow hunkered down on the edge of the helipad, its tail feathers pummeled back in the wind. They got blown out here sometimes, the captain he'd been relieving had explained. Gordon boxed the crow up and carried it to his stateroom and then had seen to it that it was ferried back on the last copter out that night. "Well, at least the crow is safe," Ellie said. "Unless he comes back," her husband told her.

Betty Bakke's husband Roy was one of the medics who hadn't insisted on flying back to the mainland the first time he'd set foot on Tower No. 4, because he believed in fulfilling his responsibilities. He'd already made master sergeant and was two years older than the captain and nicknamed for his standard advice, which was Don't Sweat It, as in, *I thought I was coming down with something but Don't Sweat It said I was okay.* He'd transferred from the navy, where he'd served on a minesweeper during the Korean conflict. He told Betty in his phone calls that the only thing that fazed him was his separation from her. She was still stuck in their old bungalow in Mount Laguna on the other side of the country with their boy. Roy had put his friend and commanding officer Captain Phelan on the phone during one call, and the captain had regaled her with stories about Roy. Roy had stayed on duty eighty straight hours with an airman second class who'd had a heart attack, and he was even better known for having after a fall stitched up his own eyebrow while everyone had watched. He'd organized fishing contests off the deck and had also radioed passing trawlers so the guys could trade their cigarettes and beer for fresh fish and lobster. He'd also put himself in charge of the 16 mm movies traded from tower to tower and had scored big that Thanksgiving by having dealt *The Vikings* with Kirk Douglas for *The Sheriff of Fractured Jaw* with Jayne Mansfield. Betty had told the captain that her husband sounded like a one-man morale officer, and the captain had answered that that was what he'd been getting at. Betty had responded that she'd heard that long separations were the reefs that sank military marriages, and the captain had laughed and had said that he was going to pass the phone back to her husband. "Sounds like she needs a house call," she heard him say to Roy.

The Navy Bureau of Yards and Docks had advised that the platform would need to withstand winds up to 125 miles per hour and breaking waves up to thirty-five feet, based on twenty years of data provided by the Woods Hole Oceanographic Institution. The main deck's seventy-foot elevation should then provide plenty of clearance. A few engineers on the design team dissented, wishing to put on the record their belief that wave heights and wind speeds should be calculated on the basis of what might be expected once a century rather than once every twenty years. They were outvoted.

To extend its radar coverage Tower No. 4 had been given a location as close as possible to the very edge of the continental shelf, which meant that just to its east the bottom dropped away thousands of feet, and waves coming from the north or east encountered that rising bottom and mounted themselves upward even higher. And in the winter storms it had weathered, Tower No. 2, in much shallower water, had already recorded waves breaking *over* its deck.

But wait, Gordon told Ellie once he'd done a little more research: the news got even worse. Because the footings were so deep, Tower No. 4's hollow legs had been designed to be towed to their location, where they'd be upended and anchored to the caissons on the bottom before the main deck was attached and raised. But because the legs had been so long the design engineers had had to use pin connections—giant bolts—rather than welds in the underwater braces. Bolts were an innovative solution, but as a modification failed to take into account the constant random motion of the sea. The oil rigs and the other two towers had used welded connections for that reason. The moment the bolts had gone in, they had begun generating impact stress around their connections. And Gordon had further discovered that during the towing a storm had so pummeled two of the legs' underwater braces that they'd sheared off and sunk during the upending, and that everyone had then floated around until the Air Force had finally given the order to improvise repairs at sea to avoid having to tow the entire structure back to shore. Then in the swells the five-thousand-ton main platform had kept smashing up against the legs, and so reinforced steel had been flown out and welded to the legs over the damage. "Okay, I think it's time to put in for a change of assignment," Ellie told him in response to that news. "Yeah, well, in for a penny, in for a pound," her husband had responded, by which she took him to mean, *You got me into this, so I don't want any complaints.*

As soon as the tower had gone operational Wilbur Kovarick had asked to be assigned to it as senior electrician so he could be closer to his family on Long Island, and Edna had been so grateful that she'd kept him in bed the entire weekend.

By the time Edna had turned twenty-six all of her friends but two had married and she had been a bridesmaid five times. She'd told Wilbur on their first date that at the last wedding if the clergyman had dropped dead at the altar she could have taken over the service. He'd been sweet and had thought she was a riot but after they had said good night she had found herself back in her little rented room with no radio or television and her three pots of ivy wishing that she'd thought to get his home address or telephone number. By the time he had called back she had had no patience for pretense and had told him to come over and when he had appeared at her door she had kissed him until he had finally pulled his face away and she had pressed her cheek to his and had said, "I'm not fast; I just know what I want," and after a moment he had squeezed her even harder than she was squeezing him. Their first apartment after their marriage had been so small that one of them could get dressed in their bedroom only if the other stayed in bed, and Wilbur had joined the Air Force so they'd send him to electricians' school.

He told her that without him the whole tower went dark and the gigantic antennae stopped spinning and she answered that that was the way she felt, too. He told her that when the diesels altered their outputs at odd intervals, the voltage changes caused the radar transmitters to sound their alarms, and every single time the threat had to be assessed, the alarm had to be silenced, the transmitter readjusted, the alarm reset, and a Threat Assessment Report filled out. Some nights he was up nineteen hours straight. Then he was so wired that he called her when he went off-duty and talked. He told her that the wind chill was so bad some days that in the sun and behind some shelter he'd be sweating in a T-shirt but then out in the wind, water would freeze in a bucket. He told her that the space heater she'd insisted he take had made his part of the bunk room a big gathering spot, and that he'd also gotten a reputation as a good egg because instead of filing a report about an airman second class who'd dropped a transmitter drawer he'd spent the night repairing it himself so he wouldn't get the guy in trouble. She asked if he'd made any friends, and though it disappointed her, he said no, not yet, and there was an awkward pause, and then he added that he *had* been getting a kick out of one of the divers who was always sucking helium out of a tank and then telling everyone "Take me to your leaders" like he was the man from outer space.

After Gordon had been on the tower a month Ellie started hearing about his friend Captain Mangual. Gordon made it sound like he'd known him all his life. "Who's Captain Mangual?" she asked him, after having waited for him to explain. "And why are there two captains out there?" He told her that Captain Mangual didn't work on the tower but on the AKL-17, the ship that supplied the tower. "And he has time to visit you on the tower?" she asked. No, they got to know each other by radio, Gordon told her. So he was quite the guy, huh? she wanted to know, and then she got even more irritated when he answered that Honey, there was *nothing* that this guy could not do.

Captain Mangual's ship was specially outfitted to unload cargo between the legs of the tower, but it had to be positioned just so, in whatever seas, and it sometimes took three hours just to get its mooring set. And it was no small ship: 177 feet from stem to stern. He had to have the patience of a saint, boy. And then he had to hold the ship as steady as possible under the crane that unloaded the cargo or personnel onto the tower. The poor crane operator would just get a load in the bucket and the boat would drop fifty feet and then come back up just as fast. And when stuff was unloaded onto the boat, the load got dropped onto this bouncing and pitching cargo area and once it was free the deckhands had to get it lashed down before it squashed them flat. Ellie said it sounded like the crane operator and the deckhands had it harder than Captain Mangual, and Gordon said No no no as though he hadn't been getting through at all, and told her that Captain Mangual was the guy who made it all possible by doing a million different things to keep the boat in that one same spot no matter what. He started to give an example and then gave up. Oh, Ellie finally said, into the silence. After they hung up she caught sight of her expression in the mirror in the foyer, and snapped at herself: "Stupid."

The butterfingers who'd dropped the transmitter drawer was Jeannette's husband Louie, and the first snapshot he'd sent back to her from the tower showed what looked like a circle of boys in lifejackets high in the air on a fairground ride, on the back of which he'd printed *On the Crane.* He'd explained later that that was how the guys got from the ship to the tower, and that spare parts and supplies were always unloaded first since if a load was going to be smashed or lost it was better that it be the Coca-Cola pallets. She asked how high the thing lifted them and he said over a hundred feet and she exclaimed that it looked dangerous and he told her that the rule was no lifting in winds over forty knots since at that wind speed the loads spun like tops. And besides, two guys were always on safety lines trying to control the bucket's swinging. She asked if they couldn't just go up the stairs. "Baby, from the ship's deck if I had a baseball I could barely hit the tower platform. And I was All-State," he said. "Does anything ever *fall?*" she asked. "I think the crane operators drop stuff on purpose to shake us up before it's our turn," he told her. When it was their turn, though, it was funny how everybody stopped joking once they were up in the air.

"So are you keeping busy?" she asked. "You know, I *am* a Grade Five, so I'm as much a specialist as the tech sergeants," he said. She told him that that was very impressive, and he answered that whenever she was ready to stop teasing him, that would be great, and she asked how he was getting along otherwise and he said the same as always: he kept to himself and didn't bother anyone. Those were his mottos, along with: stay friendly and don't question stupid orders.

The new policy was that the helicopters would bring in everything except the fuel and the very heavy equipment. The choppers never shut off their engines so while you stood there in the noise and wind the guys coming off duty had to peel off their baggy yellow survival suits and hand them over to the guys coming on, and during the ride everyone did some serious sweating and handed over some pretty funky suits. She asked if the helicopters flew in all sorts of weather and he answered that he guessed they had to, since they carried the mail and the beer. He said that you only got helicopter work in the armpits of the world, since in regular places the operating costs were too high because of everything that was always going wrong and needing to be replaced. But when the helicopters came in, the double rotors made their own storm and in the middle of all of that, this giant thing just set down as lightly as a leaf. And then you waited until the rotors lost enough speed to start drooping like they were worn out from the trip.

That night Jeannette lay in bed thinking about what a boy her Louie was, and then about another one of the boys she'd dated before him. The other boy had painted flames on his car and had asked her to call him Shiv. She fell asleep thinking of him, sitting in Louie's television chair, and when she woke, her blinds were open and an old man wearing suspenders and no shirt was standing on her front lawn and looking in at her.

The guy Louie *really* wished Jeannette could meet, though, was Frankie Recupido, one of the divers and a real Ernie Kovacs type. Louie had been told to watch out for him even before he'd set foot on deck, and it wasn't hard to see why: he was always pulling stunts like stuffing cut-up rubber bands into someone's pipe tobacco. On his first flight to the tower he'd emptied a can of vegetable soup into his sick bag before takeoff and then had pretended to throw up so he could call out a few minutes later that he was hungry before he ate it. He kept the non-coms and enlisted men in moonshine he called plonk that he made from sugar and banana peels and whatever else he scrounged from the cook. He'd gotten into fights for twice punting the basketball off the platform after arguments during games. They'd had to launch a lifeboat to recover the ball. In bad weather he went out to the railings at the edge of the platform and howled into the wind like a wolf.

Jeannette said he sounded like someone to keep away from but Louie said he was a good guy who really missed his kids. His previous station had been Guam and his family had gone out there with him but he'd been away so much in the eastern and southern Pacific that he said he'd been lucky to see them three weeks a year. Frankie said that two-thirds of the divers he knew were divorced or separated, since whenever the water heater shut down or a kid broke a finger or the roof sprung a leak you were offshore, and after a while the wife got fed up. He said that his wife had told him that for her in Guam the last straw had been the spiders that hung upside down from the living room ceiling. He said that when she'd first seen one their little girl had said, "What is that? A cat?"

Louie found it funny that the one thing that Jeannette couldn't get over about Frankie was that the nudes over his bunk were framed. When he'd told her that, she'd just kept repeating, "Framed?" until he'd finally said, "You know what? Whether or not you'd run screaming from a guy like that onshore is beside the point. Here the point is: Can he do his job?"

Because boy they needed *somebody* to be doing that job. From day one the official logs for the tower had listed unusual motions and sounds reported by personnel onboard, and the design engineers had already visited three or four times and agreed that the bracing and joints had not been as effective in stabilizing the platform as had been anticipated. They'd identified the damaged braces and pins as the most likely elements responsible. Which meant that guys like Frankie were carrying out constant underwater inspections and bolt-tightenings. The problem, the engineers told them, was that the defective portions were weakening not only their immediate area but also shifting stress onto the non-defective areas.

And even going down as often as they did, Frankie and the other divers couldn't keep up with the accumulating damage. Even in good weather the braces' movements under the constant wave loads kept wearing down the pin joints. And what would happen in *bad* weather? The engineers had already figured that one serious storm would cause as much wear on a given pin as a full year of normal weather. Frankie would tighten bolts and the next day when he checked them again they'd be so loose he could turn them with his hand. So the engineers finally came up with something new, and big T bolts were flown out and installed at the loosest points to provide more rigidity. And that helped some, but then a few weeks after that the engineers checked the thing again and word was that they'd told the Air Force that without radical measures the condition would only continue to worsen with the ultimate loss of the tower the most likely result. So above-water X bracing was designed and installed in the summer of 1960. The guys felt the difference right away but when Ellie asked Gordon why he didn't sound more relieved, he told her what Captain Mangual had told him, when he'd first seen all that new rigamarole above the surface: because it filled in the space beneath the platform with its crisscrossing diagonals, waves that would have otherwise passed underneath the platform would now collide head-on with all that brace work. When she asked why that was a problem, Gordon answered that it was like when you were standing in the surf and you saw a big wave coming: you wanted to turn sideways to it, and not expose your whole chest to the wallop.

Betty Bakke was the first in her family to hear any reports about Hurricane Donna, from a spinster aunt whose telegram announced a ruined vacation in Miami Beach, and Betty asked in her phone call to Roy that night if the hurricane was something that the men on the tower needed to worry about, and Roy answered that gee, he sure hoped not. He asked how she was holding up all by herself for so long and she said that so many people now said a version of *Poor you* to her that she really was starting to manage a tragic look. She told him she'd learned how to run the sewing machine and had made curtains and bedspreads. She said she was trying to be as self-sufficient as possible. She was doing volunteer work at the Airman's Closet on the base, stocking donated items for the E4s with dependents. He complimented her on being such a Samaritan and she said that she mostly stood behind the counter embarrassed while the less fortunate families picked over what was available. She said she never knew whether to wear her hat to work so she always carried it in her hand. It was only after they'd gotten off the phone that Betty had realized that she hadn't asked what the tower was supposed to do if the hurricane was headed their way.

Edna Kovarick hadn't heard about the hurricane until it was halfway up the North Carolina coast, but when she called Wilbur he was inside the radome watching the height-finder antenna rock in its yoke while it made its 360-degree sweep, so he had to call her back. She asked about the storm and he told her that they had an evacuation procedure in place and that if the thing got anywhere near them he was sure they'd all be safe on dry land before she knew it. Then they talked about babies. She reminded Wilbur of the story her sister had told them of carrying her infant on the train in an open wicker suitcase as a crib. Maybe they'd get started on that when he got back, he said. Maybe, she said, feeling wonderful at the notion of it, but looking at their little bathroom nook and wondering what it would be like to bathe a newborn in a shower bath.

Hurricane Donna had already killed 125 people in the Caribbean and Florida by the time Air Force weathermen predicted that it would hit the tower dead-on. The evacuation was duly ordered and the coast guard cutter along with Captain Mangual's AKL-17 dispatched from New York Harbor. But the Air Force wanted to wait until the last possible moment so that the Russian spy trawlers that were always loitering around the tower wouldn't get any free access to the classified equipment, so by the time the two ships arrived on-site the outer edge of the hurricane had hit. On the first attempts to use the crane its bucket was blown into the ocean and the guys on it barely rescued, so the whole evacuation was called off. Captain Phelan called everyone into the mess and gave them the bad news that they were going to have to ride out the storm. By that point wave crests were already visible through the windows and with every impact the whole platform screeched and groaned and jolted before settling back into its position. Before the first half of the storm was over, the flying bridge underneath had torn loose and they could see through the lower hatches that it was flailing and smashing itself against the two downwind legs, and then the eye passed over, and the storm hit from the other direction. The whole thing took eight hours and for the last three there was nothing but shrieking and grinding noises from the legs below. At one point during the worst of it Roy dropped in on the captain in his quarters and asked how long Gordon thought they'd float if they went over. Float? Gordon answered. He was hunkered down in his chair. He told Roy that the tower had never been designed for watertight integrity. For all intents and purposes it was a building that someone had hung out over the sea on stilts.

The rest of the time they talked about other subjects. Roy said that he'd heard that as electronics got more portable these systems could be airborne instead of platform-based. And what would they do with the platforms then? Maybe turn them into prisons, Gordon suggested. Roy told him that during that last really bad movement poor Laino had upchucked into the sink and it had flown back into his face. An hour before the storm's end, the two of them looked in on everyone, and then Gordon wrote in his daily log *Men's morale OK*. Once the storm was over, he added in caps *NEVER AGAIN*.

When Ellie finally got through on the phone once the weather had cleared, her husband sounded like someone who'd been hit by a car. She asked how he was doing and he told her they were all still standing, but just barely. The maintenance platform beneath the main one was gone. The catwalks above it just stopped where the waves had snapped the steel. The roof panel on the avionics hangar had rolled up like the top of a sardine can. The colonel who'd flown out from Otis had told him at the end of their inspection tour, "I can't believe you all stayed. I would have ordered everyone off." Gordon said he had just stared at him.

By their next phone call a week later the news was even worse. There were multiple fractures in the new X bracing, and Frankie and the other divers were reporting that two of the submarine diagonals in the middle tier had torn loose. That had meant a visit to the tower by the entire design engineering team. They had shown up with their Mae Wests over their business suits and had huddled for three hours with the divers in the mess and then had come to Gordon's quarters in a group with a plan for cable bracing that would extend from 25 to 125 feet below the surface and bypass the damaged tier. He said he'd asked if that would really work and that they'd all been pretty gung ho about it. They'd have to fabricate special cables with sufficient tensile strength but those should be ready by the first of the year.

By the first of the year, though, Frankie and the other divers had discovered more fractures on the lowest tiers, the 125-foot level where the bottoms of the cables were supposed to be anchored. When the engineers heard that, they threw up their hands and said that stabilizing the tower was going to be such a massive under-taking that it would have to be put off until the spring, when conditions would be more favorable.

"So they'll just evacuate you until the spring, then?" Jeannette asked Louie once Louie had passed that news along on his leave. They'd been lying together and Louie answered that he didn't see what else the Air Force could do, given the shape the thing was in. And Jeannette startled him by shouting, "Don't *lie* to me about this," and rolling away. And after he'd driven back to base, she found under her pillow a note that read *I love you SO much* paper-clipped to a booklet entitled SAFETY TIPS FOR LIVING ALONE.

A week after that Gordon woke Ellie up with a phone call at 1:00 a.m. to report that the engineers had told the Air Force that the entire bracing system on the A-B side was no longer effective and they were no longer able to give an estimate as to the tower's remaining capabilities. Maybe it still retained 30 percent of its strength, maybe 40, maybe 50. But whatever the numbers they didn't want to encourage the Air Force to think that it was safe. So the Air Force had scheduled the evacuation for February 1. Ellie cheered so loudly she woke Larry. Then she thought: that's three weeks away. Why February 1? she asked, and Gordon answered that a lot of guys were getting off the next day, but a skeleton crew of twenty-eight was being left behind to keep things going and so the Russians wouldn't swarm all over the thing the minute they left. How were the Russians going to get on it with no one working the cranes? Ellie wanted to know, and Gordon told her he'd asked his superior officer the same question. And what did he say? Ellie wanted to know. He'd said it wasn't as though the Air Force couldn't assume *some* risk here, Gordon told her. And that the only way to keep someone *entirely* safe from the ocean was to leave him on land.

So when Louie rotated back onto the tower a week after the New Year as part of that skeleton crew, Frankie was standing there on the helipad waiting to take his survival suit. After he had climbed into it, Frankie shook Louie's hand and told him that it had been great knowing him and that he wasn't coming back. And Louie said, "You mean you guys have already finished the repairs?" and Frankie told him, "I mean I'm not coming back."

Wilbur told Edna on the phone that he wasn't even supposed to still be there and that he'd been due to rotate out but that his replacement hadn't reported. He said that for the guys left behind the atmosphere was like homeroom in junior high on a winter morning: everyone just kept to themselves and those who didn't were surly. The weather was always winter morning, too, windy and dark and cold. Because they were shorthanded, he now worked as a plotter behind the radar-scope operator, which meant longer hours, which was probably good since no one could sleep anyhow.

Ellie said that Gordon had to get off there but he asked what he was supposed to do: he was the commanding officer. While she sat on the phone trying to think of what to offer in response he said that it had occurred to him that confidence was like a little air bubble that shrank every time something went wrong. He said he'd installed a plumb line in his cabin over his desk to check just how badly the tower was doing and that the plumb line now never stopped making this wild figure eight. He asked where Ellie had been when he'd called earlier and she said she'd been driving Larry around on his paper route. "Why? Should I stay near the phone?" she asked, and he said yes.

Roy when he'd seen the plumb line hadn't said anything but then had mentioned later that this back and forth was just like when you bent a wire back and forth and back and forth: sooner or later the wire was going to snap. It was a mess, all right, was all Gordon managed to say in response. Together they worked out the order of evacuation if it came down to just the lifeboats, though they both understood that in a storm trying to lower those boats would be suicide. If they were going to get off the tower they had to do it before any storm was even over the horizon. Gordon put himself in the last boat and Roy in the first, and Roy rewrote the list and put himself in the last boat as well. He could always tell when Gordon was making the best of a bad situation because whatever he was doing, he started humming.

Louie told Jeannette that now in any kind of wind or seas no one could sleep for the clanging and grinding coming from the legs. She asked hadn't they been checked and he told her that civilian contractors had come out any number of times and always said when they left that the new fix was the one that was going to work. Now whenever he talked to her she was crying. He told her he'd written a letter to the president-elect asking him to override the brass at Otis and get them off the tower. She asked what the president-elect was supposed to do and he reminded her that Kennedy was a Massachusetts guy like him. He said he'd written that he had to get off because his presence here was affecting his wife so much. That made her cry even harder. "Why did you even *report* when they told you to report?" she wanted to know, but he had to say good-bye because his time was up and all twenty-eight guys were calling home.

The weekend weather forecast for January 14 and 15 was not so good: sixty-knot winds and possibly more. The Air Force ordered Captain Mangual's AKL-17 to head for the tower, take on equipment, and stand by for a possible full evacuation. Saturday the fourteenth the sky stayed dark but the winds were manageable and the crane operators on the tower off-loaded twenty-two tons of radar equipment. And Louie traded cigarettes and some of Frankie's homemade hooch for a spot in the front of the line for the phone and called Jeannette back with the happy news that they were taking the equipment off and there'd be nothing left for him to guard and so he figured everyone would be off the tower by the next day. Late that afternoon Roy found Gordon at the edge of the platform staring off to the south at a black wall of clouds that lifted from the horizon to the top of the sky. Wilbur and Louie had pulled maintenance duty and were repainting the two lifeboats on the deck and stopped what they were doing to look as well.

"Maybe it's just a local depression," Roy told him. They could already hear the wakes of the tower's legs in the increasing currents.

Captain Mangual on the AKL-17's bridge read his weather forecast from the merchant marine, and it was bad—extreme weather conditions within twelve hours—and radioed his friend Gordon it was time to get everyone off. And Gordon reported Captain Mangual's recommendation to his superiors at Otis, who reported back that the Air Force's forecast was not nearly so dire and that the storm was going to swing wide of them and that Captain Mangual had already been ordered back to port.

But Captain Mangual refused to leave. Gordon stayed up all night checking in with him on the radio and at 0400 went out onto the platform and looked out over the sea. It was blowing hard enough that he slopped some of the coffee he'd brought with him onto his wrist. The wind was already seventy knots and building fast. The seas were already thirty feet. The lights of the AKL-17 turtled along in the distance off in the blackness and the rain, disappearing behind the wave crests. Sometimes he couldn't even see the green light atop its radar mast. Farther out, the red lights of the Russian trawlers appeared here and there in the troughs. Because he couldn't think of anything else to do he spent an hour rigging safety lines over the upper platform so there'd be something to clip onto if they had to do some emergency troubleshooting or get to the boats.

The next morning the northeaster hit. He climbed up to the helipad deck and opened the hatch just enough to confirm that waves bigger than any he'd ever seen were concussing spray even onto the radomes. Everything was already sheathed in ice. He had to brace himself against the railing because the staircase was swaying.

In the mess near the phone the guys in line gave up their place to him and Ellie picked up on the first ring and asked if they were going to be evacuated. She said the weather was already awful where she was. He told her he kept requesting evacuation and that his requests had been denied. She told him *she'd* call instead and he told her to go ahead. She shouted that his tour was almost over and he told her he knew that and that she was going to wake Larry up, and that he'd never wanted to be out here in the first place. "Are you saying it's *my* fault?" she asked, and he said that as soon as the weather let up he'd be off this thing for good, and that the poor sap assigned to take over was already at Otis.

At seven thirty the line at the phone had progressed far enough for Wilbur to call Edna. He had to shout over the awful clanging of metal on metal. "That's outside," he told her, as if to reassure her. She heard men screaming. "That's inside," he told her.

At ten thirty a huge bang knocked everyone standing off his feet. "I think I shit my pants," Wilbur told Louie once he'd gotten back up off the floor. Gordon and Roy climbed into their survival suits and humped a hundred feet of nylon rope back up the staircase to the main deck and Gordon tied a square knot around his waist and tied the other end with a clove hitch to the railing inside the hatch. They popped it open just as a wave exploded over the deck and stripped the crane box of its welding equipment. They clipped into the safety lines and crawled forward on their hands and knees. In the wind and spray it took ten minutes to get to the platform's edge and the safety netting. Their ropes whipped and spiraled behind them like they were hitched to furious animals. Roy belayed him and Gordon hung upside down over the safety netting and the gale blew him out to sea, but the knots held and after a minute or two Roy was able to haul him back in. They were both crying they were so scared. Once he got ahold of himself, Gordon lay out over the netting again to try to see what had happened below and the wind battered and spun and whirligigged him. Sleet whipped his face and while he tried to see down the waves erupted to meet him. The bigger ones propelled ice water into his suit and he could hear Roy shrieking along with him. Finally he signaled that they could go back and on the staircase they closed the hatch behind them and he gave Roy the bad news. Some of the X bracing had broken loose and was battering itself against the legs. The joints were failing and the braces buckling. Once the braces buckled the entire thing was standing on three spindly legs three hundred feet long.

Back in the mess the guys helped them out of their wet clothing and piled them with blankets and handed them hot coffees but they were both shaking so much they knocked the mugs off the tables where they were sitting. Roy lit a cigarette and it kept bobbing in his mouth. "What have you guys been up to?" Wilbur tried to joke. "Inspecting the X braces," Roy finally managed to say. "Bad day for it," Wilbur told them.

Once he'd warmed up, Roy kept radioing Otis for the weather updates. Whenever he got off, Gordon asked him if it was going to stay this bad and Roy said that it was going to get worse. Guys climbed into their berths and put blankets over their heads. They put their hands over their ears. The low-frequency beacon antenna blew away. The last wind-speed reading was 110 knots before the anemometer blew away. The ceiling on the upper floors bowed and the light fixtures popped loose and swung free. The outer walls flexed from the air pressure. The dome covering the windward radar collapsed and tore itself to pieces and blew away. Gordon recorded it in the log.

Captain Mangual radioed that the AKL-17 was now registering wind speeds of 130 knots and the seas were even uglier. He said the good news was that the wind was so hard it was blowing the tops off the waves.

Afterward Ellie and Betty and Edna and Jeannette, in the face of reporters' questions on the subject, could not themselves recall a moment when alone at their kitchen tables or back windows, in the best tradition of military wives, they refused to give up hope. But each of them remembered thinking some version of *What about me?*

At 1:00 p.m. when Ellie got Gordon's next call he told her the tower was gyrating and she registered it as a word he'd never used before. She said she'd called and called the numbers at Otis but she couldn't get through to anybody. He said he wasn't surprised and that everyone's families were probably calling. She asked if the tower would float if it went over and he told her that it would go down fast and that no one could be saved. He told her that he was worried about Captain Mangual, whose ship was overloaded and getting swamped. He'd ordered him back to port but the guy had refused the order. He said the last time he'd looked he'd seen the ship's entire bow come out of the water with one wave. "How did everyone let things *get* to this point?" Ellie shouted at him, and he answered that he could barely understand her and that she had to try to calm down for Larry's sake. She asked if the people on the ship could help him. He said he doubted they could even help themselves.

When Louie called Jeannette there was no answer so he dialed again and again and then had to go all the way to the back of the line, and when he finally did get through he shouted at her about where she'd been, and she said "I'm *sorry,*" and he told her that he'd had to tie himself into his bunk, and that he'd listened to his buddies crying themselves to sleep, and that he wanted her to find someone good to take care of her. And she said, "I don't *want* to find someone else," and he said that he had to get off because other guys needed the phone. She said, "You can't just *say* that and hang *up,*" but another guy had the phone by then and yelled for her to get off the line.

Betty's phone rang and she snatched it up and Roy told her that their relief ship was in and out of radio contact but was reporting that it was being lifted off the crests and thrown sideways into the troughs. The ship was just going to keep motoring to leeward and try to stay within range. He said that he and Captain Phelan had tried to go back out on the safety lines but between the whiteouts from the spray and the force of the water and wind they couldn't make it to the netting to see what was going on below. The deck's steel plates were vibrating. The lower storage areas were awash. But they were all hanging in there. "My one-man morale officer," Betty told him, and they'd both been surprised by her rage. But she hadn't been able to make herself apologize. Otis had agreed to try for an evacuation at the earliest lull, which the forecasters were predicting for 0300, he told her. Copters were already on high alert and ready to go. The aircraft carrier *Wasp* and its entire battle group had been diverted to their location. They just had to hang on. "For *twelve more hours*," Betty shouted. He told her that because the weather was a little better over New York, the coast guard had already dispatched the cutter *Agassiz*, so it was already on its way.

A half hour later Ellie's phone rang again and when she answered it Gordon told her that the tower was breaking up. She wailed and he told her that he'd never known he had so many religious men in his crew and that even the welders were praying. He said he kept thinking that maybe if this shitbox could last another hour the storm might blow itself out. He told her that to give everyone something to do he'd ordered them into their survival suits and all hands on deck to keep the helipad clear. He told her he had to get back up there because guys were skidding around into the nettings. He told her that she'd been the best thing that had ever happened to him. He told her to wish them all luck. She was still crying and he was helping Wilbur keep his feet an hour later when eighteen miles southeast of the tower the *Wasp*'s captain reported having turned his bow just in time to negotiate a single and monstrously large rogue wave. The crest was sixty feet higher than the ship's bridge, so he estimated the wave at 120 feet high. The helicopters strapped to the deck had been smashed into one another but the ship had careened safely down the back end of the wave, which when he'd last seen it had been heading off in the direction of the tower.

Jeannette was trying to call Louie back when Captain Mangual's helmsman was knocked unconscious and he had to take over. The seas were like one cliff after another tipping at him from all directions and between crises all he could do was observe the blip of the tower on his radar screen. At seven thirty on Ellie's clock as she sat by the phone unable to respond to her son, the blip vanished. Captain Mangual abandoned the helm and knocked aside his radar operator and watched the wand as its line of light swept through two full revolutions before he grabbed the radio and shouted, "Tower 4! Tower 4!" until his executive officer grabbed his shoulders and brought him back to the situation at hand.

Betty Bakke was trying to get rid of a worried neighbor when her husband Roy was ordered to stay with the radio in case of an update about either the weather or an evacuation and so left the deck. He'd just cinched the top of his survival suit tighter for warmth when everything lurched as though the A-B side of the tower had pitched down a gigantic stairstep and everything loose or not lashed down in the room was swept into the wall. There was a high-pitched rending of metal like train or subway brakes and he impacted the door near the ceiling. And then there was another crash and he felt the shock of being underwater and the suction of the sinking platform even inside the room. The lights flashed out and in the darkness and bitter cold he rose up on waves to the ceiling, and his head surfaced into a pocket of air.

At 2:00 a.m. when Ellie's phone rang she ripped it from its cradle on its second ring. She was still in the foyer and Larry was curled at her feet wrapped in the quilt from his bed. The call didn't wake him but his mother's screaming did. When he couldn't calm her down he fled to his room and under his bed, but then scrambled out again and found their family doctor's number in the address book, and it wasn't until the doctor arrived and Ellie was sedated that all of the screaming stopped.

Jeannette was pulled out of bed by a call from her father, who told her that a New York newspaper had called him at two thirty in the morning to ask if he was aware that the Texas Tower with his son-in-law aboard had sunk. Her father sounded put out, and when she started shrieking he was so taken aback he said he'd call her again when she was more ready to talk.

Edna dreamt of a pounding on her door and woke to realize it was happening and with her housecoat on turned on her porch light to find a man who identified himself as a reporter for *Life* magazine. He wanted her reaction to the tragedy. She made him repeat what he was talking about before she told him to get off her property as a way of not collapsing right there in front of him.

THEY WERE ALL still awake in the wee hours when the senior sonar operator for the destroyer *McCaffery*, part of the *Wasp*'s battle group, reported rhythmic tapping noises emanating from the wreckage on the bottom, as well as what the operator said sounded to him like a human voice, and the ship's captain reported that despite the conditions and the water's depth it was attempting to send down divers and requesting all possible emergency salvage assistance. Some divers had already reached the site on the bottom but had failed to make contact in the limited time they had to search. More help was on its way from multiple shore bases, but by 0330 the tapping and the other noises had stopped.

Four days after the collapse Betty was notified that divers had found Roy's body floating on the ceiling of Captain Phelan's office. He'd been still holding the radio mike. A day after that they found the body of a technician a few miles south. A copter had spotted the yellow of his survival suit. No one else had been recovered. Six months later, on a humid night in June, Edna came in from her screened porch and took a call from a man who identified himself as a fisherman out of Montauk. The man asked if she was the Edna Kovarick whose husband had been on the Texas Tower, and she was about to hang up when he said he had something for her. He had her husband's billfold. It had been dredged up inside a giant sea scallop's shell three miles from where the tower went down. He was looking at her photograph as he talked to her.

The report by the Senate Committee on Armed Services on the Inquiry into the Collapse of Texas Tower No. 4 ran to 288 pages and ended with the acknowledgment that the tower had represented a spectacular achievement but that due to various factors it had never really approached its intended design strength, and stipulated that the committee was not so much attempting to assess blame as to follow up on the dollars that Congress had drawn from taxpayers to pay for programs such as this and others deemed vital to national defense. The committee sought to protect all individuals involved, whether contractors or service personnel, where protection was justified, and in its uncovering of the facts had, it felt, afforded a proper and necessary background against which any individual who might have charges preferred against him could be tried properly. But the report in its conclusion wanted to stress that those twenty-eight men in and out of the service who had sacrificed their lives deserved the same recognition as those who had died in combat, since it had certainly been a battle station to which they'd been assigned. And the committee wanted to make clear to one and all that those men had been patriots in every sense of the word.

Ellie read the committee's report and then took it out into the backyard with Larry and set it on fire. Jeannette read it once and stored it after that in a trunk with the rest of her husband's papers. And Edna found that every time she read it she lost her Wilbur again, and so after the fifth or sixth time she stopped.

Each of them despised herself for her own contributions to the disaster. Ellie thought that her father had turned out to be right about her selfishness, and Jeannette spent weeks remembering having ever only asked about nest eggs, and Edna told friends that someone more confident would have worried less about her husband being well-liked and more about where he was stationed. And Betty kept hearing Roy's silence on the phone after she'd shocked them both with her rage.

WHAT THE SENATE report spared them was the last thing their husbands had seen that night while they slewed across the pitching and ice-covered platform in the rain and sleet and wind in their survival suits waiting for their rescue. While Jeannette and Edna and Betty and Ellie had sat by their phones castigating themselves for ever having entrusted their lives to other people's promises, off to the southeast of their husbands' platform as if in a silent movie the sea was rising, and one after the other their husbands had turned in that direction, confused that everything was black until they realized that they weren't seeing any crests or spray and that that was because they weren't looking high enough. And when they did look higher they saw, like a line across the sky, the thin white edge of the top of the wave. And they recognized it as the implacability that would no longer indulge their mistakes, and would sweep from them all they had ever loved.

Prof

by Chika Unigwe

"Prof! Good morning!" I cannot easily recall the name of this man with a raspy voice who has just greeted me but I give him a friendly wave and what I hope is a warm smile in return. Before I reach the door of my flat, I run into two more people whose greetings—even in these days—are as enthusiastic as the man's: "Prof! How you dey?" This from our Ghanaian neighbor who runs a hairdressing salon and who, after the business with the phone tower, told me that were I ever to grow my hair, he would be my personal stylist. "Our own prof! Good morning, ma!" From Njide, pregnant with her second baby. I am used to it by now, neighbors treating me like a mini celebrity, rushing to take my shopping from me, coming over to greet me, telling me their problems as if I had the power to solve them all, leaning into me as they speak as though all they had to do was touch the hem of my billowing dress and they would be healed. Frank often teased me about it, telling me that thanks to the phone tower, he was now one half of a celebrity couple.

When the cell phone tower suddenly materialized opposite our street, I told anyone who would listen that it was an interceptor, set up to connect to phones by mimicking cell phone towers and sucking up data but nobody would believe me. Rose, a woman who lived in the flat below ours, had asked me, in a rather mocking tone, if I had studied to be a spy at the same time that I was getting my degree in mathematics. Rose had laughed at her own joke and even Frank had been unable to hide his laughter. When he caught me scowling at him, he had said to Rose, "I'm sure my darling would make a wonderful spy!"

"Idleness is driving you mad, you've got nothing to do," another neighbor said, the same man who said once that, had I been his wife, he would have made sure that I had enough babies to keep me busy.

"None of this teaching rubbish," he said. "A wife should stay home and have babies!" Our childlessness, five years after we moved into the neighborhood a newly married couple, was a constant source of gossip. The fact that I taught mathematics at the university did not impress our neighbors. It did not help matters either that I had been discovered to use a washing machine for my laundry rather than join the other women in the courtyard sweating over huge basins of dirty laundry which they washed by hand. "What sort of a woman uses a machine to wash her husband's underwear?" Rose asked me once before I became the local celebrity. Without waiting for a response, she answered herself, "A lazy one!"

When I told Frank what the man had said about idleness causing me to run mad, Frank had simply said, "Ignore him. What does he know about all the work you put in for your students? What does he know about how all your intellectual pursuits keep you busy? He would be better off chasing money to raise his thirteen children!"

When he said this, a tenderness for him swelled up inside me and as I leaned in to kiss him, my Frank, the only man I ever dated who supported my desire not to have children, saying that he understood why anyone would want to put their career first, that he understood that not every woman wanted to be a mother, he said gravely, "Perhaps, you are reading too much sci-fi, seeing conspiracy theories everywhere. This tower thing, maybe you should drop it, eh?"

Yet two months later, the much respected *Daily Star* had written an article accusing the government of setting up fake phone towers around the city. The government had at first denied it but when irrefutable evidence was produced in the form of leaked official documents, they capitulated and apologized in long, officious sentences: "We live in dark and dangerous times. Boko Haram terrorists pose a real and significant threat to us and to our dear, beloved state. It is in the interest of security that the Enugu State government set up towers to collect information which has helped us forestall attacks and arrest would-be perpetrators ...

"We are a democracy and we understand that the manner in which we have gone about this might appear undemocratic and for that we wish to tender our sincere apologies. We have already begun the process of disabling those towers and are working with the state security service to find new, less invasive ways to continue to safeguard our state ...

"However, it would be inaccurate—as the report claims—to portray the state government as engaging in 'bulk collection' of the contents of communications. What data we collect is not looked at or retained unless investigators sense a tie to terror, and only then on the authority of a judge ... "

I WAS VINDICATED. The very day the news broke, Rose stood at my door with a plate of jollof rice and a crate of Maltina to "see our professor!" She looked at me as if seeing me for the first time. "You have a very intelligent wife oo," she said to Frank, her eyes beaming as if she herself were being complimented. The neighbor with thirteen children began to bow whenever he ran into me and one of his children asked me for an autograph, giggling excitedly as I, too embarrassed to refuse, signed a sheet of paper with my name. Neighbors began to seek my opinion on everything from whether to take a loan to which political party they should vote for, shouting "Prof! How are things today?" whenever they saw me. When Frank asked me how I knew about the tower, I did not tell him about the wonderful coincidence of reading about such towers in the USA in a journal one of my colleagues at the university subscribed to just before the one opposite our house went up. Or of the voices I told Frank I no longer heard, which told me, assured me in fact, that what the government was setting up was no ordinary cell phone tower.

Those voices I have heard clearly since I was sixteen and saw my best friend, Mmeri, drown in a pool. The voices—all three of them—have always been there for as long as I can remember, subdued, hardly ever making their presence known especially after Father took me to see a nice doctor who asked me a lot of questions, made notes, and who prescribed some medicines with names I could not pronounce—but after Mmeri died, they came to the fore. One of them—the little girl's—even took on Mmeri's high-pitched stutter. When there was nobody else with whom I could share the depth of my sorrow or the fears that kept me from sleeping at night, the one with Mmeri's stutter became the hands that rocked me until the fears ebbed away. When I worried that I would not pass the entrance exams to the university, the deep male one who sounded like a priest told me I had nothing to worry about. He was right. I made it into my university of choice. When my pocket money was stolen from my purse just before I had to return to school, the female one—which I imagine for some reason as belonging to a woman with a small stomach and toned thighs—whispered in my ears that my stepsister, Ifeyinwa, had stolen it. I just walked up to Ifeyinwa and demanded that she return the money that she stole from me, and she did. I told Frank about it years later, when we started dating and Ifeyinwa tried to break us up. I did not tell him about the voice identifying the culprit but about Ifeyinwa stealing my money and being too shocked when I confronted her to deny it. Frank began calling her Ifeyinwa-the-thief behind her back. He was not fooled by her friendliness and always found an excuse not to sit and chat with her when he visited, even though he talked a lot with my brother, and with me, he never ran out of things to say. Spurned, she took to calling him Talk-like-a-woman-Frank to his face, which to her annoyance did not bother Frank much. The first time she called him that he told her he liked women too much to be insulted by the insinuation that he talked as much as women did. "It's not even an insult," he said, "if you think about it." That would have been enough to shut anyone up but not Ifeyinwa, who the voice with the stutter says is "as foolish as a sheep."

FRANK DOES NOT talk much these days. I walk into my sitting room. He is sitting down—as he has been doing for the past couple of days—on the sofa. I kiss him softly on his forehead. It is like kissing a fish, his forehead is moist and cold. I say hello but he does not even look at me. He stares straight ahead at the TV, which is off. I sit beside him and switch it on. The three o'clock news—which we have always listened to together—has just begun. There is a new camp being set up in Polo Park, the newscaster—the really pretty one with long eyelashes and deep dimples whom I nicknamed The Kangaroo—says, "Even as I speak, the government is setting up isolation tents there. I have been inside one of those tents myself. I must admit to feeling a bit envious. The tent's neat, the camp itself is very clean. Bigger and cleaner than the previous camp. It is very secure. The safest place in Enugu. No crime. No power outage. No need for a generator. It is a Utopia." The camera zooms in on her carefully made-up face and she smiles an awkward smile, as if she has food stuck between her teeth. "Remember, if you or anyone you know is exhibiting any of the symptoms of the virus, please come to the camp. If you can't make it, call any of the numbers showing now, and the government will send someone to bring you. We can fight this. We can contain this virus but everyone has to help. Keep away from anyone who is showing symptoms. This is a terrible illness. It is spread through contact. Remember the three watchwords: Cleanliness. Vigilance. Distance. We can fight this. Yes. We. Can."

I turn to Frank and begin to speak but his eyes are glued to the screen, as if he were memorizing the flashing series of emergency telephone numbers scrolling the bottom. I reach for the remote control in the crack between the cushions on which he and I sit, and switch off the TV. My husband groans and sinks deeper into the sofa. I inch closer to him and stretch to take his hand. As soon as I make contact, he snatches it back as if I were a leper, and groans again. I pretend not to mind. I say to him, "You really do not believe what The Kangaroo said, do you? Utopia my nyash! You don't think that she believes it either? You could see it in her eyes. Her heart wasn't in the message."

I move back to my own side of the sofa. "Listen, do you or do you not trust me?" I have put on the voice I use when I am scolding an errant student.

Frank groans again. His breath comes in short sputters like the dying engine of a car. It hurts me to hear it.

"I hate to see you this way, my poor darling." My tone is softening at the edges, becoming fluffy, flirty even. "Do you need anything? Water? Tea?"

Frank shakes his head and sinks deeper into the sofa, the blue of his shirt segueing into the blue of the sofa so that it appears as if he were melded to the chair. He does not say anything. He does not need to. I have always been able to tell what he is thinking. I respond now to the thoughts I see darting across his mind like a restless lizard.

"Why do you want to go to that place? Have I ever let you down? Have I ever been wrong? This isolation camp is just the government's way of taking control. This disease, this Ebola, do you think it fell from the sky?" The soft edges are hardening up again. My tone is urgent. How can Frank be blind to this? "The government manufactured it to get as many people as they can sick. And then they created this camp where you can be 'cured.' I tell you, anyone who goes there is going to be implanted with a chip that will make it easier for them to be monitored. I will not let that happen to you! Have I not told you that a colleague of mine knows a doctor who is at this very moment putting final touches to the antidote? That doctor will come here and cure you."

Frank opens his eyes and turns toward me. His eyes are red as if he has conjunctivitis. His is a textbook case, ticking off all the boxes for the symptoms: Fever. Red eyes. Chills. He is shivering now, his shoulders hunched to keep out a cold that only he can feel. I miss my Frank. I miss his voice. I miss the conversations we had at the breakfast table every day. I miss the Saturday mornings we spent in bed making love with the enthusiasm of teenagers just discovering the wonders of sex. If I could take his place, I would. I would bear it better, knowing what I know. It is not fair that it is Frank who has gotten ill.

"The hunger that is hopeful of being assuaged does not kill," I tell him, hoping to make him laugh. When we had just started dating and I still lived at home, there were very few opportunities for us to get intimate. Frank always used that phrase to console both himself and me that soon, we would get our own place, get married, and be able to "do it whenever and however" we chose. It has evolved to become our secret sex code. Frank looks at me and the sadness in his eyes is so intense, I look away immediately. I get up, walk into a room, and return with a damp towel with which I begin to wash him. His face, his arms, and beneath his shorts. Every time I touch him, he flinches. Each time I shush him, placing a finger on his lips. "Please," he says, his voice so soft he might have been whispering. I work in silence starting from his head and then moving gradually to his hands and then, unbuttoning his shirt, I wash his stomach. "Please," he says again. It comes out as a whispered "plis." I begin to hum under my breath, the John Legend tune we both love:

'Cause all of me
loves all of you,
love your curves and all your edges,
all your perfect imperfections

I wash first his right leg, then the left, scrubbing the dark, rough skin of his knee, which, no matter how much shea butter I bully Frank into rubbing on it, remains dry and callused. When I start on his right foot, the woman's voice tells me it is time to remind him of things he might have forgotten. I stop humming and begin to talk.

"You're such a worry bug, my darling." I wish I could tell him about the voices, which warn me now that he must not be allowed to go to the camp. They tell me that if he goes, he will not come out alive. They ask me how many of the people I know who have gone in so far have come out. And they tell me that if Frank does come out alive, he would not come out the old Frank, he would be nothing more than a robot, implanted with a chip to control him. Either way, if he went I would lose him. I cannot bear the thought of that. All three voices assure me now that an antidote is on its way for this mysterious illness, that the antidote will be brought to my door and Frank—together with anyone else who takes it—will be saved. I trust those voices but Frank, who, when he announced that he wanted to marry me, was informed by the envious, older Ifeyinwa that I had spent some time in a mental institution and was prone to "bouts of insanity," but had not been put off, would certainly question me about the veracity of the voices. He will ask me, as he did once when he thought I was talking to myself (I had actually been dictating into my phone), if I still took pills. Those pills, which now too, the voices tell me, the government has somehow found a way to switch with their own pills so that they could rid me of the voices and better control me. Of course I am not taking them. I am not that foolish but Frank will not understand. He thinks I ought to take my medication "because it is dangerous not to." On our honeymoon, the stuttering voice had told me that the man lying in the bed with me was not Frank but a devil who had taken his place. I had to get rid of him so that Frank would return. I had to slash his throat but I had nothing sharper than a nail file in the hotel room. I had never killed anything, not even a chicken, but I straddled him and brought the tip of the nail file to his neck. He jumped up and grabbed my hands, swearing as he did so. He sounded like my Frank. He looked like my Frank. How could I have wanted to hurt him? I dropped the nail file and let him hold me. He supervised me every day as if I were a child while I took my medication, handing me the glass of water and waiting until I had swallowed the pill.

He only stopped two weeks after, when I convinced him that I would never, ever play "drug truancy" (his words) again. So what if the voice was wrong then? It does not mean that they are wrong now. What about all the times that they have been right? Even if the voices are wrong now, can I also discount the rumors going round?

AS THE WEEKS went by and the illness continued its round of the city, and found its way as a regular feature on the news, it made sense that the neighbors would seek my thoughts. Rose stopped me two weeks ago as I walked to work.

"It was manufactured by the government," I said.

"How do you know?"

"I cannot divulge my sources. If I did, I'd have to kill you." I laughed to let Rose know I was joking.

"Why? Why would they want to make us sick? What have we ever done to them? Are we at war with our own government?" Rose looked confused.

"Control."

When another neighbor challenged me and said, "But they said it was a man who ate bush meat in Liberia who brought it in here," I laughed and said, "You expect the one who seeks to control you to tell you that?"

At first, the neighbors deferred to me. They agreed with me that of course it was a government ploy. They agreed that a government that was so corrupt that even local government chairmen could afford to buy private jets would want to squash any opposition by citizens by spying on them with fake cell phone towers, that a government that has never been known for its transparency would seek total control in this way—with a manufactured virus and internment camps—that this made sense. But when Rose's son became ill—they said he began to bleed from every part of his body—Rose had him taken to the camp. It broke my heart to hear that she did not have enough trust in me, that she could not see that she was making it easy for the government to gain control of her family. "He's my only son. If he dies, my life is finished," Rose said when I asked her the next day why she had sent her son off. Not too long after that, Rose herself too became ill and was carted away. Then Rose's husband and aged mother who lived with them. And now, it has entered my own house like a sneaky thief in the night, invading Frank's beautiful body, coloring his eyes red. But I am not afraid. The voices tell me to be strong, that anytime now, a man will appear at our door with a serum that will cure Frank and keep anyone who takes it immune to the evil machinations of the government.

WHEN FRANK FIRST became ill, he agreed with me that it was just a flu. He was a nurse and even though he had helped care for Ebola patients before it became an epidemic, he had always been careful, wearing gloves and surgical mask. He gorged on Panadol and vitamin C. And then we thought it might be malaria and Frank dutifully added artesunate to the cocktail. And then when it could no longer be denied that it was the dreaded Ebola, and he still had the strength to talk, he asked me to drive him to the camp. "Let me go, please." By then my voices had warned me not to let him out of my sight, their warnings urgent and insistent, clutching me around my neck, shouting into my ears. By then too, the rumors had begun to make the round of doctors harvesting the organs of Ebola patients in their care to sell abroad. A few years ago, a private clinic on Agbani Road was closed down because it was discovered that the doctors there were taking out the healthy organs of unsuspecting patients and selling them for ridiculous amounts to wealthy clients in Ghana and Cameroon. What stops these doctors at the camp from doing the same now?

"I can't. Can't you see that my love?"

Now, he no longer has the strength to hiss out more than a "plis." I am not sure what he is begging for anymore but whatever it is, I have to do the right thing by my husband. I have to keep him home until the serum comes. He will not fall prey to the government.

I stand and kiss him on the lips.

"Do I not prove my trust in this antidote that is coming by kissing you?" I place a hand against my forehead. I do feel a bit feverish. My joints ache but I have been working hard, looking after Frank. The ache will go if I lie down and rest. I am certain of that.

The Witness and the Passenger Train

by Bonnie Nadzam

A man stands alone in the black night watching a passenger train speed past. Its yellow-lighted windows are splashed with colored hats and coats; flashes of silverware and glassware; with shoulders in black jackets and bright wool sweaters; with pointed and rounded and upturned noses. Three men in hats are drinking glasses of beer. The children dunk strips of buttered toast in cocoa. An old man snores like a happy pig, his mouth open, his giant milk-white teeth exposed. A young mother pulls a picture book out of her giant purse. Everybody on the train is warm with that consoling feeling of being on an adventure.

The man outside who sees the train knows none of the passengers personally, but they feel oddly familiar as each of their faces appears briefly before him in the dark; it is as if he does know them, the way a person can feel intimately connected to strangers in a crowd. Even though he stands apart, he recognizes he is of them, as thoughts are of words, as something is of nothing.

That he intuits this last sense at all is remarkably peculiar, because although the man outside in the dark, in the grass, cannot experience the train journey himself, it is his very act of witness that has rendered all of it—and all of them—not only material, in the first place, but beautiful, as well.

"This is brilliant work," the international public radio correspondent emphasized for the benefit of his listeners. He sat with Dr. Flame and Dr. Flame in his studio; it was a warm summer afternoon. Outside the window, green palms splintered the clear blue sky. "For those of you just joining us, we're talking about an astonishing paper and mathematical model created by the Drs. Flame, a couple of young physicists making big waves in the scientific community. Tell us, Dr. Flame and Dr. Flame—this paper presents mathematical proofs for a highly unusual idea about the nature of reality."

Dr. Flame smiled at her husband. "But one you've kind of always sensed was true, no?"

"This is totally unprecedented," the host said.

"Well. Fairly unprecedented."

"Shoulders of giants," the other Flame interjected, and put his hand on his beloved's arm.

"What's next for you two? You're a young, seemingly normal couple."

"We lead very ordinary lives."

"And yet. I wonder if you don't both feel a little bit like that man out there in the dark, set apart from everyone?"

"One of the keys to this model," Dr. Flame said, as her husband took her hand, "is that every one of us feels that way."

"Even the passengers on the train?"

"Someone on that train," Dr. Flame said, taking over for his wife, "imagines there is someone out there in the night watching her rush past."

"So what this model ultimately suggests," the correspondent guided his listeners, "is that there's some scientific ground for the old notion that the world is whatever we imagine it to be?"

The Drs. Flame laughed. If anything, they joked with each other on their way home, it was the other way around.

"There is some imaginative notion that there is scientific ground," Dr. Flame tried out, and put his arm around his wife's square shoulders, and steered with one hand. The light was changing all around them, the blue sky deepening to navy, the trills of mockingbirds slurring in the ficus trees. They had all the car windows down as they drove.

"I feel rich. Let's go to that drive-thru up the coast for ice cream."

"Shakes?"

"Malts."

"Burgers?"

"Dogs."

"French fries?"

"Definitely."

THE NEXT MORNING on the university campus they met in the office of their chair, Dr. Regula, flanked behind her desk by the president of the School of Liberal Arts and Sciences, the provost, and a man in circle-shaped glasses whom neither of the Flames recognized.

"It's not that we think you're pursuing something that isn't worthwhile," Dr. Regula told them. She did not look the Flames in the eye. "It's that it isn't science."

The Flames knew she didn't believe that. They pressed. What was unscientific about it? If it wasn't science, what was it?

"It's irresponsible," the man in circle glasses interrupted. "And dangerous."

"To whom?" Dr. Flame asked.

"You think it's philosophy," Dr. Flame suggested. "You think it's religion."

Dr. Regula looked down and folded her hands.

The provost cleared his throat. "I'll escort you out."

"We need to get our things."

"That won't be necessary."

In their car, the Flames talked it over.

"If they don't like The Witness and the Passenger Train," Dr. Flame said, glancing at his wife as he drove, "they really won't like the next one."

"You think there'll be trouble?"

"I certainly didn't expect Circle Glasses this morning."

"Maybe we should stay off the air this time."

"The Drs. Flame, in hiding."

"Well?"

"You're probably right."

They found the handwritten letter in an ordinary business envelope in their mail that same evening. It was postmarked in Minnesota, and came from an old married couple who went by Blushwort.

"Clearly not their real name," Dr. Flame said, reopening the letter on the kitchen counter.

"Clearly not."

He looked up as if searching the spackled ceiling in the kitchen. "Blushwort," he said. "*Aeschynanthus*."

"Cultivated species. Showy flowers."

"Red, orange, yellow."

"Bird-pollinated."

"Exactly."

The letter indicated that if the Flames wanted at no cost but in fact with some considerable caretaking stipend the use of nine hundred wooded acres in a private, undisclosed location and the three-story, two-hundred-year-old adjacent farmhouse, barn, silo, stable, and various modern outbuildings, they were to contact the Blushworts at the PO Box provided.

It was an uncanny coincidence—the kind that tends to make one either suspicious or suddenly full of easy faith.

"It's as if we dreamt it up ourselves," Dr. Flame said, bringing the breakfast tray into their bedroom the next morning.

"Maybe we did."

"Impossible to say." Dr. Flame buttered a piece of toast and handed it to his wife. She refilled his hot coffee from a French press on the nightstand. The sun came in at silver angles through the white sheers and piano music spilled from triangular silver speakers mounted above them.

"No, tell me my love," she pressed. "Did we invent the Blushworts?"

He took the coffee and leaned over to lightly bite her earlobe. "Did I invent you?"

"Certainly only you could have thought up such a remarkable creation as myself."

"Nice of you to say so."

"You have only yourself to thank."

So DID THE Flames go off the radar before the year was out, even as the next installment of their work was discussed on the nightly news, astonishing the astronomical community and anyone else who had ever looked up at the night sky.

In the second century, the news anchor explained, Ptolemy, the Greco-Roman astronomer, mathematician, geographer, and poet, identified a dim arrangement of stars situated between Centaurus and Scorpius and named it Nova Stella, Nova for short. It was a remarkable observation of both aesthetic and geometric sophistication, for the stars were situated such that the constellation itself appeared in the shape of a star: a shiny, metal-pointed celestial fixture that tilted up sideways with the moon and faded just before dawn. It was the kind of dazzling thing you might like to point out from a blanket in the grass on a fresh summer night—right after you finish a spread of cold chicken and June strawberries, and sharp cheddar and a buttery white wine, and the air around you smells lightly of blossoms and of the clean, freshly shampooed hair of the girl at your elbow. This is precisely when the constellation was most visible in the Northern Hemisphere.

But here was the modern-day breakthrough: the Drs. Flame found its perfect mirror opposite in what they subsequently named Nova X, just adjacent to Nova. As if the sky were a piece of dark paper a child had folded and traced.

The Flames had meant for the X to represent some kind of unknown, but the mystery was deeper than they imagined. Nova X, though many light-years farther away, was brighter and seemed, by their innovative computational reckoning, to be the original constellation. The real constellation. Nova Stella—Ptolemy's Nova—the one that human beings had seen fixed in their peripheral vision for centuries—was merely its reflection.

"TO THINK ALL this time we were looking at the reflection of a thing, and were unable to see the thing itself." From beside a telescope in his little glass office at the South Pole, the international star recorder turned to face the camera and shook his head in disbelief.

As there was no sheet of glass, or film of water, or any other smooth surface stretching through space by which such a picture-perfect specular reflection could be cast, the Flames' discovery presented scientists with a new puzzle about the physical world: What exactly was reflecting what? And how? Especially baffling was the fact that ever since the Flames had seen and named Nova X, there it obviously was, right where it had presumably always been, printed in the black sky and clearly visible to the naked eye.

"Seeing it now is like suddenly realizing something you have—somehow—always known."

"Known how? Intuition?" the news correspondent asked him. She wore a heavy parka with a fur-trimmed hood down around her shoulders, and in her gray-gloved hand held a thin silver microphone that she moved between herself and the star recorder.

"Sure," he said. "If you like."

"Dr. Flame and Dr. Flame declined an interview and have been oddly reclusive since leaving academia. Rumor has it they are privately funded for space exploration in the near future."

"I don't know anything about that."

The camera scanned the window and the frozen landscape below, the stars and overhanging icicles a jeweled ceiling above the planed and caped empire of snow. "Do you find the beauty of the South Pole comforting in what might otherwise be such a lonely place?"

The old man considered. "I find it terrifies me, this tremendous beauty. I find, sometimes, I would rather not see it at all."

"Do you know what's next for the Flames?"

He shrugged. "I cannot imagine."

*

THOUSANDS OF MILES to the north, in the Blushworts' undisclosed wooded location, the Flames were indeed preparing for a covert and unprecedented intergalactic expedition to Ardoris, a star in the constellation of Nova X that they'd named for themselves.

"It's Latin," Dr. Flame explained to the Blushworts. They were at the lunch table. It was always the biggest meal of the day, and all of their faces grew rosy as they ate.

"Latin for ardor," her husband added.

"For intensity."

"Brightness."

"Color."

"Fire."

"Heat."

"We like it," Mr. Blushwort said, with his arm around the thick, aproned waist of the blue-haired Mrs. Blushwort. She lifted the basket of bread.

"Eat eat," she said. "You need your strength. Butter?"

"Yes, please."

"More gravy?"

"Absolutely."

THE DRS. FLAME capped the Blushworts' old silo with glass to study the night sky, and had an old airplane hangar retrofitted as a space in which to draft and assemble not only scientific equipment but also the vessel by which they would travel to Nova X: a slick little white-and-silver capsule they called the *Inquiry*.

As they worked, the Flames grew closer to the Blushworts. Mrs. Blushwort kept everybody well fed: pheasant stew, grilled cheese, blueberry pie, spinach omelets, and white wheels of farmers' cheese she made and hung herself in the barn. Mr. Blushwort knew both where to find and how to fuse the rare metals the *Inquiry* required.

He practiced precision in every mundane task and was fastidious with the Flames' tools, equipment, and objectives. If the idea of visiting Ardoris had at first been his, or Mrs. Blushwort's, they never afterward imposed with their own thoughts or ideas.

"We're just here to support you," Mr. Blushwort said by way of explanation one afternoon in the hangar.

"We think of ourselves as your godparents," Mrs. Blushwort agreed. She set down a tray of black tea and fresh rolls on the workbench. "I made a rhubarb tart," she added, turning from the workbench to the Flames. "For after dinner tonight."

The Drs. Flame glanced at each other. "But that's our favorite thing," Dr. Flame said. "I mean, like our one absolutely favorite thing."

"Well." Mrs. Blushwort smiled, and lifted the glass dish. "How nice."

"It isn't nice," Dr. Flame said later. They were in bed in the old farmhouse eating gigantic sandwiches and passing back and forth a tall green bottle of beer. "It's creepy."

"I know it."

"All of this is beginning to feel very—unauthorized. Spooky."

"Shh. Listen. An owl."

"You see? That's a portent of death, my love."

"Be careful what you say. If we expect things to go badly, they will."

"I guess what I'm wondering," Dr. Flame said, "is what they're getting out of this. I mean, I get it that they like us."

"But."

"Right."

THE FOLLOWING MORNING, as if the Blushworts had overhead their entire conversation, Mr. Blushwort told a story.

Years ago, he and Mrs. Blushwort were cleaning the kitchen in the farmhouse. It hadn't had a good scrubbing in years. Just when they thought the kitchen was as clean as they could get it, Mrs. Blushwort discovered that a piece of the countertop was actually on rusty old recessed wheels, and slid right out of place. Beneath it, old peeling linoleum was seeded with mouse droppings, rimed with rust-colored stains, and caked with a film of hair, lint, and pasty sludge almost an inch thick. So, they cleaned that too. Afterward Mr. Blushwort asked his wife, now, doesn't that feel good, to know you've got everything cleaned, even the hidden places? And she answered: No. It makes me wonder what else we're missing.

"Point is," Mrs. Blushwort innocently explained, "you got to keep going."

"Pushing the envelope," Mr. Blushwort said.

"Even when you think you've already found everything."

"I guess that's something like what has us worried about you," Dr. Flame said, and she checked Dr. Flame's gaze to make sure she was speaking correctly for them both.

Mr. Blushwort laughed. "Trust," he said. "A scientist's least appreciated but most important tool."

THAT EVENING, THE Flames circled the expansive property to gulp the oxygen and observe life on earth in all of its glory—for the launch would be soon, and there was, of course, a good chance they wouldn't make it back. The crickets clicked and creaked around their ankles. On the horizon, the hemlocks and balsam trees were a soft feathery black. Bats circled above them and the night birds whirred up in the dense canopies of leaves.

"The world at night," Dr. Flame said, and put her hand on Dr. Flame's upper arm and whispered, her face pointed toward the opening in the trees. There was a coyote, standing just beyond a rectangle of light cast by their science library window. Its eyes full of green fire, its gold and brown fur matted and filthy. They often saw the coyotes—on blue sheets of snow in the night, or, as now, in summer, on the move under an egg-shaped moon. But it had never seemed to the Drs. Flame that the phenomena of the world—visible or invisible—were facts or physical forms to be taken for granted and studied, so much as they were questions posed. If their lives and all the inventory of the world in which their lives took place were equations or could theoretically be represented and modeled by equations, then this wild and beautiful creature surprising them in the circle of blue grass struck each of them as a new, heretofore unaddressed problem.

"Perhaps we've chosen the wrong destination," Dr. Flame said.

"Perhaps we're being a bit too one-to-one in our thinking."

"Looking for symbols."

"Correlations."

"Messages from beyond."

"Thinking figuratively."

"Metaphorically."

"Anagogically."

"Looking for answers."

"God forbid."

"Mm." Dr. Flame nodded and coiled a dark curl around her long white finger. From out of the dark, the deep and hollow ringing call of a loon on the lake in the woods. "We might end up creating whatever it is we think we're discovering."

"That's not science."

"No," Dr. Flame agreed. "I don't know what that is."

QUIETLY THE FOLLOWING week, just before dawn and without any fanfare, the Drs. Flame stepped into their silver suits, head to toe wearing blankets that snapped at the neck like pajamas, as if they were tucking for a long nap.

Ardoris was a distance of approximately ten light-years from home, so they expected some considerable length of travel time, but somewhere around two light-years out, the hum of the *Inquiry* ceased, and they felt themselves begin to accelerate in a direction they would have called downward if—without gravity to propel them—this had been at all possible.

"It feels like falling!" Dr. Flame shouted across the craft, buckling himself into his white co-captain's chair. And his breath caught in his throat. In her own chair, Dr. Flame was perfectly still and—it struck her husband all at once—hauntingly human. As if this were not her true form, as if he had known her as something else, and would know her again in yet some other shape. The line of her jaw, the whiteness of her cheek—ghostlike in how they brought to bear some other thing that was—how could it be so?—more vivid than his beautiful wife.

"My love," he said. She heard him, but did not respond. It was as if she were on the edge of sleep and instead of being jolted awake by this sensation of falling, she was turning right for it, pitching into it.

Later, he would say he had felt it too, but had been so fearful he'd allowed his anxiety to eclipse it. "It's just so hard," he said, "not to jump to Newtonian conclusions."

"We're so accustomed to them," she agreed. "I could feel an impact coming right here," she said, and tapped the center of her chest.

But there was no impact. The *Inquiry* began to rattle and shriek. Everything outside the viewfinder window went dark. The instrumentation indicating direction blinked in and out of operation and suddenly, everything was quiet, and still. The *Inquiry* slowed and was hovering in the midst of nothing, nowhere.

Exhausted, unable to resist, they fell asleep, whereupon they both dreamt the same dream. They would share it with each other years later, when Dr. Flame was dying, and his wife sat upright beside his hospital bed, holding his hand, her once brown hair woven back in a coarse silver braid.

"I dreamt we weren't ourselves."

"So did I."

"What did you dream we were?"

He paused as if something pained him, and looked up at his old friend. "I couldn't say."

"Not because you don't know."

"Right."

"Rather because—"

He put his finger to her lips to shush her.

Her eyes were full of tears as she put her lips to his old furry ear. "I am going to miss you so much."

When they awoke on the *Inquiry*, a younger pair of dark-haired explorers, they rubbed their eyes and crossed the room to check on the status of the instruments. Everything seemed intact. Checking the function on their scope in the giant viewfinder, Dr. Flame was looking at Planet Earth when suddenly—it was gone. The whole earth. "Oh! Darling!" She waved her hand to beckon Dr. Flame and he came over and stood behind her, then bent in and took a look.

"What did you do?" he said, straightening.

"Nothing! I don't know." She bent and looked again. "I was afraid it might not be out there. And then—it wasn't."

He took another turn at the scope and looked into the dark. His panic began to mount when suddenly he felt a little heat in the back of his head and the earth reappeared. "There," he said. "It's right there."

"Oh. Oh I must have had the setting off."

"I didn't touch the setting."

"Well what did you do?"

"What did *you* do?"

"I couldn't say."

"My God." He took his wife by the shoulders and looked into her eyes. "Do you understand what's happening?"

"No."

He zoomed in on their own faraway launchpad in the woods; she watched. The rivers were a tangle of silver string; there on the sparkling, board-hard snow was a pack of wolves, the whites of their throats visible in the night as they all had their heads thrown back, their eyes shut, their mouths narrowed and pointed like hollow weapons at the sky; and there was the little town outside of where the Flames had lived with the Blushworts, where they purchased their groceries. It was the middle of the night. Sparse, modest rooftops among the trees. No one was up and no one was out. Dr. Flame pointed his gaze at the cold bare branches of a burr oak, and the sky behind it filled with starlight, and its branches lined themselves with soft white winter birds that tipped their heads and blinked their small shining black eyes in the soft light.

"Ohhhh." She thought she understood. "Did you put those birds there?"

"What, those birds?" he asked. "I didn't make those birds."

In the next moment, the Flames saw the Blushworts far below, outside their cottage on the snow, simultaneously turning the beautiful white ovals of their faces up from the trees and the birds toward the sky, straight toward the *Inquiry*, straight at the Flames.

"Oh," Dr. Flame said hoarsely, and her knees went soft. Dr. Flame held her up.

"I think they are making us," he whispered.

The young doctors were silent a moment, but all at once, and simultaneously looking at each other with wide eyes, they remembered they'd launched in summer, but were looking down on a winter's night.

"Light-years," Dr. Flame recalled. "Time travel."

"We're looking into the past."

"Exactly so."

So they adjusted the settings on the viewfinder, entered the coordinates they wished to see, and there it was: the two slightly younger Flames in their science library two years past, peering through the telescope at that smear of sidereal light where they'd discover Ptolemy's error.

"Ah ha," Dr. Flame said, and he moved the viewfinder to Nova until, to his satisfaction, Nova X appeared beside it.

"Nicely done." She moved to kiss him, and he extended his cheek.

"But." Dr. Flame stepped back from the viewfinder and looked at her gravely.

"Down on earth we should thereby—right now—conceive of our idea to travel to Ardoris."

She thought back. Yes, that was how it'd gone. They'd found the constellation, and decided it merited a visit. "We'd come out here," she said. "Where presumably, our future selves would create Nova X. Which we just did."

Dr. Flame thought. "Say that again."

"And on that trip, at Ardoris, we'll invent Nova X." She nodded and smiled broadly. "Isn't it wonderful?"

"But my darling." He pointed to the digital map that indicated they'd fallen short by several light-years and were in a strange pocket of dark, unmarked, directionless space. "Ardoris is not where we are. In fact, we don't *know* where we are. We got stopped here by mistake."

"By accident."

"So it seems."

Inside their silver suits, the hair went up on the backs of their necks, along their forearms.

"So then, who—" He frowned. "Where," he said, and stopped. "What are we?" They stretched out their silver-gloved hands before them, turned them over in space, looked each other up and down.

"Oh my God," Dr. Flame said, seeing a crush of light outside the window screen. "My love," he said. "Look at the stars."

Moonless

by Bryan Hurt

It took some doing but I finally made a white dwarf star like they'd been making out in Santa Fe. I made mine in my basement because basements are the perfect place to compress time and space. I slammed together some very high-frequency energy waves and—ZAP!—a perfect miniature white dwarf. Even though it was very small for its type, no larger than a pushpin, it was extremely dense and incredibly bright. The star was so bright that you couldn't look directly at it. Had to look above or below or off to the side and squint. One time I set myself the challenge of just staring at it for thirty seconds. Got a big headache, huge mistake.

Density was a problem too. The star was dense enough that it drew small objects toward it. Tissue paper, curtains, the tail of my cat. Of course they all burst into flames. But at the same time it wasn't so dense that it just hovered there above my table, an object fixed in space. It wobbled this way and that, wandering the basement, knocking against the walls, the floor, the ceiling, leaving burn marks everywhere. The last straw was when it set fire to my favorite Einstein poster—the one with his tongue sticking out, his messed-up hair and goofy grin. I trapped the star in a box, put a padlock on the heavy lid.

But stars are not meant to be kept in boxes. At night I could hear it down in my basement bumping against the walls of its prison. My dreams were soundtracked by a million leaden pings. The only solution was to make another one. A second white dwarf that matched the first one exactly and set both of them into a stable binary orbit. The two stars dancing around their common center of gravity. It was a simple and elegant solution, as most solutions from nature are.

But once I had the stars locked in equilibrium, I couldn't help but notice how shabby the rest of their surroundings were. The basement's dull walls, spiderwebs hanging from the ceiling beams, boxes stacked and packed with old LPs and moth-eaten sweaters and love letters from girlfriends who'd liked me first for my ambition and then called it neglect. So I went to the art store and bought black poster board, which I glued together and strung with Christmas lights. I called the finished product the universe even though it was more like a diorama of. Still I felt the display added some dignity to the scene, my white dwarves floating there in front of all that blackness, the holiday lights shining behind. My cat liked it too. He rubbed his cheeks against the sharp corners of the universe and purred.

Exactly when it happened, I don't know. But soon little globes of matter began forming around my stars. The globes were made of drops of water from the glass I'd spilled, Einstein ashes, and fur that the stars pulled from the back of my cat, who liked to nap underneath them. There were two of them, two globes. They were more like tiny planets really, each one orbiting its own star. I put my elbows on the table and squinted at them from behind my welder's mask (for by then I'd learned my lesson). One planet was slightly larger than the other, had its own miniature moon, so I named it after a moony ex-girlfriend who liked to stare at the night sky and ask why our love wasn't as dark and infinite. The other one had no moon, so I called it Moonless.

The next time I checked on my cardboard universe even more had changed. There was a tiny flag planted on the tiny moon. Microscopic satellites orbited the planet and miniature airplanes flew to miniature cities. Each city swarmed with tiny cars with sub-atomic red-faced drivers inside. Moonless was doing even better; its civilization had become even more advanced. There were hover-cars, biodomes, black glass buildings that swooped and curved as if they'd been painted into existence. On top of its tallest mountain was an enormous telescope that was pointing at its neighbor. Operating the telescope was a tiny scientist in a tiny white lab coat, her hair twisted into a tiny but perfect black knot.

But I was not in the right mood to appreciate the wonders of my universe. I could not force myself to feel the requisite joy or awe or whatever I should have felt at that particular moment in time. I had just returned home from my laboratory, it had been a not-so-great day. First I'd been rejected by one of my lab assistants. Not even formally rejected. Asked her out and she just jammed her eyes into a microscope and hummed. Then I'd lost out on a big government grant to my chief rival, the smug molecular astrophysicist Dr. Hu. I patted him on the back and ate his celebratory cake, forced a smile with icing on my lips. Someone had dented my car in the parking lot. My cat had made a hairball in one of my loafers, which I stepped in as soon as I got home.

So no. I could not muster the enthusiasm to celebrate the triumph of my dwarves, the impossibility of their little people. What I felt instead, primarily, was annoyed.

Because take for example the planet named after the moony ex-girlfriend: here was a brand-new world, unlimited potential, infinite possibilities, and it was basically just a smaller copy of this one. Same cars, same space junk, same flag on the moon. Pretty much all the same crap except played out on an even smaller, more insignificant scale. Pathetic, really. Boring. Much like the girlfriend I'd named the planet after. After a promising start—exciting, sexy—it was a movie on the couch every Friday night, maybe with a little petting mixed in. But when I'd start taking her pants off, she'd yawn and say she liked it better in the morning when she was not tired but still half asleep. As if sex were something that happened only once a day, like breakfast or sunsets. In the end she was the one who said I didn't love her. Said that if I didn't like what she had to offer, I'd never be happy. So I flicked the moony planet into the universe's backdrop, watched it explode against the cardboard and Christmas lights. The explosion was so small that it barely even registered as a blip.

But the tiny scientist on Moonless saw it too. She blinked into her viewfinder, pushed her glasses up the bridge of her nose, then turned the telescope in the opposite direction, a full half circle, so that when it stopped it was pointing directly up at me. She wrote something in her tiny notebook, her tiny hand trembling. I didn't go back into the basement for a while after that.

But basements can't be avoided forever. When I did return—with a basket of laundry so ripe you could practically see the wafterons rising off it—I saw that the tiny scientist had built a gigantic ray gun. She was taking potshots at my Christmas lights. Zapped a light and tiny glass tinkled onto cardboard. I told her to knock it off. She zapped another one. "Or what?" she said. "You're going to destroy this planet too?" Maybe I was. I told her not to test me. "Oh I'll test you," she said. She wheeled the gun around and fired a shot that skimmed my nose. The second one hit me dead on. It stung a lot. I ducked the next salvo and raised my hand to swipe her planet out of existence. She set her chin, bracing for the blow.

But I was not a destroyer of worlds. Not really. I had destroyed one world, singular, and it was just a very small one. I hadn't even meant to create it. What I'd intended to do was make a star, a modest white dwarf, something beautiful just to see if I could do it. Maybe I also wanted to have something to show off to girlfriends when I brought them down to my basement, something that would help get them to hop into my bed. I didn't want to contribute to the grand unhappiness. There was already too much of it in this world. Just today I'd read about a kid in Ohio who shot another kid in school. In Japan someone had taken a knife into the subway and stabbed five people to death. At work I'd found Dr. Hu crying alone in a bathroom stall. He had stage four prostate cancer, inoperable, spreading.

Still, perhaps it was all unavoidable. Maybe whenever you made something—stars, planets, people, whatever—you always made a little sadness, a little death. There was no such thing as pure creation. I told the tiny scientist that I was sorry about the planet but either I was going to destroy it or I was going to be destroyed by something else. That's how it worked: that was science, that was the natural order of things.

"That's bullshit," she said. She said that I was a coward and a chicken shit. She said that her husband had been on that other planet on an expedition. I had killed him. She asked how I wasn't responsible for that. "Look," I said. "I'll make it up." I pulled some fur from the back of my cat, dunked it in some water and rolled it into a ball, which I set in orbit around the dwarf.

The ball came undone. It drifted into the star and burned to ash. "Pathetic," she said. She looked at me, angry and disappointed, just like every moony Lindsay or Sarah or Kara or Jen looked at me when something came undone between us. But it was just a little thing, an insignificant thing, barely worth dwelling on because it hardly even existed. A small planet; her husband, a small man.

"I'm sorry," I said and I guess I was. "But what do you want from me? I can't fix everything. I'm not a god."

Even then I think we both knew that wasn't true, not entirely. For after the tiny scientist grew old and died, and her children died, and her planet's sun died, and everyone died, I continued making new stars. I made white dwarves but also other types because my techniques had become more advanced. Sometimes new planets coalesced around these stars and sometimes the planets made life. I continued to flick away the inferior or disappointing ones, or I'd feed them to my cat. Of those that remained I watched tiny people spread out and inhabit all the corners of my tiny universe, until the universe became too full to contain them and so I'd wipe them all away. Sometimes there were other tiny scientists with very powerful telescopes who would look up and out at me. When they saw me there were always questions about who I was and what I wanted. Was I good or malevolent? Omnipotent or indifferent? A god of death? I was just a man, I'd say to them, just as I'd told the original scientist. But like the original scientist, the more they studied me, the more they watched, the more they became unconvinced. Not because I had power over life and death, destruction and creation—which I did. But because there was only one of me. The god of my own isolation, my own unhappiness. A man with a cat in a basement. What is a god if not alone?

Our New Neighborhood

by Lincoln Michel

When the incidents start, my husband decides that what our neighborhood needs is a Neighborhood Watch. "We need to watch our assets as closely as we're gonna watch the twins," he says, tapping the baby monitor screen. The screen is dark and blue. It shows two pale teddy bears in an otherwise empty crib.

The next morning, I come downstairs and see Donald slinking in the corner with a black trench coat and fedora.

"What do you think?"

We're low on disposable income and, as usual, he bought a size too large.

"It looks a little conspicuous," I say.

"That's the idea, Margot. I want them to know someone is watching."

My husband buttons the top button of the coat, puts on a pair of sunglasses.

As I slide the toast in the toaster, I see him out the window. He's sneaking through the bushes in the neighbor's backyard.

THE REASON WE are low on cash is that we poured our savings into buying house #32 in a neighborhood called Middle Pond. Middle Pond is located between West Pond on the east and East Pond on the west. All three are part of North Lake, which is itself a subset of the Ocean Shore suburb.

It looks perfect on paper. It has a stellar school system and all the amenities.

"Normally, I'd say we should wait and see," the real estate agent said, "but if you don't snatch this now you'll watch it go bye-bye."

Donald downloaded an app called HausFlippr that estimates property values in exclusive neighborhoods. Each time the Middle Pond score went up a full percentage point, Donald cooked rib eyes on our new five-burner grill.

He hasn't cooked rib eyes in months.

OUR NEIGHBORS ARE not as worried about the declining rating. "My father used to say, 'Markets fluctuate like fishes swim,'" John Jameson says at the neighborhood improvement meeting. It's our week to host and I'm placing triangles of cheese beside rectangle crackers.

Several of the other wives are insisting on helping me.

"We'll make sure this is the last time you host until after the miracles pop out," Mrs. Jameson says.

"Can I see?" Alice Johansson asks while lifting up the hem of my blouse.

"There's nothing to see, I'm not even showing."

In the other room, Donald is raising his voice. "Well *my* father always said you can never be too careful when it comes to property and prosperity. Plus, I already bought the trench coat."

The three of us walk back in holding the one tray.

"Okay, if it will make you feel better, we'll take a vote."

Donald is a tall, muscular man. He knows how to use his body, how to loom. The vote is tight, but Donald stares down enough neighbors that his budget is approved.

"Let's move on to the question of acceptable dye colors for next month's Easter egg hunt."

"I refuse to participate if metallics are allowed again," Samantha Stetson says. "They hurt my eyes."

THE CRIB IS temporarily in my office. This means that the baby monitor camera is temporarily in here too. It is shaped like a purple flower and situated between the plants on the windowsill. The monitor is downstairs in the living room. I've adjusted the angle of the camera so that it can see the crib, but can't see my computer screen.

I can't allow Donald to see what I look at online.

THE PROPERTY VALUES in Middle Pond are based on the reputation of the neighborhood, which is determined, in large part, by the official score assigned by the North Lake Committee on Proper Property Standards.

We are never told the qualifying factors, but judging from the way the inspectors inspect, the list is long and varied. They inspect the level of seed in the bird feeders, observe the height of the grass in each lawn, and mark down rule infractions during the games of hopscotch on the street.

Our neighbors probably thought that Donald would get bored after a week or give up when the score increased. But the score keeps declining and by mid-month Donald has an entire operation set up in our basement.

"Look at those paint stains in the driveway of the Johnsons'. And see how the Stetsons keep every curtain drawn?"

I'm maneuvering the laundry basket between his monitors and stacks of notes.

He calls me over, makes me watch a time-lapse progression of black cars entering and leaving the Jacobsons' garage.

"I'm going to see if the neighborhood board will increase the Watch's budget. I need at least a dozen cameras. What do you think?"

I want to tell him that my bladder hurts and my back aches and I don't care about the neighbors' driveways. I want to tell him that he was supposed to be helping me during the pregnancy, not getting in my way. Mostly I want to tell him that he should be looking at me, not the neighbors.

OR THAT'S WHAT I know I'm supposed to feel. In fact, I don't mind that Donald isn't looking at me. After five years of marriage, my own eyes have started wandering.

I know that every marriage goes through those phases, where you look at the other person and can't remember what you ever saw in them. I know that it will pass, and that the babies will give us something new to look at together. But they aren't born yet.

When Donald starts pinning evidence to his corkboard, I creep upstairs and open my SingleMingle account. I gaze at the pixelated men. Some of them are smiling with salt and wind in their hair. Others are introspective, reading a novel in a leather wingchair. When I click next, a new one materializes. I click next again and again and again. There is an endless number of these men. My favorites are the ones who don't have shirts on. Some even crop their heads off, leaving just their disembodied, under-tanned torsos moving across the screen.

Donald's operation starts out small, and consists mostly of warning signs that Donald posts around the neighborhood. These signs show a dark figure with glowing eyes and the words *You Are Seen.*

Nevertheless, during the inspector's next visit, while he is measuring the dampness of the cul-de-sac gutter, somebody keys the inspector's car.

THE NEXT DAY, HausFlippr changes our safety rating from A to A- and drops our overall score five points.

Donald's budget is quickly tripled.

He buys a dozen cameras from Discountsleuth.com and hides them around our property. One is slinked through the hose, looking out at the street. Two face our immediate neighbors' houses through holes in the fence that Donald drills with an old dentist drill. One is hooked to the weathervane at the top of the house, providing a rotating view of the neighborhood as the wind blows.

The cameras snake down into the basement, where they are monitored by Donald and his two interns, Chet and Chad.

I USE A fake zip code on my SingleMingle account. My user info is a lie. My height is shrunk an inch, my status marked "seductively single," my eyes labeled hazel instead of green. I use photos that obscure my features, angles that make my nose look bigger or my hair a different shade of brown.

If anyone who knows me saw my profile, they wouldn't be able to recognize me.

Still, I make sure to browse strangers in other neighborhoods like North Forest and South Beach.

A man with the username OceanShoreStud27 catches my eye. His profile doesn't have much information, but I want to know more. I plug his user photos into reverse image search, find his other profiles on other sites. His name is Derek Carrington. He's thirty-seven, a Libra, works in finance, has a blog devoted to his sport fishing catches. I check out his most played songs on Boom-boxFM and a list of every movie he's rated on Moviemaniacs.com.

What gets my heart truly racing is the satellite photo of his house. It's only a few miles away and has a back porch and a pool. I zoom in as far as I can until the pool's blue hues are giant pixelated blocks. I imagine myself sitting by the pool with Derek, our twins splashing in the abstract art.

I come.

I organize the files on Derek, zip and encode them on a folder in my external hard drive.

Then I start searching again.

"CORRUPT ASSHOLES!" DONALD is pounding his fist into the refrigerator.

He notices me in the doorway, gazes at my stomach.

"What are the three of you craving? Fried chicken? Tacos? I can get one of the interns to make a run."

I tell him Thai, and he sends Chet out. He looks at me with that serious expression he gets when he is unsure if I can handle what he wants to say. It's my least favorite expression of his.

"A dog attacked Chad when he was affixing a new camera to the yield-to-children sign. We got a photo, but none of the neighbors will identify it."

"People get protective of their pets."

"The bastards are trying to stonewall me!" He hits his own palm with his fist. "It's not just that violation, Margot. It's vandalism. Crime. Drugs. Lord knows what else."

He mistakes my bemusement for worry. He comes over and touches my stomach with the backs of his hands.

"Don't worry, I won't let anything happen to any of us."

He continues to rub my belly with his knuckles. I try to think of the last time those knuckles touched me in a place I wanted to be touched.

"I wish I could see what was going on in there," he says without looking up.

DESPITE DONALD'S EFFORTS, the incidents don't stop. Someone toilet-papers the Thompsons' oak tree. A raccoon spills garbage all across our cul-de-sac. Four yards have grown well beyond the allowable length. Donald calls in a half-dozen noise violations, but can't pin down the sources.

He has successes too. He catches the Jamesons' cat urinating on the Abelsons' rosebushes, gets little Sally Henderson to sign an affidavit that she left her Frisbee in the gutter.

When we bought this place, Middle Pond houses were valued higher than West Pond and nearly equal with East Pond. Now they are not better than condos in South Creek.

Donald takes a temporary leave from his job. Says he's going to focus on the family, on our protection. The North Lake Proper Property Standards Guidebook is a tome. Donald and his interns keep finding new rules and new violations.

Worse, he thinks the neighbors are undermining his efforts. They keep ripping the cameras out of the streetlamps and snapping the microphones on the fire hydrants.

"It's probably just the teens being teens," I say over dinner. It's the only time that we see each other anymore. I spend all of my time upstairs in the bedroom, adding men to my folder, while Donald spends it in the basement, monitoring his wall of screens.

Donald doesn't look up from his bowl of noodles. "Youth is no excuse for crime. If you don't stop them now, they'll be watching the world from behind a set of bars."

THE NURSE SQUIRTS the gel, fires up the machine.

I'm not sure what to think of the little objects on the screen. I know, intellectually, that they are our children. But they look like microbes in a microscope, inscrutable creatures from another world.

"Those are the hearts, those are the brains," the nurse is saying. She uses a little laser pointer on the screen.

"The checkup comes with prints, right?" Donald asks. "I want to be able to look at these whenever needs be."

AS MY BELLY swells, my searching habits shift. I've gotten bored gathering information on strangers in distant neighborhoods, started to yawn seeing the photos of middle-aged men next to their cars and fireplaces. I move on from SingleMingle to other, more explicit sites. Affluent Affairs, OK-Dungeon, WASPs_Gone_Wild.

I set my zip code to Middle Pond, check in on the neighbors.

Browsing close to home, I have to obscure myself further. I use photo-editing software to change the tint of my skin. I make sure that there are no identifiable objects in the background of my selfies or else decorate my wall with dime-store decorations that I throw away after a snap. I get the latest encryption software to block my IP.

The men on these sites are like me. They do not reveal their faces, don't give away identifying information.

I stare at a hand or corner of a painting caught in the background of a photo and try to figure out who I'm looking at. Is that William Carlson's untanned thighs? Do those pubes curl how I'd imagine James Jacobson's to curl? Is that edge of cheek or lock of hair one I've seen at a neighborhood meeting?

THE NORTH LAKE Committee on Proper Property Standards applauds Donald, gives him an award for excellence in property protection. Donald makes me come to the ceremony. It's the first time we've been out together in weeks. These days, the twins move so much I'm peeing every thirty minutes. For the most part I stay upstairs, logged in.

As usual, Donald's speech is overlong and mawkish, yet sprinkled with some sharp wit. I'm too far along to drink and try to will myself drunk by staring intensely at the glasses of merlot. I pee twice during the speech.

The residents of Middle Pond, however, are not happy with the Neighborhood Watch.

"You scared Sally," Hubert Henderson says when the Hendersons come by for dinner two nights later.

"She wouldn't be scared if she didn't have something to hide." Donald chews his pork chop slowly, his eyes rotating back and forth between the Hendersons.

"Look, this has gone on long enough. This neighborhood doesn't need a watch. If anything, you are making people uncomfortable and they are acting out!"

Donald gets up, wipes his chin with a napkin. He goes into the other room.

"Why, I never," Henrietta says. She turns to me. "You understand our concern, right? You have children on the way. You don't want them spied on all the time, do you?"

I'm not really paying attention to her. I'm looking at the curve of Hubert's elbow, mentally measuring the distance between moles on his neck. Have I seen those body parts digitized before?

Donald comes back and slaps down a manila folder. It's stuffed with papers and has *Hendersons* written on the top in thick marker letters.

"What is the meaning of this?" Hubert says.

When he opens it, the folder is filled with photos of him and his family. Secret shots of Sally not wiping her muddy shoes on the welcome mat, close-ups of fungal infections on the trees, stills of the cat devouring a protected songbird. He flips through them with increasing speed. "This is madness," he sputters.

THE NEIGHBORHOOD ASSOCIATION cuts off the Watch's funding, but Donald doesn't care. "It just means we are getting to them."

He shows me grainy footage of neighbors wearing black stockings on their heads and ripping out his cameras. He freezes them, puts them side by side with photos taken from their Buddy Face pages.

I lean forward, fascinated at seeing the same photos that are in my files on his screen.

The next week, Donald takes out a mortgage on our house. He puts the money into three iSpy drones. They can fly up and down the neighborhood for two hours before they need to be recharged. Each has a camera on a swivel base.

"These babies are the future of neighborhood protection," he says.

I watch the test run from my upstairs window.

Chet and Chad set up chairs down on the front lawn. They cheer each time the drones pass by.

MIDDLE POND FEELS like a ghost town. Children are no longer allowed to play games in the streets. No one walks their dogs or barbecues on the lawn. Our neighbors do not want to have every action watched, every interaction documented. They stay inside with the curtains drawn. Most of our neighbors have purchased tinted windows for their cars so that Donald cannot see how many come and go.

The only things that move on the streets are the drones humming in their preprogrammed patterns.

I can barely even move indoors. My belly is swollen, and when I look at myself in the mirror, I don't recognize who I see. I know that it won't be long before the twins are born, and that their birth will mean a change to much more than just my body or our house.

I've installed the Bread Crumb Trail app on Donald's phone. The app shows you a digital bread crumb trail to your device's location so that you can find it if it's misplaced. I use it to monitor Donald's movements, see where he is coming from or going to.

"Donald, maybe you can drive me to the movies. Have a night out for ourselves before the house is full of screams."

"Can't now, Margot. Things are coming together. I'm connecting the thread. This thing goes all the way to the top."

He is breathing heavily on the phone. We never see each other in the flesh anymore. The house is divided between our bases of operation. When I ask him for something, Donald sends one of the interns upstairs.

"The top of what, Donald?"

"You don't even want to know."

*

I WAIT FOR the drone to fly past, then close the blinds. Today, I'm finishing up my file on John Jameson. I found him on SuburbanPervs, recognized his sprinkler system in the background of an explicit pic.

It only takes a few clicks to get his credit score, high school GPA, and family tree. I put the details in my spreadsheet, gaze at the figures. You can look at all that data and the picture of a person really does emerge. It really does. I know more about Jameson now than most of his friends, more perhaps than even his wife.

Suddenly, I get a pop-up chat from Jameson's profile, SilverFoxGolfer72.

"I think you've been looking at me," he says.

I don't reply.

"I've had my eye on you too," he says.

He puts in a request for video chat.

"If you record, I'll sue."

OUTSIDE MY WINDOW, things are getting ugly. The Neighborhood Watch is opposed by a new group, the Middle Pond Citizens' Veil. The MPCV scuffle in the streets with Chad and Chet. They cover all the Watch signs with their own symbol: a child skipping rope with a hood over her head.

The exact membership of the MPCV is unknown. They wear latex masks that have been fashioned to look like Donald. I do a double take when I see them on the sidewalk in front of our house, erecting a temporary wall.

Donald responds by attaching speakers to the drones and blasting out audioclips of the neighbors admitting their violations and begging for forgiveness that were recorded during secret interrogation sessions with Chet and Chad in our basement.

Donald is secretly receiving funds from the North Lake Committee, who are concerned that the destabilization of property standards will spread beyond Middle Pond. I know this, because I've started monitoring Donald's emails—his password is shirley-andhugh2015, his desired names for our twins and the year of their upcoming births.

Donald, you are our man on the inside, the most recent encrypted email says. *Remember the three Cs of neighborhood standards: Community, Commitment, and Containment. Emphasis on containment. This can't be allowed to spread.*

WHILE I'M TRYING to use public information to answer Frederick Abelson's uCloudPhotos security questions, a brick smashes through the window. The double-wide crib is covered in shards of glass. I wobble as quickly as I can to the window and see a Donald-faced figure climbing over our fence.

There is a sheet of paper attached to the brick. It says, *Do you want out? Check [ ]Yes [ ]No. Sincerely, the MPCV.*

I think about this question for some time. Out of what? The neighborhood? My marriage? My soon-to-be-formed family? My life?

If I could go back and do things differently, well, of course I would. But isn't that true of everyone?

I mark my check. Then place the paper in a paper shredder.

THE TWINS ANCHOR me to my desk chair. I can no longer see my toes when I stand up, and the hormones and chemicals swirling inside me are making me feel as if my body is an alien vessel. The main thing it feels is hunger. Chet and Chad bring me takeout meals, but Donald remains a ghost floating in the glow of his basement monitors. I see him only through a small camera that I tucked behind the washing machine. When I installed it, I saw something that broke my heart just a little bit. Above his workstation there were two images: a map of the neighborhood and the sonogram printout. There are pins and string connecting the image of the twins to the map of our neighborhood, permanent marker notations on the side. I can't make out the chicken scrawl code.

A part of me thinks that when all of this is over, it might not be impossible for us to go back to the life we had. We could delete all the data we've accumulated, purge the audio and video. Live again like our neighbors are strangers whom we simply wave to on the street.

Why not? Every day people reset their lives, move to new towns or take up new jobs.

But then an explosion echoes down the street.

THE FLAMING CAR is not our car. Donald doesn't know what happened, and there is no clear footage as the drones were captured in nets strung between the streetlamps on the cul-de-sac right before the attack.

The explosion pulls the different factions out into their yards. The Neighborhood Watch on ours, the MPCV and sympathizers on the others. The air is thick with both tension and smoke.

"This is a declaration of war," Chet says.

"Each house is either with us or against us," says Chad.

"You two don't even live in this neighborhood," I say.

Chet scratches his ear. "Well, we get college credit if the mission here succeeds."

Donald pulls me close, moves his body in front of me as if to shield me from the neighbors' eyes.

"I'll find out who did this," he whispers to me. "I have cameras they don't even know about, feeds beyond their wildest dreams."

The driver is singed and shouting, "No, no, no! What the fuck?"

No one moves to help him. His clothes are still slightly on fire.

He looks around at all of us. He is wearing a pointed purple hat with embroidered stars. His pointer finger is outstretched and he moves it from family to family, yard to yard.

"What kind of neighborhood is this!" he screams. He says that this was only his first week driving the Wizsearch street-mapping car. Wizsearch has been expanding into online maps and is trying to get real-life pictures of every street. "It's supposed to be a public service. If you didn't want to be mapped, you could have opted out online!"

"YOU LOOK JUST about ready to burst," Sarah Ableson says. She's standing in my doorway holding a casserole dish. She lets out a high-pitched, forced laugh.

"Still a month or so to go," I say. I'm thankful that my belly is large enough to obscure my laptop screen. I reach my hand behind my back to close it.

Sarah's eyes dart around the room. She mouths something to me that I can't understand.

"I brought you my famous third trimester tortellini!" She's talking much louder than necessary. "I ate this for a month straight with both Bobby and Susan!"

She hands me the casserole tray and then slides a note into my pocket.

Sarah steps back into the hallway and scans to see if anyone is there.

"Well, I better be going. Hope to *hear* from you soon."

After she leaves, I read the note. It tells me that they know the room is bugged, so they can't talk. They want to know if I can broker a peace meeting, get the two sides to come to terms.

There is a phone in a plastic bag in the middle of the casserole. Donald won't be able to monitor it. Call us if you can help end the madness.

*

I DRAG ALL of my files—every neighbor I've gathered data on, each .doc of their life and spreadsheet of their history—and place them in the recycle bin. I tell myself that it's unhealthy to be spending so much time monitoring the lives of others, and so little time looking at my own. Plus, when the twins finally arrive, I won't have time to look up my neighbors and video chat with masked faces. I'll be shaking brightly colored toys before their newborn eyes, or watching to make sure they don't eat rat poison or loose nails.

I hover my cursor over the pixelated trash can icon. I click on it and start to sweat. I hit undo, sending the files flying back to the proper folders.

There's always time to delete them when the twins are born. I'll be able to make a clean break when that happens.

Until then, I fire up the browser, log back in.

And then one morning I wake up and the neighborhood is quiet. I don't hear the drones flying past. I don't hear Chet and Chad struggling with masked Donalds in the street. I don't even hear the sounds of cars driving quickly down the street.

I get up and pee. Wash my hands with antibacterial soap. I struggle to the window.

At the end of the street, I can see two people being shoved into a patrol car. The rest of the houses have their driveways blocked off with police tape.

I move to my laptop, start to do a Wizsearch News search for "Middle Pond." No results.

I look over at the casserole phone still in its plastic bag. I dial the preprogrammed contact, listen to it go straight to voicemail.

Then someone taps spryly on the door.

DONALD EXTENDS A handful of roses. His face is shaved and he's wearing a new suit that fits just right. He looks nothing like the disheveled figure hunched over his charts I've been monitoring in the basement.

"It's all over, baby. We won, you and me."

My heart is beating quickly and I'm unsure what combination of fear, relief, and confusion is mixing in my head.

He hugs me and tells me he's taken down the cameras and will be renting the drones out for upscale weddings for overhead photo shoots.

"The North Shore Committee asked me to give you this." He hands me a pendant of an eye surrounded by a white picket fence. "There will be a ceremony later, of course."

He pins it carefully to my blouse.

"Margot, I have to say I had my doubts about you for a little while. I thought you were looking for kicks elsewhere, but I couldn't see the big picture. Obviously you knew that I was monitoring your online activities. Your research was the key to the whole operation's success. The files you had on the neighbors exposed it all: tax fraud, drug use, and everything else we needed to take down."

Donald takes me by the hand and leads me downstairs and out onto our front porch.

"There will be a housing depression for a little while, but with the bad elements gone the market will stabilize before the twins are even in preschool."

We step out onto the trimmed green grass. I can feel the twins swimming inside me. The empty neighborhood that they will be born into surrounds us. I look at the facade of the house across the street. It is similar to our house, but different. It has the garage on the left and ours has the garage on the right.

Buildings Talk

by Dana Johnson

We called him That Fat Bastard Fatty Arbuckle because he was fat and that's all we had. We thought about trying to be above it. I know it's unoriginal and ignorant to point out the fatness of a guy that huge. But he just looked like every little thing Essex Properties Trust was doing to us. The rent being raised first 3, then 7, then 10 percent for the last two years. The shady utility company they switched to in the middle of my decade there, with all its hidden "fees," so that the cost of a five-minute shower set us back like twenty bucks a pop. I've lived with so many dudes to keep living here, the latest one, Franklin, he didn't even know of a time when stuff that was free, now costs. It's like trying to tell some fifteen-year-old about how back in the day getting your luggage on the plane cost you nothing, because it *shouldn't* have. Like the parking spot that used to be free, all of a sudden costs $150 a month to park my car that only runs some of the time. All this after the romantic years, the years when no one wanted to live in downtown Los Angeles, where your shoes slipped in blood and spit and urine and vomit, where you yelled at your dog not to sniff the needles in the gutter, because, in fact, you knew exactly where they'd been. And so they courted us, the first in the building. You're pioneers! they said all chummy and enthused, like they were letting you in on some great real estate deal, when all they were doing was making sure they didn't have any empty apartments. They even gave us duffel bags with the building's logo on it: *Banker's Loft Since 1905.* If old building management sniffed the vague scent of us about to jump ship, move to some other building that was trying to fill their apartments, winking and blowing kisses at would-be tenants with other useless but seductive merch, they got all Please sir, please don't go on us. Begged us to sign a new lease. No rent increase.

But Fatty Arbuckle. He was the most recent in a line of building managers. The others would last a while but kept being shown the door, word was, because they didn't know how to strike the balance between being nice and making money. Me, I hated him from jump because he looked like a dude in costume. And even my roommate Franklin hated him. "He is so not pulling that off," he was always saying, but Franklin was a guy with his own fashion problems that I'll tell you about in a minute. But this new manager: you're asking for resentment and hostility if you're the kind of person who wears a pocket watch and you're on the shy side of thirty. Old-timey rounded collars with thin ties, *bow* ties sometimes. Suspenders on days when he seemed to be daring us to crack behind his back about the fact that a man that fat didn't need suspenders, let alone the belt that wrapped around his body like he was caught in a black Hula-Hoop. He was never going to be one of our favorite people in those kinds of getups, but when he refused to hear our arguments about why, as longtime tenants, we should be shown the courtesy of a lower, hell, *no* rent increase, we went off the rails. Every day was all things Fatty.

My roommate and I, we sat in the office at a time for which we were made to have an *appointment*, when back in the day you could just wander in and shoot the shit over a too-small Styrofoam cup of hours-old coffee that tasted like lye. They were really doing up the historical aspect of the building, relics they'd found during the excavation and remodel, a few rusted beer cans, somebody's glasses frames. Some ashtrays. When I'd first moved into the building, I tripped out over all these old things because they were proof that some guy I didn't even know cracked himself open a beer and enjoyed it and smoked a butt and lived his life. It was like he raised a can for me, the guy way in the future, and said, Life's a bitch and a laugh so, aw, fuck it. What are you gonna do? Look, I know, it's not like they raided some pyramid tombs and pulled up King Tut, but it was something in a city that never feels that old, according to a bunch of dummies who don't know jack. I don't know, my father's father's father was a bricklayer somewhere in England, okay? And in 1905, some dude laid down some bricks and built a really cool building, not some tan, nondescript stucco crap you can find anywhere around town, but *this*, Banker's Loft. Lately, though, the beer cans and whatever were just looking like stuff. In the rental office the walls were covered in grainy sepia-toned wallpaper with blown-up images of Banker's Building in the past, before it was lofts, when it was just offices where some guy working toward the next payday punched a time clock. We sat there without being offered our lye coffee and Fatty was all business. "What can I help you with today?" He leaned back and made a little steeple with his fingers.

We were there because we were done with the 10 percent increase business. We had to talk this through like reasonable people. Any lunatic would have agreed: that was *so* much more money every month. Were they even for reals?

"So," Franklin started, all reason and politeness. "We've lived here for like, what? Eight years?" He looked at me and I nodded. Actually, he was my fifth roommate in ten years. Nobody liked to stick around too long. The idea of a loft that wasn't theirs, with rent being raised willy-nilly just *whenever*? Turns out people didn't really like that. Eventually they always ended up telling me in one way or another, It's been real, rolling their dollies of hastily broken-down IKEA furniture down the marbled hallway. Franklin was only on his second year but I'd thought he'd be good ammo against Fatty Arbuckle, since they were representing similar decades, was my thinking. Franklin twirled the corners of his mustache, turned up on the ends in backward Cs. This all of a sudden frustrated me, this fashion problem that I mentioned earlier. He put wax on it. I *had* been cool with that, which is embarrassing to admit, until seeing him with Fatty Arbuckle made me feel like I was the anachronistic freak who wandered in from the future, in a strange costume of black Converse, jeans, and white T-shirt. Maybe I had. It *was* kind of a *Happy Days* look somebody pointed out to me. Franklin coughed. "I'm sure you know that already," he said to Fatty, "how long we've been here. *He's* been here," he corrected, tilting his head sideways at me and stammering. He was starting out with no conviction. Dude, my eyes said, focus. I was going to use his barbershop quartet ass and then maybe not be all, Dude, don't move out when he decided to move on. I had decided that right then. His limp handshake had foretold this moment, my moment of losing faith in the guy. But I don't have that kind of emotional intelligence when I need it. Not when rent is due.

Fatty Arbuckle looked at Franklin and then at me. His kept his eyes doing that side-to-side thing like we were a tennis match and his smile was spooky as hell, a puppet smile or something. Still as a photograph. It never changed.

"Yeah," I said, trying to recover the fumble. "I think loyalty should count for something. Never missed a payment. I break down all my boxes when I get deliveries. I'm the kind of guy that picks up other people's trash, even. Walking down the hall? I see like a cigarette butt or something? I pick it up." Franklin turned to look at me and telepathed the fact that we both had stepped over dog shit in the hallway that some d-bag had left behind walking his dog. But come on. You have to draw a line. "So," I said, "not that you owe me, *us*, anything, of course. A courtesy. That's all I'm asking. As someone who has been a solid, reliable tenant."

Fatty looped his thumbs under his belt. Sat up straight. Smiled his frozen-in-time smile. "I understand you have been a good tenant. Essex Properties respects your tenancy. But we cannot make distinctions between tenants. Those who have lived here for a long time and those who are new."

"Old management did," I said, and Franklin nodded, even though he was just passing through and didn't know shit about old management and new.

"That was then, and this is now," Fatty said. He shrugged, but his face still had that mask smile. I studied the rolls of his neck, wanting to work my way into them, to the bony, chokeable part. "Look," he said, holding his palms up. "This is a corporation. What-ever the market dictates, that is what we do. As long as the price of rents goes up, so, too, will the rents at Essex Properties Trust." He delivered this brutal honesty with a dimpled smile and I realized that he didn't look like Fatty Arbuckle at all, but Hardy from Laurel and Hardy. We'd gotten our fat guys mixed up from the very beginning.

"So, that's it?" I looked at Franklin but his eyes said, I got nothin'.

"You're welcome to consider other rental opportunities," Fatty said.

"You mean like move?"

"I mean that you may find other, more suitable, arrangements for your situation," he said. His eyes were brown and shiny and full of comedy.

"I'll let you know what we decide," I said, trying to sound tough and savvy, as if he was in danger of losing me, as if he needed me, as if I wasn't just a part of a long line of people who had lived lives in apartments, gotten screwed over by some landlord or another, and moved on, part of a long line of people and their ghosts, in a building that was built before movies had sound.

I LOOKED ALL this stuff up. I may be cashing this week's check on Friday and broke by Monday, driving a forklift at FedEx, a waiter before that, McDonald's and Burger King when I was kid and didn't know any better, but now I know how things work. If a building is refurbished in LA after 1990, even if the building is old as hell, like my building, it doesn't count for rent control. So Fatty or Hardy or whatever his name was had some legs to stand on with his smarmy ultimatums. If I didn't like it, I was "free" to leave because now there were plenty of what looked mostly like twenty-five-year-old kids with mysterious jobs that paid them in buckets of cash so that they could afford $3,000 rent. Everybody was a *stylist* or blogger or some crap. *Downtown.* Me, I was forty. And yes, I'd had it good for most of my years in the building and, after all, I was one of those kids ten years ago, moving in and pushing out people who lived downtown before anything was refurbished, when they paid $300 dollars a month for rooms and walked down the hallway to take a dump and brush their teeth. I had no business complaining about being chased out. Still. I'm asking. Where are people supposed to go?

Where *do* they go? Does it really come down, always, to the cold, cold, hard, hard cash? I know. Where have I *been*? But I'm telling you. Down in the lobby they had this old-timey directory with folks' names that used to live and work in the building. Crazy names with eight vowels in a row followed by ten consonants. *Long*-ass names. That directory? That's some scary stuff right there. Who wants to get off the elevator and look at the names of ghosts every day? My point is this: people's time in places has got to count for something. You don't just yank the lye-tasting coffee out of a guy's hand after ten years. I blamed Fatty Hardy for his Essex Properties corporate humanity-killing policies. All this was his fault with that ventriloquist dummy smile of his. That was what I thought at the time, but now I know I just needed somebody to pay for the injustice of some people being rich as hell and other people being forty years old with rotating roommates. I started watching the guy more closely, revenge in my heart. Nothing crazy like a mysterious pratfall down a flight of stairs or busting his noggin on a slapstick banana peel in one of our ancient, tiled hallways. Just a little humiliation to take him down a peg. Let him have the feeling of staring at a wall with suspenders and dimples.

I tried to get Franklin on the case, too, but the disassembled IKEA furniture writing was on the wall. He wasn't going to be my roommate for much longer. He was already making noise about how the extra 10 percent was going to be steep, and he didn't know, so on and so forth. "I dunno know, man. Kinda steep. I can check out Culver City for that price. It's supposed to be pretty chill over there."

When I watched Fatty Hardy, as it turned out, I learned a thing or two, for real. Dude was ruthless. Turns out, we got off light in his office. That was him being warm and hospitable. He was tearing the work crew new ones on the regular, but only when he thought he wasn't being watched. When he didn't think eyes were on him, he played the warden. "Javier. Get this mop and broom out of the way. We're always *showing*, you know that." Or "Hector. Don't you ever leave the security desk for longer than five minutes. We need someone present *at all times*." One time he caught me looking at him. He was yelling at Janet. Nice. Always talked about how hot it was in the lobby, didn't I think? She always wiped down the fake red velvet in the elevators. People wrote *fuck you* with their fingers and drew uninspired dicks that were majestically lit by the halogen lights in the ceiling of the elevator. One day she forgot to use the lemony-smelling stuff to cover up the funky smell of dogs too big to be living in apartments in the first place.

"If I get in another elevator," he said, pointing a finger in her face, "and it don't smell like lemon? We're going to have a problem."

"Yes, sir," Janet said, nodding, and some braids fell out of her scarf and onto her face. Hot. She was hot. Not a part of the story. I'm just saying. Right when I stopped looking at Janet, though, was when I saw Fatty Hardy see *me*. Up popped the puppet smile. But before that, there was a moment. Maybe he saw what he looked like through my eyes: a guy way too big to be looming over and pointing a finger at a woman who happened to be not his color. Yeah. It looked bad. My eyes agreed with his eyes. But then the moment was gone and we were back to the dimples. He gave me a nod and strolled back to his office. Another time, in the lobby, I watched him bend over to pick up a piece of something on the floor, and when he bent over, his ass looking like a pinstriped mattress, I was hoping so bad that his pants would split straight down the middle with the loud sound of ripping sheets, laugh track in my head. But no luck. When he stood up and turned around, what he saw was a dude staring at his ass. His eyes got small, trying to figure out my motives, but this time he didn't even bother with the nice act. He nodded, his lips pinched together, and gave me a look that said, Why should I be nice to you, you goddamn pervert?

STILL, I GOT what I thought I wanted. I saw Fatty Hardy go down.

There's this big conference room in the lobby, with glass walls so you can see in. Whoever's in there working or whatever. It's supposed to be for anybody in the building, but I never see anyone but the old guys who own the building in there. About four months after Franklin and I dropped our pants, bent over, and got charged another 10 percent, Fatty Hardy was sitting in the room with three guys with white hair, striped oxford shirts. I was sitting in one of the truly stupid, overlarge silver chairs that were supposed to be all about deco elegance or something, pretending to go through my mail. Franklin buzzed himself into the lobby just then and sat on the arm of my chair.

"What are you doing? You never sit down here." His eyes followed mine. "What's that all about?" He tilted his chin toward the conference room. There was lots of hands waving, nods, staring into space, notes being taken. "I'm trying to see," I said. I was talking out the side of my mouth, trying not to move my lips.

"Are you purposely talking like that? What are you, some spy now? Nobody cares," he said. "They can't even hear us." He looked back at the room. "Jesus. Look at the sweat on Arbuckle. It's really coming down."

"Hardy," I said.

And then, the conference room door opened and the old guys came out, all of them wearing pleated khakis and loafers. I don't know what got into me, but right then, I would have taken Fatty Hardy's suspenders and rounded collars over any one of those guys' bread-colored pants and loud Easter-looking shirts. Timeless. One of them patted Fatty Hardy on the back. He shook his hand

and said the worst words in the world that one human can say to another human. He said, "Good luck."

BUILDINGS TALK. THAT'S the cool thing about them in case you don't live in an apartment. It's true: Maybe I don't really know anybody in a building of what? Three hundred lofts or something? But how do I know all the stuff I know? That's what I'm talking about. The building's got a big mouth. That's how I know that Fatty Hardy lost his job and that's how I know he lost it by trying too hard to hold on to it. The dudes in the khakis weren't fucking around. They wanted mo money, mo money, mo money. They made Fatty Hardy the enforcer, but that was his doom. So many people said, What do I need to pay another $200 a month for? I'm out. I saw it coming, myself. The big turnover. From my apartment window, I could see into the windows of so many empty apartments across the way, and those windows looked like eyes staring right back at me like, What are you looking at? You're next.

Maybe a week later, Franklin and I went downstairs to the bar underneath the building. It's the oldest bar in LA, built in 1908. They sell French dip sandwiches and cocktails that are tasty, but me, I'm not the mixology-type guy. I'm just a straight-whiskey-in-a-glass-no-ice-type guy. I just like places with liquor. But I tell you the thing I like best about the place downstairs: it's the first place in LA that had a check-cashing service, way back in the day. I like the idea. You get your check cashed, get yourself a sandwich and a nice pop of something not fancy but strong, and you're good to go.

When Franklin and I got downstairs we saw right away, bellied up to the bar, there was Fatty Hardy. There were exactly two seats left, of course, right next to him, and so Franklin pretended that he had to tie his shoes when we were walking up to the bar, I guess so I'd have to sit next to him. Jackass. That made me get to him first but then I took the seat next to the seat *next* to Fatty Hardy, because Franklin's no chess player. He couldn't see the move after his. "Jerk," he said as he sat down.

"What?" Fatty Hardy halfway turned to Franklin and took a sip of something brown.

"Oh. No," Franklin said. "Him. I was talking to him." He pointed his thumb my way.

Fatty leaned over. When he saw it was me, he held his glass up in a toast. I didn't know what *that* meant. It gave me the creeps. He and I? We were not cool. We were definitely not *down*. He was *not* my peeps. Thanks to him, around the same time the next year I'd have another roommate, this one with a 1980s Mohawk and those fucked-up plugs in his ears that stretched them to shit.

But a funny thing happens when you drink with somebody. You get to be somebody's history, the memory of a stranger. That night we had some laughs sure, but also, I remember this: we were steady getting drunk but I was getting sad. Fatty Hardy kept saying, "You're all right, the two of yous" and "That looks all right, that mustache" to Franklin. Fatty Hardy kept putting his sentences out of order and sounding weird like somebody's grandfather from the old country. I started missing him already and that was good, I guess, because I never saw the guy again. And my new roommate, I can't say to him and have him understand, no matter how big his drooping ears are, I can't say, "'Member that one manager? Fatty Hardy? That belt he used to wear? *Damn*."

That night was a good night. The backbar is old, dark and oaky-looking, soft lights and the names of guys from years and years ago who drank enough to have their names up there from 1908 to now. The music was good. First Bowie then Aretha, then Zeppelin. In the mirror of the backbar, I could see the framed black-and-white photos on the wall behind us, people who were history looking back at us in the mirror. One of them looked like Marilyn Monroe.

"Marilyn Monroe!" I turned around and pointed. There was a guy next to me with a huge Afro. "Naw, dude. That's some other lady that just look like her." He pointed at me. "James Dean!" "No, no, no," his friend said. He pointed at me and covered his mouth with his fist. "Oh shit. You know who that motherfucker look like? What's that dude on *Happy Days*?"

"Screw you guys," I said. I was so faded. Franklin was working on some girl with a ring in her nose, I remember that, and by then Fatty Hardy was gone. Vanished. I said it again. I said, "Screw you guys!"

"Man," the guy next to me said. He pulled on my T-shirt. "Sit your drunk ass down."

"No," I said. "No! My name is Marty Allen Jones and I been living here for ten years and I'm going to live here for ten more, maybe even forever, and I'm home and ain't going nowhere!"

Lifehack at Bar Kaminuk

by Mark Chiusano

When Anderson arrived at the bar for the new-employee welcoming event, he knew already that it had been a mistake. He searched the room a little warily. There in the far corner, where tables were available for reservation, were the members of the small start-up he worked for, gesturing wildly at each other. Before Anderson could think better of it, Griff, the marketing coordinator and second-most-recent hire, spotted him and raised both hands in victory greeting. In doing so, he accidentally sloshed excess beer on the seat that had been kept vacated, Anderson supposed, for Anderson.

Anderson walked to the seat and claimed it. There was a general howl of greeting, and he was instantly regaled with some story that he had missed, while he had been in the office working—where had he been, by the way? Why hadn't he come down earlier, like a true red-blooded American? Anderson, you work too hard! Anderson, in fact, had been more or less twiddling his thumbs up in the sleek offices that they shared with a few other start-ups, full of quiet glass doors and elegant secretaries, some of them male, but no books other than the ones that the start-up that Anderson worked for kept piled on their secretary (female)'s desk, color-coded in the general arc of a rainbow and spread out edge to spine. The company was called FicShare. The idea behind it was that people could use the content on their Kindles or iPads that their friends or family weren't using—they could stream it, like Slingbox did for TV. At the moment you were limited to a maximum of five Share-Buddies, but the plan was for up to ten. The online interface was much slicker than the regular e-reading experience, and the ultimate goal was a community of readers, sharing and recommending texts. Marginalia would be transmitted, and book chats were easy to initiate. Anderson was the editorial side of the start-up. Sometimes, Anderson worried that if it really succeeded like everyone else in the company thought it would, it would destroy the reading economy. It's just like a library, they reassured Anderson, and that and stock options made him feel slightly better.

It wasn't as if he was flooded with better offers. FicShare was the highest-paying employer he'd ever had, combined with the fewest responsibilities. His job was to curate the selections, in addition to writing short blog posts about the books that users were using, and generally manning the content that kept FicShare's website fresh and new. This was all quite simple and he usually knocked off most of it by around 11:45 in the morning (the programmers never got in until ten, so neither did he). He took a long lunch and walk around noon, often to the water, where he leaned against the railing's edges and pondered throwing himself in—to swim, not Virginia Woolf. He'd stare, happily/melancholically, out toward New Jersey. By two he was back in the office, playing solitaire or skimming an old paperback or tapping out a blog post on Ian Fleming, while the headphoned programmers pounded wordlessly away.

Anderson turned his attention to Griff, the new marketing coordinator, who was trying to engage with him. Griff had graduated from some fancy school, Duke or Dartmouth, only three or four years ago. Anderson had known from the moment that he met him that he was different from the programmers, who most often opened up only when they were drunk or taking a break from work—Griff talked your ear off 24/7. Though Griff's resume (Anderson had snooped: he had a thing for resumes) claimed that he was proficient in JavaScript and C++, Anderson tended to doubt it, no matter what it was worth—or guessed he was proficient only insofar as could be accomplished by a class or two as an elective at whichever bucolic campus he'd been spawned on. He had worked for an event-planning company before this, high-end, proselytizing for an app someone else had created.

Time, Griff said profoundly in Anderson's general direction.

I'm sorry, asked Anderson.

Griff's watery smile wavered a little. 'Bout time, he said. That you made it down here, he continued, when Anderson hadn't added anything to their rather one-way conversation.

Busy day at the office, Anderson said. I hear that my brother, said Griff. Griff usually wore polo shirts tucked into extremely neat, probably expensive jeans, and today he had added a blazer.

I'm gonna grab a drink, Anderson said. Then he said, his voice a little lower, Any tabs open? Sometimes the founders, Nikil and James, would come early to slip a card onto the bar, and then leave. The bar owners were trustworthy enough that they could pick it up, more or less unabused, when they came back in the morning. Anderson had met the pair of them at a bookstore reading where he was filling in as a moderator. It was the most work he'd done in weeks, other than transcribing conversations for a reality TV show. The reading was for a paltry book, a regular MFA collection of short stories, that he'd read the first three-quarters of the night before. We're looking for someone of your caliber, Nikil and James told Anderson, while the author's friends and family crowded up around the writer afterward, gushing and not buying books. Anderson didn't think at the time that maybe they meant someone of medium-level caliber. Anderson's then-current bio, chalked in next to the writer's, hardly visible over the erasure of the true moderator's more eye-catching credentials (*New York Times*, FSG), said simply, "Freelance editor." They gave him their shared business card, which felt slim and small in his pocket. When he interviewed, he was surprised by their wide-ranging knowledge of American and international literature, and their seeming commitment to education and the literary sphere. They were in discussions with PEN International, they said. Truthfully Anderson wouldn't have said no to any offer at that point. He had been on the verge of writing to his old dissertation adviser to see what she thought about getting the band back together once again.

Tab, Griff asked innocently. What is this bar tab you speak of? Perhaps you mean the credit plastic in your wallet at the moment, kind sir? This was Griff's idea of humor. Anderson had made the mistake of telling him once that though he was most familiar with contemporary literature, his favorite book of all time was the *Morte d'Arthur.* Just let me know before I buy us both a drink, Anderson said. Now we're talking, Griff said, grinning. Then he leaned close to Anderson. Nikil stopped by but he was pretty flustered, he said. He continued: Apparently she didn't take the job.

This was mildly interesting to Anderson. It was, in point of fact, the reason for this happy hour—held in honor of the number-one newest hire, fresher even than Griff. Every time FicShare hired a new employee, they held a bit of a gathering at the Kaminuk or a similar SoHo bar, *before* the employee started work. After he or she signed a contract of course, but before their first day. The idea was, according to James and Nikil, that the post-first-day drink felt somewhat apologetic, or carrot-at-the-end-of-the-stick: work hard, drink a little. Hold the welcome celebration before, and the employee was already a part of the family. It wasn't a bad philosophy, as with most things that Nikil and James thought of. Anderson's own ceremony had been pleasant, a bit like an initiation, like something out of Jules Verne, or one of Somerset Maugham's spy stories. That was the way tech people felt about the things they did, sometimes. Griff hadn't been there yet, which might have been part of it.

She fled the coop, huh, Anderson said thoughtfully. Wasn't interested, yeah?

Griff got into the rhythm. Too good for us, I suppose, he said.

What was she supposed to be doing again, asked Anderson.

Griff drained his beer. Oh she was a star man, he said. Triple threat. I can't say more than that. It's too heartbreaking. He gestured at his empty glass.

Anderson took it to the bar and set it down softly. The bartender, who looked strangely content and upbeat for this hour of night and this location in the Manhattan universe, whisked it away. What's the poison friend, he said, a little knowingly, it seemed to Anderson. Anderson looked at the sea of ten-dollar beers whose names were written in grainy colorful chalk on the board above him. He still couldn't quite shake the price shock that came from being a freelance copyeditor full time. You got any happy hour specials still, he asked.

The bartender looked dramatically at his watch, though Anderson well knew it couldn't be earlier than eight or eight thirty. For you, he said. Why not. Two of whatever it is then, Anderson said. Actually, he said, make one of them a Bud Light. That's actually more expensive, the bartender said. That's fine, Anderson said. It seemed to be the way the world was going.

Don't I know you from somewhere, the bartender said to Anderson as he passed off the drinks. I don't think so, Anderson said. Hmmm, the bartender said. He swiped Anderson's almost brand-new credit card. Well, he said. Open please, said Anderson. He took the drinks back to the table.

It could have been a worse group of people, Anderson considered. He'd heard of worse things happening to professionals his age, that was for sure. It was a small company still, a true start-up. Nikil and James had the buoyancy of youth and positive thinking about them, backed up by what seemed to be a true intelligence—they were double-edged, perhaps was a good way to think about it, the type of people who at any stage in human history would have been at the top of their pyre or pyramid, however the age went. They might have been shamans, soldiers, explorers, nuclear physicists. Because it was 2014, they were start-up CEOs. And they'd gathered a good group around them, most of whom were clustered around the table. There was their second-in-command, the austere Zoe, who'd streamlined the initial code base enough to cut battery usage by 30 percent. She seemed to have no background but a very bright future, and the short haircut she often sported in addition to her clipped, complete lack of interest in him was an unbearable but low-grade attraction to someone like Anderson. Arrayed to Zoe's right were Tim, Mike, and Anita, three hardworking programmers who hadn't gone to fancy schools like Griff or Nikil and James— they'd learned their programming on the side, or had always been good at it, or went to Hacker School after leaving dead-end jobs in reception (that one was the lovely Anita). In a previous age they might have been construction or quality-control engineers, rolling up their sleeves to really get their hands in the business. Anderson had a soft spot for them, for Tim's and Mike's matching thick Boston accents, which jibed well with Anita's New York one—not many people who Anderson interacted with had a New York accent anymore. She lived in Staten Island, and drove to work every day—James and Nikil paid for her parking garage. They had recently promoted her to project manager, and the other two programmers had taken it remarkably well, it seemed to Anderson. They'd bought her a cake in the shape of a blank triptych science board—"Project!" they shouted gleefully when she took the tinfoil off. They seemed happy together. They all made upward of 150K a year, though, which couldn't hurt.

Anderson put the Bud Light in front of Griff's hand, and explained that they had been all out of anything else. He had expected to get a cheap thrill out of the prank, but Griff just slumped down a little, almost imperceptibly. Perhaps he hadn't drunk much Budweiser in college. Here Griff, Anderson said, just kidding. The Light's for me—better digestion. Griff lapped up the cold IPA.

Anita, flanked by the other programmers, was leading the table in conversation. The way I see it, she said, better member of no team than halfway part of this one.

Hear, hear, Mike and Tim muttered gruffly.

The new programmer, Griff told Anderson unnecessarily. Anderson raised his eyebrows in acknowledgment.

Where's a better place to work, is all I'm saying, Anita said. There was an upturn to the end of her sentence, but it was a statement as opposed to a question. Zoe expressed her agreement, in the reserved, quiet way she had. Anderson wouldn't have been able to say how she did it. The tilt of her chin?

Truth, she added.

You know, Griff chimed in, bigger's not always better. Less cuts of the same pies.

Fewer, said Mike and Tim, almost simultaneously.

Huh, asked Griff.

Fewer cuts, explained Mike kindly. Right Anderson?

Anderson pulled down a gulp of his beer. He's got you there Griffin, he said.

All I'm saying is, Anita continued, I don't understand why Nikil and James were so torn up about this chick. Anita had strong, shapely forearms, which nestled confidently on the table while she made her point. Zoe bristled a little.

Know what I mean? Anita said, directing herself toward Zoe. It looked like Zoe, as usual, knew more than she was letting on.

She was an exceptionally good candidate, Zoe said evenly, by way of explanation. Anderson waited, but like a minimalist short story, it seemed like that was all she was going to give them.

She came highly recommended, Zoe added, when it seemed like it hadn't been enough. The table waited.

Nikil and James had been pursuing her for a long time, Zoe finished, in a concluding kind of way. She shrugged and raised her glass, some kind of brackish wine. To the future, she said. And to FicShare.

To FicShare, the rest of the company chimed. Anderson felt himself going along with it, the way he went along with the river waves he watched, every lunchtime, leaning over the railing without jumping in.

EVEN THE STRANGE bartender could no longer pretend that it was happy hour. At a certain point in the evening Zoe had been a mensch about it and thrown down her own credit card—was it a company card? Did the company have those? Nobody quite knew—and bought the last few rounds for the cohorts. Anita, Mike, and Tim were the heaviest drinkers, quietly getting to the bottoms of their glasses as if they were adventure novellas. Zoe carefully drank the same brackish wine without any discernible exterior difference.

Griff got sloppy, like the college kid he had been. Anderson was embarrassed to realize that he himself was getting a little sloppy, but there was nothing to be done about it at that point. He'd get home, heat up some old pasta, try to read a little more of *Crime and Punishment*, which had been bookending his bed stand for the past several months, before he'd inevitably give up and watch television. Sometimes he had dreams, on particularly warm nights, of a FicShare fairy creeping into his studio apartment and wrenching the unread Dostoevsky from his care. Others need it better, the FicShare fairy would say in a singsong way.

The chair did not squeak as Anderson pushed it away from the table, letting himself up. The bottoms must be covered with something, or else the floor was more forgiving than he'd thought it was, when last he'd stood up on it. A good lifehack for the bar, getting rid of all that excess noise, Anderson considered. Lifehack was a new word he'd picked up from Mike and Tim, which he struggled to use correctly. Room, Griff pronounced grandly as Anderson got up. This time he and Anderson were on the same page. Bathroom. He nodded. They pushed themselves away from the table silently and ventured to the men's.

Anderson and Griff stood at adjacent urinals. In the middle of his piss Anderson felt himself drawn to check his cell phone, but he resisted the urge (it was a recipe for further sloppiness), and instead happened to glance toward Griff. When he did he noticed the pained expression on his colleague's face.

What's the matter, Anderson said, almost horrified. He couldn't believe that he was about to have a urinal conversation with the guy. Griff continued shaking his head and staring into the blank monitor screen of the urinal.

She was supposed to be beautiful man, he said. The new hire. Talk about one who got away. For a moment only the sound of their quiet piss streams interrupted Anderson's silence. This always happens to me, Griff said, and for an awful moment Anderson thought that Griff might be about to cry. They washed their hands together at the sink, the water cascading around and getting the fronts of their shirts wet. The bathroom was dark and smelled strongly of ginger beer. Griff didn't meet Anderson's eyes.

When they exited the bathroom, Zoe was the only one waiting for them, sitting at the table and tapping on her phone. The guys went home, she said. I don't think they're gonna let Anita drive. She smiled in her thin way. Anderson wondered if he'd ever have a chance dating her. He wasn't sure how much they had in common—her favorite author on Facebook and the FicShare landing page was Ayn Rand, favorite book was *The Right Stuff* (one for two, at least)—but he admired her quiet competence, the elegant way she sat at her computer desk. Anderson spent a lot of time looking through the interior glass walls of the office. Anderson tried to project all his possibility into a smile. Griff broke the moment with a burp.

I should take off, Zoe said, and went to the bar to close out her tab. She did so quickly, while Griff and Anderson watched—it was almost as if the bartender had had her card ready, a pen prepared for her to sign. After she did so she looked back, and gave them a small wave. Her small tote bag bounced softly against her back as she left.

Well, Anderson said, another night in suck city. Griff laughed uproariously. That's really funny man, Griff said. Where you come up with these things? Anderson accepted the praise. Here's to tomorrow, Anderson said. Tell me about it hombre, Griff said. They were walking to the door when Anderson remembered that he'd left his tab open, his shiny new credit card in the bartender's clutches. He'd finally responded to one of those countless spam ads after he'd gotten the job—he felt like a member of capitalism once again. I've gotta close out, he told Griff, and he backslapped him. See you tomorrow. Griff nodded a little and kept walking. Anderson felt strangely buoyed—it was, he realized, that he'd both remembered about his credit card and also had succeeded in not taking the train the few stops to Brooklyn with Griff. Although surely Griff would have taken an Uber. Hell, he might have too.

Anderson made the universal symbol for check-please at the bar, and the bartender came to him immediately. The check was right there for him, and an uncapped pen, all ready to go, but before Anderson could reach for it the bartender bent toward him and whispered in his ear. You're going to get an email tonight, the bartender said, portentously. She will contact you.

Anderson backed away, his fingers still curled around the pen. Now he really felt like a Maugham story; maybe Ashenden. What are you talking about, he said, a little thickly. The bartender backed away, and smiled as if he hadn't heard him. He made the check-please sign back at Anderson, and walked away to the other side of the bar.

Anderson waited for a moment and watched the bartender. He signed the bill, and made sure to pocket the new credit card. He looked toward the bartender one last time to see if he might divine any special provenance or helpful assistance but the bartender refused to meet his eyes. There had been no customer at the other end of the bar—the bartender was leafing through the pages of a book. Anderson wanted to ask him what he was reading—it was a habit that Anderson found hard to drop. He'd always considered that he could judge a person by their paperback choices. This had changed in recent years with e-readers. There was only so much consumer difference between iPad and Kindle. But just as Anderson was opening his mouth the bartender shook his head warningly. Anderson, a little disconcerted, took his leave from the SoHo bar.

As IT WAS wont to be on summer evenings when the night air is cool and welcoming and the subway itself is fetid and warm like the day that has already died aboveground, the Broadway-Lafayette station was dark and crowded, and Anderson waited twenty-five minutes for the next train. He had forgotten his book at the office, and though he tried to read a couple more pages of the always-waiting *Crime and Punishment* on his iPhone, through software Anita had introduced him to, which allowed you to read the same book on all your devices, he soon gave up. He wasn't sure if it was the translation, the device, or just him. Also, he couldn't get the bartender and his strange warning out of his head. When the F finally came, it was empty; not as in loosely populated but almost entirely empty, only its ghost lights on, like the garbage trains of 3:00 a.m. The crowd at Broadway-Lafayette surged on anyway, and Anderson followed. The train paused a little in the station but the air-conditioning worked and eventually it closed its doors and continued on.

Back at his apartment, Anderson heated up the days-old pasta he'd been not much looking forward to. He wasn't much of a cook, and in his freelance days he'd been forced to enjoy his own cooking more than he would have liked to. The pasta was left over from a restaurant that Anderson had been to one night the week before, after work. He'd left the office, gone to the restaurant, thought about nothing, sat with no one, and before he knew it it was ten o'clock and he brought the rest of the meal home to his quiet apartment, where he had immediately fallen asleep.

Pasta devoured, Anderson checked the locks on his door and changed into a sleeping T-shirt and clean boxers. He settled himself into the armchair beside his bed, and rather than cracking the desperate old copy of Dostoevsky that had been darkening his bed-side, he reached for a copy of *The New Yorker* that he'd picked up on a whim one subway ride. It was neither new nor old. This was the perfect age for a *New Yorker*, he considered. He had always felt an aspirational tug to read *The New Yorker*, to sit somewhere and read the magazine from beginning to end. Including the dance reviews that he might not have paid any attention to otherwise. He could envision himself doing this someday, some weekend when he was married to a Zoe-like figure and he was the editorial director of a fresh new imprint, maybe e-only at that stage in the game. He would page through the magazine, knowing all the writers, many personally. Anderson opened the magazine, and made it all the way through the Talk of the Town, skipping the economics column (naturally), and starting the short story. But it was a light first-person piece that had the problem that many first-person pieces had in recent years, in Anderson's opinion, that they mattered only to the first-person in the story and their creators themselves. They didn't have the elegance, the everyman quality, of third-person nar-ration. In the middle of the story Anderson lost interest for good, and closed the magazine.

Usually Anderson tried to go to sleep without checking email. He'd come to understand that it messes with your natural sleep pat-terns, that it opens some pathways that healthy sleep depends on having closed. But tonight Anderson pulled his laptop off the shelf where he kept it next to his bed, and signed into his Gmail account. There were the usual promotions from Amazon and BookBub, and news alerts from a local news website he'd signed up for long, long ago. Nothing of interest. Perturbed, Anderson pulled up a new tab to get into his office email system, which was something he *very* much tried to avoid on a regular basis. He gave them enough hours of the day. He typed in his ironic password—DownAndOutInNYC—and the colorful green design of the FicShare page appeared before him. There was an all-staff email from Griff about some new e-reading app he'd seen on the train that night. Nikil had responded, "Interesting." Zoe had sent out the daily schedule for the upcoming day. But nothing particularly intriguing. Anderson even checked his spam folder.

There's no other way to put it: Anderson felt a little down. As usual, there was nothing special in his life. This was nothing new. He found his surprises in literature, not real life. Even his reading choices confirmed it—he looked, dilettante-like, for amusement, rather than deep vertical mastery of any particular author or period. It was why he'd drifted out of graduate school to New York City in the first place. Anderson looked at the clock on the upper right-hand corner of the screen—it was 1:00 a.m. Easy to get down on yourself at a time like that.

Anderson closed down the laptop, slid it back on its shelf, took a lingering look at the forlorn-looking Dostoevsky, and shut off the lights.

He was awoken with a rap on his window. He had been in the middle of a dream in which he and Anita were staring at a computer monitor, forearms bumping, and Zoe had her hands on their shoulders, staring disapprovingly. This was all par for the course for Anderson. Anita reached for the computer screen and tapped it with her fingernails. Again and again. Finally Zoe reached forward and did the same, but harder this time, so that in his dreamworld the screen Anderson was looking at shivered and broke. He woke up. There was someone tapping on his fire escape.

He got out of bed. With the lights off, he had a pretty good view of the outside, once he pulled the curtains apart. Leaning against the fire-escape railing, hand poised to knock once again, there was a woman. She was dressed in slacks and a button-down shirt, which seemed to Anderson improbable for a cat burglar or nighttime strangler. Her posture prefigured not danger or anxiety but almost normality, even out there on the fire escape. The woman nodded at him, gesturing the window up. He unlocked it and lifted.

Higher, the woman said, in a friendly but impatient way. He pushed it as high as it would go, and the woman ducked her head underneath. He gave her a hand as she hopped down next to his bed.

Shut that, the woman said, and keep the lights off. Wait, she said, as Anderson opened his mouth to begin with one of various pressing questions. The woman took a cell phone out of her pocket—it looked like an iPhone but a bit heavier-duty. She brought it to life with a few touches of her meaty fingers and a beam extended from it. She swung it 360 degrees around the room. Then she consulted with its glowing screen and, satisfied, returned the phone to her pocket. Okay, she said. Then she froze again. No. Her eyes had lighted on a plastic cup that Anderson had carelessly left on his bedside table, gifted from some takeout place down the street. The woman peered at it, sizing up the angle from it to the window, and in one motion reached it, snatched it from its perch, and crumpled it to a loud nothing of grainy plastic in her hands.

Jesus, yelped Anderson. Microphone, the woman explained. Or, it could be anyway. All they'd need is a laser pointer and a clear view from across the way. The woman scowled out the window from whence she'd come, as if these laser demons had been right behind her. I have to say I'm a little confused, said Anderson. Don't you have P2P, the woman said indignantly. The blank look on Anderson's face would have told her what she needed to know. It's a security system, sighed the woman. Anonymous peer-to-peer secure communication. I thought everybody knew about that these days. Anderson, however, didn't.

Can we turn a light on, Anderson asked. The woman responded by retrieving her cell phone from her pocket and tapping a few times. The ceiling light, and also Anderson's reading lamp, flickered on. Anderson eased himself back onto his bed. This is all quite a lot to take, Anderson said.

He closed his eyes for a moment. When he opened them, the woman was still there, indeed, was peering down at him concernedly. It gave him a good chance to take the measure of her. She wasn't exactly beautiful, which is another way of saying that she matched Anderson. She had thick limbs like he did, a wide, angular face that in some lights could seem strange or intriguing. She seemed to have the beginnings of a paunch around the waist, just like Anderson had begun developing recently. He would say it had been the switch from earning his money hand-to-mouth to FicShare's custom of leaving Nutri-Grain bars all around the office desks. But really it was his lack of self-control.

I'm the new hire, the woman said, with an air of explaining the obvious. Or, former, she added. Svetlana, she said, waving her hand in an awkward but pleasant hello. Great bookshelf, she said, I love Malory too. Anderson, Anderson said stiffly, a little behind.

Let's get going, she said, gesturing toward the doorway. It's fine, it's not bugged after all. Anderson stayed where he was, although she didn't look back to see if he was following. She didn't seem to be the type of person who successfully waited for answers or orders. Only at the doorway did she turn around.

What, she said, do I have to make the whole speech now? Aren't you even a little bit curious? Look, I promise to have you back in bed in an hour, if that's what you want to do. Her eyes twinkled a little.

Anderson considered. If he was in danger he probably would have felt it already. There would be plenty of time later for regrets. It wasn't like he had to be at work early in the morning. Svetlana, sensing what the small movements that Anderson was committing were pointing toward, opened the door soundlessly. Anderson gathered his keys and wallet—Svetlana wagged a finger when she saw him reaching for his cell phone, which he dropped—and, on a whim, traded the phone for the copy of Dostoevsky lying to the side. Anderson carried the book against his wrist, and the weight of it, the half-fresh paperback pages, felt comforting as he ventured into the unknown.

OUTSIDE, ON THE corner of the block of Anderson's apartment, a white car was waiting. This furthered Anderson's sense that he wasn't in danger, immediate anyway, and besides, Svetlana was the one driving. She pulled a slim ring of keys out of her pocket as they approached. Anderson opened the back door. I'm not a taxi driver, she said, indignantly. Or a cop. She grinned.

The car bounced along the recently unpaved streets of Brooklyn—Anderson's neighborhood (not Anderson exactly, but his immediate peers) had been pressuring the city government to re-level their relatively bucolic street, as if there weren't enough problems elsewhere. Someone with a sense of humor in City Hall must have given the okay to get started, but not permission to finish. The hot exposed street was sticky and vaguely sewage-smelling in the summer days. But soon they reached the Manhattan Bridge, by the good offices of wide Flatbush Avenue. As they crossed the great river, Svetlana began to fill Anderson in.

FicShare is a dangerous entity, Svetlana started. It's not alone in its danger, but that doesn't make it innocent either. She had a stirring, sugary voice. Maybe it began in an innocent, positive way, she said—maybe the idea really did come from a library. That was partially why I went through the interview process, Svetlana said, gunning the gas to get through a red light off the bridge, to hear Nikil and James in their own words. She looked over at Anderson. It's seductive, as I'm sure you know. I can see them thinking about it while sitting on some leafy steps outside an actual library, wherever they went to college. Anderson knew it was Stanford (he'd seen their resumes too), but he didn't mention this to his confident driver.

I don't think I need to play out the numbers for you, Svetlana said. Sure, maybe this gives a relatively underprivileged kid the opportunity to read a few more books—that's assuming they've gotten their hands on an e-reader in the first place, and haven't heard of a public library system, which does this for free anyway. And maybe it spreads awareness of an author, and someone, some-where, actually buys the book, physical or digital, that supports their bottom line. But you know the real drill. The only people who will actually use FicShare are people like us, people like Griff. It sounds sexy and hip and like a new way forward, in lots of ways. But people will start feeling good about *thinking* about all the reading they can do and they won't actually do any of it. And all there'll be will be VC funding and some nice offices, Svetlana said. Another reason to be glued to our device. Anderson was pleased, among all this, that Griff's proclivities traveled before him. And so it'll be one more trap, snaring us in the digital space, Svetlana said.

They coasted through the streets of Chinatown. The people I work for, Svetlana said, don't want this to continue. It doesn't matter who they are, or how many of us it takes. There is a silent majority of us. A person wakes up in the morning and discovers—well, nothing particularly earth-shattering, just that they can't continue with it any longer. Not with life, although that's a part of it, but everything—the constant connection. Pinterest, Facebook. The fact that the first thing this person reaches for every morning is their cell phone because it has become their alarm clock, and then, because they've reached for it, they start checking things, before their bleary eyes have even adjusted to another morning—email, work email, various sites, Snapchats. In this way this person or persons feels that they are missing the advent of sunlight, the nape of their lover's neck; the puffy-cheeked entry into daily existence. They sometimes forget to go to the bathroom first thing, as they had usually done, sometime in the distant past. They can hardly remember their old daily routines. Anderson did, in fact, know what the woman was talking about. He agreed, in a sort of begrudging way.

I'm bringing you to meet some people, Svetlana said. They'll have some requests to make of you. They're fellow souls, you'll see. You'll feel right at home with them—she nodded at the paperback Anderson was carrying, like a talisman or spirit pole. We've taught ourselves to survive in this world, Svetlana said, but we want to change it. We want to pause it, is a way of thinking about it, she said. Suddenly there were the lights of Broadway, the empty but half-lit stores of the street's southern section, mannequins gesticulating in the moonlight, and before Anderson had much more time to process anything they had arrived, back at Bar Kaminuk where he'd started his then-uneventful night.

Svetlana parked in a bus stop and they left the car. Don't worry, she said, there won't be any cops coming by. She moved confidently and methodically, Anderson noted, like a former athlete, or someone who had cottoned to manual labor late in life but well. The lights were off in the bar except for one, all the way in the back, and Svetlana and Anderson eased their way through the quiet door. Inside, the bartender was sitting more or less where Anderson had left him, still reading something or other, and next to the bartender stood Zoe.

Hello Anderson, the bartender said with a smirk. Zoe! said Anderson. Are you involved in this, he said, and she gave a small nod without changing her expression. Svetlana reached over the bar to shake the bartender's hand, and nodded at Zoe. Svetlana took her heavy-duty cell phone out of her pocket and waved it around once more—it beeped when she got to the bartender, and the bartender pulled his own phone out of his pocket and apologized. He got up and Anderson watched him go to the refrigerator behind the bar, where he tossed his phone in and closed it. Svetlana took a seat on the stool next to Zoe, and Anderson remained standing, as if at an interview.

Zoe has been very helpful to us, Svetlana said, in monitoring FicShare. But soon she will be moving on. It's all it takes, one woman or one man, some serious conviction—Anderson could tell that Svetlana was just starting to get warmed up. She seemed to have a nervous tic of continually rolling her sleeves up, even as they kept falling down. Anderson had noticed her doing it about four times already. And now the burden has come to you, she continued. It's time to shake off your lethargy. Time for you to step out of your quotidian existence. You are old world but you are also new. You are a guardian but an innovator too. Time to decide to make something of yourself, for this and all ages. Very soon—

But at that very moment the door of the bar slammed open. There was no high-end creaklessness now—it slammed and banged. Inside ran four hooded figures, dressed all in black—were they armed? Anderson couldn't say. The lights had suddenly shut off again, and the room was plunged into darkness and delirium. Anderson felt a hand on the back of his neck, urging him down, coolly, softly, almost pleasantly, though urgently. As he crouched, heart banging away somewhere around his throat, he turned and saw that it was Zoe, and she had her usual grim expression on her face. He realized that, whatever else, he trusted her. He didn't know why, but he realized now that he always had. The little grimace she made, unconsciously, while she was typing, in the office; the way she bit her bottom lip while she read something, almost whispering it out loud. They crouched together, and Anderson closed his eyes. He clutched the Dostoevsky to his chest.

When he opened his eyes again, the lights had come back on. The sounds had stopped, and Svetlana and the bartender were leaned up against the bar, plastic zip cuffs around their wrists, dark material blindfolding their eyes. Zoe, Svetlana called. Anderson? Do they have you too? Zoe looked at Anderson and slowly shook her head. Anderson didn't say anything. Two of the hooded figures took charge of the captives, and began to perp-walk them out the employee exit of the bar. As she went by, Anderson could smell a whiff of something off Svetlana's body—sweat? Fear? But she went toward her fate stoically, her sleeves hanging loosely around her cuffed wrists.

When the captives and the first two figures were gone, and the door shut softly behind them, the remaining figures removed their hoods, and Zoe stood Anderson up. Well done J, the first figure said. Anderson watched him carefully, as the shadow of the hood fell away from his face. It was Nikil.

Good work, Zoe, Nikil said quietly. She never suspected. Zoe nodded almost imperceptibly. We've been very successful here tonight, said Nikil.

As if on cue, the three leading members of FicShare looked to Anderson. Zoe's bracing arm left Anderson's back. Once again he had the feeling of being at an interview, or else a firing squad.

This is bad business Anderson, James said. We wouldn't want an employee who's dissatisfied at the company. You know what I mean. He looked to Nikil, who agreed.

Of course, continued James, we haven't been entirely honest with you either. With many of our employees. We have certain connections with a larger start-up, one which doesn't have a public name yet, but which very soon will be changing the way we think about lots of the regular aspects of our lives. James looked quite earnest, the way promotional material does.

One vast connection, he continued. One large multiplier. One—

All right J, Nikil said sharply. This is all quite beta.

James came down to earth. We'd like for you to be a part of it. We value you at FicShare, we really do. The books, the stories—you keep us grounded. Will you stick with us a while longer? He, Nikil, and Zoe stared out at Anderson. Zoe held her hands motionless behind her back.

Anderson considered. Should he answer truthfully? What he wanted was a steady job, a decent apartment. Room for his books, nicely constructed bookshelves, and most of all, time to read from them. He realized, deep down, that he didn't mind office work, much as he complained about it. It was a routine for him, like life. It kept him connected to some larger role, the possibility for some great advancement. And, he figured, everyone else was doing it. Once, when he was just out of college, there'd been an opportunity for him to go to an island off the Finnish coast and work in a bookstore for eight months, room and board included, but he'd decided against it. His life was like that. He shrugged off the unusual, and the strange. These thoughts flashed through his mind, like end-of-life, like a montage, like the flip-book public art installment that the B train passed on the Brooklyn side of the river when going over the Manhattan Bridge. It was a painting, lit from behind, covered with strips of black metal, so that when the train sped past it, it jumped and buzzed almost like a movie. He knew it well—he could see it before him. Anderson closed his eyes. He felt like Griff, nearly weeping in the clean SoHo bar bathroom.

I'll see you all in the morning, Anderson said, pointedly. I don't suppose I'll recall much of what you might call a very dream-like night. Nikil nodded swiftly, James pressed Anderson's hand into a quick handshake. It's for the best, Nikil said. Undoubtedly, answered Anderson.

He was almost to the door when Zoe called out to him. Wait, she said. You forgot this. He turned around. It was the Dostoevsky. He took it from her grasp. Her face was impassive, grave. Without saying anything, he left the bar. Outside, he hailed a cab—the subway would have been a nightmare at this hour, whatever hour it was. He didn't know, because he didn't wear a watch anymore. He didn't have his cell phone, so he couldn't tell the time—nor could he call an Uber. But the taxis were out in full force on the vacant streets of lower Manhattan, even at that hour, shuttling from the hotspots of northern Brooklyn and the centers of commerce, industry, and culture on Wall Street, Midtown, Murray Hill. The taxi that picked Anderson up stank inside of old cigarettes and bad bread, and old, mildewed leather jackets. By the streetlights of the city that never sleeps around them Anderson opened his copy of *Crime and Punishment,* and began reading. St. Petersburg. Islands and canals. A policeman and a public park. Fallen women. He forgot to tell the driver to avoid the unpaved street just before his building. They bounced to the end. He paid the driver, walked the quick stairs to his apportioned room, closed the window that he'd left a little open, and settled into the armchair next to his bed to continue reading. By the time morning came, stark and resolute, Anderson had finished the book.

Making Book

by Dale Peck

The sun beat down so hard it almost had a rhythm to it. I mean, the sun's rays pounded against the top of my head like the bass track on a gangsta rap single, boom-*boom*, boom-*boom*, boom-*boom*, boom-*boom*, and I could almost believe that the angelic visions in front of my eyes were being forced out of my brain by the relentless heat: acres and acres of barely covered baking flesh, virtually motionless in the foreground but undulating in the distance, where thousands upon thousands of swimmers rolled in the surf like potatoes floating to the surface of a pot of boiling water; and it was just as I hit freeze frame that Ace Ferucci stuck his naked white ass in front of the camera, and, at the same time, my mom called my name. And I mean Ace's ass in freeze frame was bad enough, but then my *mom* too.

"Fuck off!" I yelled at the TV in general and at Ace's ass in particular, but with the video paused and the television suddenly silent—there *had* been a bass track, courtesy of these two like totally obnoxious dudes who'd been next to us on the beach, but it disappeared when I paused the video and I could almost see my words carry past the television to my door, and then push on through to my mom on the top of the stairs.

"Boo?" she called again, a funny, half-worried, half-peeved sort of undertone to her voice, and then she knocked on my door. It must've been about five, I guess, sometime after school but before their bridge game, and thank God—I mean *thank God!*—I hadn't really had a chance to get into the video yet. "Boo, I wondered if I might..."

She eased the door open, but by then I'd composed myself and was staring at the TV and trying to make my face look like, *Ah, summer*—which "summer" was a shot of Ace's ass I barely had time to fast-forward past before my mom's head appeared in the doorway. She held the doorknob in one hand and a drink in the other, and for a long time she just looked at the TV. Ace was gone, but in his place was this like totally stacked brunette, or, really, just her chest, which in context was even more incriminating than Ace's ass. My mom looked at the TV, and then she looked at me on the bed with the pillow on my lap, and when I followed her eyes down I saw that I was holding the remote so hard my knuckles were white, and I dropped it like it'd burned me. "Boo," my mom said. "Boo, could you come downstairs for a moment? Your father and I have something we'd like to discuss with you."

I was so relieved I practically thanked her. They were in the living room when I came downstairs. Even I have to admit we've got a pretty fantastic living room, which is centered around these two absolutely amazing Chippendale sofas facing each other. I mean, my dad restores furniture for a living, and he'd done nothing but the best job on those sofas. In particular the leather on them was like butter, which on the one hand feels especially soft but on the other hand means you sort of have to watch yourself when you sit on them, or else you'll just like slide right off them. But anyway, my mom and dad were sitting on the one sofa and I sat down on the other one. In between the two sofas is this coffee table which my dad always calls "contemporary" to the sofas—which means it was made at the same time they were, but he's not sure *who* made it—and like *right* on top of the coffee table was a pair of underwear, and the fly was facing up, and like right *on* the fly were these stains. The underwear was mine, the stains were mine too, and if I mention that I was fourteen then I don't think I have to say anything else.

"Have a seat, Boo," my dad said, even though I was already sitting down.

I guess right off I should mention that my parents more or less never called me Book, ever, unless they were mad at me or introducing me to their friends.

And I guess, saying that, that I should also say how it is I ended up with such a dumb name. See, my parents aren't just bridge players: they're bridge *fanatics*. They've played bridge every Tuesday against Angela and Tony Ferucci since like way before I was born. I don't really play bridge myself—I've watched them a lot, but the one time I asked them to teach me they laughed and said I should call them again when I'm like thirty—so if any of you play bridge I apologize if I'm getting this all wrong. Anyway, what happens in bridge is, you make your bid by taking six tricks on top of the number of tricks you bid for, so to take a bid of, say, five clubs, what you really have to do is take eleven tricks, which is actually a hard thing to do, and, I mean, whatever, if you don't get it it's not really important. What's important is that those first six tricks are called *book*, and when you take these tricks it's called *making book*.

Supposedly it was my mom who was struck by the phrase. Like I said, my dad's a furniture restorer but my mom's an editor, so I guess it makes sense that she was the one. I mean, my dad's not particularly articulate if you know what I mean: Have a seat, Boo, when I'm already sitting down, and like that. *Making book*. They used the second word for my name, my real name—I didn't start using Booker until this year—but I bet it was the first word that really got them. See, my mom edits this food magazine you've probably heard of even if you've never read it, but the only reason she edits it, she once told me, is because she can't write a decent sentence to save her life, and she can't cook either. What she does have is great taste, in food and writing both, which is why her magazine's so famous. My dad's got kind of the same relationship to furniture. I've seen him take what looks like a bundle of wood and turn it back into a two-hundred-year-old Louis Quatorze dining chair—which he then sells for like an *amazing* amount of money—but whenever he tries to make something himself it's a total disaster. I guess what I'm trying to say is that my parents have never been able to *make* anything, except me.

"How's school, Boo?" my mom started things off, and she reached for her drink. My mom always allows herself two drinks before dinner—she calls them "aperitifs"—and I was guessing from the little wobble in her hand as she picked up the glass that she was already on her second one. The glass was sitting right next to the underwear on the table, but she just picked it up and drank from it and put it back down on the table as though the underwear wasn't even there.

"You want to put a coaster under that?" my dad said. He himself was holding his beer in his lap. "I mean, the wood."

"I'm sure it'll be fine," my mom said.

"It'll leave rings. That table was a lot of work, I could sell it for a mint."

"Well, *okay*," she said then, and then she sort of looked around for a coaster but there wasn't one, and I guess she didn't want to get up or something, and so what she did was, she picked the drink up and put it down on my underwear.

No one said anything for what seemed like a long time.

"Boo," my mom finally said.

"Look, Mom, we talked about it already. In school. Health class. I know all about it. Everything's fine, really." And then I remembered: Tuesday. "Hey, won't the Feruccis be here soon?" By which I didn't actually mean Mr. and Mrs., but Ace, who always came over with them.

THAT SUMMER THE Puerto Rican girls had straightened their hair like Mariah Carey but the white girls were still frizzing their hair out with big perms like, I don't know, like the women on *The 700 Club* or something. What can I say, Long Island. But straight or frizzy they were all in bikinis—the one-piece was definitely out—and one of the two brunettes sunbathing in front of us was lying on her back, sucking in her stomach and making these like finger-paint-type designs in the baby oil and sweat that puddled around her belly button, and her friend was on her stomach and doing this thing where she hooked a finger through the string that ran around her hip and pulled up on it to cover the top of her ass, after which she'd slide a finger under the seat of her suit and pull it down to cover the bottom of her ass, and I tell you what, I could've watched her do that *all day long*. But instead Ace came running up from the dunes and said he'd got an idea, come quick and bring the camera and tripod, hurry up Book, we haven't got all day, and what could I do? Ace saw me looking back at the two brunettes and just sort of smiled and said what he had in mind was way better than that. What he had in mind, he said, would keep me warm all winter long

*.

"Boo," my mom said now, like I hadn't said anything. She smiled, and took a drink, and when the glass was in her hand you could see that it had left a little hollow ring on the front of my underwear, and when she put it down I could see that she was careful to put it down in exactly the same spot. "I'm sure that your health teacher was able to give you a perfectly adequate technical explanation for the changes occurring in your body."

"Technical," my dad sort of threw in.

"No, really, Mom, I mean, thanks, I appreciate it, but you should get ready for your game."

"Nevertheless," my mom went right on, "your father and I feel it is our duty to provide you with a warmer, more emotional rationale for what's going on."

"Emotional," my dad threw in. His beer was empty but he took a little pull from it anyway. He looked at his watch. "The Feruccis are due in about an hour."

My mom picked up her glass again. "I found this in your hamper," she said, and I guess it must've been that I didn't really want to focus on the underwear or whatever, but I was kind of confused for a minute.

"Your glass?" I said.

My mom tittered then, which is what she calls it, which when I asked my dad what she meant he said it was sort of the sophisticated way to chuckle.

"No, no, the glass was in the cabinet," she said. She hadn't put her glass down and she took another sip. "I mean your underpants."

My dad: "The underwear."

All three of us kind of looked down at them. The front was pretty much wet from my mom's drink, which unfortunately brought out the stains all the more, and my mom, I guess since we were all looking at the underwear, she didn't put her glass back down but instead took another sip, and then, when nobody said anything, another, but by that point her glass was empty and she just looked over at the bar. She didn't get up though, just looked back at me.

"I'm sure it must seem a bit overwhelming to you," she said finally. "I mean, the changes. But your father and I are here to assure you that the things that are happening to you are perfectly natural, and that these processes, which must seem a bit"—she paused long enough to look down into her empty glass, and then she settled for a word she'd already used—"over*whelm*ing," she said, and kind of shrugged, "they'll all work themselves out in time, and come to seem perfectly natural."

"Perfectly natural," my dad threw in at that point. I'm not sure if he meant to clarify what my mom was saying or if he was just repeating her. He looked at his watch again. "Forty-five minutes, really." He spoke to my mom this time, and I knew that he wanted to get this over as much as I did.

My mom was looking at her drink again, and then she looked at my dad, and then she said, "Maybe just this once. Another aperitif."

"I could go for a beer myself," my dad said. "Boo, what about you?"

I'd've loved a drink, but whatever.

My dad went over to the bar to fix new drinks, and while he was up my mom and I just kind of smiled at each other. I mean, she kind of smiled a little bit, and then I kind of smiled back at her, which made her smile a little more, and so I felt like I had to smile even more back at her, which of course only made her smile even wider, and so on, until by the time my dad came back we were both grinning like circus monkeys.

"Ho ho ho," my dad said. "What's the big joke, huh?" He sat down and then he set the drinks on the table, but right off the sound of the glass on the wood must've made him realize that he'd forgotten to bring coasters because he immediately picked them up, and he sort of held them for a moment, kind of half getting up and then sitting back down again and getting up and sitting back down and then finally just handing my mom her drink and putting his beer in his lap.

At that point it was starting to look like this was going to take all night, and the thought of Ace Ferucci walking in and seeing my underwear on the table was making me kind of panicky. But the new drinks seemed to speed things up, and I guess, well, the long and short of it was that the books my mom had read were all about making sure your pubescent adolescent takes responsibility for his or her new feelings, by which I'm pretty sure they meant being careful when you have sex, but my mom and dad, you know, being more practical people, kind of reduced it all to would I please make sure that if I had any further "accidents" as the stains had come to be referred to then would I please make sure I soaked my underwear in a sink filled with water, cold water, hot would only set the stains, cold water with a capful of bleach in it, so that this wouldn't happen again, by which I think they meant the stains and not the conversation, but whatever. I was all ready to get up and grab my undies and go back to my room—it must've been well after six by then—when my dad kind of put his beer down.

"Boo," he said. "There is one more thing."

Well. I guess I should've realized that the whole set-up was a bit much for a laundry tip. I *mean*.

THE THING ABOUT Ace is that he's always had good luck with girls. On the one hand he's so big and on the other so sweet and dopey, and so whatever, what I'm saying is that it wasn't long before he came back to the dunes with this girl in a yellow bikini with this totally eighties-ed out short spiky haircut that actually sort of looked good on her. From where I sat I couldn't really see her face—especially since Ace's was more or less glued to it—but I could see his hands, making like Lewis and Clark and exploring her entire body. Ace was good. He'd told me the secret: never let your hands sit too long in any one place, that way the girl'll never have an excuse to push them away. And like I said, Ace's hands were busy, traveling from top to bottom and back to front, he kept constantly moving so the girl never got like nervous, like some girls do if you cop a feel while you're making out. Which I don't think this girl would've gotten nervous anyway: her hands were as busy as Ace's, and if anyone seemed a little put off it was him, what with me in the bushes with the camera and the girl's hands snaking inside the back of the loose waistband of his Jams, and through all this the two of them were doing this sort of slow descent to the blanket, like, first one of Ace's knees went down, then one of the girl's, then Ace's other knee, then the girl's, and so on, until eventually they were stretched out on the blanket and somehow even while doing that Ace had managed to untie the neck string of the girl's bikini top, and two tiny triangles of fabric hung below her breasts like banana peels. It wasn't until Ace, you know, actually laid himself right on top of her that I could tell the girl was reaching her stopping point, and thank God *she* did or I don't know what I would have done. Before she left I heard her say that she went to Coram and Ace said maybe he'd drive over there one day and the girl sort of smiled and said she was going to have half days on Tuesdays all next year. When she was gone Ace just fell down on his back with his arms and legs spread wide open, and I was about to slip out of the bushes when he made this noise, it sounded just like a hungry dog watching someone open up a can of food that they then, like, eat themselves, and this noise stopped me dead in my tracks.

*

MY MOM STOOD up now.

"Boo's right," she said. "I really *must* call Angela and Tony." Meaning Ace's parents.

"Barbara," my dad said. Meaning my mom, who was heading for the door.

"It will only take a moment. It's Angela's turn to bring the wine, and you know how she always 'buys' that same terrible Chianti. I know they're Italian, but still."

My mom supplied the quotation marks with her fingers. And even though I knew she was just trying to create a diversion, it was also true: Mrs. Ferucci did always bring the same kind of wine, and just one bottle at that. By now it should be pretty obvious that one bottle wasn't going to go very far in that crowd—believe me, the Feruccis could match my folks drink for drink any night of the week.

Before she called Mrs. Ferucci my mom came back over to us and just sort of dropped her empty glass in my dad's lap. "You two carry on in my absence," she said, and then she marched unsteadily out of the room.

When my dad got up to "refresh" her drink—that's another word my mom always puts quotation marks around—I grabbed the underwear off the table. They didn't really fit in my pocket and so I just stuffed them down the front of my jeans and kind of pulled my shirttails over the little bulge they made.

If my dad noticed the missing underwear when he got back with the drinks he didn't say anything. He sat back down, and nodded his head at me. I nodded back and then he nodded again, but I remembered the smiles thing with my mom and so I forced myself to look down at the coffee table. That's when I saw the videotape. I guess my dad must've grabbed it when he got the drinks. It was just an ordinary videotape, I mean, there was no reason why it should've creeped me out the way it did, except maybe the way it was placed between my mom's glass and my dad's beer exactly where my underwear had been, and then too there was the fact that the tape was labeled *Making Book*, which the ink was kind of faded and the label half peeling off, but you could still read it.

Making Book. No quotation marks.

The phone was just in the other room, and my mom's voice came sailing through the door.

"Angela? Barbara Davis here." My parents have known the Feruccis since way before I was born, but my mom still always uses her full name when she calls them. My dad once said this was a sign of my mom's insecurity, to which my mom said drinking was a sign of insecurity but using her full name on the telephone was simply good manners.

"I've discovered the most *amazing* Camembert," my mom was saying, which I suppose is the sort of thing you'd expect to hear from an editor at a food magazine. "It's so creamy it's like *pudding*. Anyway, I was thinking that a Le Grand Cru Saint-Émilion would be perfect with it, you know, something just *full* of tannic acid. Oh, well, Chianti. Did you by any chance try that Zinfandel I—well, if you've already been shopping. I'm sure that would be fine. No, no, don't bother. We don't want to hold up the game, after all."

At the word *Chianti* my dad looked at me and nodded, and, unable to control myself, I nodded back. We were just about to go into the whole marionette routine when my mom came back into the living room. My parents both picked up their drinks and I sort of fluffed my shirttails over the front of my jeans, and the first thing my mom did was ask me how "Ace" was. She always does the quote thing with Ace's name too, because it's not actually his real name, which is Tony, like his dad's. Anthony. My mom says the Feruccis gave Ace his nickname just to imitate us, meaning the bridge thing,

I guess—meaning *making book*—because *ace*, besides being a card, is also a kind of title that really good bridge players get.

"He's fine, I guess."

"Tony was saying Ace was going to start on the football team this year." This was my dad.

"I guess." I was pretty sure Ace was only second string, but it wouldn't've been the first time Ace's parents had overstated the case—or mine for that matter. Mr. Ferucci certainly knew *I* hadn't made the team, which I'd only tried out for because my dad more or less insisted, and so I just nodded at the video on the coffee table, which was covered with water rings. "What is this, like, a tape of you guys playing bridge or something?" At which point my mom tittered so loud it was practically a guffaw.

"Well, no," my dad said. "Not exactly."

"Really," my mom said. "Is this really, I mean, do we have to do this?" But my dad, like I said, he doesn't really say much, but when he does set his mind to say something there's no stopping him.

"I think we are in a position to offer Boo a unique gift," he said. "After all, how many people can say they actually know where they actually come from?"

Well, right then who flashed in my mind was Ace Ferucci. Ace's parents, according to my mom, liked to think of themselves as "liberal," which is how my mom characterized the fact that they'd videotaped their son's being born. They played it for me once about a year ago, and I mean, it—I mean, the tape—it was kind of interesting and all, but still, every time I looked at Ace I just had this vision of his face all covered with slimy goo. And plus too, and this is something I didn't realize, but the umbilical cord looks like a *hose* growing out of your stomach when you're born, and that is just *gross*.

"A *unique* position," my dad was saying, or saying again.

"I would hardly call it *unique*," my mom said. "It was more like *missionary*."

"A special gift, to help you through what you're going through right now."

"But really," my mom tried one more time. "We should be discussing that weak no-trump opening. Angela and Tony will be de*fense*less against it."

"*A special gift*," my dad repeated, "to help you understand where you come from."

My mom just kind of sighed then, and held up her glass, which it seemed like she'd drained pretty damn quick. "You want to know where you came from, Boo?" She kind of waved the glass a little. "Look no further," she said. "Boo," she said, "you came right out of this glass, which if you get right down to it is where most children come from."

"Barbara."

My mom made her noise, but she didn't say anything.

"Maybe we should just play the tape," my dad said.

At this point I was too freaked out to say anything, and so when my dad asked me to put the tape in the machine I just did it. In our house the TV and the VCR are in this mahogany armoire my dad restored, a pretty fancy piece of work with burled columns on the sides and a relief running along the top of it—the rape of the Sabine women, which why you would want to carve that in an armoire is beyond me—and so anyway I put the tape in the machine but I didn't start it, just brought the remote back to my dad, which he held in both hands the way you might hold something you wanted to buy but knew was too expensive. And then, you know, then I guess he decided that whatever it cost it was worth it, and he started the tape. And what was on the tape was my parents. And they were . . .

Well, like I said. The tape was called *Making Book*.

*

I SUPPOSE I should've come out of the bushes then, but I didn't. And Ace didn't call out to me or anything. He just lay there on the blanket looking up at the sky and I just stood in the bushes and listened to the thin whir of the camera. This went on for a while actually, until Ace reached down to like fix himself in his shorts, and, you know, I hadn't paid much attention before but once he put his hand down there I could see that he was, you know, hard. Still. He sort of angled it down one leg of his shorts, but even before he could finish that tiny movement he froze, and I realized two things: that he'd forgotten I was watching him for a moment, and that he'd just remembered. And what was even stranger was that for a moment I'd forgotten I was watching him too, if you know what I mean, and then when he froze I remembered too that I'd been watching him the whole time, and that I was, well, I was . . . I mean, my shorts were a little constricted too. And so whatever, anyway, for a moment Ace's whole body was as rigid as the thing he was holding in his right hand, and then, slowly, he relaxed but he didn't let go. He relaxed, and his body seemed to sink into the blanket and the sand beneath it, and then, when it had settled, I saw that his hand was sliding the fabric of his shorts up and down, just a little bit, but his hand was squeezing hard and he didn't stop, and if I listened really hard I could hear that same boom box playing out on the beach and if I listened really, *really* hard I could hear the movement of Ace's shorts. He stopped soon enough. By which I mean he didn't "finish," just stopped, and then a moment later he rolled over on his stomach and pretended to be asleep. But even that took a moment of squirming, his ass lifted slightly as he twisted around trying to get comfortable, and meanwhile I just waited in the bushes until the tape ran out. I had set the camera to the slowest recording speed so it took another two hours before the machine finally clicked off, by which time Ace really was sleeping, and when I woke him he didn't mention anything, and he never asked for a copy of the tape either.

"WE HAD QUITE a few tapes for a while," my dad told me, "but we got rid of all the duds after a while." He explained to me how they were almost positive this was the right one. They'd been really careful, he said, plotted out my mom's cycles and things, made sure that whenever they, I mean, whatever, that they always had the camera running.

My mom rolled her empty glass between her palms.

"It's a good thing I didn't let you get that Beta camcorder," she said, "or we would never have been able to watch this." She made her noise then, twice, and said, "On second thought."

I guess the thing that amazed me most was that after a few minutes it didn't seem so strange. I mean, it was kind of like it was with Ace: I almost forgot who it was I was watching, and that they were right there. And my parents had their own bathroom and everything, we were hardly the show-and-tell kind of family, but even so, I'd seen them both naked a few times, and like once or twice I'd heard them through the wall. This just kind of like, I don't know, put it all together.

"Your mother and I weren't exactly young when we had you," my dad was saying. "We'd waited a long time. We both had our careers, and we wanted to be sure we could provide for you, bring you up comfortably."

It was weird the way he said that, as if they'd known who I was going to be before they even had me.

"I guess we were just kind of filled with the specialness of it all, and it kind of occurred to us that we could, we should share that specialness with you. So."

"Actually," my mom said, "we were trying to think of a way to one-up Angela and Tony and their little monument to Anthony's entry into the world." She looked at my dad to see if he would contradict her—if he would, say, point out that the Feruccis would have filmed Ace's birth sometime after my parents made this video—but he didn't say anything. "Well," she said eventually, "if no one is going to refresh my glass." She stood up, very slowly, and made her way to the bar, but then as it turned out she just walked right past it and out of the room, leaving my dad and me alone with the videotape.

He kind of looked at me, and smiled, but he didn't say anything else.

On the tape my parents did what you do. They were sweet about it, which I guess made me happy, I mean, it wasn't wham bam thank you ma'am. I can't believe I just thought that about my mom. At any rate, I'm not going to go into what all they did, but one thing, my mom was on the bottom, which I remember learning was better for conception, which I didn't know if my parents knew that or if that's just how they took care of business, and I didn't ask either.

Toward the end my mom pulled my dad's ear close to her mouth and you could see her whisper something but you couldn't hear it on the tape. My dad kind of nodded, and then a moment later he started calling out, "I'm making a baby, oh yeah, I'm making a baby," and my mom started calling, "Oh yeah, make that baby, make that baby," and so on, "I'm making a baby," "Yeah, you make that baby," which was what I focused on, because if I'd focused on anything else I think I would've just died.

That's when the doorbell rang.

My dad and I kept looking back and forth at each other and at the television. We were stuck in that loop again, and nothing could get us out of it. On the tape my parents were almost finished—I mean, you can just tell that sort of thing—and the doorbell rang again, just as my mom appeared in the doorway, and that broke the spell. My dad and I both jumped up.

"Isn't someone going to—" she began, and then she saw that the tape was still playing. "Oh my God!" she said, and then she looked at me and pointed. "Oh my God!" she said again. "He's gotten excited!"

I looked down. My shirttails had fallen open and the bulge made by the extra pair of underwear stuffed down there seemed *really* large.

"No, Mom, it's just—" I reached into my jeans, and my mom kind of screamed. She put her hands over her ears for some reason, and ran from the room.

On the tape my parents were just kind of lying next to each other, and then they kind of rolled over to face the camera and said, "I think we made a baby that time." They were both all sweaty, but at least they'd pulled the sheet up.

The picture disappeared then, and I turned and saw my dad with the remote in his hands. I had the underwear in my hand, and we kind of looked back and forth at what each other was holding, and then my dad shrugged, and I shrugged back, but we both just shrugged once.

"Hello?" Mrs. Ferucci's voice came from the foyer. "Anyone home?"

I chucked my underwear in the armoire with the television and closed it. My dad looked around for some place to stash the remote like it also was some incriminating piece of evidence, but then he smiled goofily. For just a moment, though, I'd thought I'd seen him consider stuffing it down *his* pants.

Mr. and Mrs. Ferucci walked into the living room, followed a moment later by Ace. His round cheeks were red and his upper lip was wet with sweat.

"Richard?" Mrs. Ferucci said. "We rang the bell, but no one—" She held out a dusty bottle of Chianti.

"We heard noises," Mr. Ferucci said then. "What the hell's going on in here, an orgy? I thought we were here to play cards."

He laughed then, one of those really loud Italian belly laughs, and in a minute my dad was laughing with him and it was almost easy to believe that nothing had happened. My dad handed me the remote control and then took the wine from Mrs. Ferucci. He actually kissed the bottle and said, "*Magnifico!*" and then he sent Mr. and Mrs. Ferucci to the game room to get everything set up while he went to find my mom. "Shuffle along, shuffle along," is what he said, and everyone laughed again like it was some really clever pun. When they were gone Ace pointed to the bottle on the coffee table.

"Looks like we missed a party." He tried to make his voice deep but it cracked on the word *party*.

The remote in my hand was wet with sweat, I wasn't sure if it was mine or my dad's, but when I looked down at it I saw that my hands were actually shaking. I was so keyed up that I wanted to jump up and down, scream out loud, laugh like a maniac, I wanted to grab Ace Ferucci by the collar and kiss him like my father had kissed Mrs. Ferucci's crappy bottle of Chianti.

Well, no. Not exactly like that.

All of a sudden I understood how it was that my parents had come to make that tape in the VCR. Not, I mean, the one-upmanship thing my mom had mentioned, or my dad's "special-ness" bullshit, but just the particular blindness which comes over you sometimes and practically forces you to do something you wouldn't normally do. I imagined Ace must have felt the same feeling that day in the dunes, just as Ace's dad must have felt it when he pointed that camera at his wife in the delivery room. And I say I understood it but I didn't really. I *felt* it.

"Yo, Booker man. What's going *on*?"

And I mean, *Ace*. He was one of those people who take up all this room in the world without ever really *doing* anything. I'd always thought of him like a snowman: all the fun was in making him what I'd wanted him to be. But now I realized he could actually *do* something.

I looked down at the remote in my right hand, but even as I looked I felt my left hand float up like it was the most natural thing in the world for me to do and land right on Ace's shoulder. I even squeezed. I practically kneaded Ace Ferucci's shoulder, and beneath my hand Ace's skin felt soft and pliable as clay.

"Booker?" Ace said. His voice was confused, but he didn't go anywhere.

From the game room, the faint sound of shuffling was drowned beneath another of Mr. Ferucci's belly laughs. Our parents, I realized, might have been dealing out the first hand of the evening, but they'd made book a long time ago. They had, and Ace and I had as well. Now it was time to take our first trick.

My hand seemed almost superhuman now. It turned Ace and steered him toward the hall.

"Booker? What's up?"

And I didn't answer him because I didn't actually know what was going to happen, but I was sure about one thing: the camera was going to be turned off.

Dinosaurs Went Extinct around the Time of the First Flower

by Kelly Luce

Mr. Ukaga wanted her on the horse again.

It was their fourth meeting, the most Tara had seen any client. Usually after the first time they asked for someone else. She was bad at escorting; she wouldn't have actual sex—she drew the line at blowjobs—and tended to ask too many personal questions. But Mr. Ukaga was consistent in his choice of her and of other things, too. Always the same love hotel, always Tuesday; the only variety came in his choice of room: Dungeon or Wild West. Tonight he'd picked the latter and when she arrived she could tell he'd rented the room an hour early, as usual, to prepare.

On the side table near the door were an array of lipsticks, a sleek vial of French perfume (Espion), a container of loose powder, and a huge puffy brush. The perfume always made her sneeze.

The leather-padded pony had been dragged to the middle of the room. Mr. Ukaga paced around it in his fuzzy robe. He shivered in greeting as she removed her heels and set them against the wall, toes pointing toward the door. A crocheted cover—green cactus, charmingly lopsided, on a yellow background—hid the unsightly fire alarm. In the Dungeon room, the alarm cover image was of a skull and crossbones. Tara imagined the love hotel owner's wife sitting down with her needles, producing this custom décor so that even emergency equipment would not distract from a client's fantasy.

The horse, with its wooden head, drawn-on eyeballs, and mane of black yarn, looked like it belonged in a kindergarten. Except for the hole, the size of a tea saucer, cut out of the center of its back.

She peeled off her pants and zebra-print thong and straddled the horse. He never wanted her to wash first. Her feet dangled a few inches above the concrete floor where Mr. Ukaga kneeled, naked now except for his kneepads and the classic, bulky Polaroid camera hanging around his neck. His face was cast upward as if waiting for a vision of Yahweh. She sat up straight and spread her legs and leaned forward a little, making sure her entire crotch pushed through the hole.

He moaned as he moved into position directly under her. She felt his breath on her like a curious finger. Then he began to take pictures.

She tilted her head back. Her breasts looked great in the ceiling mirror. Solid C-cups, resting coolly in the lime-green satin bra she'd lifted from Sogo last week. Dropping ninety bucks on a bra was a waste, especially when the only person who'd see it was ambivalent about tits.

"How do you call this?" he asked from beneath her.

He made her list all the English names she could think of. Cunt. Poontang. Pussy. Slit. Twat. Muff. Cooze. She began making things up. Juju-gum. Washiki. She used words from her GRE prep book: Conflagration. Affable. Magnanimous. He liked that one, magnanimous. "Magnan-i-mous," he said, gazing between her legs, snapping photographs. She could only hear what was happening beneath her: the click of the shutter, the whirring of the machine spitting out a photograph, and the tap of it hitting the floor.

After ten minutes, they moved on to the lipstick, powder, and perfume. He was fussy about her sneezing and brought a mask so she didn't succumb to the unladylike affliction. The only thing he didn't photograph was the finale, oral sex. Was he embarrassed? His cock—well, she'd seen larger turnips. Which made blowjobs a cinch. Sucking him off was like working a cough drop that didn't dissolve. He usually came, politely pulling out right before, after a minute. Then he collected his photographs, paid her more than was owed, and urged her to get home safely.

THE ZEBRA-PRINT THONG was the first thing she'd stolen. She took it because it was overpriced at ¥4800, and because it seemed too insubstantial to be owned. She ripped off the Sogo tag, stuck it behind the dressing room mirror, and put the thong on beneath her regular underwear. When she opened the curtain, there were no clerks or police waiting. It was like her coworker had said: *In Japan, foreigners are the most visible group, but the least seen.* No one gave her so much as a look as she strode awkwardly out of the store. In the crowded Shibuya station bathroom she removed the thong and spun it around her finger. It reminded her of a helicopter propeller before takeoff. She felt more powerful and free than she had in a long time. There were a dozen women in the bathroom with her, hundreds of people in the station, thousands on the city streets above, and not one could see what she was doing; not one knew what she'd managed.

*

THE ASSIGNMENT HAD started out like any other, an email from Mimi that she read on the staff room computer while sipping green tea during lunch. The drink's bitterness felt healthy.

He wanna tall French girl. You can pass, yeah?

I only took a year of French.

He don't want talk, he wants tall. Six feet.

I'm a five-foot-ten Canadian Jew.

You wear heels, yeah? Set you up for 7pm. He's nice guy. Speaks some English and works at Kawasaki College. Physics department.

Her train was delayed and when she arrived at their designated meeting spot, outside a shuttered bank, she spotted him pacing. His hands were balled up in his pockets. She rushed over, apologizing in Japanese, English, and as an afterthought, French. He looked her over and said in Japanese, "Too many relationships begin with the words 'I'm sorry.'"

She liked him.

He looked her over, nodded, and jerked his chin toward a cab waiting at the corner. As they got in, he put his hand on her leg. "How tall, without shoe?" he whispered in what even she could tell was terrible French.

She exaggerated her height to make up for her lateness. "*Cent... quatre-vingts centimètres,*" she replied.

He sighed and, thankfully, switched back to Japanese. Her being late was a great turn-on, he explained. He loved the suffering it caused him. He loved imagining her in her bathroom, powdering her armpits, spraying perfume on her wrists, slipping on a delicate pair of panties, applying lipstick, blotting it. Would she let him photograph her doing these things? "*J'adore les femmes françaises,*" he whispered.

She pushed out a laugh, panic beating in her chest. She didn't wear perfume or lipstick and she had never heard of powdering one's armpits. "*Mais oui*," she managed, looking into her lap.

SHE DIDN'T KNOW what he did with the photographs. Kept them in albums, maybe—hid them away, a secret pleasure he might visit in the night while his family slept. Or he could be posting them online at a fetish site, getting "likes" and comments from viewers around the world. She wondered what they'd have to say about her labia, her untamed pubic hair, her arid armpits.

Though it was taboo during these gigs, she couldn't stop herself from asking about the wives and children she knew must be stashed away in an apartment or house in this compartmental city. It was one thing she liked about Tokyo, the cubby-ness of it, the ease with which one could get lost yet still feel part of things. No one on the planet knew where she was. She could look without being seen.

When she'd asked Mr. Ukaga after their third meeting if he had a family he replied in English, "There are two daughters." He didn't offer anything more. Something about his tone, his face when he'd spoken, the phrasing—"there are," not "I have," as if to distance himself from them, or to acknowledge them in the smallest way possible—left her with nothing to say. She finished dressing. As she left, he handed her his business card and told her that his hobbies were opera and cooking.

She walked back to the station that night instead of taking a taxi. Though cab drivers were the most discreet people in a city full of discretion, she couldn't shake the feeling that she'd be discovered moonlighting in this not-quite-legal profession. It was strange: ever since Mr. Ukaga had started taking the pictures, she'd felt different. Not just more visible but more solid. As if he were bringing her to life with his gaze.

*

THE MORNING AFTER their fourth encounter, she took a walk through Shimabukuro to the gleaming Sogo building. First stop: women's clothing. She bought a thick black sweater with skulls embroidered across the chest—not her style, but that didn't matter since she'd be returning it later. The salesgirl stapled the receipt to the outside of the large plastic Sogo bag and Tara continued shopping.

In the imported candy section, which smelled like strawberry Suave shampoo, she slipped a pack of root beer gummies into the bag on top of the sweater. She rode the escalator to the second floor and in the electronics section added two CDs (Catalonian music, a mix of up-and-coming Japanese songwriters) to her take. The small items slid into the folds of the sweater. Undetectable. The paid-for sweater was like a lead vest at a dentist's office: it protected what was underneath it.

She walked the floor, ending up in accessories. Cheerful pan-pipe music descended from a place too high up to see, like a light snow you didn't notice until it accumulated on your sleeve. Tara felt happy there in that huge store with its unending square footage and its bright lights and hum of commerce and things upon things upon things in all their colors and crispness, waiting to be touched, to be used, to be made valuable. She slid a scarf from a rack. It was blood red with turquoise specks. She wrapped it around her neck, fluffed it. The soft material reminded her of Butterball, her child-hood cat. She'd mistreated him, tugged his whiskers, tossed him high into the air and onto the couch, rubbed his belly too hard. But he still curled up in her lap afterward. Yes, she'd used him for her own amusement.

That was the thing about being objectified, she thought. It implied usefulness, purpose. She picked up a thick plastic coin purse with a cartoon daisy on it. Printed across the bottom were the words, *Dinosaurs went extinct around the time of the first flower.*

She took the scarf into the dressing room along with three pairs of lace panties. With nail clippers, she snipped the tags off the panties and put them on over the underwear she was already wearing. She left the dressing room, put the scarf back, and went down the escalator. She lingered near the sales bins at the front of the store. Her heart thundered. The store was crowded; no one looked at her despite her height, her light hair. Despite five years in the country, she couldn't understand them fluently, couldn't read most of the signs around her. She'd been in a sensory-deprivation tank once during college—an experiment in the psychology department that'd paid eighty-five dollars for half a day's work—and living in a foreign country was not unlike the hour she'd spent in the tank.

Her blood was fuzzy. She walked toward the sliding doors. Stepped outside. Her immediate desire in these moments was to look at every item she'd stolen, admire it, feel like life had bestowed a bonus. But she knew better. She kept walking, step, calm step, step—

A hand on her arm. Its grip was not light.

"*Issho ni kite*"—come with me—said a woman's voice, and she was pulled back into the store.

By THE TIME the worst was over, it was almost 9:00 p.m. She'd been sitting in a back room on the first floor of Sogo for almost three hours. The police had come, taken down her information, her foreign registration number, grilled her about connections to violent criminals. They made her show them the contents of her bag but let her remove the panties behind a screen. She paid for the items she'd stolen with cash from her wallet. They said in Japanese, then wrote down in English, what amounted to: "We can take you to jail, or you can call someone to pick you up if you promise never to come back."

The only numbers in her phone were work-related, along with a few coworker acquaintances, an Australian ex-boyfriend, and her ninety-two-year-old neighbor who came over at least once a week to bring homemade pickles and ask her to turn down her music.

Then she spotted Mr. Ukaga's card in her wallet.

He showed up within an hour, quite a feat considering he'd come from work in Ikebukuro during rush hour. He spoke authoritatively to the fat woman who'd grabbed her arm. They bowed to each other but the woman held her bow longer, and lower. A young security guard fiddled with the computer. After a second, a black-and-white image of Tara appeared on the screen. She was in the candy section, holding the gummies. She looked 100 percent guilty.

Her face burned. How could she have thought she was being smooth?

How could she have thought no one was looking?

Mr. Ukaga watched the video intently. When she slipped the candy into the bag, he murmured. Both she and the security guard glanced at him. Only Tara noticed the slight bulge in his pants.

IT WAS A Friday, but he took her to the love hotel anyway. "I will pay twice," he said. She asked if they could stop for a bottle of something stiff and he had the taxi driver wait at the curb while he fetched champagne from an import shop. He popped the cork in the back seat. It was the first time she'd had the real stuff, direct from France.

"What's your first name?" she asked after a long swig. Bubbles spilled over the bottle's rim and onto her blouse. She didn't care.

"Toshio."

"Toshio, what do you do with the pictures of me?"

He motioned for her to drink more. "I throw them away when you leave, of course. It would be unwise to be found with such things."

She was deflated. His reasoning made sense, though. Why had she expected him to treasure these grotesque images? These disembodied parts that were scarcely identifiable? Why had she assumed his fetish was in the keeping, not in the doing?

At the hotel, they went through the routine: horse, makeup, perfume. He in his robe. Pictures of everything. He'd planned this, she realized; he'd brought the supplies when he came to pick her up at the store.

She'd stop this job. She didn't need the money. She *liked* the money—loved it, even—but every part of it now felt tedious. From her knees, she said, "Did you know? Dinosaurs went extinct around the time of the first flower."

"What a thought," he said, scooping the Polaroids from the ground. She thought he might throw them into the trash immediately now that the secret was out, but he only set them on the side table beside the lipsticks. "The first law of thermodynamics."

"Conservation of . . ." she began, forgetting the rest. She sank to her knees. But he stopped. Walked to the door, slipped the cactus cover off the fire alarm. He laid his hand on the red, exposed box.

"It's emergency. Ha. Ha. Come to Pah-ree?" His prick softened into a sleeping mouse.

"Paris?" She smiled.

He hopped, hand on the alarm. "Yes, yes. Bring magnanimous."

"Is this a role-playing thing?"

"No play." His face was serious. "We go."

She didn't understand. Was this a game? His price for having rescued her today? If so, she had no idea what the rules were. How to please.

"We could go. But we'd need to study. You know I'm not really French, and they hate when you can't speak their language."

"It's okay! Bring magnanimous. Dinosaur. Flower. *Dee-no-sare! Fleur!* Does not matter."

She thought about what he'd said—*there are two daughters*. He hadn't mentioned a wife.

What if he was serious? What if she dropped her assistant teaching job, her shoe box apartment with its frayed and molding tatami, her GRE test date in Osaka, already paid for? She could reschedule the test in Paris. She could study at a sidewalk café, sipping wine, eating a beignet, watching people go by.

She heard the familiar *click-whirrrrr* of the Polaroid. Mr. Ukaga did not wave the photograph in an attempt to make it develop faster. Instead, he stared into it. He leaned close to the fire alarm.

"Toshio?"

He did not respond. A full minute passed.

"Toshio?" She was worried. "Let's talk. I need to think about Paris. Okay?" She took a step toward him. He looked up at her, looked at the photo. Looked at her. Then he pulled the alarm handle. A deafening blare filled the room. It was so loud she could feel it in her chest, on her skin. She threw her hands over her ears and ran for her clothes. Harsh yellow safety lights flooded the room, making it look like what it was: an unfinished concrete box. She picked up the cactus cover and slipped it into her bag.

He was oblivious to her as she dressed. Completely naked, he sang along with the blaring alarm tone, matching its pitch with a

Pavarottian bellow. His belly was round and puffed and smooth like a drum. His mouse penis slumbered in its shadow.

"Are you okay? Get dressed—someone's probably coming!" she yelled. He continued to sing. She looked at the photo in his hand. Her face, mouth slightly open. There was nothing special about it.

She left him there, the drone of the alarm so loud it felt like it was coming from inside her head. Even as she emerged out of a side door, even as she made her way down the dark avenues into the bright ones, did that alarm sound in her mind.

Ether

by Zhang Ran

translated by Carmen Yiling Yan and Ken Liu

I

All of a sudden, I'm thinking about an evening from the winter when I was twenty-two.

A pair of pretty twin sisters sat to my right, chattering away; at my left sat a fat boy clutching a soft drink that he kept refilling. My plate contained cold chicken, cheese, and coleslaw. I don't remember how they tasted, only that I'd reached for the macaroni and dropped some on my brand-new pinstripe trousers. I spent the entire second half of the meal wiping at the crescent-shaped stains on my trousers as the chicken cooled on my plate, untouched. To hide my predicament, I tried to strike up a conversation with the twins, but they didn't seem very interested in college life, and I wasn't knowledgeable about ponytail-tying techniques.

The dinner seemed to last forever. There was one toast after another, and I would raise my long-stemmed glass with whomever was standing, and drink my apple juice, perfectly aware that no one was paying attention to what I did. What was the banquet for, anyway? A wedding, a holiday, a bumper crop? I don't recall.

I sneaked peeks at my father, four tables away. He was busy chatting and drinking and telling dirty jokes with his friends, all his age, with the same thick whiskers and noses red from too much alcohol. He didn't glance at me until the banquet was over. The fiddler tiredly packed his instrument, the hostess began to collect the dirty dishes and glasses, and my inebriated father finally noticed my presence. He staggered over, his bulky body swaying with every step. "You still here?" he slurred. "Tell your ma to give you a ride."

"No, I'm leaving on my own." I stood, staring at the ground. I scrubbed at the stain on my trousers until my fingers were numb.

"Whatever you want. Did you have a good time talking with your little friends?" He looked around for them.

I said nothing but clenched my fists, feeling the blood rush to my head. They weren't my friends. They were just kids, eleven or twelve years old, and I was about to graduate from college. In the city, I had my friends and my accomplishments. No one treated me like a little boy there, seating me at the children's table, pouring apple juice into my long-stemmed glass in the place of white wine. When I walked into restaurants, a server would promptly take my jacket and call me mister; if I dropped macaroni on my trousers, my dining companion would wet a napkin and gently wipe it clean. I was an adult, and I wanted people to talk to me like one, not treat me like a grade-schooler at some village banquet.

"Fuck off!" I said at last, and walked off without looking back.

I was twenty-two that year.

I open my eyes with effort. The sky is completely dark now, and the neon lights of the strip club across the street fill the room with gauzy colors. The computer screen flashes. I rub my temples and slowly sit up on the sofa. I down the half glass of bourbon resting on the coffee table. How many times have I fallen asleep on the sofa this week? I ought to go online and look it up: What does holing up at home in front of a computer and falling into dreams of bygone youth mean for the health of a forty-five-year-old single man? But the headache tells me I don't need a search engine to know the answer. This aimless way of life is murder on my brain cells.

<Hey, you there?> Roy's words appear on the LCD screen.

<I'm here.> I find half a cigar in the ashtray, flick off the ash, and light it.

<You heard? They opened a discussion group on how to tell the difference between bluefin and southern bluefin tuna sashimi by sight,> Roy says.

<Did you join?> I exhale a mouthful of grassy smoke from my Swiss-manufactured cigar.

<Nah. It looked even more boring than the last discussion group. You know, the "Long-Term Observation of the Probability Distribution of Heads vs. Tails in Coin Flips" group.> Roy adds an emoticon: a helpless shrug.

<But you joined that one.>

<Yeah. I flipped a coin twenty times every day for fifteen days and reported my results to the group.>

<And then?>

<Turned out we got closer and closer to 50%.> Roy sends me a pained smiley.

<You knew that would happen from the start,> I say.

<Of course. But it's so boring online that you have to find something or other to do,> Roy says. <Want to join the "Visually Differentiating Bluefin and Southern Bluefin Tuna Sashimi" group?>

<I'll skip it. I'd rather read a book.> The cigar has burned to a stub. I pick up the whiskey glass and spit out foul-tasting saliva.

<Books, magazines, movies, TV . . . they all drive me crazy. The sheer dullness of everything will be the death of me.> Roy taps out a sticker—a big period—and disconnects.

I close the chat window and sign into a few literary and social network sites, hoping for something interesting to read. But just as my online friend said, everything seems to grow duller by the day. When I was young, the Internet was full of opinion, thought, and passion. Exuberant youths filled the virtual world with furious Socratic debate, while the brilliant but misanthropic waxed lyrical about their dreams of a new social order. I could sit unmoving in front of a computer screen until dawn as hyperlinks took my soul on whirlwind journeys. Now, I sift through front pages and notifications and never find a single topic worth clicking on.

The feeling is at once sickening and familiar.

On a social media site I frequent, I click the top news article, CITIZENS GATHER AT CITY HALL TO PROTEST HOBBYIST FISHERMEN'S INHUMANE TREATMENT OF EARTHWORMS. A video window pops out: a gaggle of young people in garish shirts, beers in their left hands and crooked signs in their right, standing in the city square. The signs read SAY NO TO EARTHWORM ABUSE, YOUR BAIT IS MY NEIGHBOR, EARTHWORMS FEEL PAIN JUST LIKE YOUR DOG.

Did they have nothing else to do? If they really wanted to march and protest, couldn't they have found an issue actually worth fighting for? My headache is returning in force, so I turn off the monitor. I flop onto the worn brown couch and tiredly shut my eyes.

2

In the scheme of an enormous aggregation of resources like this city, a low-income, forty-five-year-old bachelor is utterly insignificant. I work three days a week, four hours a day, and my main duty is to read welfare petitions that meet basic requirements and pick the ones I empathize with most. In an age where computers have squeezed people out of most employment opportunities, using my "emotional intuition" to approve or deny government welfare requests is practically the perfect job, no training or background knowledge required. The Department of Social Welfare thought some measure of empathy was needed beyond the rigid rules and regulations to select the few lucky welfare recipients (from petitions that had already passed the automated preliminary checks, of course), and therefore invited individuals from all strata of society—including failures like me—to participate in the process. On Monday, Wednesday, and Friday mornings, I take the subway from my rented apartment to the little office I share with three coworkers in the Social Welfare Building. I sit in front of the computer and stamp my e-seal on petitions I take a liking to. The quota varies day to day, but my work typically ends after thirty stamps. I use the remainder of the time to chat, drink coffee, and eat bagels until the end-of-shift bell rings.

Today's a Monday like any other. I finish my four hours of work and swipe my card to leave. I walk toward the subway station, not far away, the gray granite edifice of the Social Welfare Building behind me. The performer is there at the subway entrance as usual, a one-man band whose repertoire consists of ear-splitting trumpeting accompanied by a monotonous drumbeat. As always, he glares at me balefully as I approach, perhaps because I haven't given him a cent these few years. It makes me uncomfortable. The trumpet begins, the sound of a cat scratching at a glass pane. My lingering headache from yesterday begins to stir. I decide to turn away and catch the subway one station up.

The ground is still wet from the drizzle earlier this morning. Ponytailed youths whiz by me on skateboards. Two pigeons perch on a coffee shop sign, cooing. The storefront windows reflect me: a thin, balding middle-aged man in a yellow windbreaker that used to be fashionable, with a brandy nose just like my father's. I rub my nose and can't help but think of the father I haven't seen in so long. More precisely, I haven't seen him since the banquet when I was twenty-two. My mother sometimes mentions him in her calls: I know that he still lives at the farm, that he's raising cows, that he's kept a few apple trees to brew hard cider, even though alcohol has destroyed his liver, and the doctors say that he can't drink again till science can cure his liver cancer.

To be honest, I don't feel a bit of sorrow for him. Although my red nose and big-framed body are all inherited from him, I've spent my adult years trying to escape his shadow, trying to prevent myself from turning into a fat, selfish, bigoted old drunkard like him. Today, however, I find that the only thing I've successfully avoided is the fat. The greatest achievement of his life was marrying my mother. I don't even have anything close to that.

"Stop right there!" A shout cuts short my self-pity. Several figures in black hoodies are sprinting my way, dodging and weaving through traffic. Two cops waving police batons stumble past braking cars in hot pursuit. One blows his whistle; the other is shouting.

The drivers' curses and the blaring of horns fill the air. I press myself against the coffee shop window. *Keep out of trouble.* In my mind's eye, I see my father's cigar-yellowed teeth flash amidst his whiskers.

The people in black hoodies knock over the trash bin by the street. They run past me—one, two . . . a total of four people. I pretend I don't see them, but I notice that they're all wearing canvas shoes. They're all young. Who hasn't worn dirty canvas shoes in their youth? I look down at my own feet, encased in dull brown leather lace-ups. The surfaces of my shoes are covered in creases from long wear, like the wrinkles on my forehead I try valiantly to ignore when I look in the mirror.

Suddenly, someone's hand blocks my view of my feet. He's reaching into the pocket of my windbreaker, pulling out my right hand. I feel strange tickling sensations—he's drawing something on my palm with his finger. Surprised, I raise my head. In front of me is the fourth person in black, small and thin, his eyes covered by his hoodie. He rapidly sketches something out on my palm, then pats my hand. "Do you understand?"

"Hurry!" the other three people in hoodies are hollering. The fourth person tosses a glance back at the steadily nearing police and leaves me to run after his friends. The cops are right behind, puffing and panting. "Stop right there!" one of them shouts hoarsely. The other has his whistle in his mouth, blowing raggedly. I'm certain they turn and look at me as they pass by, but they don't say anything, only run into the distance, waving their batons.

The pursuers and the pursued turn the corner at the flower shop and leave my sight. On the damp street, the cars begin to move again, the pedestrians weaving among them as if nothing had happened. But the warmth of a stranger's fingertip still lingers on my right hand.

3

"The usual?" the waitress in the diner below my apartment asks me. Her smile doesn't reach her eyes.

"Yeah," I say automatically. "Wait, add smoked salmon to the order." The waitress, who has already turned and started walking, makes an okay sign over her shoulder.

"Did something happen? You changed your order." Slim is a coworker at the Social Welfare Building, and my only acquaintance close enough to call a friend. He has the ability to sniff out the pheromones other people give off without fail. In the five minutes since he's sat down, he's identified a middle-aged virgin, a pair of gay paramours, an aging housewife desperate enough to bed the pizza boy, a debauched teenager buying beer with his big brother's ID card, and a sexually fulfilled paraplegic.

"For real, though, how would someone in a wheelchair have a fulfilling sex life?" I pick up my beer glass and take a sip.

"The higher the paralysis goes, the more likely he's impotent." Slim gestures at his own spine with a long, crooked arm. "Anyway, what about you? You've met the one, haven't you? She's a blonde, right?" His grayish eyes gleam with the pleasure of prodding at my privacy.

"Stop kidding. I ran into some demonstrators this afternoon. You know, the sort of hooligans you see crying out on the news for earthworms' rights." I shake my head. "Thanks," I say, taking the plate from the waitress. A meatball sandwich with pickles on the side—my dinner, forever and always.

"Kids with too much time." Slim shakes his head. "Speaking of which, did you know . . . the word 'potato' comes from the Arawak language of Jamaica."

Dimly, I think his voice sounded strange just then, when he was saying the second half of his sentence, as if something got stuck in his throat or the cold beer caused a relapse of my tinnitus. "No, I didn't know. Not that I'm interested in some language no one speaks anymore." I stick a slice of pickle in my mouth.

Slim widens his eyes in surprise. "You don't care about this?"

His voice is back to normal. It was tinnitus, then. I should go see a doctor, if I haven't reached my health insurance coverage limit this year. "I don't give a damn," I say with my mouth full.

"Fine, then." He lowers his head and toys with his beer glass. The waitress brings his dinner to the table, and passes me my smoked salmon as well.

"Seriously, you two should go out and have some fun. Go to the strip club or something." The waitress looks at our expressions, frowns, and leaves.

Slim and I wordlessly turn our heads toward the gaudy club front across the street. I take two fries from his plate and stuff them into my mouth, then push my smoked salmon toward him. "Have you felt that we haven't had any interesting topics to talk about lately?" I say.

"You're feeling it too?" Slim exclaims. "Beyond the sex lives I've sniffed out, I can barely find anything to talk about. I've found conversations so boring these last few years."

"Maybe we're just getting old?" I unhappily retrieve my right hand from the plate of fries. There's a noticeable age spot on the back of my hand. It appeared just recently, awkward like the stain on my trousers the year I was twenty-two.

"I'm only forty-two! Jiménez was forty-one when he won the Wales Open!" Slim cried, waving a french fry wildly. "The drudgery of work is making us this way. It'll all be different once we retire. Don't you agree, old buddy?"

"I sure hope so," I answer distractedly.

4

I drink two more bottles of cold beer tonight. Waves of dizziness assault me once I'm through my apartment door. I make for my bedroom and collapse on the bed without bothering to shower.

The sheets smell strangely earthy. I don't know if it's because I haven't changed them in so long, but on the bright side, the smell makes me think of the farm when I was little—not the farm that reeked of my father's animal stench, but from before he started drinking, before he started abusing my mother. I'm thinking of the tranquil, peaceful farm where my mother, my sister, and I lived.

I remember playing with my older sister in the newly built granary, airy and filled with the clean fragrance of earth and fresh-cut wood. Sunlight spilled in through the little loft window, accompanying the smell of the cookies my mother baked.

When we got tired from running, we sat down with our backs against the wall. My sister pulled my right hand over. "Close your eyes," she told me. I obediently shut my eyes, the sunlight glowing dusky red on the inside of my eyelids. My palm tickled. I giggled and tried to pull my hand back. "Guess what word I'm writing." My sister was laughing too, her finger scratching around on my palm.

I thought a bit. "I don't know. Write slower!" I complained. My sister wrote the word again, more slowly.

'Horse?' I answered, looking at her.

"That's right!" My sister laughed and ruffled my hair. "Let's play again! If you can get five words right, I'll let you ride my pony for two days."

"Really?" I excitedly closed my eyes.

My palm started to tickle again. I barely held back my giggles. "It's . . . 'crow' this time?"

"That was 'road,' dumb-butt!" My sister flicked my nose, laughing, and jumped to her feet. "First one there gets the biggest frosting cookie!"

"Wait for me—"

I stretch out an arm. I open my eyes to fluorescent lighting and the ceiling, one corner stained with water. The family living above me forgot to turn off their bath tap again. *I'll get the apartment managers to teach them a lesson this time*, I think, realizing that I've woken up from my dream of childhood. My shirt smells sour from alcohol after a day of wear. My neck and back ache from my awkward sleeping position. It takes me five minutes to sit up, look at the alarm clock, and see that it's only one in the morning.

I feel better after a shower and a few glasses of water, but I don't feel like sleeping anymore. I put on pajamas and sit on the living room couch. I flick on the TV; as usual, there's nothing interesting at all on the late-night shows. As I flip through the channels, I notice the ugly blotch on my right hand again. I scrub at it with my left hand, even though I know something like that can never be rubbed off.

The sudden faint itching on my palm makes me shiver. *Wait, what's this feeling? I—I recognize it from the dream, my sister scrawling childish characters on my hand . . .*

Today at noon, the stranger in the black hoodie wasn't tracing some mysterious symbols or gang signs on my palm.

He was writing. No, *she* was writing. The stranger was a woman. The black hoodie hid her other features, but that slender finger couldn't have belonged to a man. What did she write?

I frantically dig out pencil and paper and set them on the coffee table. I try with all my might to recall what I felt. The last word had been written by my sister before . . . yes, it was "ROAD."

I write "ROAD" on the sheet of paper.

There was another word in front of it. She wrote it quickly, very quickly. From my long years approving petitions, I've found that people will write words with pleasant associations that way, fast and fluid, words like "smile," "forever," "hope," "fulfillment." She wrote a short word, standing for something good, with two vowels . . . Aha! EDEN. That's right, the garden of paradise.

I write "EDEN" before "ROAD."

Even before those words came a string of numbers, Arabic numerals. She wrote them twice over for emphasis. I wrinkle my brow, carefully recalling every movement of her fingertip. 7, 2, 9, 5?

No, the first number traced the outside edge of my palm, so there should have been another bend at the end. It was 2, then. 2, 8, 9, 5. I check my recollections again. That's it.

I write "2895" on the left.

The paper reads "2895 EDEN ROAD."

I flop down in front of the computer, open up a map site, and enter "2895 Eden Road." The page shows Eden Road to be on the other side of the city from me, far from the downtown area and the slums near the financial center. But Eden Road doesn't have a 2895. The building numbers end at 500.

I rub my temple, translating each number back to a sensation on my skin, a tingling line traced on my palm. I stare at my hand. 2, 8, 9, that was right. 5 . . . Oh, of course, it could have been an "S." I type in 289S Eden Road, and the map site shows me a four-story apartment building halfway down Eden Road. It's at the outskirts of the city, forty-five kilometers from here. "Got it!" I triumphantly smack my keyboard and leap to my feet, only to fall back on my ass, dizzied by the blood rushing into my head.

What would I find there? I haven't a clue. But I do know that in the forty-five years I've lived by the book, I've never had an adventure where a woman in a black hoodie left me a contact address in a cloak-and-dagger manner—well, my path never seemed to cross with the ladies at all, loser that I am. Something interesting has finally appeared in my dull and listless life. Whether driven by the urging of my hormones, as sharp-nosed Slim would say, or my aroused curiosity, I decide to put on a windbreaker and go to 289S Eden Road to find something new.

Don't make trouble, kid. As I prepare to leave, I see my father in the mirror opposite the door, his belly bulging, a bottle of gin in hand.

Oh, fuck you. I stride out the door like I did twenty-three years ago.

5

I own a motorcycle, long unused. In college, I was as captivated by the latest high-tech toys as all the other young people were: the newest phone, tablet, plasma TV, electricity-generating sneakers, high-horsepower motorbike. Who doesn't love Harley-Davidson and Ducati? But I couldn't afford such expensive brand-name motorcycles. When I was twenty-six, I found a Japanese exchange student about to return home because his visa was expiring, and at last managed to buy this black Kawasaki ZXR400R with only eight thousand miles from him. She was in excellent condition, her brake disks gleaming like new, the roar of her exhaust pipes mesmerizing. I couldn't wait to ride over to my friends and show her off, but they'd long since grown bored of motorcycles. They came to the bars and talked about women with their brand-new Mercedes-Benzes and Cadillacs parked outside.

From then on, I didn't really have friends anymore. When I put on my tie and rode my Kawasaki to work, everyone would look askance at me and my ride, smacking of youthful rebellion. In the end, I gave up and locked my beloved motorbike away in storage. There she stayed as I grew older and met one failure after another in my career. In the blink of an eye, I'd turned into a forty-five-year-old single alcoholic. Sometimes, on a sunny day, I'd ask my beloved Kawasaki as I cleaned her: *Old buddy, when do you want to go out for a ride again?* She never answered me. Every time I thought I could work up the courage to take her out for a ride, the grotesque mental picture of a balding middle-aged man hunched over the sleek motorcycle turned my stomach. It reminded me of the sickening way my drunken father would self-assuredly hit on every woman he saw.

I make my way down the battered apartment stairwell and unlock the dusty doors to the public storage room. I find my motorbike half buried in empty beer cans and pull the tarp aside. The Kawasaki 400R's jet-black paintwork is covered with dust, but the tires are still full of air, and all the gears still gleam with oil. I uncap a small spare gas can and pour the contents into the tank, then turn the key, testing the ignition. The four-cylinder four-stroke engine howls to life without hesitation. My old buddy hasn't let me down.

"Asshole, do you know what time it is?" When I walk my motorbike out of the storage room, a beer bottle smashes to pieces at my feet. I look up and see the landlady yelling from the second-story window, a nightcap on her head. I don't apologize like I would usually do. I just get on my motorcycle and rev the engine, the roar reverberating up and down the street. I loose the clutch at her shouts of, "Are you crazy?" Amidst the squeal of tires and the smell of burning rubber, I whoop with excitement, and my apartment and the strip club retreat from me at breakneck speed.

The wind howls. I'm not wearing a helmet; I feel the air resistance mold the flabby flesh of my face into comical shapes, and the hair I grow long for my comb-over whips behind me. But I don't care how many people might be around at one in the morning to see an ugly middle-aged man racing by on a motorcycle. At this moment, the endless monotony of my life has at least been broken by thirst for the pursuit of happiness.

The ride is over too quickly. The sign for Eden Road appears before I've had my fill of racing through the empty city streets. I decelerate and shift to second gear, turning my head to read the numbers on the doors. Looking at the map, I see that the subway and light-rail stations closest to Eden Road are two kilometers away; this is a place forgotten by the city's development. The street isn't wide, and dingy old cars line both sides of the road. The run-down three- and four-story buildings beyond them are crammed against each other, the majority looking more dilapidated than my own apartment building. Most of the streetlights are dark, and the Kawasaki 400R's headlamps sketch an orange halo against the black street. A feral cat jumps out of a trash bin, eyes me, and pads off.

At this point, I've calmed down enough to wonder whether crossing the city at night for an unfamiliar district in search of a stranger's cryptic address was a rational decision. Every telephone pole could conceal a knife-wielding mugger, maybe even a black-market doctor in search of organs to steal. I want to escape my dreary life, but I definitely don't want to escape it only to end up as a gory crime-scene photo in tomorrow's newspaper.

I decelerate as much as I can, but it's too quiet here, and the rumble of the Kawasaki's engine sounds louder than a B-52 pressed back into active duty. Luckily, at this point, a bronze doorplate appears in the headlights: 289A/B/C/D/S EDEN ROAD.

I stop by the roadside, kill the engine, and turn off the head-lights. A deathly silence instantly engulfs me. On either side, Eden Road has fallen into darkness. In front of the door to the apart-ment building at 289 is the only light, a weak incandescent lamp; its shade wobbles in the wind, making muffled metallic scraping noises.

Dammit, I should have brought a flashlight. Cold sweat seeps from my back. *Right, my cell phone. My cell phone.* I pat my wind-breaker all over and finally find my old-fashioned phone in an inner pocket. I turn on the flash; the football-sized spot of white light comforts me somewhat.

I walk up and gently pull open the doors to 289 Eden Road. The doors aren't locked. The glass pane in one door is broken, but there's no glass on the floor.

It's even darker inside. My cell phone barely illuminates a long-unused front desk with a yellowing ledger tucked behind it: this used to be a hotel. There are stairs on the right. I walk closer, shining my light on the walls. The letters A through D are written crookedly on the walls, followed by an arrow pointing up. There's no "S".

I point my cell phone light up. The stairs lead into a pitch-black second floor, and I can't see anything. *Don't make trouble!* my father repeats idly. I wave the irritating memory away. When the beam of light swings behind the staircase, I see that there are no stairs down. Typically, there would be a closet in the triangular region below a set of stairs, and I spot its door, painted discordantly green. The doorknob is unexpectedly shiny, seemingly at odds with the dilapidated building around me.

I step toward the door, my old brown leather shoes tapping against the badly worn terrazzo. The brass doorknob is as smooth and oily as it looks. I try to turn it. There's no lock on the door, and I push it open, revealing a long set of narrow stairs. My cell phone light doesn't penetrate far enough for me to see how deep they go.

I don't hear anything. It's as quiet as a grave. Should I go down? I weigh my options, looking at the battery-percentage icon on my phone display. I make up my mind and start down.

The stairs are only wide enough for one person, and the walls press in on me. I shine the cell phone at my feet and count about forty steps before a wall appears in front of me, where the stairs double back. I continue forward—down toward the center of the earth, I suppose.

It's not a fun experience. My heart thumps loudly, and my blood presses at my eyes. The sound of my footsteps bounces off the walls, echoing at times in front of me, at times behind me, and I look back more than once. Another forty steps later, my cell phone reveals a green wooden door ahead, slightly ajar. A big brass letter hangs on it: "S." No light shines through the crack.

I'm here, then, at 289S Eden Road. For a second, I'm not sure if I should knock. If the strange woman's message was intended as a personal invitation, I'd be amiss to come at two in the morning, whether I knocked or not. If the message was an invitation for some sort of secret organization, how else was I supposed to enter? I lick my dry lips. I need a glass of whiskey. I'd even settle for beer.

I push the door open all the way and walk in. All I see is darkness. I raise my cell phone in my left hand to better illuminate my surroundings. In that moment, my scalp prickles so hard I can feel the plates of my skull being squeezed together. I can't help but turn my tensed neck like a searchlight, shining my phone over each corner of the room.

This is pretty big as basements go, the walls plain, pipes and concrete everywhere, the air damp and moldy. A couple dozen—maybe a couple hundred—people in black hoodies sit cross-legged on the floor, hand in hand. No one's talking. Even the sound of their breathing is as faint as the beat of a mosquito's wings. Their eyes are closed.

My light shines on one face after another. Under the hoods, there are men, women, old people, young people, whites, blacks, Asians, and on each face is the same eerie expression of joy. No one reacts to my unexpected entrance; their eyes don't even move under their eyelids. The air in the basement congeals in my lungs. I stand frozen at the doorway, my throat working uselessly.

I need a drink. In my mind's eye, my father always carries that bottle of gin, the clear alcohol sloshing against the glass. I'll leave here first. Get out, ride my motorbike back to the apartment, then pour myself a full glass of whiskey. I swallow, feeling my Adam's apple bob jerkily, and start to back out of the room, slowly, one step at a time. I reach out my right hand to pull the door shut. I stare at my hand to avert my gaze from the strange gathering, at the ugly splotch. I'll go to the hospital tomorrow and get that damn laser surgery done, I decide, and have a doctor look at my tinnitus while I'm there.

Then a hand suddenly descends onto mine. The black-clad arm comes from the other side of the door, and the fingers are slender but strong. I feel every hair on my body stand on end. The cell phone falls from my left hand and goes dim. I'm left in darkness. I can't move. I can't think.

A finger gently reaches for my palm. The familiar tingling sensation begins again. It is the mysterious woman from yesterday; I think I can read her fingerprint from her fingertip. Or is it just bioelectricity? I mentally read the words she writes: "Don't be afraid. Come . . . share . . . transmit."

Don't be afraid. Share what? Transmit what? Did I miss words between these? The hand pulls me forward, and I follow unthinkingly with clumsy steps, reentering the silent room. The air is like thick printer's ink. The mysterious woman tugs me through the darkness slowly, toward the depths of the room. I'm afraid that I'm going to step on one of the sitting strangers in black, but our circuitous path is free from obstacles. At last the woman stops and writes, "Sit."

I grope around, but there's nothing around me. I sit down on the ice-cold cement, my eyes wide open, but I still can't see anything. The woman's breathing flutters at the edge of my hearing. Her left hand still rests against my palm, cold, the skin smooth. Her finger starts moving. I close my eyes and read the words she traces onto my palm: "Sorry. Thought. Knew. Don't. Afraid. Friends."

"Sorry, I thought you already knew what this is about. Don't be afraid. We're friends. We're all friends here." With a bit of imagination, her touch could be translated into eloquent words. I still don't understand why she didn't just talk, but this isn't bad either. My fear melts away like hail in sunlight. Slowly, I adjust to the blinding darkness and the touch in the center of my hand.

She moves closer and finds my left hand, pressing my finger against her right palm. I understand immediately. I write in her palm, "I'm fine. This is one heck of an experience."

"Slower," she writes.

I slow down and write one character at a time, "I'm. Great. Fascinating."

"You learn fast." She draws a shallow crescent shape that I interpret as a smiley.

"You. Meet. Here," I write, followed by a question mark.

"Yes, the society meets daily," she replies.

"What for? What kind of organization are you? Why did you invite me?"

"We hold discussions through finger-talking. You'll love it. I saw you on the street staring at that window, lost in thought, and supposed you must be lonely like me. You must find the world so dull."

"Me? Yes, I suppose. To tell the truth, I do find life stifling. But before I met you, I never thought to do something about it."

"Start now, then." She draws another smiley. It's at that moment that I think I've fallen in love with her, even though I've never seen her face, never smelled a woman's perfume on her.

"What am I supposed to do now?" I ask.

"Members arrange themselves in a circle, each person linked to two others. Write with your left hand and let someone else write on your right. Whatever you want to hear about, whatever you want to say, is up to you. I left the ring just then to meet with you," she replies.

"I think I understand the gist." I think some more. "Then I won't be able to converse with someone like I'm doing now? I can only speak to the person on my left, and listen to the person on my right."

"That can't be helped in the general gathering. But privately . . . whatever you want."

"If—just out of curiosity—I were interested in the person to the right of me. If we alternate writing between my right hand and his left, couldn't we have a one-on-one conversation?"

"That's not allowed. The rules of the finger-talking gathering require facilitating a unidirectional flow of information. But you can make a topic and transmit it so that the person you're interested in joins."

"I don't understand."

"Say you want to talk about the president with the person on your right. Spread the topic 'What does everyone think of the president's foreign exchange reserves policy?' to the person on your left. They might add in their viewpoint, or transmit the original topic unchanged. When the topic goes around and reaches the person to your right, he can now give you his opinion. Finger-talking gatherings aren't meant for dialogues. The fun lies in sharing thoughts and transmitting opinions. I've been told this resembles the old, extinct topological structure of the Internet."

"Sounds complicated." I don't understand why they had to invent such a strange mechanism for having conversations. There are plenty of forums and discussion groups on the Internet, and chatting over a beer at a bar is even better. But since my bizarre experiences have led me to this mysterious gathering, I'm not going to pass on a chance to try it out. "Can I join the gathering right now?"

"There's too much info being passed around for a beginner. Your slow speed of transmission will clog up the entire circle. We use a lot of abbreviations and references to increase efficiency, and you'll need time to learn them," she replies, and spends the next five minutes demonstrating those special abbreviations. "You don't seem like a newbie," she says, surprised at the speed at which I pick them up. She draws a big letter P to represent sticking out her tongue.

My sister's and my little secret, I think.

"Don't worry, let me try it."

"Okay," she says eventually. "I'll move to your left. We'll step forward three steps to one of the nodes in the ring. Pat the shoulder of the person on your right, and he'll break the connection. Take his left hand in your right hand. Remember, you have to be quick."

We exchange positions. She holds my left hand in her right and leads me forward until I can dimly feel the body heat of the person in front of me. I kneel, feel someone's shoulder come into contact with my hand, and pat it. The person immediately moves to the right to leave me a spot. I sit down with the woman hand in hand, and the person finds my right hand and takes it.

The hand is a man's, hard and knobby and powerfully muscled, but his finger is astonishingly nimble. My palm is instantly covered with rapid writing. He's so fast that I can't even identify every letter. I focus on capturing the keywords and abbreviations, and guessing the meaning of the sentence from there. Before my brain has time to take in each message, the next sentence assaults me— my skin evidently hasn't become sufficiently sensitive for the flood of finger-talking information. As I frantically decipher the words, I pass on what I can to her on the left. "Opposition party . . . scandal . . . resignation crisis . . . secret police . . . pursuit . . ." I can only retransmit some of the keywords in the message, but I'm hooked. No one brings up politics in my online groups anymore. I want to add my own viewpoint for her, but the next message has arrived already. "Spaceplane wreck . . . Jamaica. Scandal. Fuel leak. NASA's lost government support? Russian attack." The first part is the topic, and after it are everyone's opinions. I think I'm getting used to this method of receiving information. She's right, I'm not a newbie. But the fingers on my left hand can't quickly and clearly transmit information no matter how hard I try. After a few attempts, I write dejectedly, "Sorry."

Her palm is cool and smooth, like the fresh new blackboard in my elementary school classroom. In response, she extends a finger and stealthily writes three words on my left hand: "I forgive you."

I can feel the corners of my mouth lift. "You just told me this is against the rules," I write.

"You're getting better." She breaks the rules again and adds a smiley face.

6

Knocking on my door wakes me. I cover my ears with my pillow, hoping that whoever is at my door will go away. But five minutes later, I have no choice but to put on a night robe, shuffle into my slippers, and walk toward the living room. The knocker is persistent but unhurried. I look out the peephole; the brim of a policeman's cap blocks my view. "Damn," I mutter. I unlock the door and open it. "What can I do for you?"

"Good morning." The cop leaning against the wall takes off his cap and shows me his badge. "Can I have five minutes of your time, sir? It's purely protocol," he says listlessly.

"Sure, five minutes." I return to the living room and flop down on the couch. I pour myself half a glass of bourbon. The clock reads

Tuesday 1:30 p.m., and my night of tossing and turning has reactivated my headache. I pour the amber-colored alcohol down my throat and exhale slowly. My computer screen brightens: Roy left a message. <I joined that discussion group after all. It's a little more interesting than I thought.>

The cop looks to be about thirty, short, with an old-fashioned mustache. He makes himself at home in my armchair. He looks around, sizing up my little apartment. "Nice place."

"It was nicer twenty years ago," I reply.

The cop sets his cap on my coffee table and takes out a tablet and stylus from his pocket. After a moment of consideration, he tosses them aside and falls against the armchair's backrest. "Even I know this is completely pointless," he sighs.

"Just doing your job, right?" I say sympathetically.

"Yes, job." He frowns as he unwillingly picks up the tablet. "Let's see . . . you work at the Social Welfare Building. Mondays, Wednesdays, Fridays," he reads.

"That's right," I reply.

"You're forty-five and single. Last year, you were convicted of medical insurance fraud and sentenced to two weeks of community service." He sounds mildly surprised.

"The hospital got my coverage limits wrong! They apologized afterward," I explain irritably.

"We received a complaint today at 1:12 a.m. saying you were disturbing the neighbors?" The policeman idly combs at his mustache with the tip of his stylus.

"Uh . . ." Remembering the experiences of last night, I feel a surge of apprehension. Is the cop's visit tied to the finger-talking gathering? I don't think sitting in the dark in large groups and scribbling against one another's palms is illegal, but my instincts tell me to say nothing, to keep this secret. *Don't make trouble*, as my father used to say to me. "I had some beers last night. When I woke, I thought I'd take my motorcycle out for a spin, nothing more. I apologize if I disturbed the neighbors."

"I see. You were taking your motorcycle out for a spin." The cop lethargically writes something on the tablet. "I understand a man's need for adventure. Well, that's it, then. You know we don't take those neurotic old ladies' complaints too seriously, but protocol is protocol." He stands, sticks his cap under his arm, and stuffs the tablet and stylus back into his pocket.

"That's it?" I stand, in disbelief.

"Thank you for your cooperation," the cop recites, and turns to leave. I follow after him with my whiskey glass in hand. Just as I prepare to close the door, the short policeman turns and raises his black eyes to mine. "Right, you didn't take your motorbike anywhere you shouldn't go, I hope."

"Somewhere I shouldn't go? Of course not," I reply quickly.

"Oh, your motorcycle went southeast, out of surveillance camera coverage. You must have come across some really unique little neighborhood. Crime rates may have fallen to their lowest in fifty years, but in my job you learn that there's still all sorts of bad people in this world. Have a nice day, sir." He pats my shoulder with a not-quite smile, puts on his cap, nods in farewell, and trots down the squeaking wood steps.

I slam in the deadbolt and lean against the door, gasping for breath. Was the cop really on to something? Are the woman and the finger-talking gathering doing something illegal? *That's right. I'm an idiot.* I smack my forehead, remembering that when I met her yesterday, she and her friends were being chased by two policemen.

I need to see her again. The strange and strangely fascinating conversations of the finger-taking gathering ended at three in the morning. The people in black hoodies streamed out of the spartan basement of 289S Eden Road in silence, and I lost her among the crowd. I obeyed the rules of the gathering and didn't call out for her. Later, I realized that I didn't even know her name.

I need to see her again.

7

By the time I log in, Roy has left. I sigh and turn off my computer.

The finger-talking gathering begins at midnight. I've never waited so anxiously for sundown. I stand up, sit down, change the TV channel, sit blankly on the toilet staring into space. I repeatedly check my watch. To while away the time, I take the Bolívar No. 2 cigar I've secreted away for so long out of the humidor. I open the precious aluminum cigar tube, carefully cut the closed end, and light it with a match. I take a deep drag and exhale it slowly. The rich, intense smoke of the premium Cuban cigar makes me dizzy with pleasure, but guilt quickly follows. A thirty-dollar cigar? I don't deserve it. A thing so splendid should remain forever in my crude humidor, to be admired from a distance the same way as the beautiful Kawasaki.

And my motorcycle . . . it functioned less smoothly on the ride home, the engine coughing weakly. I think the aging carburetor's losing efficiency; my old buddy's getting along in years, after all. I ought to use a safer, less traceable method of transportation to go to Eden Road. I turn my mind to that problem, idly clicking the TV remote through channels. The TV shows are as boring as the Internet. None of the topics from yesterday's gathering appeared at all, never mind the accompanying bold discussion and critiques. Impatient and restless, I suck away at my cigar until the stub burns my fingers, then go to my bedroom and dig in my closet until I find a dark blue hoodie from my college years. I put it on, flip up the hood, and walk in front of my mirror.

The wrinkled hoodie bears the image of Steve Jobs—someone this generation of young people might never have heard of—printed in black and white on its front. It fits well: I haven't gained a pound since I graduated. From the depths of the hood floats the bloodless, hollow-cheeked, baggy-eyed face of a middle-aged man. It tries to smile, but coupled with the big brandy nose, the smile looks comical.

This is why I long for the finger-talking gathering. In darkness, no one needs to see your ugly face. All you have is the touch of a fingertip and a thought put into writing. I push back the hood and carefully comb my hair to the right, but I can't cover the balding top of my head no matter what I do.

The sky is finally dark. I stack crackers and cheese, press down, and heat them in the oven. Then I open a bottle of beer and have myself a simple dinner. The cheese gives me heartburn. I can't suppress the pounding of my heart. In my hoodie, I pace in the living room. The TV shows some guy with too much time carrying a massive sign in front of City Hall. The protestor is surrounded by a sizable audience, but no one seems to be joining him. I think I see a few people in black hoodies in the crowd. Is it them? I toss down the remote and pull up my hood, determined to go take a look.

There aren't many people on the subway. A number of them pretend to be watching the commercials on the display screens while secretly sizing me up.

Two teenagers with fashionable mushroom-shaped hair discuss me quietly. "Who's the guy on that old geezer's sweatshirt?"

"Some religious leader, probably. Like Luc Jouret or something."

"Uh, who's that?"

You're half right, ignorant kids. I pull my hood lower. In my time, Steve Jobs was as good as a religious leader, until the Internet degenerated into senselessness and everyone tossed aside their complicated smartphones for basic phones that could only make calls.

I arrive at the city square half an hour later. The protestor stands in the middle of the brightly lit lawn. His sign is ridiculously huge, covered with several rows of garishly colored writing. I can't see what it says with my deteriorating vision. Is this a side effect of overdrinking, like the tinnitus? My mother says that my father is blind as a mole now. I can't imagine what he looks like, what remains of his bushy beard, red face, brawny arms, his massive beer belly, and I don't care to find out.

A crowd has gathered to watch him from afar. A few cops are leaning against the side of their police car, chewing gum. Skater kids are showing off their tricks on the steps. In front of a TV van, a reporter and a cameraman are chatting. In contrast, the protestor seems all alone. I walk closer, squinting at the sign. The red text on the top reads, WOOD-BURNING FIREPLACES ARE THE LEADING CAUSE OF GLOBAL WARMING. Below it, FOR EVERY TRADITIONAL FIREPLACE YOU TEAR DOWN, MOTHER EARTH LIVES ANOTHER DAY is written in blue.

I wrinkle my brow. The First Amendment wasn't made for idle crap like this. Where are the incisive opinions from the finger-talking gathering? I approach the crowd, trying to find the people in black hoodies, but at this time the police come up and ask the protestor to leave for the sake of the grass, and the crowd disperses too. I can't find anyone I recognize. Two cops turn their gazes on me questioningly. One of them points at the portrait on my hoodie, and the other guffaws in realization. I quickly turn and leave.

Without thinking, I ride the subway eastward and get off at the terminal station. I hail a taxi, telling the driver, "289 Eden Road."

"Eden Road?" the driver grumbles. "I hope you're planning to tip well."

The car turns onto a side road. The city around us grows more and more run-down, and the streetlights dwindle. When the taxi stops in the middle of the darkened Eden Road, my anxiety and hope rise as one. "Thinking of going elsewhere, pal? I know some good hotels." The taxi driver takes my fee and opens the door for me.

"No, it's fine. I like quiet." I get out, shut the car door, and wave. The taxi's taillights brighten, then quickly diminish and disappear into the distance. It's nine o'clock right now, but Eden Road is already silent as a grave. I walk toward the front door of 289 Eden Road with its missing glass panel. After some thought, I open the door and enter.

I know I've arrived too early, but I thought that the anticipation would add to tonight's gathering. Like yesterday, my heart is thumping, but this time it's out of excitement rather than fear. I find the door at the back of the stairs by the light of the wobbly incandescent lamp and turn the brass doorknob. The dark, narrow forty steps appear before me. I've lost my cell phone, and neither do I have a flashlight. I adjust my hood, close my eyes, and walk into the deepening darkness. One, two, three, four, five . . . thirty-nine, forty. There's a wall in front of me now. The stairs double back here. I grope around, exploring with my right foot until I find the next stair. One, two, three . . . thirty-nine, forty. Both my feet are on flat ground. The green door with the brass letter S should be in front of me. Filled with hope, I reach out.

My fingers touch cold concrete.

Have I misremembered? I summon last night's experiences to my mind. There was only this door at the end of the stairs. This door, and nothing else. I'm sure of it. I clearly recall the gleam of the brass S. I shuffle to the left and right, but touch only concrete wall on either side. The place directly in front of the stairs, where the door should have been, is also rough wall. The stairs have taken me to a dead end.

I can feel the blood pounding in my head. My ears feel hot, and the headache is returning. *Calm, I tell myself. I need to calm down. Breathe deeply. Breathe deeply.* I take off my hood and suck in a slow breath. The cold, damp basement air fills my lungs, and my overheated brain cools down a little.

Once I've taken a few minutes to calm down, I start to look for the vanished door again, but there are no signs that there has ever been a door here. The rough wall scrapes my fingertips raw. I sit down, despairing.

Where are your friends now? My father's face appears in the darkness, sneering carelessly.

Shut up! I yell. I bury my head in the crook of my arm and cover my ears.

I told you, don't make trouble. My father wipes a trickle of beer from the corner of his mouth. His breath is hot and foul. His arm is around my sister, whose blue eyes glisten with tears. My mother is to the side, crying.

Shut up! I scream.

You're eighteen now. Get the hell out of my house. Get a job, or go to your goddamn university, but I don't have to let you live under my roof anymore, my father roars, throwing the suitcase at my feet. My sister hides herself in the kitchen, tears running down her face as she looks at me. My mother is holding a pot; her face is expressionless.

Shut up! I scream hysterically.

I don't know how much time has passed. You can't tell time accurately in the dark. It might have been a nightmare, or maybe I never fell asleep in the first place. I stand up slowly, letting the wall take some of my weight. I've been curled up too long; every joint cries out in protest. All I want to do is go back to my little apartment, down a big glass of whiskey, no ice, and turn on the TV.

Forget my absurd dream from last night. Forget the lingering sensation on my palm. Forget that there ever was such a thing as the ridiculously named finger-talking gathering.

I stride forward. My left foot strikes something. It rolls, then glows to life, a spot of white light illuminating the narrow space. It is the cell phone I lost at the door last night, my ridiculed, one-of-a-kind old-fashioned smartphone.

It wasn't a dream. Strength surges into me instantly. I pick up the phone; the battery is almost depleted, but it's enough to let me properly examine the wall in front of me. *Yes.* This portion of the wall is brand new, troweled together in a hurry with fast-setting concrete. Where the wall meets the floor, I see a wooden doorframe buried in the depths of the crack. The door is there, just hidden by people trying to keep it secret.

I knock on the wall and find that the cement is too thick for me to break through. The people in black hoodies weren't some hallucination. They simply changed their meeting place and forgot to tell me. I comfort myself with that.

I wait there until two in the morning, but no one comes. I climb back up the stairs, walk to the subway station two kilometers away, and hail a taxi back to my apartment from there. Step by step, I climb up the squeaking stairs. My thoughts are in a muddle, but I still need to work Wednesday morning. As I open the door to my apartment, I plan to drink a glass, take a shower, and get some proper sleep.

I freeze at the doorway. Someone in a black hoodie is sitting on my couch.

8

I pick up the e-seal and stamp the social welfare petition on my display: a newly immigrated family with six children. The green indicator light on the e-seal turns red, telling me that I've used up today's approval quota. I relax into my chair and work the cramp out of my wrist. There's still half an hour until my shift ends.

The pretty blond girl who shares my cubicle stands up to invite everyone to her birthday party. "We'd . . . welcome you too, if you have the time," she says belatedly to me, out of what I know is forced courtesy.

"Sorry, I have an important date the next day. But happy birthday!" I reply. She visibly gives a sigh of relief and puts her hand to her chest. "Thanks. That's a pity. I hope the date goes well."

To a girl her age, I'm from another generation, and I understand an out-of-place old man at a party can be a disaster. But the date wasn't an empty excuse. I can still feel *her* message on my right palm: "Tomorrow in the city square at 6:00 a.m."

I don't know how she found me, how she got in my apartment, or how long she waited there. After a moment of surprise, I walked over and took her hand. The neon lights of the strip club flashed through the window, splashing her black hoodie with radiant colors. I still couldn't see her face properly. "Sorry, we changed the meeting place. We couldn't contact you in time," she wrote.

"Did I cause trouble for you?" I asked.

"No. The situation's complicated. Only a few core members went to the finger-talking gathering just now. We've had some internal disagreements." At the end of the sentence, her finger tapped out a few hesitant ellipses.

"About what?"

"About whether to do something stupid." She drew two wavy lines under "stupid."

"I don't understand," I wrote honestly.

"If you're willing to listen, I can tell you how the finger-talking gathering came to be, how we're organized, the struggles between the factions, and our ultimate goal." She wrote it in one long sentence.

"I don't want to know," I replied. "I don't want to turn these interesting conversations into politics."

"You don't understand." She drew a greater-than sign, a sigh. I realized that she expressed even the most basic emotions through writing. "You must have noticed how the Internet, TV, books have lost any semblance of intelligence."

"Yes!" I felt a rush of excitement. "I don't know why, but every topic worth arguing over has disappeared. All that's left is pointless bullshit. I've tried tossing provocative topics out in discussion more than once, but no one would reply. Everyone's more interested in sashimi and earthworms. I noticed it years ago, but no one believed me. The doctor gave me pills to get rid of the hallucination. But I know this isn't a hallucination!"

"It's not just these. Conversations with friends and the things you see on the street are becoming as bland as the Internet and the media."

"How do you know?" I nearly stood.

"It's all a conspiracy." She pressed hard writing this, hard enough to hurt.

"A conspiracy? Like the moon landing thing?"

"Like Watergate." Her writing grew agitated, harder to decipher.

"I think you need to tell me everything."

"Then we'll start with politics."

"Hold on . . . when's the next gathering? Can I join?"

"This is what we're arguing about. Those in support of action think we should hold our next gathering in a public place, like the city square. We shouldn't keep running and hiding. We should show what we believe in, no compromises," she told me.

"I'm guessing that the police don't like you guys very much." I once again recalled the first time I saw her, chased by two panting cops.

"They don't have anything on the organization as a whole. It's just some individual members who have criminal records, especially the activists," she answered frankly.

"You have a criminal record?" I asked, curious.

"It's a long story." She was unwilling to say anything more.

I worked up my courage and asked the question at last. "What's your name?"

Her finger stilled. I tried to scrutinize her face under the hood, but the hoodie concealed her face entirely. It even hid any sex characteristics. I suddenly realized that my only evidence that she was female was her slender fingers. She could just as easily be a young man, I thought, though my heart utterly rejected the idea. I wanted her to be a woman like my big sister, flaxen-haired and soft-voiced and a little mischievous, freckles scattered over the bridge of her nose. The sort of woman I'd been seeking all my life.

"You'll know it in time," she said eventually, avoiding my question.

"Actually, I'm more curious about" —the exquisite sensation of my left finger on her right palm was interrupted by the sudden howl of a police siren approaching rapidly. She straightened, alert, and pulled her hood lower. "I'm leaving now," she wrote rapidly. "If you want, be there tomorrow in the city square at 6 a.m. Remember, this is your choice. This is your chance to change the world, or more likely, regret it to the end of your days. Either way, don't blame anyone else, especially not me, for your own decision. And I might as well add, I think bald men are sexier."

She squeezed my right hand with her delicate but strong fingers, got off the sofa, and vaulted out of the living room window.

I hurried over to look down. She'd already climbed down nimbly from the fire escape and disappeared around the corner. I touched my balding head, somewhat dazed.

9

For a variety of reasons, I sank into a deep depression the year I was thirty-seven. The landlady persuaded me to go to her shrink, threatening that if I didn't get treatment, she'd kick my ass out of the apartment. I knew that she just didn't want me to OD and leave my corpse in one of her rooms, but I'm grateful to her all the same after the fact.

The man was a Swede with a beard like Freud's. "I'm not a psychologist," he said, once we'd talked some. "I'm a psychiatrist. We don't consult here. We fix problems. You'll need to take medications if you don't want to dream every night of your sister's grave."

"I'm not afraid of pills, doctor," I replied. "As long as the insurance covers it. I'm not afraid of dreaming of the sister I love, either, even if she crawls out of the grave every time. I'm afraid of what's happening around me. Do you feel it, doctor? Tick-tock, tick-tock, like the second hand on a clock. Here, there, endlessly."

The psychiatrist leaned over, full of interest. "Tell me what you feel."

"Something's dying," I said in a low voice, glancing around me. "Can't you smell it rotting? The commentary on the news, the newspaper columnists, the online forums, the spirit of freedom is dying. It's dying en masse like mosquitoes sprayed with DDT."

"All I see is the advancement of society and democracy. Have you thought whether some paranoia-inducing mental disorder may be causing this suspicion toward everything, including the harmonious cultural atmosphere?" The psychiatrist leaned back, fingers interlaced.

"You were young once too, doctor. You once had the courage to question everything." My voice rose anxiously. "Back then, when we didn't know who we'd become, but understood who we didn't want to become. When there were battles and heroes all around us."

"I reminisce sometimes of my youth too. Everyone should. But we're all grown people now, with responsibilities toward our families, our society, even our civilization and our descendants. I suggest you take these pills regularly when you go home to get rid of your unreasonable fantasies. Find an undemanding job, fish on the weekends, take a vacation once a year. Find a nice girl when the time is right—we haven't discussed your sexual orientation yet, I realize, please don't take that the wrong way—and start a family." The psychiatrist put on his glasses, flipped open his notebook, and cut my protests off with a hand before I could voice them. "Now, let's discuss the problems relating to your father and sister. Your childhood traumas had significant influence on my choices of medication. Is that fine with you?"

The treatment was effective. I gradually grew used to the tepid TV programs and online forums. I grew used to society being peaceful, simple, nice, indifferent. I grew used to seeing the shade of my father, and tried not to argue over things past. Then this person in a black hoodie barges into the monotony of my bachelor's life and hands me a choice, a choice whose meaning I don't understand. But I do know that finger-talking has brought me a sense of groundedness I haven't had in a long time, made the things I felt that slowly died off eight years ago return from the grave like beetles bursting from their underground cocoons in spring.

I don't know what "tomorrow in the city square at 6 a.m." will signify. Normally, when I'm faced with a choice, I toss a coin. The answer naturally appears as the coin whirls through the air:

Which side do you hope will land faceup? But this time, I don't toss a coin, because when I get off from work, leave the Social Welfare Building, I unthinkingly walk in the opposite direction from the subway station. Next to a spinning pole, I push open the glass door. I say to the fat man across from the mirror, "Hey."

"Hey, long time no see." The fat man waves me in. "Same as usual?"

"No." I smile. "Shave me bald. The sexy kind of bald."

10

I startle awake at 3:40 in the morning and can't sleep after that. I take a hot bath, change into my Steve Jobs hoodie and khaki pants, put on my sneakers, put in my earphones, and listen to the metal bands of olden days. At 5:00 exactly, I leave Roy a message, drink a cup of coffee, and leave my apartment. The sun hasn't risen yet. The early morning breeze caresses my freshly shaved scalp, cooling my feverish brain. I take the first subway that comes, unperturbed by the strange looks I get from the sparse fellow travelers. At 5:40, I arrive at the city square. I stand in the middle of the green. The streetlights are bright, and the morning mist is rising.

At 5:50, the streetlights go out. The first ray of dawn illuminates the thin mist. People are slowly gathering. Someone in a black hoodie takes my right hand, and I pick up the arm of the stranger next to me. "Good morning" spreads palm to palm. More and more people are appearing in the city square, silently forming themselves into a growing circle.

At 6:10, the ring stabilizes with more than a hundred people in it. The participants of the finger-talking gathering begin to rapidly transmit information. I close my eyes. A drop of dew falls from the brim of my hoodie.

The person to my right is an old gentleman, by his flabby skin and the refined construction of his sentences; the person on the left is a well-preserved lady with a plump, smooth palm and a large diamond ring on her finger. The topic arrives: "Compared to the gutless bands of today, what bands ought we to remember forever?"

"Metal. U2. And rock and roll, of course." I immediately add my own opinion.

"The Velvet Underground."

"Sex Pistols."

"Green Day. Queen. Nirvana."

"NOFX."

"Rage against the Machine."

"Anti-Flag."

"Joy Division."

"The Clash."

"The Cranberries, of course."

"Massive Attack."

"Hang on, does dance music count? Add Pussycat Dolls, then."

I grin knowingly. The second topic appears, then the third. I've missed this sort of easy, organic discussion, even if it's via a mode of information exchange out of a kids' game. The fourth and fifth topics appear. My fingertip and palm are hard at work, avoiding typos while trying to use as many abbreviations as possible. I think I'm slowly mastering the skill of finger-talking conversation. The sixth topic appears, followed by the seventh. This seems to be the bandwidth limit for finger-talking gatherings. The commentary appended to each topic steadily grows until everyone interested has finished speaking. The creator of the topic has the right and responsibility to end its transmission at a suitable time to make room for a new topic. The first and third topics have disappeared.

The second topic, on the First Amendment, is still gaining comments. The creators of the other topics independently choose to stop transmitting. Only the second topic is left in the circle, and the participants come to an unspoken agreement to stop carrying the topic itself, transmitting the commentary only to save bandwidth.

It's an inefficient use of the network to transmit only one data packet at a time. Someone realizes this and starts a new topic in the lull. The network is occupied once again, but soon the data clogs up at one of the nodes.

A memory from my distant college years suddenly surfaces. "Let's look at a now-obsolete network topology structure," the network systems professor had said behind the lectern, "the token ring network, invented by IBM in the seventies of the last century." So the finger-talking gathering was really an unscientific token ring network reliant on the members' responsible behavior. I hurriedly finish sending the enormous data packet of the second topic and use the bit of free time to consider how the system might be improved.

A very brief message appears. It's uneconomical, I think, but its contents make me gape. "To the sexy bald guy: my name is Daisy."

I can feel the serotonin forming in every one of my hundred billion neurons, the ATP sending my heart pounding furiously. Every living bit of me is jumping and hollering in victory. In the place of this message, I send out: "Hello, Daisy."

The size of the second topic has slowed down the network so that it takes me ten minutes to receive the data from upstream. It's clear that someone's stripped down the commentary to the second topic to the essentials. After the compressed file is my topic "Hello, Daisy" and its legion comments. "We love you, Daisy." "Our daisy blossom." "Pretty lady." Then "Hello, Uncle Baldy!"

I recall how I looked in the mirror before I left home: my skinny body, drooping cheeks, red nose, and comical bald head, my outdated sweatshirt. I look like a clown. I smile.

I'm writing my reply when a commotion ripples through the network. I open my eyes. The sun has long since risen, and the mist has disappeared without a trace. Every blade of grass in the city green sparkles with dew. The members of the finger-talking gathering have formed an irregular circle, linked hand in hand into a silent wall. Many people watch from a distance: morning joggers, commuters on their way to work, reporters, policemen. They look perplexedly at us, because we have no signs, no slogans, none of the characteristics they expect of a protest.

A police car is stopped at the edge of the green, its exhaust pipes billowing white smoke. The car doors open, and cops get out. I recognize their leader, the short policeman who interviewed me. He's still wearing the same apathetic expression and walking with the same careless swagger. He strokes his neat little mustache, considering us, then makes a beeline for me. "Good morning, sir." He takes off his cap and presses it to his chest.

I look at him and don't say anything.

"I'm afraid you're all under arrest," he says without energy. Six hulking black police vans glide silently into the city square. Riot police in full gear flood out, approaching us with batons and riot shields raised. Our onlookers don't react at all. No one shouts, no one moves, no one even looks in the direction of the neat marching phalanx of riot police.

I can tell the people beside me are anxious by the sweat on their palms. The second topic's data package has disappeared. A single short message replaces it, traveling at the highest speed our network can sustain.

"Freedom," many fingers write rapidly and firmly into many palms.

"Freedom." Our eyes are open. Our mouths are shut.

"Freedom." We shout to the black machinery of the government in the loudest form of silence.

"I love you, Daisy." I send my last message before the riot police slam me roughly to the ground. The network has collapsed. I don't know if the message will get to Daisy. Where was she in the network? I don't know. Will I ever see her again? I don't know. I've never really seen her before, but I feel as if I understand her better than anyone.

Don't make trouble. My father looks down at my squashed face. The riot cop is doing his best to mash me and the lawn into one.

Fuck you. I spit out grassy saliva.

II

I'm getting ten minutes on the phone, and I don't want to waste them. But besides Slim and Roy, I can't think of anyone to call. Strangely, Slim spends the call talking about the Arawak language of Jamaica. Roy doesn't pick up. I put down the receiver, at a loss.

"Hey, old man, how much time do you have left to waste anyway?" The line behind me is getting impatient.

I dial the familiar number without thinking. Like always, the phone rings three times before someone picks up. "Hello?"

"How are things, Mom?" I say.

"I'm well. How about you? Do you still get the headaches?" Through the receiver, I hear the scrape of a chair being dragged over. My mother sits down.

"I'm much better nowadays. And . . . and what about him?" I say.

"You never ask about him." My mother sounds surprised.

"Ah. I was just wondering . . ."

"He passed away last month," my mother says calmly.

"Oh. Really?"

"Yes."

"Do you have anyone to take care of you?"

"Your aunt is with me. Don't worry."

"His grave . . ."

"Is in the church cemetery. A long ways from your sister."

"That's good, that's all I wanted to make sure. Then . . . have a good weekend, Mom."

"Of course, and you too. Good-bye."

"Bye."

She hangs up. I rub the age spot on my right hand as if trying to wipe those memories away. My father, reeking of alcohol. My sister sobbing, my mother growing withdrawn and numb. The memories from my college breaks are far enough downstream in my life that they no longer seem so unbearable. "Old man, time is money! Tick-tock, tick-tock!" The person behind me taps at his wrist, imitating the tick of watch hands. I hang up the receiver and walk off.

For lunch, I end up sitting next to a red-haired guy with a man's name tattooed on his face. His arms are garishly patterned, as if he were wearing a Hawaiian shirt. "That guy's gay! Don't go near him. And don't let him grab your hand," the Mexican who shares my cell warned me—I'm guessing he meant well. I take my tray and move a bit aside.

Redhead scoots closer, smirking. "Want to share my goat milk pudding? I'm not a big fan of lactose."

"Thanks, but I'm fine," I say as politely as I can.

Redhead reaches over. I snatch back my hand as if jolted on a live wire, but he manages to grab it anyway. He grips my right hand tightly and tickles at my palm with a fingertip.

I can feel every hair on my body standing on end. "I don't think I'd be very suited to this type of relationship. If you don't mind . . ." I struggle in vain. The bystanders are laughing raucously, smacking the dining tables like a drum.

The sensation becomes familiar. It's finger-talking, the same abbreviations, rapid and precise. "If you understand, tell me."

I calm down and give Redhead a careful look over. He still wears the same stomach-turningly lecherous expression as before. I hook my finger and tell him, "Received.

"Thank God!" His expression doesn't change, but he writes an abbreviation for a strong exclamation. "I've finally found another one. Now, after lunch, go to the reading room. The philosophy section is against the east wall. No one ever goes there. On the bottom of the second shelf, between Hegel and Novalis, there's a copy of the 2009 edition of *Overview of the History of Philosophy.* Read it. If you don't understand how, pages 149 to 150 explain the basics. I'll contact you afterward. For reasons of safety . . . I suggest you prepare to be thought of as gay. Now, hit me."

"What?" I say, caught off-guard.

Redhead leers with utmost lasciviousness and reaches for my ass. I flail out a fist and punch him in the nose.

"Ow!" The bystanders burst into laughter so loud the guards look our way. Redhead scrambles upright, a hand over his bleeding nose, and leaves cursing with his meal tray.

"What did I tell you?" My cellmate appears with tray in hand and gives me a thumbs-up. "But you've got guts!"

I ignore him and stuff food into my mouth. Once I finish, I go to the reading room alone. On the bottom philosophy shelf, between Hegel and Novalis, I find the clothbound 2009 edition of *Overview of the History of Philosophy*. I sign it out from the librarian and take it back to my cell. The Mexican isn't back yet. I lie on my cot and flip open the heavy covers. I don't see anything special. From a glance, it's just a yawning pit of references and citations.

I flip to page 149, and see that someone's replaced this page. In the midst of headache-inducing philosophy-related proper names is a sheet of yellowing paper clearly torn from another book. The front is covered with completely irrelevant medical information on joint protection, while the back is mostly methods of head massage and corresponding diagrams. At the bottom is a three-hundred-word simple overview of a newly invented type of low-error, high-efficiency Braille. However, the development of more practical visual surgery techniques led to the decline of Braille, the book informs me. The new type of Braille was made obsolete before it was ever implemented.

Oh, of course. Braille. I shut the book and close my eyes. The outside covers only have the big embossed gold lettering, but on the inside cover, I find little bumps arranged in some sort of dense pattern. If you weren't paying attention, they'd seem like some oversight in quality control left the paper unevenly textured. I refer to the instructions and slowly decipher the Braille. The information is heavily compressed; it takes me almost two hours to understand the text on the inside cover.

"The finger-talking gathering welcomes you, friend," the unknown author greets. "You've certainly felt the changes, but you don't understand them. You're lost, angry, considered crazy by other people. Maybe you've bowed to the way things are. Maybe you're still looking for the truth. You deserve the truth."

I nod.

"This was an enormous program. The secretly ratified Thirty-Third Amendment allowed the formation of a Federal Committee for Information Security to filter and replace information that could pose a threat to social stability and national security. After lengthy test trials, a high-efficiency system called Ether slowly came together. At first, Ether only functioned to automatically monitor the Internet through network and Wi-Fi equipment. All text, videos, and audio it considered to be subversive would be put through hacking, sampling, and semantic network analysis. Once it found the forum hosting it, Ether would infiltrate all related conversations on that server. Everyone except the poster would see an altered post. In addition, the poster would be recorded by the database. For example, if you posted the topic "Senatorial Luncheon," it would be flagged as harmful. Ether's supercomputers had free legal rein to override all network firewalls, and would intercept the data packet at the interface and replace all keywords. Everyone else would see your topic as the uninteresting "KFC Super Value Lunch." This way, the federal government gained total control over the Internet. The tragedy is that most people never realized what had happened. They only pessimistically believed that the spirit of liberty was gradually disappearing on the Internet—exactly what the government wanted."

I feel a chill at my back. The Mexican comes in at this time and throws his dirty towel on my stomach. "Buddy, you should join the group exercises now and then."

"Shut up!" I yell with all my might. The Mexican looks blankly at me. His expression shifts from surprise and anger to fear. He looks away, afraid to meet my bloodshot eyes. My fingers move shakily across the flyleaf of *Overview of the History of Philosophy*.

"Following the success of Ether, the federal government's control over radio, television, and print was a foregone conclusion. The few members of the media who refused to collaborate with the Information Security Bill were isolated using a technology from the same origin as Ether. Nanoelectronic technology had been used to tamper with data exchange, and the people in power soon realized that nanobots could similarly tamper with data exchange through visible light. Seven years after the enactment of the Thirty-Third Amendment, they decided to release nanobots into the atmosphere. These tiny machines could remain suspended in air, using the silicon in soil and construction materials to self-replicate until the desired density was achieved. They were simple devices, activating once they reached the requisite density. They would detect subversive text—information in visible light waves—and subversive speech—information in sound waves—replace them with harmless data, and log their source. They could adhere to printed text and signs, polarizing light so that all observers besides the source would receive false optic data; they could alter the spread pattern of sound waves so all listeners except the source received false acoustic data. Since the source can receive the sound traveling through their bones, they'd hear the message they intended. These little demons floating in the air made Ether omnipotent and omnipresent, like the mysterious substance undetectable to mankind that the philosophers said occupied all space—the original ether."

I remember the psychiatrist's words: "All I see is the advancement of society and democracy." I clench my fists and grind my teeth hard enough to be audible.

"This is the era we live in, friends. Everything is a lie. The online forums are lying. The TV programs are lying. The person speaking across from you is lying. The protesters' signs raised up high are lying. Your life is surrounded by lies. This is a golden time for the hedonists: no conflicts, no war, no scandal. When the conspiracy theorists are locked away in the mental hospitals, when the last revolutionaries fade away in front of their lonely computer screens, only our fragile and perfect tomorrow awaits. We will dance our stately, well-mannered waltz at the cliff's edge, build our magnificent castle on quicksand.

"Who am I? I'm a nameless soldier, one of the criminals who created Ether. I'm not important. The important thing is that you should see these changes. You should know the truth. Now the truth is yours, and you can choose the path that lies ahead. Our fingers are our most precious resource, because in the next twenty years, within the range of foreseeability, nanobots won't be able to deceive humanity's sensitive sense of touch. If you make the choice, you can join the finger-talking gatherings through your mentor at any time, and enter the last and only resistance group under Ether's omnipresent surveillance. You will enter the only truth left in this world of lies.

"The finger-talking gathering welcomes you, friend."

I close the heavy covers. Thoughts and images are stringing themselves together in my mind. I've seen the truth, but I have even more questions now, and only whoever wrote these words can answer them. I brush my palm across the short gray bristles of my scalp, knowing I've already made my choice.

At dinner, when I see Redhead, I make a beeline for him and take his hand. The cafeteria is instantly in an uproar. We're going to be the butt of every joke, but I don't care. I write in his palm, "I'm in."

His smile is full of stories. "Welcome. The first gathering is in two days during group exercises, northeast of the woodwork factory. Our internal publications are in the philosophy section, second shelf, bottom layer, flyleaf of Nietzsche's collected works. Right, there's a flax-blond, freckled young lady in the female wing who wants me to ask "the sexy old bald guy" how he's doing. I think I'm talking to the right person."

I gape.

In that moment, I think of many things. I don't think of how to change the world with our primitive method of communication, but of all the things my father left me. I thought my father's beatings and curses had made me incapable of loving, but I've found that love is a piece of the human soul that can never be cut out, not just the tremble of hormones. I'd so hated my father, tried to reject every memory that included him year after year, but I've found that the child of an abusive father doesn't have to stay broken. The pain at least is real. I hate lies, even well-meaning lies, more.

I need to do as I did twenty-three years ago. I need to shout as loudly as I can to the guy trying to control my life, "Fuck you!"

She gives me courage, flax-haired, blue-eyed her. I grip Redhead's hand tightly, as if I can feel the warmth of her body through his skin. On our palms are written love and freedom, burning hot. Love and freedom, searing through the skin, branding the bone.

"I love you, Daisy—not you, don't get the wrong idea." Under countless eyes, I write it on Redhead's palm.

"Of course." Redhead is ready with his familiar, mischievous smirk.

Drone

by Miles Klee

The president's coma had taken a turn for the worse: she was dead. The VP shot himself before they could do the oath. Whoever came next in line met the void, called the wars off, and undid the draft. Those of us in the last week of boot woke at dawn, synchronized, to find the top brass had already split.

First thing we did was whoop it up. Then we showered and set out for the women's barracks to get it on. The women had had the same idea. We collided over the mortar range, which was dry and pockmarked and not ideal for fucking, but in the party that ensued we all got laid except Taylor, who despite running fifteen miles a day could just not stop being fat.

Taylor's fatness was a joke at first, when he couldn't keep up, but soon the joke became myth. We punched him on the pretext that he couldn't feel. A lady soldier half wearing my camo rode me in the hot dead grass, and I saw Taylor taking shade under the only tree, massaging feet that must have hurt like hell under all that weight.

The party depressed me after two days. By then I honestly couldn't believe I was me. I hiked to the airbase and hitched a plane to Jersey. Except it was resupply to Jersey the goddamn island. I got to London and fit a southie crew that mugged tourists in the Elephant and Castle pedways. Other gangs raped down there; we mugged. We'd rip cams and phones from helpless fingers to fence in Camden for hash. I beat up an Italian for his hat.

Hash didn't go far. Kyle burned through it so quick that we had to keep pace to smoke our share. My name is Kyle too, so they called me Kyle the American. Didn't like sharing my name, not with a gobshite who smelled of rotting vegetables. When the hash went, a game began: first to say "Morely's," the name of the foul kebab stand, had to walk down there and buy kebabs for all.

"Cah need another hit," Aliza was explaining. "Sorely."

"Ap!" Vernon pointed, and the rest of us shouted also, except Kyle the Englishman, who'd pushed a drunk banker in front of the Jubilee that day, fled into the two o'clock drizzle, all of it on CCTV.

"What," Aliza said. She wrote poetry that I read when she'd gone, because I am a sensitive monster. It was okay. The whole UK was okay, except for a low and troubling drone in my head. Anything not loud was a whisper.

"You said . . . it," I said.

"I didn't say Morely's!" she cried.

O, we howled. Howled more when she returned with kebabs. It plays in the mind like I was howling at this weeks later, well after the gang dissolved, when I was tackled and hooded in Paddington by men I never saw. I thrashed and screamed it was just panhandling, but the hood was soaked in fumes and it was a purple bloom that answered.

"You're awake," I was told. I tasted my snot and spat. It hung inside the hood with me. The bustle of Paddington had silenced. Ears felt pressure: we were in the air.

"Son, relax. Not so bad as that. Just there's protocol for recovering property. You ain't the first, and it's worse if we don't scuttle."

"Not your prop, Yankee cunt."

"Oh Jesus," the other man laughed. "You didn't pay for that accent coach I hope."

"Son," said the nice one. *Son*. Didn't load me up or push me out and I don't like the ones who did. My sister was into the money machine, she was set. I had a cousin who played pro tennis. Me, I was swimming in my own skull, no idea who to blame. "Face it. The company *trained* you. They own what's there, see? Invested."

I decided I wouldn't speak. We landed and shuttled to a camp that from smell I'd say was downwind of Philly. Looked around and if I looked as sorry as this lot I was sad: everyone had a black eye or slung arm. None could meet another's gaze.

A drill sergeant came into the tent and told us we were deserters, degenerates, subhuman retards for supposing the military disbanded in peacetime. Deserter with some teeth knocked out said he'd been discharged for self-harm. They hauled him off and told us to wave good-bye for good.

We were too tired not to.

The weird passed again into normalcy. There were meals. The exercise was good, body juiced at the lack of dope. I shared a triple bunk with Wilt and Johns, always together and much alike, so I never clicked who was who—we were pals. After we'd got some shape back they fitted us for flamethrowers. It was fun torching the straw men, but our fuelpacks weighed a motherfucking ton.

Job was to penetrate some pines and flush out the ferals who lived there. Halfway through, the officers stopped calling them "ferals" and starting saying "mud eaters." The mud eaters, inbred swamp trash that walked on all fours, had killed a resource exploration crew. With rocks.

The story made us mad. Wilt or Johns said they put drugs in the food, a dose of giddy insomnia. Johns or Wilt disagreed with Wilt or Johns, said they put a hard drive in each head they buzzed. I had to admit, the barber nicked me bad. An elsehood had driven me since, some cloud of simple demands.

We slogged through muck with flamethrowers and chased whatever ran. The muddies didn't eat mud; they were covered in it, camouflaged. Wilt and Johns, walking shoulder to shoulder, had a snake pit open under their feet. By the time we got a rope down, the bodies lay together, puffed with poison.

A fox shadowed me for a whole day's march. Except that was back in London . . . The animal had trotted soundlessly along a low stone wall that bordered the gardens of Borough High, perfectly happy to stroll at my side. The sun was the sun the day my brother got into Canada, so bright and close it went through the leaves. We flipped a coin and it rolled into a storm drain, so I told him to hop in the trunk.

It's true I was beyond sleep, but this was a bit much.

Adults couldn't be taken alive. A TV show laid claim to captured kids. We saw a taping as reward for abundant kills and captures. Behind the waxen flesh-colored host sat a wall of acrylic glass. Behind that: adolescent savages fought predators and extreme artificial weather as though their lives depended.

A female unit was half the audience, so the hour was seized by handjobs and clit rubbing. At one point a girl I'd yanked from a tree—receiving a kick in the larynx—ignored the fire-making tools and stood there in her frosted chamber, gazing over the moany lot.

I went around bleachers to the rear control room. The man and woman inside didn't see. They weren't talking about my muddie, down there on the stage. Woman worked the panel while the man just watched.

"Thought we could offset the cost of short-life organic LEDs with energy savings," she said. "They're efficient but decay fucks it up."

"You say organic?" the man wanted to know.

"Next-gen won't rely on polyanilines in the conducting layer."

God, I could have strangled them for saying these things, but I blacked the fuck out somehow. Rebooted choking on an oxygen tube they were trying to shove in.

"Hello, never mind," said one of the doctors. The tube slid out. I rasped and retched a bit and rolled over on my side. The room was silver. I glitched out again.

The world underneath me tilted. A boat. Some boys were huddled off at a porthole, discussing where the boat was pointed. South, they mainly agreed.

"Word banged round the muddies had a natural cancer defense, insurance lobby said wipe out."

"Christ. Extinction duty."

"How far you bolt, Saul?"

"Vancouver. It was beautiful. Did a hooker and she came in three languages. They caught me at the zoo watching penguins."

"Look who's up."

"Ey," I said. "Real penguins?"

"Real enough, buddy."

Destination we heard topside: Nicaragua. Vessel a destroyer, the USS *Spangled*. Here to dismantle the Zero Cartel with *local cooperation*. Commanding officer touched his face, hid beyond it.

He dreamt of a classical democracy that worked, that was not crippled by its weak. If he could strike us from history, fine.

First run became a classic botch. Signal flew; we opened fire on a salvage tub and killed four civilians, one pregnant. Smuggling themselves up Mosquito Coast. We waded through their sorry possessions.

"They shouldn't've," the commander began, confused. He never told us his name or rank, paranoid even for his kind. "Insurgents." He had us heave bodies overboard.

"Sir?" I said. "There's a war?"

"Agitators in the wild, that's all."

Plain old rogue economy, working places the capital couldn't. And the villagers were loyal. When we landed in a port town, it was to explode their illegal lobster fishery.

"Don't think so," said Saul before he swallowed the charge that splattered the deck with his self. Almost did the same but for some alien snag in my action. It was curious, now: whatever I saw or touched—ocean spray, my own hands—I sensed a simulation.

Cargo flowed out of the rain forest in canoes, shielded by triple canopy that satellites couldn't see through, into open water. We floated at jungle's edge in skimcraft, hoping couriers might blunder at us. Finally some wake. We thought the fins were sharks. Dolphins, it turned out.

"Been getting aggressive," our captain said. They began to breach as gray liquid missiles, knocking men into the water with their tails so that others could drag them down to expire beneath the waves. One landed square on the deck, flipped about, snapping her nubby white teeth.

No, this never happened. I was gone.

Wrong: I was here, reaching for a white preserver. They pulled me out of a life, they must have, though nothing about that life would assemble. I was crushed under the weight of things or falling through their total absence.

You'll stay, a distant quarter of me said. You'll steer out. You do not want for courage.

I crawled around the kamikaze dolphin to the dash. I threw the accelerator, and soon we slammed into beach, where two or three of us climbed over the prow and lay breathing on the sand.

It was tropical night when one of us spoke.

"I'm for disappearing."

Waited for my own agreement, but I was disappointed.

"Your call," said the disappearing man. The jungle swallowed him.

The stars: how I hated them. A star doesn't have to know itself.

That faraway part of me spoke again, a subzero voice that echoed down the spine. It said I had rested enough, and to run. Back toward some rendezvous, an outpost—the loving arms of the company. But what did this voice imagine running to be? Did it really suppose I could *run*?

We wouldn't ask if you couldn't, it said. You do magnificent work.

You are one of a kind.

Transcription of an Eye

by Carmen Maria Machado

ANNOUNCER: You are about to enter the courtroom of Judge Judith Sheindlin. The people are real. The cases are real. The rulings are final. This is Judge Judy. Sakshi Karnik is suing her ex-girlfriend, Lola Zee, for the balance of a loan, and an assault. Lola says the money was a gift.

BYRD THE BAILIFF: Order, all rise. This is case number 109 on the calendar in the matter of *Karnik v. Zee*.

JUDGE JUDY: Thank you.

BYRD THE BAILIFF: You're welcome, Judge. Parties have been sworn in. You all may be seated. Ladies, have a seat please.

JUDGE JUDY: Miss Karnik, according to your complaint, you and defendant used to be in a relationship, and while you were in a relationship, you loaned her an amount of money for the purposes of some sort of—event. Soon afterward, you broke up. You would like your money back for that and also payment for some damaged property. You also claim that the defendant assaulted you, and you feel like you endured a lot of pain and suffering, and also you needed some treatment, so you'd like compensation for that as well.

SAKSHI KARNIK: That's correct, Your Honor.

JUDGE JUDY: So before you broke up, you were in a relationship with Miss Zee for how long?

SAKSHI KARNIK: Yes, I—

JUDGE JUDY: Please speak up, I can't hear you.

SAKSHI KARNIK: Two and a half years, Your Honor.

JUDGE JUDY: Can you please tell me, first, about the money that you loaned her.

SAKSHI KARNIK: She asked me for money to throw a party.

JUDGE JUDY: A party? What kind of a party?

SAKSHI KARNIK: A birthday party, Your Honor. In her honor.

JUDGE JUDY: And when was this?

SAKSHI KARNIK: July 7, Your Honor.

JUDGE JUDY: July 7 of—what year?

SAKSHI KARNIK: Last year.

JUDGE JUDY: Go on.

SAKSHI KARNIK: And she said she wanted her guests to have everything. She wanted to afford them pleasures. And so she sent me away to buy them, the pleasures.

JUDGE JUDY: She sent you—to the grocery store?

SAKSHI KARNIK: Yes, Your Honor. She wanted game hens. Cornish game hens.

JUDGE JUDY: So you bought her groceries?

SAKSHI KARNIK: Yes, Your Honor.

JUDGE JUDY: And you brought them back?

SAKSHI KARNIK: Yes, Your Honor. I bought and brought them. Cornish game hens. Sage. Honey. Salty cheeses. Fragrant pâté. Vodka. Feta-stuffed olives. Not blue cheese because why do you hate me, do you hate me? Do you wish me dead? Flustered potato chips.

JUDGE JUDY: Ruffled potato chips?

    SAKSHI KARNIK: Those too.

JUDGE JUDY: Then what?

    SAKSHI KARNIK: She glazed the hens. She glazed them with oil, roasted them in the oven. She cut them in half with her shirt off. Her breasts were—

JUDGE JUDY: Excuse me?

    SAKSHI KARNIK: She cut into them with kitchen scissors. Into their breasts. Their bodies all grease and tendon and whistle-slicked. She wrestled with their gristle until they were vanquished. Flecks of salt and oil on her skin. In half. She cut them in half. Then she folded them together and let the sides drop down like a trap, released. You understand.

JUDGE JUDY: I certainly do not.

    SAKSHI KARNIK: What I'm saying is, afterward, after she left me, and found me, she whispered into my hair that she loved me. That she was sorry.

JUDGE JUDY: For not paying you back for the groceries?

    SAKSHI KARNIK: For everything.

JUDGE JUDY: But she never paid you for those groceries?

SAKSHI KARNIK: No.

JUDGE JUDY: What else, Miss Karnik? Any other expenses?

SAKSHI KARNIK: One morning I woke up and I was outside on the glass. The grass. It was wet. My teeth tasted like fillings. She was inside, in bed. A coyote slunk by, and I said sir, is it not too close to dawn to be out here, your kind? And he said ma'am, is it not too far from kindness to be out on this lawn? And I said touché.

JUDGE JUDY: Wrap up your story, Miss Karnik! How is that an expense?

SAKSHI KARNIK: My clothes were ruined.

JUDGE JUDY: Why were you out there?

SAKSHI KARNIK: She said that I had thoughts about others. That I wanted to leave her. That I was thinking about other people during—you know.

JUDGE JUDY: No, I don't know. During what?

SAKSHI KARNIK: Sex, Your Honor. She would grab my chin and say, "I can see you somewhere else, who are you thinking about fucking? Come back here, love me." And I would drift away. But only after. Never before.

JUDGE JUDY: Tell me about the assault.

SAKSHI KARNIK: And then I started getting sick. She made me sick.

JUDGE JUDY: What do you mean, she made you sick? When did she make you sick?

SAKSHI KARNIK: This morning, this beautiful autumn morning. I woke up, the air was thick and the color of honey, but darker, like a tamped-down sunrise. The window glazed with rain. I opened up the front door. Outside, it was chilly and wet. Golden leaves were pummeling off the trees, whizzing down into the brilliant green grass like bees, and the air leaked and loosened. Part of the sky was amber sun, part of it was dense, black clouds, and thunder snarled over-head. It was like some alien world being birthed, or perhaps coming apart—the end of its days. Then the light dimmed, the sky became grayer, and realness seemed to seep back into the air. When I left to go to work, my car was covered in splayed maple leaves that clung wetly to its sur-face like so many starfish.

JUDGE JUDY: On that morning, she made you sick?

SAKSHI KARNIK: Yes. She had one. I turned my face because I did not want it. But then she kissed me and kissed me and then there was this thing on my lip. This red thing. It was hot. It bloomed out of me.

JUDGE JUDY: I don't understand.

SAKSHI KARNIK: She said, don't you love me?

JUDGE JUDY: I still don't understand.

SAKSHI KARNIK: A fever sore, she gave me a fever sore.

JUDGE JUDY: A cold sore.

SAKSHI KARNIK: I'd never had one before but then she gave it to me.

JUDGE JUDY: You don't know that she did that, or that she even did it on purpose. Everybody gets cold sores. My grandkids get cold sores! Did she give them cold sores, too?

SAKSHI KARNIK: Probably not, Your Honor.

JUDGE JUDY: So you got a cold sore. So what?

SAKSHI KARNIK: And then it began to bubble and blister and then it erupted.

JUDGE JUDY: So. What.

SAKSHI KARNIK: And there was an eye there.

JUDGE JUDY: You got one in your eye?

SAKSHI KARNIK: No, Your Honor, when the blister burst there was an eye inside, watching me.

JUDGE JUDY: I don't understand.

SAKSHI KARNIK: It was her eye. She had always kept it on me but now it was there, in the open.

JUDGE JUDY: In the sore?

SAKSHI KARNIK: In the sore.

LOLA ZEE: If I may, Your Honor—

JUDGE JUDY: Hup hup hup hush.

LOLA ZEE: But Your Honor—

SAKSHI KARNIK: Rolling around as if the tender rim of the wound was a socket. Every time it blinked, I felt the nerves fire. It wept, sometimes. Infectious tears.

JUDGE JUDY: What happened next?

SAKSHI KARNIK: I felt like I was unraveling. I was ugly, watched. I begged her to make it go away. It knew what I was thinking. Knew I was afraid. I said please, please let me have my own mind back. I wept. It read my mind, betrayed me. I fell down in a street, crying. Eye was responsible.

JUDGE JUDY: You were responsible?

SAKSHI KARNIK: No, eye.

JUDGE JUDY: When you say that it read your mind—

SAKSHI KARNIK: It knew. It knew what I did in my room, alone. It knew what I read. It knew everything new. And she knew. Before she could possibly know.

JUDGE JUDY: What happened next?

SAKSHI KARNIK: And then the eye began interfering with my own eyes, like a signal. It interfered with my reading.

JUDGE JUDY: What do you mean?

SAKSHI KARNIK: I would try to read and the text would be blackened out, like a hand had gone over with a censor's hand. And it could read my thoughts and perceptions. It discerned and influenced like a king's mistress.

JUDGE JUDY: What did you do next?

SAKSHI KARNIK: I went to a woman who lived deep in South Philly, who was rumored to know how to make the eye go away.

JUDGE JUDY: And?

SAKSHI KARNIK: I found her. She told me to run.

███████████████████████████████████
███████████████████████████████████
███████████████████████████████████
███████████████

JUDGE JUDY: Did you █████████████████

SAKSHI KARNIK: I tried. I followed her directions exactly. I ██████ the goose. I cut its throat on the ██ moon and then █████ the bird, ate it █████ lying on the ██ where Lola and ████ once come, ██ come, and come, █████ burned sage, and rubbed orange █████ my hair and kissed the ground and licked my palms and prayed for deliverance. I wanted to be free. I needed to be.

JUDGE JUDY: What?

SAKSHI KARNIK: Free.

JUDGE JUDY: What did it cost you?

SAKSHI KARNIK: More than I had.

JUDGE JUDY: And then what?

SAKSHI KARNIK: Nothing. Nothing happened. It stayed there.

JUDGE JUDY: It's not there anymore!

SAKSHI KARNIK: You can't see it, but it's there. It's like the morning after a fine meal, and as you drowsily floss, you rock a sliver of basil leaf, which had been wedged between the cloven hooves of your teeth, into your mouth. And then among the notes of blood and wax, there is a sweet bite of herb, a memory.

JUDGE JUDY: But where is it?

SAKSHI KARNIK: It's hiding, Your Honor. It's shy.

[*Titters of laughter from audience*]

JUDGE JUDY: All of you, shhhh! I will kick you out. [*To* LOLA] All right, your turn. Uncross your arms! Now, tell me about this party.

LOLA ZEE: It was my birthday and I wanted to celebrate.

JUDGE JUDY: And how did you want to celebrate?

LOLA ZEE: You know, choice booze, choice food, choice weed.

JUDGE JUDY: Wipe that smirk off your face! She might be crazy but you've got an attitude and I don't like attitude. Byrd here will tell you that I hate attitude.

BYRD THE BAILIFF: [*Inaudible*]

LOLA ZEE: Sure. So I was going to buy all of the groceries and stuff but then I had stuff I had to do and she offered to buy the groceries. So she bought the groceries.

JUDGE JUDY: Did she offer, or did you ask?

LOLA ZEE: Oh, she offered.

JUDGE JUDY: Then what?

LOLA ZEE: She bought the groceries.

JUDGE JUDY: And you never paid her back?

LOLA ZEE: It was a gift. She was my girlfriend at the time.

JUDGE JUDY: Did she ask you to pay her half?

LOLA ZEE: Nope.

JUDGE JUDY: When did you and Miss Karnik break up?

LOLA ZEE: About a month later.

JUDGE JUDY: Miss Karnik, I'm afraid I can't award you anything. These groceries were—well, you bought the groceries. Presumably as a gift for the defendant's birthday. This cold sore was not an injury.

SAKSHI KARNIK: Fever sore, Your Honor.

JUDGE JUDY: Fever sore, cold sore, what difference does it make what it's called? It's the same thing.

SAKSHI KARNIK: It makes a difference to me, Your Honor. The cold lays the body low. The fever burns the body bright. One is submission. The other, resistance.

JUDGE JUDY: Well either way, it's not an assault.

SAKSHI KARNIK: But Your Honor—

JUDGE JUDY: Did you miss work?

SAKSHI KARNIK: No.

JUDGE JUDY: Did you go to the hospital?

SAKSHI KARNIK: I tried, but eye wouldn't let me.

JUDGE JUDY: Were you afraid for your life?

SAKSHI KARNIK: [*No response*]

JUDGE JUDY: Miss Karnik, I—

SAKSHI KARNIK: She doesn't need to pay me. No one needs to pay me. Just take it out. Please take it out. There's nothing between it and I, between eye and it. We are inseparable. I want to be separated. Eye does not, but I do.

JUDGE JUDY: Miss Karnik, you're no longer dating Miss Zee.

SAKSHI KARNIK: Not her. It. Please. Please. I need justice from the state.

JUDGE JUDY: From the state?

SAKSHI KARNIK: For my state.

JUDGE JUDY: Miss Karnik, I feel for you. This was obviously an unpleasant situation, one that you should be happy to be free of. But there are no damages here.

SAKSHI KARNIK: Your Honor—may I show you something?

JUDGE JUDY: No funny business, Miss Karnik.

SAKSHI KARNIK: On my life, Your Honor. None.

JUDGE JUDY: Fine. Byrd, take that from her. Miss Karnik, what is this?

SAKSHI KARNIK: A vial of my tears, Your Honor.

JUDGE JUDY: You know, Miss Karnik, they don't keep me up here because I'm beautiful. They—

SAKSHI KARNIK: I know, Your Honor. I wish I could say the same.

JUDGE JUDY: What do you want, Miss Karnik?

SAKSHI KARNIK: Anything, Your Honor. A dollar. A nip of thread. A piece of paper that says "You were right to trust." It's the symbol that matters, Your Honor. My honor, Your Honor. You understand.

JUDGE JUDY: Miss Zee, reach into your pockets.

LOLA ZEE: What?

JUDGE JUDY: Your pockets. Am I speaking English? Your pockets. Turn them out. What do you have there?

LOLA ZEE: A peppermint wrapper. A paperclip. A condom. A— another condom. A penny.

JUDGE JUDY: Please give her the penny and the paperclip.

LOLA ZEE: I don't—

JUDGE JUDY: Byrd, please take the paperclip and the penny. There, Miss Karnik. Are you satisfied?

SAKSHI KARNIK: Yes. Thank you. On the matter of the eye. The one that remains inside?

JUDGE JUDY: Miss Karnik, there's no eye. We're done here.

BYRD THE BAILIFF: Parties are excused, you may step out.

Final Interview:

LOLA ZEE: I don't know what she's talking about. She's crazy.

SAKSHI KARNIK: I'm not crazy, I just want to be alone again. So does eye. We are tired of each other.

LOLA ZEE: Whatever, yeah, I've moved on, no biggie. Got a new girlfriend.

SAKSHI KARNIK: Sometimes, I wonder if the eye is just below the surface, waiting.

LOLA ZEE: It's not like I did any of that stuff anyway, she's just crazy.

SAKSHI KARNIK: How else did she know that I think that fig seeds explode in between my teeth like tiny glass beads? How else would she know I knelt down in front of the mirror and spread? Why else would I have listened, and listened, long beyond the edge of my patience or understanding? How is it possible that love can stretch so thin, so long?

The Taxidermist

by David Abrams

Tucker Pluid stared at the hollow eyeholes, trying to decide. Blue? Hazel? Or the old standard, amber?

He pinched the bridge of his nose. This was important. Whatever he chose for Herman Knight's elk meant, essentially, that was the color of eyes the animal was born with. It didn't matter if no one ever saw a blue-eyed elk before. If that's what he glued in the head, then by gum, that's how it was when Knight shot it and dragged it off Arrow Mountain. Besides, from all he'd heard about the schoolteacher, Tucker doubted he'd even notice anything wrong with the head.

"A blue-eyed elk would serve the son of a gun right for getting lucky his first time out," Tucker said aloud in the dead silence of his workshop. His voice was muffled by the feathers piled in soft mounds, the furs folded and stacked like blankets, and the naked Styrofoam mannequins stored in a jumble along the west wall.

At forty-eight, Tucker Pluid was no longer embarrassed by the sound of his spoken thoughts. He'd worked alone in the drafty plywood-walled workshop for so many years, it had ceased to worry him. His trailer was on the outer limits of Flint where not even the strongest Wyoming wind could carry his voice into town.

He picked up a handful of glass eyes, most of them the tame amber the hunters expected; but a few of them were brighter and more exotic—the color of showcase gems or Caribbean lagoons. He shook them across his palm like dice, trying to decide.

For Tucker, this was the most critical step in the mounting process—never so crucial as that moment with that head, Herman Knight's elk head.

Herman Knight was sleeping with Tucker's ex-wife and that made all the difference in the color of eyes his elk received.

There was another reason Tucker held the glass eyes in his hand for so long, clicking them back and forth. Once the eyes were in place and Herman came to collect his elk, Tucker could watch his ex-wife's lover as if through a hidden security camera. He would retreat into his workshop where he would pick up a freshly labeled jar from the shelf above his workbench. Inside that jar would be the elk's real eyes and when Tucker Pluid so much as laid one finger on the glass of that jar, a lightning bolt would pass down his arm and shoot straight up his spine. Then he would close his eyes as the vision, sharp as the bitter smell of cordite, burst free in the back of his head. This was his gift from God: to peer into the homes of Flint through the eyes of the animals he mounted.

One year ago, at the beginning of moose season, Tucker Pluid was sitting in the congregation of the First Baptist Church of Flint when a tremor passed along his network of muscles, lit up his brain.

It was like, he later told the stuffed heads, the pews were wired with joy buzzers.

Tucker listened as the Reverend Donald Dodge read straight out of God's Word: "For His eyes are upon the ways of a man and He sees all his steps." Like a flaming meteor striking the earth, the verse lodged in his head, scattering all other thoughts. He'd been troubled by thoughts lately, plagued by dreams in which he seemed to have turned into a camera poking in and out of scenes from what looked liked TV sitcoms but that were, on morning-after reflection, actually the homes of his friends and neighbors. And now this verse from Reverend Dodge's lips seemed like a revelation, a clarity to the muddle. If he hadn't been sitting in the middle of church, Tucker Pluid would have clapped his hands together, loud as a gunshot, and shouted, "That's it! The eyes, the eyes!"

He held himself in check until he dashed home to his workshop and fished in the waste bucket behind his trailer until he stood there holding the antelope eyes—scooped out of Frank Withers's kill the week before—in the palm of his hand. The eyeballs were a soft, sticky mess, but he'd closed his fingers over them and concentrated.

After an initial, startling blur of sagebrush and black hooves in his peripheral vision, Tucker's sight sharpened and changed. He stared at Frank sitting in his kitchen. One forearm rested on the blue-checked oilcloth, the other hand stirred his coffee then tapped the spoon delicately on the rim. Frank took a sip and Tucker saw the tiny beads of light brown coffee clinging to the tips of his mustache hairs. Frank looked up along the wall where Tucker was perched, staring googly-eyed, and raised his cup to the freshly mounted antelope head. He smiled and said, "Looks like the ol' Pecker Factory's still in business, pardner."

Marilyn, Frank's wife, entered the kitchen. Her hair was tousled, as if she'd spent a restless night in bed. Frank turned to her and said, "Heckuva buck, isn't he?"

"If you say so, Studley," Marilyn purred as she dropped two slices of wheat bread in the toaster. "What say you to a little more, um, exercise?" Then, with a smile and a cocked eyebrow, she brought her hands to the belt of her robe, tugged once, and let everything fall open to her husband.

Tucker dropped the eyes on the workbench. They made a soft, spongy splat when they hit. He was too afraid to touch the eyes again and so he left them there like that for the rest of the day, the filmed-over pupils staring off in opposite directions.

Tucker was afraid of what he'd seen in Frank's kitchen, but he was equally afraid to turn away from what God was offering him. Two weeks earlier, the Reverend Dodge had delivered a sermon about the gifts God plants in every person, Christian and sinner alike, and though some people waste those talents, burying them in the earth and going on about their business, God's ultimate desire is to see those gifts used to glorify Him. Really, it was just a simple matter of cultivating the gift so that God would be fully pleased with Man.

The Reverend Dodge had been so earnest during the sermon, his face straining and his eyes shining, that Tucker wracked his brain for two weeks, studying himself in the mirror several times every day to figure out what gifts God had given him, Tucker Pluid, a battered old rodeo star who now made his living sewing up other folks' dead animals.

Then, when the Reverend Dodge read that verse about the eyes of God, it was like the Lord Himself snapped a puzzle piece in Tucker's brain. When he rushed home and touched the antelope eyes, he knew he'd found his gift.

At first he was skeptical, thinking he must be under some sort of spell—maybe Shirleen had gone to consult with a voodoo specialist during one of her shopping sprees to Denver. He didn't think she would, but he also wouldn't put it past her.

But, he reasoned, the magic was too authentic, too startling to be anything but something released directly from the Hand of God.

Over the past year, Tucker had learned his gift was by no means an exact science. Sometimes all he saw was a confused tangle of pine branches, magpie tails, and steaming dung piles. Sometimes all he heard was the exploding crack and then everything—the sky, the sage—was rolling uphill away from him.

However, most of the time when Tucker Pluid closed his eyes he was in the homes of his customers. He saw his banker, Glen Hume, frowning over crossword puzzles while his wife Gloria sang hymns in the kitchen and fixed a meal that sizzled in the frying pan. He watched Bill VanSant, hosting a cocktail party last New Year's Eve, reach up and stick his pinkie finger in the snarling nostrils of the wild boar he'd shot on his trip to Texas. His guests blew party favors at him and laughed as Tucker sneezed at his workbench.

Tucker stayed up long into the night, letting his eyes roam every corner of Flint. He'd wake up in the morning, head throbbing, and reach for a pair of eyeballs like a smoker reaches for his first cigarette of the day.

There was Edith Pond sitting on her sofa, watching Cary Grant movies around the clock after her husband died; Chance Gooding Jr. making out with Roseann Hume on his father's bed while the seven-foot rattlesnake Chance Sr. shot the previous summer coiled like a spring on the nightstand beside the bed; Juanita McPherson folding laundry and singing along with a John Denver album on the turntable; Ringo Smits copying his girlfriend's homework; the 6:00

a.m. regulars at the Wrangler Restaurant drinking coffee, smoking cigarettes, and staring up blank-faced at the wall of heads behind the counter.

Tucker preserved the dead animals' eyes in baby food jars. By now, he had several shelves of labeled jars, each with its own pair of eyes floating in formaldehyde like large pearl onions. He no longer needed to hold the hard, slippery eyes in his hands—he had only to touch the jars to start seeing through the walls of Flint's homes.

Eventually, Tucker limited himself to one pair of eyes a day. "After all," he said, "there's only so much of Flint a fella can take."

When he had time to think it through, Tucker Pluid had a pretty good idea he knew exactly when God first handed him this gift (though he hadn't recognized it for what it was back then).

It came at the end of his rodeo career—that hot afternoon in Billings, Montana, when the black, dusty hoof crashed down on his head, leaving a deep purple dent between his eyes; when everything—the sun, the foaming nostrils of the bronc, the pennants waving like colored hands from the announcer's booth—flicked off like a light switch.

He'd struggled up from the anesthetic two days later to hear a doctor telling Shirleen that he would never ride horses again, at least not like that. "We will want to keep a very close eye on him to make sure the concussion doesn't clot his brain," the thick voice said.

Shirleen told the doctor, "I've told him time and time again. This rodeo business . . ." She shook her head then said, "He looks like an overcooked noodle laying there, don't he?"

Five minutes later, after a long silence in the room, he felt Shirleen bend over him on the hospital bed, smelled her flowery Avon perfume, and heard her say, "I've had it with you."

Tucker's vision was gray and the edges tingled with broken dots for nearly a week. Now, looking back, he was certain God was fooling around with his eyes back then, fine-tuning the gift.

It was, as the saying goes, both a blessing and a curse. Three months ago, he'd received his greatest revelation from the tiniest pair of eyes—two little pebble-shaped globs from Tom Shane's three-pound cutthroat trout.

Tucker Pluid watched Tom straighten the fish on the dining room wall. "What a beaut. That Pluid sure does nice work. Doesn't he do nice work, hon?" He turned to his wife who was sitting on the davenport cross-stitching.

"Nice work on fish, maybe, but he's not so good with the people in his life."

"What's that supposed to mean?" Tom said.

His wife shrugged and licked the tip of her thread before poking it into the eye of the needle. "I hear things."

"What kind of things?"

"Things in the beauty shop, 4-H meetings, the post office. Things about your taxidermist's ex-wife."

"Shirleen? What about her?"

"How she's carrying on these days."

"Aw." Tom waved his hand in dismissal. "She's always carried on. Ever since she left him. Why she did that, though . . ." He trailed off and shook his head.

"Oh, we women know." Tom's wife chuckled and stabbed the needle back and forth through the linen.

"Huh?" Tom turned completely from his fish, the fish Tucker was inside, and looked at his wife. "C'mon, Maggie. What's with Shirleen? Why'd she do it?"

His wife sighed and let her stitching drop to her lap. "If you really have to ask, there's no way you'll ever understand."

"What's that supposed to mean?"

"It means that men like Tucker Pluid will never change. They're the tired old men of the West who never stop believing that work is the only thing worth living for."

"Well, sure—"

Maggie was on a roll and wouldn't be stopped. "To them, just putting bread on the table is more important than who's sitting around the table. Eventually, life gets the better of them, punches them down, and they just wither up and blow away."

Tom was silent for a few moments then, his voice higher and thinner, he said, "I'm not like that, am I, Mags?"

Tucker never heard her response because he slammed the jar onto the workbench with such force the tiny trout eyes swirled around in the formaldehyde, chasing each other like frantic tadpoles. He watched them for a long time, until they settled to the bottom of the jar and he could forget about Shirleen talking about him in the beauty salon.

"I never asked for this," he'd tell the wood ducks, bighorn sheep, and largemouth bass on his worktable. The animals, in various stages of preparation, stared back at him, mouths closed and nostrils shining with shellac.

To stop touching eyeballs would be to disappoint God, he thought. God was up there watching him watch Flint and yet He offered no relief for all that Tucker Pluid saw. Tucker walked around town much more slowly this hunting season, wary of nearly everyone he met. When he saw Danny Kingston in the post office or Bret Meyer in the aisles of the grocery store, Tucker shied away, trying not to look at the hands he knew slapped the women and children late at night when the shades were pulled. Then there were those who cheated at pinochle or lied about their sex life to the others in the office. Tucker was especially shocked to see those in his own church—the ushers, the deacons, the pillars of the congregation—who never even cracked open their Bibles until Saturday night.

"God," Tucker whispered in the silence of his workshop, "preserve me from their unrighteousness."

Once Tucker swore off the eyes for a week after the morning he sat down next to Charlie Holt at the Wrangler's coffee counter and heard him tell Shellie, the counter waitress, about the operation his wife needed. "It's some newfangled procedure she says will help straighten her spine. She's had that slump ever since I can remember. Now, after all these years, she says there's this doctor over in Casper who can fix her up good and she don't even have to go under the knife."

"Modern medicine's something else, isn't it?" Shellie said, freshening their cups.

"I tell her I'll do whatever it takes to make her happy," Charlie said with a shy grin. "Wish I could go, but it's right in the middle of deer season."

Tucker knew Charlie was worried about putting meat on the table this year. It had been a slow summer down at the appliance store and he was sitting up late at night, hunched over the desk in the den, surrounded by his big game trophies from past seasons. While he fiddled with the calculator and shipping invoices, his wife was up in their bedroom underneath the whitetail deer placing calls to her lover in Casper. She cupped her hand over the phone and whispered dirty talk so pornographic that she blushed between her soft giggles.

Charlie was still telling Shellie about the miracle operation when Tucker got up from the counter, put his money beside his coffee cup, and left without saying a word.

For seven days, Tucker Pluid avoided the eyes, afraid of the pain he might bump into. He threw himself into his work, filled his nostrils with the smell of chemicals and cured hides, spent hours polishing antlers, painted as many lifelike expressions onto the dead faces as he knew how.

"Everything's fine, don't worry about me, I'm holding steady," he told the heads on the table.

Then, on the seventh day, his hand brushed one of the baby food jars and he saw, without warning, Jacqueline Rodgers, the young cashier at Flint Foodland, sitting naked in front of her mother's vanity. As she looked in the mirror, she brushed her waist-length hair with a silver-backed brush and hummed a hauntingly beautiful song, a hymn Tucker recognized from church. He knew he'd never be able to watch her scan his groceries again without thinking of her long hair and milk-colored skin. He listened to Jacqueline sing for nearly five minutes before he released that jar and started touching others on the shelf.

Sometimes Tucker Pluid thought he would go pleasurably insane with all he knew and he wondered if God, the All-Seeing, ever had enough of the folks living down here. "Someday," Tucker said, "I bet His head's gonna explode and all the stars will fall out of the sky."

Tucker Pluid finally decided to give the elk one blue and one green because a freak of nature was the only thing Herman Knight could ever kill.

He pressed the eyes into the head so hard and for so long he thought the glass was about to break under his white-nailed fingertips.

He relaxed his grip. The elk stared at him, lop-eyed and unperturbed.

"Just wait!" Tucker shouted at the elk head. "Just you wait and see. In a few days you'll be up there on his wall and then"—Tucker got nose-to-nose with the elk—"then we'll know what's really going on, won't we?"

Tucker's head pulsed and he ran his fingers through his thin, graying hair. He thought of Knight's apartment—spare and unfurnished in his imagination—and he felt an anticipation building in his veins like he hadn't felt in years, since he was straddling the chute, poised for that one instant above the restless back of the bronc.

He paced the workshop. His bum leg throbbed like a heartbeat.

Herman Knight took up with Shirleen two months ago, at the start of hunting season, when he met her at a parent-teacher conference to discuss the plummeting grades of Shirleen and Tucker's son, Jack.

Jack Pluid sat in a corner of the room and scowled behind the latest issue of *Heavy Metal* while his teacher and his mother talked about him. He propped the magazine in front of his face and pretended to read, but listened to every word they said in their low, conspiring voices.

Herman Knight was Flint High School's newest English teacher and when he spoke to Shirleen about her son he wore a tie that cut into his neck and made his eyes bulge slightly. He sat at his desk and said, in a tight, rasping voice, "Let's talk about your son's progress."

Shirleen, sitting in one of the student desks, said, "Progress? I'll be happy if you can just keep him from dropping out."

"He's doing fine, really. We're studying subject-verb agreement and he doesn't seem to be having too much difficulty. I understand his grades in the past have been rather low, but I think we can pull those up this semester."

Shirleen leaned forward so that Herman Knight could clearly see down the cleft of her half-buttoned shirt and said in a breathy voice, "You wouldn't lie to me, would you, Mr. Knight?"

Knight cleared his throat, put his eyes elsewhere. "Herman, please."

"Are you sure you're telling me the truth about my son, Herm?"

"Let me be perfectly honest with you, Mrs. Gerstein."

"Ms. Gerstein. But I'd prefer Shirleen."

"Shirleen," Knight said and got up from behind his desk and sat next to Shirleen. He looked directly into her eyes. "You have nothing to worry about with Jack. I'll keep pushing him forward."

"What a relief," Shirleen said, putting her hand to the bottom of her neck and releasing a nervous laugh. "Here I was, all uptight about this conference, thinking this new English teacher I'd heard so much about was gonna put him in a slow readers' program or something."

"No, nothing like that," Knight said.

"I'm so relieved," Shirleen said, her voice low and purring.

"We move on to predicates next week."

"Predicates? They sound dangerous."

"Oh, they *are*," he said and they both laughed, Shirleen leaning farther forward and Knight's eyes pulled downward, watching the way the front of her shirt bobbled.

Shirleen's conference had gone overtime, cutting fifteen minutes into Gloria Hume's session. When she and Knight spilled out of the room, giggling like schoolchildren, there was Gloria tapping her foot and checking her wristwatch.

That night, Shirleen went home and played all of her Nat King Cole albums while downing a six-pack of beer.

Tucker learned all of this from Jack. For once, he was thankful not to have a stuffed animal mounted in the English teacher's room.

Tucker got most of what he needed to know about his ex-wife from his son. He and Shirleen hadn't spoken to each other since the divorce, that day they left the Sublette County courthouse together and his bum leg suddenly gave out on him and he scraped his knuckles on the sandstone brick facade when he reached out to support himself. Tucker Pluid stood there for what seemed an eternity sucking on his knuckles and watching her car drive down the street, the brake lights flaming to life at the stoplights. Tucker Pluid stood there waiting for God to interrupt the eternity, to reach down with His hand, to turn her car around in traffic and steer her, like a miniature toy, back to him.

Since then, he'd often seen Shirleen around town, but for years she ducked his attempts at conversation and gave him the cold shoulder when they were standing in line at the post office. Soon, Tucker gave up trying and eventually he stopped waving at her when he passed in his pickup truck.

"So what do you think?" Tucker asked his son. He was sanding the nose of a mule deer mannequin and Jack was leaning against the doorway with his hands in his pockets.

"About what? My grades?"

"No," Tucker said. "About your mother and your teacher."

Jack shrugged. "He's an asshole."

"Don't use that kind of language in this house."

"All right, he's a prick who thinks the world revolves around his prick."

"Jack, I'm warning you—"

"What*ever*, Dad. You asked, I told."

The two of them fell silent, listening to the rasp of sandpaper. Jack was leaning against the shelf full of jars and though he had never asked his father about the eyes, Tucker knew his son wondered about them. Tucker Pluid longed to share his gift with him and often prayed that God would reach down and touch Jack, too. Then Tucker would pull a certain jar from the shelf and press it between Jack's fingers until his son was able to see the children spilling through the halls of Flint High School, the metal lockers banging and the voices crushing all other sound from the air. If he held the jar long enough, Jack might see the teachers coming from their rooms once the halls were quiet, locking their classroom doors behind them and rinsing out their coffee mugs in the teachers' lounge. In that particular jar, there were four eyes and they belonged to the heads of the two wild mustangs mounted above the school's trophy case. Painted on the wall between the horse heads were the words: WELCOME TO FLINT HIGH SCHOOL, HOME OF THE 1979 CLASS AA HIGH SCHOOL RODEO CHAMPS.

Jack did not ask to hold the jars. Instead, he said in a low, flat voice, "I think he's gonna start shacking up with her."

Tucker Pluid blew the dust off the deer's nose. Tiny drops of his spittle darkened the Styrofoam. He thought about rain hitting this deer's nose during a lightning storm in the valley. Then, he wondered if the deer would actually feel those drops since his nose was always cold and wet.

Tucker Pluid sighed. He knew so little about the ways of animals.

"You hear what I said, Dad?"

"Yes." He turned to Jack with a fallen look on his face. "I heard." He got up from the stool. "Tell you what, let's go heat up that frozen pizza now."

Five weeks after his talk with Jack, when Herman Knight pulled into Tucker's driveway and gave two short taps on the horn of his Toyota hatchback, Tucker felt a tingling in his guts like he hadn't felt since that Sunday in Reverend Dodge's congregation.

He stopped in the tiny living room of his trailer and peered through the small, unwashed window before going outside to meet the man.

Herman Knight had called a day earlier and they'd arranged the delivery of the elk.

Knight got out of his car and came toward the trailer. He was a small man, thin in the chest, with pale, acne-pitted cheeks. Tucker Pluid relaxed a little—but not completely.

He swung open the door. It banged against the side of the trailer as if caught in a hard gust of wind.

"Oh," said Herman Knight. "There you are. I've brought the elk."

Tucker grabbed for the door and pulled it shut behind him gently. He hadn't meant for it to be that loud and dramatic. "Let's go take a look," he said.

Together, they walked to the rear of the hatchback.

"I brought the whole thing."

"I can see that," Tucker said.

The entire carcass, bled and gutted, was stuffed into the car—the hatchback tied down over the splayed legs, the cream-colored torso twisted and pressed up against the side windows, the head and antlers jammed into the front passenger seat. Tucker noticed a growing rip in the upholstery where the seven-point rack had dug in. A plastic tarp was spread in the back to catch any still-seeping blood.

Tucker had already heard stories from his other customers of how Knight dragged the elk halfway down Arrow Mountain to the road where the Toyota was parked. In spite of himself, Tucker Pluid marveled at the schoolteacher's apparent strength.

"I didn't know what you'd need, so I brought it all," Knight said in a high, raspy voice. "This was my first one, you know. Since I'm new in town, I wasn't sure where to take it. I asked around and heard you do good work."

"That so?" said Tucker.

"I've never killed anything like this before, but I was surprised how easy it was. I just stepped out of my car and saw him up near the trees." Knight fumbled with a knot on the hatchback's tie-down rope.

"Here, let me," said Tucker and he sliced the cord with the knife he carried on his belt.

"Thanks. So, when I saw him, I grabbed my rifle. I made sure I was far enough off the road and then I put the rifle up to my shoulder and *boom!* it was all over, his legs just kicked out from under him. It was pretty messy—blood everywhere. All very Hemingway-esque."

"That right?" Tucker said. He pulled the elk from the rear of the car, grabbing the hind hooves and tugging until the shoulders flowed out in a tumbling rush and the antlers clattered against the chrome bumper. The car sprang up, free of the dead weight.

The two of them stared at the elk as if it were a puddle of spilled coffee there in the gravel driveway.

"I cleaned him out myself," Knight said. "Like I said, it was my first one so I hope I did okay."

Tucker knelt and examined the ragged knife cuts running down the belly. "Seems fine," he lied. He looked up at Knight. "All I really need is the head and part of the hide back to the shoulders." He drew a line across the creamy coat with his finger.

"I wasn't sure so I brought the whole thing."

"What are you going to do with the meat?"

Knight shrugged. "Don't really need it. I eat out a lot."

"Well." Tucker scratched the back of his neck though it didn't itch. "I know a few folks in this town could use half an elk in their freezer this winter."

"Doesn't matter to me. I was just going for the trophy."

Knight's voice had a high-pitched, spoiled-kid quality that irritated Tucker. He scratched his neck again then went inside the trailer for a handsaw. When he returned, Knight said, "You're Shirleen's ex, aren't you?"

"Yep," said Tucker. He knelt and ran his hand along the dark neck, feeling for the vertebrae.

"She and I met at school. I've got your son in my English class."

"So he tells me."

"You two have talked?" Knight seemed surprised, then worried.

"A little. He only comes over every now and then. He likes to watch me put the animals together." Tucker filleted the hide away from the shoulders and neck then started to saw.

"I'll be honest with you," Knight said. "Shirleen and I have gone out for a couple of drinks."

"That so?" Tucker hacked through the neck, secretly touching the elk's sticky eyeballs as he worked and feeling a special thrill of anticipation at the flood of images inside his head. He saw Flint far below, shrouded in early-morning haze. He stood on the rocky slope of Arrow Mountain, grass in his mouth, steam rising from his black nostrils. His harem, the half-dozen female elk, lingered in the trees, watching him eat.

"She doesn't talk much about you," Knight said.

Tucker severed the head and set it aside. "Well, I don't think much about her either." He stood, putting the weight on his good leg.

"She said you used to be a rodeo star."

"That what she said—a star?"

"I think those were her words. Maybe not."

There was a long pause as both men stared again at the carcass, now abbreviated and less graceful.

"Well." Herman Knight patted his pocket and pulled out his checkbook. "How much do I owe you for the deposit?"

Tucker named the amount and waited for Knight to write the check. Tucker put the check in his shirt pocket; then he asked the schoolteacher to help him drag the carcass around to the winch at the back of the trailer where together they hoisted it aloft so it could bleed out.

Tucker offered the use of his sink to wash up, but Knight just looked at the blood on his hands, smiled, and said no, he'd leave it there for Shirleen to see.

After the Toyota drove away from his trailer, Tucker went inside, dug out the eyes with his index finger, and dropped them into a jar with a flourishing sweep of his hand.

AND SO, TUCKER Pluid set to work, burying himself in fur and bone and viscera. This was his busy season, when the men, women, and children came down from the hills around Flint, carrying deer across their shoulders, clutching fistfuls of sage grouse by the legs, hauling moose on sledges pulled behind ATVs. They came to him in earnest, looking at him with shy smiles, punching him lightly on the shoulder, telling him they couldn't wait to see him work his magic. Tucker nodded, grinned, assured them he'd do right by all their hard work—because hunting *was* hard work: high-stepping through endless miles of sage, snow, and downed trees; fording icy streams; toting food, weapons, tents, and emergency gear on serious weekend trips into the valleys beyond the mountains; sitting still as stones even in wind and needle-sharp rain; watching, watching, watching. Let's face it, hunting could kill a man's soul as sure as any firefight in Vietnam. It was Tucker's job to reward that hard labor with a work of art that re-animated the dead on a canvas of thread, glass, Styrofoam, and wire.

Tucker bent over his worktable. He carved, he stitched, he glued. There were so many new orders, so many fresh-kill animals, he almost couldn't keep up. The bodies piled up, the stink filled his small trailer, and still he worked as fast as he could, plunging his fingers into chest cavities, snipping, tucking, gluing, painting. He ate his dinners alone under the cone of his work light, stopping every now and then to pull a long bristly hair off the end of his tongue.

All the while, an elk sat in the corner of the shop, watching him through hollowed-out eye sockets. It said everything with its silence.

"Yes," Tucker whispered in response. "You're next, you son of a gun. You're next."

TWO WEEKS LATER, it was Shirleen who made the trip out to Tucker's trailer. He stood in his living room and watched her pull into the driveway, gravel crunching beneath the Toyota's tires. Tucker turned away from the window and looked at the elk head leaning against the inside of his front door. The fur still smelled of glue and the painted muzzle could stand another hour of drying, but he was anxious to get rid of the mount, to get it inside the schoolteacher's house. His mouth felt full of cotton, as if he were about to take the wildest ride of his life.

"She's driving his car," Tucker Pluid told the elk. "That's not a good sign."

The elk seemed to smile with his blue and green eyes, though his muzzle was clamped shut in a neutral expression. Tucker grasped the head by the large branches of its rack and brought the face up to his eye level. He had done his best work on this head, adding a barely noticeable curve to the neck and cocking one ear at a forty-five-degree angle as if the elk were listening to a rival bull's challenging bugle echo off a canyon wall at the moment he was shot by Herman Knight. Tucker liked to think this bull had been about to draw a breath for a louder, more operatic reply.

Shirleen sat in the Toyota, watching him watching her. Exhaust smoked up from the back of the schoolteacher's car.

Tucker walked out of the trailer and carefully carried the elk head to the passenger side of the car. Without turning off the engine, Shirleen got out, holding her unzipped coat together with one hand, and walked around to open the door for him. Tucker placed the head in the seat, facing forward. On impulse, he strapped the seat belt across the elk's neck so it wouldn't roll on the drive home. He stepped back and Shirleen closed the door with a hard thud that got muffled in the cold November air.

Then they turned and spoke to each other for the first time in more than a decade.

"Well—" Tucker said.

"So—" Shirleen said.

Tucker looked down at his boots, his left leg half cocked to one side. "I hear our boy's starting to improve with the English language."

"We're working with him," Shirleen said.

"'We'?" Tucker said, looking up along the length of her body until he met her eyes. I shouldn't have done that, he thought. I should just look away and forget about those legs, those hips, that rib cage.

"Jack's teacher and I," Shirleen said. Her warm breath steamed the air between them. "Herman and I."

"Well, whaddaya know," Tucker said. "Is he a nice fellow?"

"Fuck you, you son of a bitch," Shirleen said.

"Please," Tucker said with a wince. "Don't use that kind of language."

Shirleen continued as if she hadn't heard, the breath leaving her mouth in sharp puffs, like a teapot finally coming to boil. "You goddamn son of a bitch. You stand there and act like you don't know a thing, but you know everything, don't you?"

"Flint's a small place," Tucker said, trying not to smile. "I can't help but know everything."

"Yeah? Well, you don't know the half of it," Shirleen said, her words tumbling out like guts from a knife-slit belly. "Herm's not like you. He's got goals. He's going someplace. This teaching job here, it's just a stepping-stone for him, that's all. He's a forward thinker. Always leaning into the wind. That's what he tells me. *Lean into the wind.* You, you always got blown around like tumbleweed. And you can just wipe that shit-eating grin off your face because you know what I'm talking about, Tucker Pluid."

He swallowed and heard his throat click. He hadn't expected any of this—Shirleen coming out instead of Knight, then suddenly attacking him. Now, he just wanted to get rid of the elk.

"I never wanted to come out here today," Shirleen said, as if reading his thoughts. "I even told Herm not to come out here in the first place, but he said it would be good therapy. He said if I came out here, it'd be like leaning into the wind."

"He said all that?" Tucker said.

"Yeah." A strange expression crept over her face. She dropped her hand and her coat fell open. "Hey. I just realized something."

"What?"

"Look at me, Tucker."

He looked.

"I'm still standing, aren't I?"

Indeed she was. She stood with her hands on her hips, the coat fallen open to reveal more of the soft curves that kept him awake, delirious, all those nights since their divorce.

"Aren't you cold?" Tucker asked her. "Do you want to come inside and warm up?" His voice hitched with agony even as he said this.

Shirleen tipped her head back against her collar and laughed. Tucker grew dizzy at the sight of the muscles along her throat pumping up and down, the tiny chin bobbing and the sensual plumes of breath at her lips. His leg trembled.

"You know what?" Shirleen said when she'd caught her breath. "He was right. This was better than I thought it would be. I actually feel good." She twirled around, dancing a short jig in the gravel driveway. "Woooooo! No more pussyfooting around town for me."

She stopped and stared directly at Tucker, her eyes shining like chips of glass. "You can do what you want with your life, but I'll tell you one thing, Tucker Pluid: I've had it with you." She pointed her finger at him and he felt himself deflate with each poke. "I mean I've really, truly had it with you. Once and for all."

She skipped around to the driver's side, got in the still-running car, her new lover's car, and backed out of the driveway. As the car retreated, the elk head stared at him with its odd eyes.

Tucker Pluid walked back into the trailer, forgetting to shut the door so the cold air rolled in like fog around his legs. He moved around the tiny kitchen, putting a frozen dinner in the microwave though it was still the middle of the afternoon. When he ate the dinner, he discovered a hard, unthawed spot in the middle of the food, but he continued to eat, pretending not to notice.

He wiped his mouth, got up from the table, and walked back through the trailer to his workshop, the cold, foggy air from outside chasing him down the narrow hallway.

He stared at the row of jars, at the pairs of eyes floating in each one. He knew every one of those eyeballs intimately, he'd removed them from the sockets himself, as gently as a gardener lifting potatoes from the ground. He'd labeled the baby food jars, but after so many months there was no need for that anymore. He knew where every pair of eyes would lead him.

He thought of the breasts he had seen, the bare, saggy buttocks flashed during early-morning trips to the toilet. Tucker thought about the arguments, the dirty jokes, the cruel asides, the gossip, the injuries, the infidelities, the petty malice, the defeats, the triumphs at someone else's expense. All that sinning. Tucker stood there in his workshop, his eyes sweeping across the row of jars, and for the first time in months, he felt weakened by all that he knew. He trembled to think everything he'd preserved in his jars was just one small drop in the mighty brain of God. Even if he had the eyes of every animal killed on Arrow Mountain by every hunter in Flint, there would still be events beyond his control.

"There are some things we'll never know," he murmured, without realizing he'd spoken. "Shouldn't know."

He looked at the newest jar on the shelf.

Then Tucker Pluid told himself: If I do this, if I touch that jar and close my eyes and think about the inside of his house, I will be tortured beyond repair. He remembered a cowboy he knew on the circuit, a shy bull rider from Rawlins who always stood on the outside of conversations but watched everyone with moist, caramel-colored eyes. One time, he let go of the halter and got tossed between the horns like a rag doll. No one knew why he'd unwrapped the rope from his hand, but they'd all stood there near the chutes and watched him do it. While the bull rider was in the intensive care unit, the doctor came out and told the other riders who were standing there holding their hats, "I'm sorry. It's no use. He's beyond repair."

Tucker thought of that cowboy now for the first time in fifteen years and he felt something inside him drain away.

One day, before he was broken across the horns of the bull, the rider with the soft brown eyes told Tucker that knowing the bull or the horse you were about to get on was the worst thing in the world. "If you've been on his back before," he said, "then you know what to expect. You end up anticipating which direction he'll kick and your body leans that way, but then when his legs shoot out in a different direction—snap! Off you go."

Tucker took a deep breath and looked up at God.

"God," he said, "the gift is too large. Take it back." He was sorry for talking to God like that, but there was nothing else he could do since Shirleen had shrunk his world that afternoon.

Tucker Pluid reached up with both hands, fingers clammy with sweat, and grabbed a pair of baby food jars. For an instant, his mind hummed and brightened, crazy with images: Jacqueline Rodgers brushing her hair in a waterfall over her breasts, Herman Knight and Shirleen locked in a never-ending embrace in the apartment's living room where Tucker recognized two hunting prints he used to own now mounted on the wall opposite the elk head.

Then Tucker raised the jars above his head and sent them splintering to the floor. He reached for another and another and another until every jar was gone and he stood, panting, hearing only the ragged breath in his throat and the wind shaking the plywood walls of the workshop. Then, Tucker Pluid, the broken cowboy, the great preserver of all things dead and wild in Flint, covered his face with his hands and sobbed while, at his feet, hundreds of eyes looked up at him.

Second Chance

by Etgar Keret

translated by Miriam Shlesinger

On the face of it, it seemed like just another service—innovative, revolutionary, monstrous, call it whatever you want but when you came right down to it, Second Chance was the greatest economic success story of the twenty-first century. Unlike most great ideas, which tend to be quite simple, the idea behind Second Chance was a bit more complicated: Second Chance gave you the opportunity to go to one particular critical moment in your life, and instead of having to choose either one road or the other, you could continue along both. Can't decide whether to have the abortion and drop your boyfriend, or to marry him and start a family? Not sure whether you should start from scratch overseas, or stay put in your dad's business? Now you can have it both ways. How does it work? Well, it's like this: You've reached the most important crossroad in your life and you can't make up your mind? Just head for the Second Chance outlet nearest your home and give them a full rundown on your dilemma. Then choose one of the options, whichever you want, and keep on living your life. Don't worry, the other option, the one you didn't choose, doesn't disappear. They have it running on one of their If-Only-I'd computers (Reg. Tr.), carefully keeping track of all the variables. Once you've gone through your life in full, your body is taken to one of the Road-Not-Taken halls (also Reg. Tr.), where the entire data set is fed into your brain in real time, and kept alive through a unique bio-electronic process developed expressly for this purpose. So actually, your own brain can give you the experience of the other life you could have had, down to the last detail.

Miri or Shiri? Teary or cheery?
Placid old age or perhaps hara-kiri?
A child or a pup? IVF or adopt?
Move to Miami or pick up where you stopped?
At Second Chance, whatever you do—
You can have your cake and eat it too.

It's perfect. Seriously. Nothing cynical about it. It's a fabulous concept. I mean there aren't many inventions that actually succeed in meeting some human need. Ninety-nine percent of them are just some ugly combo of pushy marketing and spineless consumers. And Second Chance is clearly in that single significant, useful percentile. Except what does that have to do with Max?

Our Max lived his life straight as an arrow, fast as lightning, no ifs, no buts, at least until now. Max's dad—well, that's a different story altogether. Max's dad not only opted for Second Chance, he never stopped talking about it either: "If it weren't for that rotten Second Chance, I'd never—and I do mean never—have married that revolting mother of yours," he'd tell Max at least once a day. "I swear, sometimes I feel like putting a bullet through my head, just so I can finally make it to Road-Not-Taken." (By the way, a bullet through the head specifically is a very poor choice. Second Chance assumes absolutely no responsibility for the quality of service in case of major damage to cerebral tissue.) Max knew that his father didn't really mean it, and he hoped that his mother realized this too, but even if she did, it didn't make his dad's behavior any less upsetting. "If he'd taken the Second Chance in connection with my being born instead," Max tried to console her, "he'd have been just as obsessive: 'I feel like putting a bullet through my head just so I can relive my life without that egotistical kid. If I went and died tomorrow I bet he wouldn't even bother coming to the funeral.' You know how Dad is, it has nothing to do with you."

The truth is that his mother really did opt for Second Chance in connection with having him, but she was tactful enough never to let on about it. In her case, the Road-Not-Taken would have led her to a quick divorce, a successful business venture, and a happy second marriage. No harm done, she'd get a chance to live that life too.

Max had always preferred women who were curvy, tan, with big tits and thick lips. And Shana, who was very very pretty, by the way, was the complete opposite. She was skinny, flat as a board, and her lips were about as thick as a credit card. But love, as the saying goes, is blind, and Max fell in love. Before the wedding they didn't opt for Second Chance, or before the twins either. Max was against it in principle. He said people ought to assume responsibility for their own decisions. And as for Shana, she'd already wasted hers long before that on a previous boyfriend, whose proposal she'd turned down in her regular life. The thought that after her death she'd experience marriage with someone else was pretty frustrating as far as Max was concerned, but it was also motivational. And the need to feel that he was the right choice often drove him to be a better husband.

Years later, about six months after Shana had used up her first chance and had left Max on his own, his grandchildren asked him what his Second Chance had been, and he said he hadn't had one. They didn't believe him. "Grandpa's a liar," they shouted. "Grandpa's embarrassed." People had almost stopped using Second Chance by then, and had moved on to Meeny Miny Mo, which gave you an intriguing third option to explore, at no extra charge.

'Cause two birds in the bush
Can't beat three—all for you.
Meeny Miny and *Mo*
Nothing different will do.

Strava

by Steven Hayward

Strava is a smartphone application invented by Michael Horvath and Mark Gainey, a pair of friends who were crewmates in college and missed competing with each other after they moved to different cities. Early in 2009 they realized GPS data had become specific enough to identify climbs based on elevation and distance and that it should be possible to record people's times and compare them. This is what Strava does. It tracks your movement. It tells you how fast and how far you ride and compares you to the rest of the world. You upload your data and it takes your measure.

The application launched in early 2010 and now has about ten million users worldwide. I am one of them. My name is Tim Babcock, and I'm forty-four years old. This puts me at the very edge of the thirty-five-to-forty-four age bracket on Strava. Twenty-nine days from now I'll turn forty-five and expect to see a consequent jump in my Strava ranking.

I am not, ordinarily, a competitive person. As a child I was the sort of kid who had his nose perpetually stuck in a book. I'm an English professor by profession. I do not play football or baseball. I am a poor swimmer. But who among us cannot be swept up in something larger than ourselves? Who among us does not want to win?

STRAVA WAS BROUGHT to my attention by my new physician, Smith Barnard. At the time I was sitting on the edge of an examination table in my underwear in his Colorado Springs office. It was my first appointment with him.

Colorado Springs is a city of a half-million people built into the foothills of the Front Range, an hour south of Denver. The people who live here tend to be part of two distinct though occasionally overlapping groups: they are either in the military or are ex-Olympic athletes. Smith Barnard belonged to both groups. He'd been a reserve on the 1992 Olympic volleyball team, and had spent two years training in Colorado Springs, at the Olympic Training Center in the center of the city.

Though Barnard went to Barcelona with the rest of the team he did not actually get on the court. Nor did he even get into uniform, though he appeared briefly on national television, sitting in the stands in a patriotic sweat suit, clapping in an encouraging way. This information is readily available. Anyone can view the videos on YouTube. I have not spent a lot of time watching those videos, but I have seen the evidence. Smith Barnard, no matter what he might say, is not an actual Olympic athlete.

When pressed he'll assert that the fact that he didn't see any actual volleyball action didn't bother him. He knew he was going to enlist and that while enlisted he was going to go to medical school.

His army life lasted a decade, during which he was stationed at various bases around the United States, including Fort Carson in Colorado Springs. When he left the service he came back to the Springs where he planned to open a practice, get married, maybe have a couple of kids. Which is what happened, more or less, except for the getting married and having kids part. Meghan met him in Natural Grocers buying protein powder in bulk. I don't know exactly what was said but she came home telling me that she'd found me a doctor.

Meghan is my wife.

I had not entered Barnard's office that day with a specific complaint. The appointment had been made at Meghan's insistence. She had become worried about my *inertia*—that's her word for it, not depression—and I appeased her by going for a physical. She had been impressed by Smith Barnard and said I should give him a chance. My current doctor didn't seem to be having much success improving my condition, she pointed out, and it was clear I needed to do something. The week before I'd come in to have my blood taken, and now Barnard had my file open in front of him.

It was not, I could tell, good news. In person Barnard is imposing. Six foot four, square jaw, blue eyes, shaved head. With his white coat on, he looks like Mr. Clean, only cleaner.

"These are not good numbers," he told me.

I was unsurprised. I am the sort of person who has long ceased to possess good numbers and I am at peace with that. Once upon a time my numbers were okay, but even then my good numbers were of the temporary variety. I have a memory of my childhood pediatrician remarking to my mother that perhaps I should ease up on the waffles. Matters have not improved, but I have ceased to be cowed by the dismayed look that passes over a doctor's face—something involving the eyebrows, a sort of facial throwing up of the hands—when confronted by my medical records for the first time.

But Smith Barnard did something different. "See for yourself," he said, and held the file open for me to see.

I found myself staring at a chart delineating four categories: underweight, normal, obese, and morbidly obese.

I nodded gravely, though the chart made no sense to me.

"This is you," said Smith Barnard. His finger lay atop an oversized dot firmly in the middle of the quadrant labeled "morbidly obese."

Despite a lifetime of humiliation in doctors' offices, I was momentarily speechless. How does one gracefully respond to the news that one is morbidly obese? Is it appropriate to weep inconsolably? Fall on one's knees and beg forgiveness?

I did neither; I argued the point. The process of arriving at morbid obesity, I observed, should be more gradual, more in keeping with the manner in which the weight has been accumulated: skinny, not so skinny, *not* skinny, perfect, *maybe* a little heavy, a *little* heavy, *heavy*, *quite* heavy, quite heavy *indeed*, obese, and then, a condition almost impossible to contemplate, *morbidly* obese.

I said this to Smith Barnard.

"Is that a joke?" he asked.

I confirmed it was a joke.

"I'm glad you can joke about this," he said.

I couldn't tell if he meant it or not.

"Give me your phone," he said. I unstuck my legs from the examination table and got down on the cold floor. The phone was in the front pocket of my pants. When I gave it to him he handed it back immediately. "Unlock it," he said.

I did as I was told.

"This is Strava," he said, banging away at the screen with his index finger.

I watched him install the application. When he was finished he handed the phone back to me and there descended into the office an awkward silence that I recognized immediately as the same silence that descends at the end of Chekhov plays as the characters contemplate their impossible future. It is the sound of a way of life ending.

"It's not just about getting into shape," he said. "It's about getting moving. That's what you need right now. Motion."

"Were you ever actually in the Olympics?" I asked him.

"I was on the team, if that's what you mean," he said. "But we're talking about other things."

I nodded in the direction of a large photograph of him spiking the ball. "Is that a picture from the Olympics?" I asked him.

He closed my chart. Then he said: "You're going to love Strava, Meghan does."

I stared at him.

"It's all she talks about," he said, then laughed.

I laughed back, but the fact is that until that moment I'd never heard of Strava.

CARL "KIP" FILMORE was a forty-one-year-old project manager from Piedmont, California. He was married with two children, a steady job at Assurant Health, and was well liked by his friends and coworkers. He died suddenly after a gruesome cycling accident that occurred while he was descending a road near Mount Davidson in the San Francisco area. As awful as the accident was, the events leading up to it were unremarkable, even mundane. He hit the brakes with slightly too much force and lost control. Though it is difficult to know what exactly happened, police determined that he had not been hit by any car, nor had the crash been the result of some obstruction in the roadway. A car had pulled out and stopped. That was it. It distracted him, momentarily, caused him to brake a little too vigorously and that was all it took.

According to Strava, Filmore was doing at least twenty miles above the thirty-mph limit. Previous to that afternoon he had been the KOM record holder for that descent and, earlier that afternoon, had learned that someone had clocked a better time.

KOM stands for King of the Mountain. In Strava language it means that you're winning. Not the winner. There are no winners in Strava because the race does not end. Someone can always show up to unseat you. Clock a better time.

Strava is a Swedish word. It is a verb meaning "to strive."

After leaving Smith Barnard's office I considered going by the college, but thought better of it. I was still on a leave of absence and knew that my presence might be disconcerting to some. The details behind my decision to take a leave need not detain us here. Suffice it to say I was under a great deal of stress and I do not respond well to stress.

Instead, I went home and dug my bike out of the back of the garage. It was a steel-framed ten-speed that lacked even toe clips. I couldn't remember the last time I'd ridden it. Miraculously, the tires inflated and the pedals turned. I decided to ride it to the park at the end of the street. Some part of me felt certain that Smith Barnard had installed Strava on my phone because he was sure I wouldn't use it. He'd sounded encouraging, like he was trying to help, but there was something about the way he pushed at my phone, prodded it with his index finger like he'd have preferred to knife into it, that made me think otherwise. The house Meghan and I live in is located halfway up a long hill. That means it takes about a minute to get to the park—it's downhill the whole way—and much longer to get back.

This is what it's like to own a bike in Colorado Springs. You're either going up or down a mountain. The fact is I couldn't make it home. Eventually I got off and walked my bike up the hill. When I got to the house I uploaded my data to Strava and it was then that I noticed that Smith Barnard had sent a request to "follow" me.

This is the verb. On Facebook you "friend" someone; on LinkedIn you "connect." Follow is what it is people on Strava do to one another.

As I stood there sweating in the driveway, it occurred to me that under normal circumstances, in any other year, I'd be about halfway through my Milton course, giving my lecture on the question of free will and predestination and the Miltonian understanding of it. Free will, I would be telling the students, is the ability to make a choice between two actions. You have the free will to choose to jump off a cliff or not. Once you make the choice to jump, you can't stop falling.

MEGHAN IS A medic in the Canadian army stationed in Colorado Springs to look after the sizable Canadian contingent of soldiers stationed there because of NORAD. Actually, she's an obstetrician, but if you were to meet her—say in downtown Denver, say on the sixteenth floor of an upscale apartment building at a cocktail party that you've been dragged to by a colleague to celebrate the launch of a local poet's work—that is precisely how she would put it. She would say "medic" and then wait while her interlocutor got a far-away look in his eyes as he pictured her darting selflessly between foxholes, kneeling down in the dark, muddied earth, staring into the despairing eyes of a soldier.

"Really," I said. "A medic?"

"Actually," she said, "I catch babies."

Her tone was dismissive. I thought: this is what it's like when you are a soldier. Babies aren't born. They're caught. Then back to the battlefield.

"What's a medic like you doing at a poetry reading like this?"

"A girlfriend of mine is a girlfriend of the girl who copyedited the book," she said. She held in her hand a glass of white wine. Stemless, untouched.

"I teach English," I said.

"So you're a writer?" she said.

"I teach the Renaissance," I said. "There is a difference."

"Still," she said, "it's literary."

She raised the glass of wine to her lips and took a small sip.

Instead of a glass of wine I realized that I held in my hand a paper plate stacked with cheese. The reason: I'd been standing in front of the cheese plate when it dawned on me that the colleague with whom I'd come that night was more interested in the mediocre local poet whose book was being launched than she was in me. Of course she was somewhat younger than me, but I had believed, however foolishly, that a connection was possible. This realization was followed by a wave of dismay and it was then that my eyes alighted on the cheese.

Under normal circumstances—in a less fragile state—I would not be the sort of person who would ever do such a thing. But I was not quite myself. Meghan seemed to perceive this—to see something my colleague had not—and looked at the cheese on my plate for a long moment. I prepared myself for a negative reaction but it did not arrive. She winked, reaching out to take a single cube of cheddar, lifting it to her lips to take a single bite out of its corner. A discreet, tiny dent.

Then she replaced the piece of cheese on my plate. Her eyes were locked with mine the whole time. Without breaking my gaze I took the cube she'd bitten into and swallowed it whole.

"You want to get out of here?" she said.

It was, simply, a very forward thing to say. I was taken aback. I have grown used to such things. That is Meghan. She moves quickly.

The next thing I knew we were out in the hallway, in an embrace, but the elevator turned out to be broken. I pushed the button, then hit it again. Nothing. I was prepared to go back into the cocktail party, if only temporarily. The host would make a call and technicians would be dispatched. Meghan, however, was undeterred. "Catch me if you can," she said, and ran toward the exit sign at the end of the hall. She pushed the door open and ran down the stairs.

I sprinted after her, calling out for her to slow down. She did not. Below me I could hear her heels clicking against the concrete. I realized she was serious. If I didn't catch up to her—if I didn't catch her—before she reached the ground floor, she'd be out the door and I'd never see her again. Now with real desperation, I quickened my pace—I was running, jumping down two and three sets of stairs at a time. I was gaining on her, I believed, though it was hard to tell. Meghan is fast. And thin. Looking at her undressed what strikes you is the way the bones of her shoulder blades protrude upward, as if they had at one point considered extending out into wings. She was a swimmer originally—200m IM—but in her thirties she turned to triathlons. If we had been moving in the other direction, I would not have stood a chance. But gravity was on my side. I was gathering momentum and by the time we rounded the corner on the third floor, I could see the blond of her hair flashing, hear her laughing.

"Stop," I called out, winded. One floor remained. It dawned on me that I was not going to be able to catch her, and was about to give up when I tripped. I felt my left foot hit against my right calf and then, suddenly, I was airborne. I flew by her, smashing into the exit sign above the doorway. The last thing I remember before the back of my head hit is the look on her face as I sailed by her. I'd beat her down; she was impressed.

She rode with me in the ambulance and we were married a couple of months later. It was good, for a while. For almost three years. Then she met Smith Barnard. I imagine they both had protein powder in their hands at the time, or else not quite yet. Perhaps they were both standing in front of the protein powder section, making the kind of obscure deliberations that one makes when buying protein powder.

Colorado Springs: city, so called, of champions.

THOUGH MOST OF the photographs of the horrific bike accident involving Carl "Kip" Filmore have been suppressed by the family, there were witnesses and many of them used their phones to photograph a scene that would soon become almost mythic. Filmore, it seems, after braking, went over the handlebars and skidding along the pavement. It was his face that hit the ground, and on which he skidded, for some thirty meters. This is how fast he was going, the velocity required to maintain his standing as KOM on Strava.

Doubtless the gruesomeness of what happened is part of the reason why the incident has achieved such notoriety. It is hard to look at the photographs of the faceless, clearly screaming dead cyclist. All it took was an unlooked-for car pulling out a little too suddenly. It could happen to me, you find yourself thinking. It could happen to anyone.

When Meghan arrived home from catching babies that evening she was surprised to learn about Smith Barnard putting Strava on my phone. She was pulling her biking shorts over her lean legs, and seemed confused about what exactly had happened.

"He made you give him your phone?" she said.

"He installed it *himself.*"

"That's pushy," she said.

"*He's* pushy."

"He's intense." She didn't look at me. "It's part of his training, he's that person."

"Don't you think it's strange he's not married?" I said. "I mean, in his office there are no pictures. Not of anyone. Not even a girlfriend."

"Why would anyone put pictures of his girlfriend in an examination room?" she said. "I don't have a picture of you in my office."

"A guy like that?"

"What do you mean a guy like that?"

"He's Ajax," I said. "Seriously."

"Ajax?"

I took a breath and started to explain but she raised a hand. "I'll get the footnote later," she said. Then she sighed. "Maybe he's just waiting for the right person."

"To catch up to him, you mean," I said.

Meghan was tying her shoes and said nothing.

"That was a Strava joke," I told her.

"Got it," she said. Now she was putting on her bike helmet.

"He's already following me," I said. "On Strava. He follows you, but you know that."

"He follows a lot of people," she said.

"Why didn't you say anything about it?"

"About Strava?" She gave me a frank look. "Why would I tell you anything about Strava? You haven't got off the couch in three months."

"I *have* a bike," I said. "I went for a ride today. Two miles, two hundred calories."

"The calories thing is always exaggerated," she said.

I told her about the ancient tires inflating. "Isn't that amazing?"

"It is," she said, though she had clearly stopped listening to me. The last thing she did before leaving the house was pick up her iPhone off the kitchen table and open Strava. "You're following me?"

"You have to accept it though," I said. "You have to agree to me following you."

"I know how it works," she said.

"Maybe we can go for a ride together sometime," I said.

She tapped her phone. "There," she said. "Happy?"

THOUGH IT DOES not appear in the pages of the *OED* it is generally accepted that the word *gamification* makes its first appearance in the English language around the year 2002. Coined by a British computer programmer named Nick Pelling who designed a number of early video games—including Invader and Hedgehog—it refers to using game thinking and game process to solve problems and improve performance. If you think you're playing a game, you perform at a higher level than if you think you're working.

"Even if you have hundreds of friends on Facebook and you told them about your great ride today," Michael Horvath—one of Strava's creators—is quoted as saying, "only a handful of them are going to care about it in the level you described. Strava gives you a way to really focus in on the friends in your life, the people that you are following, or the people that are following you, and to share this important part of your life with them."

AFTER MEGHAN LEFT the house, I opened up Strava and looked at her profile. Here is a list of the things I learned about my wife:

1. She owned *three* bikes: a "Focus Izalco Pro 2.0" (on which she had ridden 1,208.8 miles), a "Gary Fisher Hifi Deluxe 29er" (420 miles), and a "Stumpjumper FSR Comp" (233 miles).

2. She rode about five rides a week, averaging sixty miles a week though often exceeding that.
3. Her longest climb was 1,345 feet.
4. She "and one other" scored a KOM on a section of road called Sunrise Decent.
5. Sunrise Descent is a stretch of road two miles long that Meghan ("and one other") had covered in just over two minutes' time. This means she had been going almost sixty miles an hour.
6. As fast as she had been going, the "one other" she was with had been going just a little faster. She seems to have eased up at the end, at the steepest part of the descent. He did not. If anything, he accelerated and, consequently, scored the KOM, not her.
7. The "one other" was Smith Barnard.

ONE OF THE many factors contributing to Strava's popularity is that it enables you to "track your effort" with precision. In addition to the duration of your ride, the distance covered, and the calories expended (however inflated), you can *also* track your "Energy Output" ("a factor of how much you're pedaling," says the Strava website, "how fast you're pedaling and how much force you're exerting on the pedals"), your "Average Power" ("expressed in W," Strava will tell you, "a measure of how much energy you are placing into the pedals"), and your "Suffer Score," which is an analysis of your heart rate data ("By tracking your heart rate through your workout and its level relative to your maximum heart rate," Strava says, "we attach a value to show exactly how hard you worked. The more time you spend going full gas and the longer your activity, the higher the score. The more time you spend coasting, or resting, the lower the score").

In other words, if you stop pedaling—if for any reason you get off your bike—Strava knows. Looking at my own abortive rides I could see clearly the moment when I gave up each time. When I failed to get up the mountain. As humbling as it was to see my inadequacy catalogued with such digital accuracy, my humiliation was tempered when I noted that Smith Barnard—and Meghan— habitually did the same thing. Though capable of meteoring down Sunrise Descent they almost invariably paused—sometimes for a significant interval—on the way up. This is the sort of data that Strava provides you with.

I will admit that I am no stranger to humiliation. Indeed, there is nothing easy about having been made to take a mandatory leave of absence. There are the endless hearings, the repetitions, the reiterations of who said what and the implications. By the end of the process a great relief descends. Much of that relief has to do simply with not having to tell the story any longer, to make any further admissions. A colleague, yes, and yes there was a tenure process involved, a romantic attachment also, yes presumed, yes now in the past, and yes I accept full responsibility.

And at some point one has to tell one's wife.

"What did you do?" said Meghan. This was a Friday. She'd just got back from a ride and was in the process of taking off her biking helmet. As usual she was flushed.

"It just happened," I said.

"What happened?"

"The fact is," I said, "I don't know where to start."

"Start at the start," she said.

It might have been over then. I can see that now. Three months pass and she comes home from Natural Grocers. "I found you a new doctor," she will tell you.

"I'm fine," you tell her back.

"I'm worried about your inertia," she'll say. That's her word for it.

A KEY ASPECT of Strava's functionality is a mapping function which allows one to plan rides in advance and follow the rides of others. According to Strava, there are two routes that Meghan (now my ex) traveled, on bike, from our driveway to Sunrise Descent. The first, less direct, less arduous route is a ten-and-a-half-mile climb at a moderate-level thoroughfare known as Gold Camp Road. The other is an almost impossible climb up Bonne Vista Drive. I had driven up it a couple of times—most recently with Meghan's parents (she had been driving)—to show them the views from the top of the Cheyenne Mountain. Though I labored mightily, I soon gave up and I thought to turn off Strava, but didn't. There was nothing to be ashamed of, I told myself, even Smith Barnard and Meghan had had to rest—often for a substantial interval.

Indeed, Strava showed me the approximate spot where the two of them tended to give up, in front of a sprawling, palatial home that looked down on the whole of Colorado Springs. A massive American flag flew in front of the house. It was a magnificent vista; I can see why they stopped, I remember thinking, at which point the garage door of the home began to move.

Thinking I had lingered too long, that it was the owner of the house, some Republican with a shotgun charging out to tell me to get off his property, I began to continue my arduous climb up the hill. But instead of an enraged landowner, out of the garage came a helmeted figure in blue-and-white cycling gear, a gleaming weightless road bike in tow.

"Don't worry," he said, satirically, as he mounted the bike, "it's all downhill from here."

It was then I recognized him. "Okay doc," I said.

"Tim?" said Smith Barnard. "Is that you? How'd you get up here?"

I gestured to my bike. "I was doing okay to begin with," I said. "But we all need to catch our breath somewhere. This is a popular spot."

If he made the connection, I didn't see it. He took off his sunglasses. "I'm impressed."

"You told me to change my life," I said, and gestured to my drenched T-shirt. "This is what that looks like."

"Good for you," he said.

Then we stood there for a moment.

"This is a big hill," I said. "I don't know how you guys do it. You and Meghan I mean."

"Is that your bike?" he said. "How old is that?"

I said I didn't know. "The tires inflated," I said.

"No wonder you can't make it up this hill," he said. "You need a better bike. You know what, I'm going to give you one of mine."

"No need," I said.

"I insist," he said. "It's the least I can do."

"The least you can do?"

It took him a second. "For getting you on Strava," he said. "You wouldn't be here, if not for me. I take full responsibility."

"Keep your bike," I told him.

"Look," he said. "I know you're not working."

Now it was my turn to nod and say nothing.

"Anyway," he said, and seemed about to say something else, but changed his mind. "I'll drop it by." And a moment later he was gone, pedaling with ease up the mountain. Watching him glide up the hill, I found myself wondering why he had needed to stop. Maybe it was Meghan who'd had to stop that day.

I kept on pushing my bike up hill and at some point a blue blur that I understood was Smith Barnard swished by me, shouting to me to keep going.

I got to the top forty minutes later then coasted down to the bottom of Sunrise Descent.

"Coasted" is decidedly the wrong word for it. It was a descent that frightened me to death. You start at the top and plummet. As harrowing as the first two-thirds of the ride is, as steep a descent, it is nothing compared to the final third where there is a precipitous, numbing drop. When I arrived at the bottom I threw down my bike and vomited. It was hard to imagine what it would take to be King of the Mountain on such a stretch of road. But Smith Barnard had done it. Tucked himself into a sleek hurtling blur. He had done it.

When I got home Smith Barnard's bike was waiting for me at the house, propped up against the front of the garage. Meghan pulled up shortly afterward. Whether or not he had called her—warning her I suppose—I don't know, though I expect so. These are the things that become part of the public record. They will come out at trial. Cell phone records. I expect to be a suspect. I also expect there will be no actual evidence.

Meghan saw Smith Barnard's bike in the driveway. "Is he here?" she asked, and I saw it in her face. She had imagined this scene. Practiced her reaction. It was just his bike, I told her, he'd given it to me. Then I watched her face change. If I didn't know before I knew then.

The key point to make in the teaching of *Paradise Lost* is that Satan's escape from hell will never happen. Hell is not a physical location, you tell your students, it is a state of mind. He carries it with him.

I said nothing. Gave no indication whatsoever that anything had changed. That I had done the math. Uploaded the data. Seen the leaderboard. Not the next day and not the day after. On occasion I would take the bike Smith Barnard had given me and ride it, allowing Strava to take my measure, though it became a somewhat more lonely endeavor.

Meghan told me she'd grown tired of it, being always in a race, and though Smith Barnard said he was planning to do the same, he didn't. Perhaps it had something to do with being the King of the Mountain. It is not something you let go of easily. On occasion I would see him whiz by me, a blue-and-white blur, poised in headlong descent.

Going at that speed, everything is a fine calculation. Anything can throw the rider off the bike. Over the handlebars and into the concrete. A rock in the roadway, a car pulling out unexpectedly, there is so little margin for error. This morning I got in my car and drove to the top of Sunrise Descent and floored it, all the way to the bottom.

Faster than humanly possible. I uploaded my ride. King of the Mountain.

Then I drove back up Sunrise Descent. Not to the very top, or even the middle, but to the bottom third. The steepest part where those descending it are nothing but speed and reflexes. The point of the descent where touching the brakes at all becomes a risky proposition.

I don't know exactly what happens when you lose your KOM. If it's an alarm that goes off, or if you get an email notification. Maybe both. Soon enough Smith Barnard will find out.

It is only a matter of time. I'm keeping the engine running. It won't take much.

We Are the Olfanauts

by Deji Bryce Olukotun

U have to whyff this.

Cant.

Y not? 😞

Just cant.

Shes bak.

Dont care. Send it up.

I pasted in the link anyway, ignoring Aubrey's decision.

www.olfanautics.com/13503093!hsfi9hhhh

I knew she would whyff it eventually. One click and you were there. You might as well download it directly into your brain, and with a whyff the effect was nearly as instantaneous. I played the video again to confirm that it was as special as I remembered.

Close-up of a desk. Glass top on a chrome frame. On the desk, a knife, a leather strap, a small glass bowl, and the girl's wrist. Light tan skin. The whyff: hints of lilac, clearly the girl's perfume.

She holds the knife in her palm and waves her second hand over it, like a game show hostess displaying a valuable prize. Then she stabs the tip of her finger with the knife and lets her blood trickle into the bowl. The whyff is not of pain, or the metallic scent of blood. It smells like the richest, freshest strawberries, collected right there in the bowl. And you can hear her laughing.

I should say that the girl *appeared* to stab the tip of her finger with the knife. You see, there was no proof that she had actually done it. When I slowed the video down, and advanced it frame by frame, her index finger and thumb obscured my view at the exact moment of puncture. She might have stabbed her own finger, or she might have somehow burst a capsule of fake blood with her fingers. Or, more likely, based on the whyff, a capsule of concentrated strawberry essence. It was the work of either a skillful illusionist or a deranged sadomasochist. With my Trunk on, it smelled hilarious.

Aubrey eventually messaged back: **Told u to send it up.**

What abt the whyff??

Send it up.

Shld Private Review.

Send it up.

Cmon, grrl. Strawberries!

This was the second video this user had posted, and each had ended with a whyff that completely subverted the image of the video with humor. It felt like she was playing with us, questioning whether we would believe our eyes or other senses. Wasn't that reason enough to Private Review? To talk it through? Last week, Aubrey and I had met in the Private Review rooms twice. I wasn't going to let her ruin my discovery, though. Instead of sending it up, as she had ordered, I posted the link to ALL-TEAM. Immediately I heard gasps in the cubicles around me.

"Oh, shit, Renton!"

"She's back!"

"Aw, man, I bet she's hot!"

Then they went back to their keypads and we began a group chat.

You gonna send it up?

What do you think?

Think we shld.

You smell the strawberries?

I thought it was raspberries.

You cant see the wound.

She a kid?

No, shes 18+.

You hear her laughing?

Crazy grl.

I let the discussion go on for some time as the team chatted amongst themselves, enjoying the fact that with every passing moment the post was staying online, and some new stranger could appreciate its artistry. There was something beautiful about the glass and the steel and the blood. Only the essentials, the sterility of the table against the violence engendered in the blade. The whorls in the redness as the blood filled the bowl, the burst of strawberries and the laughter, ethereal, hovering above it all.

In the end someone sent it up. I wasn't surprised. We were paid to be cautious, to keep the slipstream of information flowing at all costs, even if it meant removing some of it from the world.

OUR TEAM WAS based in a multibillion-dollar technology park fifteen kilometers outside Nairobi, and our data servers, which would have made us liable under Kenyan law, floated above national airspace in tethered balloons. The Danish architect had modeled the

Olfanautics complex after a scene from Karen Blixen's novel, as if that was what we secretly aspired to, a coffee ranch nestled against the foothills of some dew-soaked savannah. The cafeteria was intended to replicate the feel of a safari tent. Catenary steel cables held up an undulating layer of fabric, which gleamed white in the midday sun. In reality, the tent was the closest I had ever been to a safari. I only left Nairobi to go rock climbing.

Aubrey found me as I was ordering a double veggie burger with half a bun and six spears of broccolini. I could tell from the few frayed braids poking out of her head wrap that she had not slept well last night, nor had she gone to the campus hairdresser to clean herself up. I reached for her thigh as soon as she sat down but she swatted my hand away.

"I told you to send it up."

"Nice to see you, too, Aubrey," I said.

"I'm your boss, Renton. If I say send the video up, then send it up. You're making me look bad."

That was the problem with dating your supervisor. She thought any discussion could be resolved by pulling rank. "Didn't you whyff the strawberries? They were hilarious, hey. That girl's an actress or something."

"We don't know that, Renton. She could have really been cutting herself. Or someone could have been forcing her off camera and layered in that whyff afterward. We don't even know if she's a she. It could be a man."

Aubrey always pulled her liberal philosophy on me, as if I couldn't trust my own nose.

"The metadata said she was a twenty-four-year-old woman," I said. "I looked at the time signatures. The whyff was recorded simultaneously."

"The signatures could have been spoofed."

"That's only happened once."

I wasn't concerned about speaking to Aubrey so intimately in the cafeteria. No one would have believed that we were together, because for all appearances, I was a handsome young Kenyan man with his pick of eligible women, and Aubrey was a frumpy foreigner from Somewhere Else. But they were using the wrong sense when they judged her.

"Aubs, maybe you should eat something."

"We can't Private Review anymore, Renton."

"Here, have one," I offered. I liked to eat broccolini from the spear to the tip, leaving the head for last.

"Those rooms are set aside for us to do our jobs."

"It's high in folate. And iron."

She glanced around. "Would you stop bloody ignoring me!"

"I think you need to eat something."

"I don't want any of those bloody things. They're not natural. They were invented by some scientist."

"At least it's food." I showed her the screen of my Quantiband on my wrist. "Says I need five hundred milligrams of iron today, and these will give me a thousand. Don't shoot the messenger, hey. I do what I'm told."

"Just not when your boss is the one telling you," she said, and walked away. Only after I had finished my broccolini spears did I realize that she hadn't been wearing her Quantiband.

THAT EVENING I tried to forget my conversation with Aubrey because I wanted to be totally focused on my Passion. In three years, I planned to free-climb the sheer granite face of the Orabeskopf Wall in Namibia, one of the most difficult routes in southern Africa, and I had meticulously plotted out my conditioning, fitness, and routes with my personal fitness instructor, whose name was

Rocky. You see, because of our work on Trust & Safety, we were afforded certain additional privileges: a trainer (mine was Rocky), a psychologist, a full-subscription Quantiband, an additional five floating holidays, a stipend of OlfaBucks that we could use at the gift shop, and access to a sleep specialist. The company would support one Passion for each of us. It could be running a marathon, completing a competitive Scrabble tournament, or stitching a quilt. What mattered was that you chose a Passion with a measure-able goal. That's why I loved my Quantiband: it calculated my heart rate, blood pressure, distance walked, calories, alertness, mood, sleep quality, and even the frequency with which I had sex. When I was treating my body well, my Quantiband felt as light as air, but it could constrict itself around my wrist like a snake when I veered off my programmed routine.

My role at T&S was fairly simple: to respond to content flagged by our users that violated our terms of service. Olfanautics was the global pioneer in scented social media. Our whyff product allowed users to send scents to people around the world. It was originally a stand-alone device that utilized four fundamental scents—woody, pungent, sweet, and decayed—and combined them proportion-ately in a spray to mimic real scents, but few people could afford to buy it. As the technology grew better, and tinier, Olfanautics became a standard feature of smartphones that could also record video and audio. Many users would whyff frequently at first and then save it for special occasions, like showing off a fresh-baked pie during the holidays, or sharing a vacation by the beach. Some users would turn off the feature when they wanted more privacy but most preferred to have the ability to whyff, if they might need it, than not to have it. Then there were people like me who whyffed incessantly, who became so enthralled by the unlimited palate of experience that we sought out its very source.

My main job was to monitor the whyffs that users considered suspicious or objectionable. I did so through my Trunk, a tube that looked like the oxygen mask of a fighter jet pilot. Between each whyff, the Trunk would inject a neutral scent to cleanse my palate. You see, scent is determined more by your tongue than your nose— think of how hard it is to taste anything when you have a bad cold—and all of us on my team had a significantly higher number of papillae on our tongues than your average user. In another era, we might have been perfumers selling bottles of lavender along the cobblestone of Grasse. Today we were the Olfanauts. We transported our users safely and peacefully to exciting realms of discovery. So went our tagline.

I loved our tagline.

The video-safety team would pull down the usual garbage: sexual content, violence, self-mutilation, and child pornography. But sometimes people would inject a whyff into an otherwise normal video. A video of a birthday cake might stink like feces, or a trickling stream might reek of decomposition. Usually these were hatchet jobs that were crudely added to the video, and our software would automatically flag the whyffs because of their metadata. Occasionally we'd come across a whyff of skilled artistry, when the scent would waft through the Trunk like a sublime wind. Like the girl with the knife.

When I couldn't decide on a case by myself, I could present it to my supervisor, Aubrey, and then she had the option of sending it up to the Deciders—members of the legal and marketing teams back in Denmark. Only Aubrey had ever met them, although we had all been flown to Copenhagen for orientation when we were hired. (That was a legendary trip, hey.)

Rocky was waiting for me at the gym when I arrived. He was a grizzly, colored South African with a bursting Afro and wind-seared skin. He claimed to have broken thirty-two bones, fifteen of which he had shattered on the same fall in the Dolomites back when he was a competitive climber. He wore glasses with thick black plastic rims that he had owned for so long that they had twice gone into, and out of, fashion while they were still on his nose. He'd switched from rock climbing to bouldering after he had gnarled his right leg, and I had seen videos of him skittering under impossible slabs of granite like a dassie.

I began strapping on my harness.

"Wait, wait, bru," Rocky said. "Let's hit the fingerboard first."

"Quantiband doesn't say I need to get on the fingerboard until next week. I'm supposed to climb."

"That thing doesn't know how to climb."

"It knows how to measure my progress. That's what it's supposed to do."

Rocky sighed. "All right, big man. Think you know what you're doing? Give this route a try, then." He hooked me into his carabiner and illuminated a green climbing path for me to follow on the wall.

I gleefully dipped my hands in my powder bag. I love the smell of the powder as I grab the first holds. It smells like freedom, hey, as if I am climbing toward my dreams. Before long I had pulled myself about thirty feet off the ground. Then I got to a problem that I couldn't navigate. There was a nasty slither of a hold that I thought I could crimp, and as I dug my fingers in, my hand stiffened from fatigue and my feet slid out from under me. I tried to dyno my hip onto the hold but it was too late. And I was falling rapidly toward the mats below.

My head snapped forward so hard that my nose bashed into my kneecap.

"Got ya!" Rocky said. He gradually lowered me to the ground.

I clutched at my nose as he unclipped my harness. I could feel numbness spreading along my eye socket.

"You all right there, bru?"

"No, I'm not all right! Why the fuck didn't you catch me earlier, Rocky?"

Rocky recoiled: "Why the fuck did you fall?"

"I couldn't crimp it. The route was too hard."

"Here, let me look at your nose. Come on, move your hand out of the way." I let go, and the blood rushed in painfully. "It's all right, bru. You're not bleeding. It was a light knock."

"Bloody hell." I was relieved but I could feel my nostrils filling with something. Mucus? Blood? The air was already starting to feel stale. It was as if the smells were slipping past me, as if the room were coated in a skin of mud.

"You weren't prepared for it, bru," he went on, tapping his temple with his finger. "It was a simple problem. It wasn't your finger strength but your mind that failed you."

I didn't like Rocky's tone. I paid him to help me fulfill my Passion, not to cause me more problems. I was in line for a promotion soon. "How am I supposed to go to work tomorrow if I can't even smell your stinking breath? You made a mistake, Rocky. Just admit it."

"That's kak. I'm not the one who fell."

I began tapping away on my Quantiband. "Says here that I shouldn't have been doing this route for three weeks. This wasn't part of the program. I could report you for this."

Now I had his attention. "Calm down there, bru. There's no need to report it."

At Olfanautics, the numbers didn't lie. The Quantiband would have measured the speed of my fall in meters per second as well as my rise in pulse. If I could show, objectively, that someone had put my work at risk then he would be dismissed immediately. The same went for all of us.

"Why shouldn't I report you?"

"Because then you wouldn't get any better at climbing. I wanted to challenge you, bru. You can't control everything when you're out there. That's part of climbing."

"But it's not part of the program. The program says I get better in three weeks. That's the whole point. If you want to challenge me then put it in the program."

"Come on, let's forget it, Renton. You're right. My mistake, bru. I put in the wrong route." He tapped on the wall and illuminated a yellow route, one that I had already successfully completed twice before. "This is what the program wanted, right?"

He grabbed for the carabiner on my harness, but I pushed his hand away. "No, I need to get some ice for my nose."

"Come on, bru. Your nose is fine. You took a small knock, is all. Let's hook you in. Yellow's still a bastard of a route. You haven't even free-climbed it yet."

It was so easy to screenshot my Quantiband, and even easier to send it to security. I looked at him blankly as if I didn't understand, buying time. He began pleading with me to hook me in, insistently, pathetically even.

"What are you waiting for, Renton? It was a simple mistake. Let me hook you in!"

"No, it's too late."

Olfanautics allowed only the perimeter security to carry guns. So the ones who arrived wielded batons, but the effect was still intimidating enough to prevent Rocky from putting up any sort of struggle.

"You think the Orabeskopf Wall gives a shit about that thing on your wrist, bru?" he shouted back. "You think that thing is going to save you when you're on the wall and a vulture starts pecking at your fingers? That's what happened to me! I was like Prometheus, getting my liver pecked out by an eagle, bru. I didn't have one of those kak wristbands. I let it eat my own hand and then I climbed up that wall! The Orabeskopf says fuck-all to your wrist! That wind will tear you off that route and splatter your brains in the sand!"

But I'd heard that story about the vulture many times before, and it didn't scare me anymore. My Quantiband told me that there was a one in ten million chance of it ever happening to me. I had whyffed some terrible things during my time at Olfanautics—ritual dismemberment by a militia in Bukavu with a volcano looming in the background, a woman being raped on a frozen canal in Ottawa, and once, a manhole cover in Nagoya crushing an old nun on the sidewalk after it was ejected by a blast of gas. If Rocky had whyffed these things, too, he might have left with a little more dignity. The world was not a fair place, and I was the one who helped people forget that fact. As soon as he had left, I put in an order for a new fitness instructor.

EXCEPT FOR THE death of the nun in Nagoya, which crept into my dreams and made me sad in a way that I don't think I'll ever understand (the ferocious spin of the manhole cover, the febrile skull), I had learned to forget the horrific smells that permeated my Trunk. I had trained for months at Olfanautics to expunge them from my mind, and the regimen had worked for the most part. You have to let things go, you see.

But I hadn't finished my climbing routine, so I felt edgy when I took the shuttle back to the Olfanautics housing complex, and my nose hurt like hell. The pain from my fall had spread from the base of my skull to my shoulders, and seemed to be wrapping itself around my chest.

My apartment had two bedrooms, a small balcony, and one and a half bathrooms. Behind it was a tolerable view of a tennis court surrounded by electrified razor wire. My unit was subsidized so it was still cheaper than living in the city, and I was permitted to invite guests, usually my parents, to stay with me for six days per month.

Aubrey was sipping on a beer at the living room table when I opened the door.

"What happened to your face?"

"Took a fall at the gym."

"What about those bandages?"

"It's to keep my nostrils open. Doctor said there might be some temporary blockage." When she didn't say anything, I added: "I should still be able to put in my shift tomorrow."

"I'm not worried about that anymore."

Her face was as distraught as when we'd met in the cafeteria. If she'd been wearing her Quantiband, it would have been twisted tight around her wrist like a tourniquet. But she still didn't have it on. Maybe it was that sense of freedom that made her come over to me. Because the next thing I knew, she began opening the buttons of my shirt. I didn't stop her. Aubrey was the most beautiful woman I had ever met. Her natural odor was enough to turn my head, and she layered on essential oils so that she was a fragrant mosaic, a true artiste who could compose entire olfascapes of inspired brilliance. I had never been able to resist her. On our first secret date, she had guessed what cologne I would wear and applied an extract of argane nuts on her skin, so that when we touched we smelled like buttered popcorn. I found other women repulsive by comparison, as if they had showered themselves in crude perfume.

But as she slowly peeled off my shirt, my bashed-in nose seemed to be obscuring everything. "I can't smell you."

"Then feel me."

In the Private Review rooms, Aubrey and I would sniff each other more than we licked or kissed, and this took time. When we were really horny, we'd inhale each other's most private scents—our groins, armpits, and anuses—like animals in the throes of estrus. But with my swollen nose I felt clumsy, as if I were watching myself make love from a distance, and my fingertips couldn't make up for the lack of sensation. Aubrey, on the other hand, enjoyed every second of it. She lingered over my bandages and wrapped herself around me. Then she dug her hips into mine until she came. Even with her breasts flopping against my face and her full buttocks in my hands I couldn't stay aroused without my sense of smell, and we both gave up trying.

As we lay on my bed, Aubrey announced: "This isn't working." She always said depressing things after sex.

"It's my fault. I couldn't get into it."

"No, Renton. I mean us. I'm your boss. We can't do this anymore."

I turned to face her, suddenly concerned. "What do you mean?"

"The Deciders know."

"You told them?"

"No, the Private Review rooms are all monitored. They've known for some time and they confronted me about it."

I tried to remember everything we might have done or said to each other. She normally made me take off my Quantiband in the Private Review rooms.

"Did they whyff it, too?"

"I don't think so—at least, I wouldn't see the point of that. They tracked our bands to see how often we were meeting. I clearly violated my terms of reference. I'm your boss and it should never have happened. I've got to go see them tomorrow."

"They're flying you to Copenhagen?"

"Yeah."

"That's a good sign, right? They wouldn't fly you up there if they wanted to fire you."

She considered this. "I suppose so."

"Why did you come here tonight, Aubs?"

"I wanted to do it one last time."

I rose from the bed to look out the window. Beyond the tennis court were rows upon rows of sagging acacia trees that the Danish architect had planted all around the campus, but the soil was too damp for the trees and their roots were slowly drowning. I had never liked them. Their pollen gave me sneezing fits. If I had my way, I'd have them all cut down. "How can you say it's the last time? How is that fair? Shouldn't I also know when it's the last time? You can't break it off and say it's the last time without telling me!"

"I'm sorry, Renton. It's not just the Deciders. It's—it's the unreality of it."

"Was it the video of the girl? The strawberries?"

"No, that's not it."

"I meant it as a joke. There's no need to break up over a thing like that."

"You know what I spent this morning doing? Watching a woman eat a goat alive. She had filed her teeth into points, Renton. Like a vampire. Even had the makeup on. Her girlfriend—I think that's who it was—was screaming at her to eat more. Shrieking at her to eat more. The poor beast was pinned down by stakes and the girl was tearing into its belly. The stench! Of piss and shit, the goat was in so much pain it was expelling what little bit of life it had left in it. Trying to die."

I had never seen Aubrey cry before, and I feared what it might mean.

"Who would do such a thing, Renton? To a harmless animal? I vomited into my Trunk it was so disgusting."

I could see that she wanted me to feel what she had felt, smell what she had smelled, but I couldn't let her get to me. Every Olfanaut who burned out tried to drag everyone else down with them. The psychologists had taught us it was called transference. I began searching desperately for my Quantiband, which she must have torn off during sex.

"Why don't you go see the psychologists, Aubs? That's what they're there for."

"They wouldn't understand."

"Of course they would! Mimi helped me with the nun thing. I'm sure she can help you with whatever is bothering you."

I found my Quantiband beneath my sock at the foot of the bed. I didn't remember taking the sock off, because I was still wearing the other one.

"Mimi can't help me, Renton. She can't help a thing like that. Tell me, when was the last time you left the campus?"

"I go to the Rain Drop all the time."

"That's still on the campus!"

"So what? It's a bar. I like the people there. We have a lot in common."

"I mean, when was the last time you went downtown? Or anywhere people don't have to whyff a conversation?"

"My family doesn't live downtown. They're out in Kibera."

"That's not my point. What we see all day—it's not right. We made love over a Nazi book burning last week. A bloody book burning."

"We took that video down, Aubrey. We prevented the rest of the world from smelling that filth. That's something to be proud of. Sure, we had sex in there but we did our job in the end. That's what matters. We have one job here, and we do it right. I'm sure that's all the Deciders care about too. That's why I fired Rocky."

"What are you talking about?"

I hadn't meant to tell her, because I knew she'd try to make me feel bad, but now it was too late. "He put me on a dangerous route. That's how I hurt my nose."

"So you fired him?"

"Of course! Rocky had it coming to him, Aubs. I'd told him a thousand times that we had to follow the program. It's not my fault he can't listen to directions."

"That's what I mean by unreality. So what if you hurt your nose—he has a family! How will he survive without this job?"

"What about *my* family?" I grabbed a glass from the kitchen, and filled it in the sink. "Do you realize this is the only neighborhood within twenty kilometers where you can do this? Drink water straight from the tap? My parents drive here for their drinking water. I'm putting my sister through school. I pay for every funeral in my family. That's as real as it gets." I pointed to my Quantiband. "This says right here that I was climbing the wrong route when I fell. Rocky hurt my nose, the tool of my trade. I'm in line for a promotion now and I can't take the risk. I need someone reliable. Trustworthy. I don't need his bloody war stories. I need someone safe. Who can commit to the program."

Aubrey stared at me blankly for a few moments. "You don't see what this does to us, do you? Today was my big test to determine if I could join the Deciders. And I failed it, Renton. I failed it horribly. Because I told them that if I had my way I'd exterminate those girls from the face of the earth. I wasn't thinking about justice. I was thinking about revenge. Revenge on behalf of a mangy fucking goat."

I drank my glass slowly, trying to taste the filtered water. They ran it through reverse osmosis and then a layer of sand, which normally gave it a delightful mineral quality. But I couldn't taste a thing.

"You're not going to get a promotion, Renton. Look at yourself in the mirror and then take a look at management. I recommended you twice but they said you don't have the pedigree. When was the last time a local was promoted?"

Now I knew Aubrey was planning to move away all along. And she wanted to hurt me while doing it, whatever for I had no idea. That was what happened in the videos. That was what those people did to each other. Even after all we'd been through, I refused to let her do this to me. It was the slippery hold on the wall. The tumble from the granite, the brains in the sand.

"I'm going to be the first one, then."

You can't let it all weigh on your shoulders. That's what Mimi had told me about the nun. You've got to let things go.

I snapped my finger. "I know what's changed—it's you, Aubrey."

"Me?"

"Yes, you need a new Passion."

"You weren't listening."

"You made that short film last year, right? That was too close to home. We whyff videos all day, hey. You've got to choose something else. Something that really gets you chuffed! Like writing a book. Or dancing. You've got to focus on the positive, Aubs! Think of all the value we're creating for our users. Think about how we protected them from that Nazi video. We saved a little bit of joy for two billion users around the world. We have to celebrate that! You can't dwell on these things. We're watching so no one else has to!"

As I went on like this, Aubrey's face brightened, and before long she seemed to be coming around to the idea. So I was surprised, when I pulled her in for a kiss, and she said: "If evil is humanity turned against itself, Renton, then who are we?"

"We're the Olfanauts," I said proudly.

Aubrey left Olfanautics two weeks later, and she was kind enough to say good-bye to me. She also transferred me all of her OlfaBucks, which would allow me to order something from the gift shop, and I think she knew, in her heart, that I would spend it on a Hyperlite Bivouac that I had told her about a few months ago, which I planned to use when I free-climbed the Orabeskopf Wall in Namibia. I won't lie—I started dreaming about the nun again as soon as Aubrey left, and I had to work extra hard at my Passion to get that old woman to leave me alone in my sleep. It's funny how sometimes you only understand what people mean well after they say it. Because I realized that Rocky had been right all along, that I had to be like Prometheus giving the fire to humanity, and that I couldn't worry about some bird pecking at my fingers as I made my grand ascent.

Viewer, Violator

by Aimee Bender

Welcome to this last stage of the exhibit. You've been a very attentive group and I've enjoyed our time together. If you wish to use the restroom, it's down this hall on the left; if you're using the ladies' room, they've asked us to remind you to knock before you open the stall door as some of the locks in there are faulty. Are we all back now?

Good. This is the final piece we will discuss today. Take a long look. It does indeed resemble things we all have drawn as children; we are not claiming this to be the strongest piece in the collection. We hung it up because of its extraordinary way of coming into being. Yes, I do realize your grandson could do just as well, indeed we have children who take classes here who are much more astute already. I should show you the deer-in-the-meadow painting done by our prodigy, Isabelle, who is ten now; it is really a thrill, the way the spots on the deer relate to the sunspots on the meadow. She has an excellent sense of composition. But this one came to us by uncommon means, which is why we hang it last.

I will tell you, of course. Please stop whispering back there.

It was the third or so week since the museum had re-opened, for as you may know, we had to close down for several months last fall due to a problem with people touching the work. We had an influx of visitors who liked to feel the texture of the paint or the slopes of the sculptures and we were not equipped to deal with them. I myself was shocked it was a problem at all but believe it or not, one man actually *licked* the Degas bronze replica of the ballerina with her arms behind her back. Left a tongue mark right on her left breast. Embarrassing for everybody, if you ask me, but suddenly it seemed dire that we implement some sort of security system to protect ourselves, which took months to install. The museum head—who I will tell more about in a minute—she was at the front lines of museum security, and she thought we could affix automatic cans of Mace inside the walls next to the paintings. That seemed legally problematic but we modified her idea for safety and now, if you move up into the ten-inch range, the art will sound a small alarm. The ringing? Yes. In each room. I've grown to like it, it sounds to me like tossing rocks in a pond. You folks have been quite well behaved and putting your hands in your pockets is a fine way to temper any urges. As I often say, art is for looking! Your ears get music, your nose gets perfume, your mouth gets food, and if you really want to touch things, for goodness sake, you may purchase some six-dollar clay in the gift shop.

We'd been back open going on three weeks when the museum head got a notice for a large package arriving in her upstairs office. The museum head is a very busy woman and she couldn't be bothered while the men from the delivery company lugged it in to her. It was wrapped in brown paper and they said it was from a wealthy benefactor, all the way from Georgia, who'd heard "what was happening" and wanted to offer up a gift. Now, the museum owner had many phone calls to return, and she was puzzled by the delivery because who was this benefactor from Georgia anyway? And really it is sensible in this day and age to consider the possibility of bombs. So she signed the package away and listened for ticking and then made her phone calls. She is not a very curious woman by nature, and she was at that time going through a divorce, so she clearly had other things on her mind as she did not open the large package all day long. It was hard to overlook, I tell you, being over three feet tall and four feet wide, but she did not even peek until nearly the end of the day.

The museum was clearing out by then, and she told me she could hear, even from her office, the little ringing pings coming from the near-touching of the paintings downstairs, alerting security, and this made her feel that her expensive renovation had been worth it. Do you folks know what fingertip oil does to a painting? Erodes like mercury! Destroys those brushstrokes! It's some kind of miracle that we don't rot each other merely by shaking hands.

The museum was slowly clearing out. It was getting dark early, a night of a new moon, and she decided she would now open up the packaging of the mysterious gift. And so she, being a meticulous person, as you have to be if you are going to run a museum, took her pearl-handled letter opener and gently sliced open the brown wrap. And underneath it was a very large canvas, and on the canvas was ... what? Can you guess?

No.

Not what you see here, no.

It was a simple painting, though, a simple black-and-white line work, appealing for a small measure of time, but like we've said, something you've often seen done better I'm sure by your gifted grandchild.

She read the attached note.

I hope this will address the problem, it said, in typed writing, signed by an unreadable scribble.

Now. There are certainly many kind benefactors of this museum, perhaps some of you are some of them, but we get our share of pranksters as well. Once, one of our leading donors sent a penny in an envelope with a letter that said it was art, and that it cost a thousand dollars. He laughed like a maniac on the phone when she called him to ask. So when the museum head read this typed note, she wasn't sure what to do with it. Was it real? What problem? she thought, vaguely insulted. Then she remembered the people touching the paintings and thought perhaps it was a mock painting, meant to be touched. But she didn't believe in those either. There are children's museums, she sniffed to herself, and there are adult museums. If she had her way completely, perhaps the gallery would be like a planetarium and you'd look at the ceiling through a telescope to observe the paintings hung up as if they were stars.

She lugged the painting into the hallway, called custodial services to come pick it up, and left the office for a while. She tended to work late those days—it's difficult to go home when your home is newly emptied. Or so I imagine. She was gone for about an hour, perhaps to go cry in the restroom. This is a recent divorce. I met him once before at the holiday museum party, and he seemed perfectly pleasant. Conservative. Ordinary. He had one of those jowly faces that seem difficult to shave, like skin-water under the rudder of the razor blade. They weren't rude to each other but very rarely did they act like a couple, if you want to know my opinion. You could always see the space between them. Anyway, he was the one who asked for divorce, which came, apparently, completely out of the blue. She confided in me that she's dismayed at how many people have accidentally burst in on her in the restroom stall, and found her squatted on the toilet seat, crying.

So off she went, and came back, perhaps with a tissue in hand, an hour or so later, and she was irritated to see that the painting was still in the hall. She went in to call janitorial again, but as she angled toward her office, she passed the painting and thought to herself that she didn't recall there being a circle in the top left-hand corner before. Just an hour or so ago, she had remembered it as a square. Certainly she wouldn't confuse a square with a circle, she thought—it's the difference between the window and the moon—but now, sure as anything, there was a circle of black paint smack in the left-hand corner. She admonished herself because for a museum director, as with a geometer or carpenter, to confuse the two is to degrade your job. Plus, she is not an unobservant person. She can recite the accessories that other women wear to parties years after the fact. Marie Snaper? Red coral earrings, which was environmentally wrong. Elaine Fitzgerald? Fake sapphire on the wedding finger implying, she said, a fake marriage. I must add that she has told me some of this in confidence, so I would not suggest asking her about it. But mainly, the circle she saw now had really seemed to be a square before, and she wondered if this was the psychological effect of weeping—it softened the corners of the world.

Settling back at her desk, she continued her list of objects she would keep and objects her husband would take. Downstairs she could still hear that faint ringing of bells, like sitting atop a church. She put down a few books on her husband's side, and then felt exhausted. On her way to the balcony to smoke a cigarette, she glanced at the painting again. The circle was still a circle, which pleased her, and she was about to step away when she noticed that there seemed now to be darker wavy lines at the bottom of the canvas. She stared at them for a minute. She really did not recall seeing these darker lines before. True, she had spent most of her time looking at the upper half of the painting, but regardless. Was someone actually drawing on the canvas? And if so, who? This was absolutely unacceptable; *drawing* on a painting went along the lines of standing in the middle of a recital hall during a concert pianist's concerto, and screaming. Who would ever want to do a thing like that? Even if this was no worthy piece of art! The principle! Or was she going insane? Was her mind going wavy, making wavy lines where previously they were straight, or where previously there had been none? She waited for a janitor to turn the corner, sheepish, with a paintbrush in hand, all set to be fired, but the hall was empty.

She went home that night, which she said was a normal evening. She came back the next morning and said it was a normal morning, except for the fact that the painting was still in the hallway and therefore janitorial services had still not come by. It was only when she went for her daily trip to the bathroom that she returned, tissue in hand, to find the painting, still in the hall, now covered with bold lines, striped, as if the former painting of the circle and wavy lines had been put in jail.

This chilled her to the core, but she is a woman of quick recovery, and she sucked in her breath, stormed into her office, and called custodial services.

"Right this instant!" she yelled into the phone. "All of you! Now!"

There was steam, I'm sure, billowing in her lungs.

She stared at the painting, at the thickness of the stripes, which were well-defined and expertly done. It was hard to imagine who could've done that so quickly and still made such a fine job of it. Despite herself, she felt a glimmer of admiration, which she pushed right down as she stood outside her door, toe tapping. The elevator opened and the custodial staff walked down the carpet. There were seven of them, and just as a side note, it's interesting to know that they all happen to be related.

She walked a bit to meet them, and had them line up right there in the hall. I have now heard eight different versions of this story, but here's the best I can do to re-create it for you.

Her jaw was set.

"First off," she said, "I ASKED YOU TO MOVE THIS YESTERDAY!"

A bold young man with sideburns raised his hand.

"We came up yesterday," he said. "Right when you called. But there was nothing here."

There was a murmur of agreement from all except the museum head.

"Then you ALL need to get your EYES examined," she said. "My next question is this. Which one of you arrogant people thinks it is okay to draw on ANYTHING in this museum? You can't draw on ANYTHING. Because even if it is a bad painting. No drawing. Never. Is that clear? We will wait here until someone confesses. We will wait here all day. We will wait here until you die of dehydration if we have to."

The seven janitors looked puzzled. They all looked puzzled in a similar way, due to their genetic coding for the word *puzzled*. The head, the patriarch, who had been taking care of the museum building now for nearly fifty years, raised his hand.

"Ma'am," he said. "When you say drawing on something," he said, "what exactly do you mean?"

"On the canvas of course," she said.

"Someone may draw on it?"

"Someone DID draw on it," she said. "Someone put that painting in jail. As of yesterday, the canvas had no stripes at all."

"Ma'am, which canvas are you talking about?" he asked again. Behind him, his nephew tittered.

The museum head blew air through her teeth. "The ONE," she said, turning around, "the ONE that is RIGHT BEHIND ME."

And as she turned around, ready to stomp her feet, ready to raise her voice to the roof, she looked at the canvas again, and fainted dead away into the waiting arms of the seven attending janitors.

They caught her long before the floor did. Carefully they laid her on the carpet.

"Is she sick?" asked the nephew.

"She's crazy," said the cousin.

The patriarch thought no, and he was relieved when she fluttered her eyes open and straightened her skirt.

"Ma'am?" he asked.

She waved her hand weakly at the painting, and the janitors all looked but they did not know what it was she wanted them to see.

For the canvas, now, was blank. Not covered with white paint, not painted over, just blank, as if no one had ever painted anything on it at all. No sign of the stripes or the circle or the wavy lines. Nothing. The museum head put her head down on the carpet, and asked each of the janitors if, when they walked down the hall, there had been anything on that canvas. They said, all seven at once, No. They said it was the first they'd seen of this canvas and it had nothing on it any more than a baby's bottom might. She said she did not understand. Did they see anyone walking by with paint remover? she asked. And they said no, they would've smelled that a mile away. One sniffed the canvas and said it was as sweet-smellingly fresh as a rose. They said drawing on a canvas was certainly a bad idea, and they would've moved it yesterday had it been there. Seven heads hovered above her, with seven similar looks of concern and barely detectable impatience. They helped her up and locked the canvas in her office at her request and she took her purse on her shoulder and they sent her home early and went back to tending and keeping the lines and corners of the building.

She claims she slept all night that night. As soon as she got home, slept and slept. But several of us got messages on our machines from her at around 2:00 a.m., quiet sleepy messages all about the painting and this sad bewilderment. I erased mine, it was too embarrassing, but some of the less kind employees who have wanted a raise for years have kept theirs for possible later blackmail.

That night at the museum, someone touched the little Degas ballerina again. No licking this time; instead, someone stroked her curved bronze neck with fingers coated in peanut oil. The bells rang and rang but the guard was in the bathroom at the time and missed it. By the time the guard was back, the Degas was already covered in sliding sweeping tracks of oil and the gallery was empty. You could only hear the swing of the back door.

Creepy, I know.

The museum head returned the next day and found the canvas leaning against the file cabinets in her office. It was still blank. She dragged her desk to the side and sat directly across from the canvas and stared at it. She stared at it the entire day. From nine in the morning until two or so in the afternoon, she was glued to that chair; I walked by and I saw it. Her phone would ring and she'd answer and write down notes but her eyes did not leave that painting.

But for all her good watching, nothing happened. It was only after she went off to the bathroom, not even to cry this time, just to use it, that she returned and saw the new pattern through her office window. She ran inside, dashed in to see the new box and arc and little dancing lines, the precise pattern you see now. Yes. Exactly.

And she fell to her knees, asking it to change in front of her. She was desperate to see it happen. She talked to the painting so long that anyone who wanted to hear her could've just walked by. I happened to, yes. It was disturbing to see, someone pleading like that is always disturbing to see, and of course especially disturbing if they are pleading with things inanimate. The security guard, Lola, went upstairs, shaken, all set to confess that she had missed the Degas-touching but the museum head waved her off and said it was fine, fine, whatever. She said clean off the oil with a damp rag and some soap. The bells were ringing and you could hear another security guard talking loudly downstairs, but the museum head didn't seem to notice or care. All her energy was focused on the painting and asking it to shift that box into a circle, to make a tiny line—anything, AN-Y-THING. She sat there the whole day, ordered food on the phone without moving her eyes, and stayed there the entire night. She spent about three days staring at that painting. Alarming; we were all distressed by it. Her hair was falling out, or maybe it was just unbrushed. Her husband delivered the divorce papers in person and tried to talk to her but she wouldn't even look at him. She held out her hand and he placed the papers in them, and she nodded to the painting and he left. Downstairs, someone actually lifted the Degas ballerina off her platform to the loud ringing of many bells and was halfway out the parking lot with it when the youngest janitor screamed "THIEF!" and the thief dropped the ballerina and ran. We didn't catch him. The ballerina was facedown in the grass and has a small dent on her toe shoe from the fall. The reason you didn't see her up today is because we thought it'd be best to keep her in storage for a while until this whole thing blows over.

On day three of her observation, on who knows how many energy pills, the museum head called all us staff up on the phone and said we had better clear a space for the painting, the most important space in the gallery. Last, on the tour line. Here. "Do it today please," she said, slurring her words from exhaustion. This certainly did not match our carefully discussed plans to put our best Vasily Kandinsky last, since it is such a sizzle of a grand finale, but we made the space and painted the wall ecru behind it, and then she called up the electronics store and installed a video camera directly across. Up more. Yes, the glint? There. She kept her eye on the canvas until the camera was up and rolling. It goes to one of those security TVs in the basement, and if you want to check on it, it's on twenty-four hours. With help from three of the janitors, she moved the painting downstairs and hung it up and then went home to sleep and sleep.

It hasn't changed once.

She wants to catch it on film but it hasn't even changed a centimeter and I don't think it will ever again. Would you? The whole thing makes me tense. Whenever she dies or if she quits, if I am still alive, I think I will snap off the camera right away and give the poor painting a break, but until then, she has us all under oath that we will leave it on all the time and if we were to violate that oath and turn the camera off, not only are we fired, which might not be so bad, but there's some city policy that requires a huge fine. And let me tell you people, a museum salary does not leave room for huge fines. And since it's a camera, you're sure to get caught if you do it because she has bolted it in there with titanium cords.

I do sit up sometimes at night feeling bad for the painting; one wonders about the health of us docents sometimes, spending all day with all of this art. But it does not seem like a good life for a painting. Worse than a zoo, in a way.

The Degas ballerina's toe is being restored and you'll be able to see it on Level Two in about a month. We'll have our burliest guard watching it. And good question, we did call the Atlanta benefactor, but he just babbled on about guns and defense funding. He had no memory of sending the package at all. And yes, the museum head's divorce did come through. I saw them on the last day they saw each other, maybe forever. He went up to her office again, I assume to collect those papers, or maybe just to say good-bye. I happened to be up there at the drinking fountain—it was a very warm day and I was very thirsty and the best drinking fountain happens to be right next to her office. So I happened to overhear. He said, "Good-bye," and she just smiled at him. They didn't hug. He said, "I know it'll take time," and she just smiled at him. He said something else then that I didn't hear because in a gigantic ding-dong, all the bells went off down below, louder than ever, all at once, and I had to run downstairs. It was craziness, when I arrived. Pandemonium. On the first floor, a whole team of rebels—four people, grown adults, three men, one woman—had taken off their clothes and were making love with the Jackson Pollock. I ran in and the security guards were securing three of the people, all nude, and the last one was still wriggling on the painting, humping it, eyes closed, kissing the dribbles of paint. A security guard seized this last one, called the police, and the art experts ran in from their offices and began looking closely at the painting with magnifying glasses to see if it was stained. The male rebels were still erect so it appeared likely that no one had reached a climactic point yet, which was very good news, though as they perused the painting, in the lower right quadrant one expert located a possible foreign blob of gray-white material. He blew his whistle. "Violation!" he yelled, pointing. "Press charges!" he said. The guards pulled the delinquents away, in handcuffs, down the hall. They were yelling back, all the way down the hall. "But it inspired me that way!" one nude guy was yelling. "It aroused me! You're telling me I'm just supposed to LOOK at that thing?"

The museum head did not come down. We handled that one on our own. We are considering building a glass case, but the board is waffling.

So, yes, it has been quite a year. Very eventful. I appreciate your attentive listening. I highly recommend the gift shop, on the left, for the end phase of your visit. There are silkscreened T-shirts, and high-quality mugs and umbrellas. We also have an unusually fine selection of magnets. They are tiny and detailed and they will stick nicely to your refrigerator and hold up photos of your loved ones. Bring art into your homes, people. Thank you, again, for your interest and continued support of our museum.

Thirteen Ways of Being Looked at by a Blackbird SR-71

by Paul Di Filippo

> Among twenty snowy mountains,
> The only moving thing
> Was the eye of the blackbird.
>
> —Wallace Stevens,
> "Thirteen Ways of Looking at a Blackbird"

1

We stopped digging vertically in our pursuit of a life free from surveillance when we reached one mile straight down into the bosom of the earth, and began to excavate laterally. With that single perpendicular shaft the only access to our refuge, we finally felt safe from all prying eyes dominant on the panopticon surface. Now we could begin to build our surveillance-free society.

The big boring machines opened up huge caverns, all connected in pleasing and harmonious arrangements. A ceaseless stream of chewed-up rock ascended the shaft in conveyor buckets, while an equally endless stream of equipment and supplies came down. We installed fusion power plants that brought to life the natural-spectrum lights affixed to the cavern ceilings. Programmed to replicate the eternal cycle of day and night, they would provide comfort and familiarity. Smaller lights mimicked the constellations when the large lamps were turned off.

We tapped underground aquifers for more water than our population could use. Air-filtering and air-regeneration machines were installed. Lacking weather and enjoying a perpetual ambient temperature of seventy-five degrees Fahrenheit, we were able to build simple, delicate houses. Nudism was encouraged. Vast hydroponic systems and mushroom farms were established, along with aquaculture tanks and herds of some small animals for meat production. Supplies and items we could not manufacture would continue to arrive, thanks to funding from a secret self-sustaining foundation aboveground. All our well-off members had to tithe.

Finally, the new world was ready for its immigrant population to arrive.

Our pioneering settlers passed through the stringent inspection. No cameras, no communications devices, no recording devices allowed. There would be no Internet, no broadcasts, no telephones to tap. Our government was a benevolent anarcho-libertarianism with an emphasis on minimal interference with the rights of citizens. All social and civic intercourse would occur face to face, and when one wished to be alone and private, no one would monitor or intrude.

For the first six months our paradise rolled along smoothly.

But then people began to complain of feeling spied upon. An unmistakable feeling.

We examined our lone connection to the surface world, but found that no intrusive devices had been stealthily inserted. We reluctantly performed exhaustive searches of every house and storage facility underground, and came up dry of spy bugs.

And then someone noticed a camera lens in the *floor* of our world. Soon, many others were found, and eventually traced to their source.

Yes, all the old legends were true. Deros, C.H.U.D.s, and Mole People all existed, flourishing down below our level, and they wished to know everything about us. We had moved into a neighborhood that boasted more suspicious eyes focused on our every move than we had ever experienced in the open air.

We filled in our caverns and returned aboveground, where at least the spying was performed by our own kind.

ll

The discovery of the secret to the compression of matter allowed the creation of miniature humans: perfectly proportioned, naturally functioning men, women, and children only three inches high at most. These Tom Thumbs and Thumbelinas, these Stuart Littles and Borrowers, were initially heralded as the saviors of the planet. By shrinking in size, they would consume many fewer resources. This assertion was true, and many socially responsible volunteers stepped forward to be shrunk. But a corollary, at first unnoticed, was that maintaining surveillance of these tiny beings was much harder.

Public CCTV cameras did not possess enough resolution to track the mannikins, and the tiny people could conceal themselves in a practically limitless range of common places. They did not emit big heat signatures on infrared monitors, or disturb pressure or motion sensors. They were, in effect, invisible.

Human nature dictated that there would inevitably be bad apples among the mannikins. Theft, sabotage, and, ironically, spying by the mannikins soon became rampant.

The authorities had only one solution: to create a class of humans even smaller than the Tom Thumbs, and use them to surveil and control the first-generation mannikins.

As of today, the latest iteration in the multiple generations of tiny people has reached atomic size, and subsequent generations will be stopped only by the firm boundary of the Planck level.

"Great fleas have little fleas upon their backs to bite 'em, /And little fleas have lesser fleas, and so *ad infinitum.*"

III

When I got home from school, I put my phablet down and it yelled at me.

"Excuse me, Mr. Johnson, but exactly where do you think you're going?"

The festering voice was that of one of the myriad assistant festering principals at festering Boomgarden High School, Ms. Daggett. Each of the one hundred assistant principals had the task of monitoring twenty students. That accounted for the whole population of Boomgarden High. The authorities kept track of us 24/7 through the government-issued phablets. The machines could never be shut off. They recorded all the swipes and taps, spreads and pinches we made, which were analyzed by intelligent software for anything forbidden. Their cameras and microphones remained continually activated; there was no power-off button. We were told never to be farther away from our festering phablets than ten feet. The only time we could be separate from them was in the bathroom. And even then we had to leave them right outside the door.

"Gee, Ms. Daggett, I was just going into the kitchen for a snack."

"Very well. But don't dawdle! You have four point two five hours of homework tonight, and then studying for your AP exam."

"Yes, Ms. Daggett." Satan rot your festering soul!

At the fridge—the phablet still had a line of sight on me from the living room, so I didn't have to tote it—I thought about how I might be able to thwart the damn machine so that I could sneak out to see my blazing favorite band, Llama Iguana, in concert tonight. I couldn't damage the phablet, or I'd have to pay for it. Actually, of course, my parents would end up paying, and they wouldn't be too happy about that. I wasn't savvy enough to hack it. And I couldn't pull a Tom Sawyer and get someone else to do my work, because Ms. Daggett would be alerted to a stranger's face in one of her twenty windows.

I finished a quart of milk and half a box of Oreos before I got a brainstorm.

"I'm back Ms. Daggett. Here I go. I'll start with algebra."

I stared into the phablet's camera with a real intense look of concentration, but I didn't actually touch the screen. Ms. Daggett went away to focus on other kids for a while, and when she returned she was obviously puzzled and angry.

"Mr. Johnson, you haven't done a lick of work. Why is that?"

I put on my most innocent look. "But I have, Ms. Daggett! I've gone through twenty problem sets—oh, damn, all my work just vanished! And now there's a message on the screen with a lot of obscene emojis! Can't you see it? It says, 'Tough shit from the Honker Union.' Ms. Daggett, the Chinese ate my homework!"

Ms. Daggett flipped out. "They've gotten past our firewalls again! God knows what they're doing in our system right now. Mr. Johnson, put your phablet in its Faraday cage so it goes blind and deaf. I have to call Principal Finney this minute!"

I did as Ms. Daggett ordered, changed my shirt for a Llama Iguana one, and left the house.

God bless foreigners and paranoia!

IV

The rise of biometrics as a means of identifying individuals and tracking them caused many strange behaviors. But perhaps no phenomenon was weirder or more gruesome than eyeball spoofing.

Reliance on scanning a person's irises to formalize their identity naturally led to measures to counteract or confuse or convince such systems. Simple contact lenses failed to trick the devices, as did artificial constructs, and eventually people realized that only living organic human eyeballs could fool the machines.

The savage surgical theft of eyeballs became a shocking trend, as rampant as the theft of credit card numbers had once been. The iris was the key to unlocking all of a person's wealth and information. And employing a stolen optic to register an innocent dupe as the perpetrator of your crime—entering a bank past its scanners under pretense, in order to rob it, say—was a default criminal move.

But soon, waving a detached eyeball in front of the scanners was technologically precluded. Only an eyeball firmly socketed would suffice.

Underground clinics arose to meet the demand, the science of whole-eyeball transplants having been recently perfected. (The banishment of many forms of blindness was almost overlooked in the clamor about eyeball thefts.) At first criminals could often be recognized as the possessors of two differently colored eyes, and innocent individuals with this condition were needlessly stigmatized. But the adoption of contact lenses by savvy crooks ended this easy-identification aspect of the crime wave.

Reluctantly, defeated organizations began to abandon this particular method of biometric security.

But the adoption of gait-and-stance recognition metrics hardly improved matters.

But that remains the theme of another historical account.

V

When aliens eventually landed on Earth, and First Contact was finally a reality, no one initially predicted that their arrival would destroy civilization in precisely the manner that occurred. The extraterrestrials seemed friendly and harmless, and indeed their intentions were honest and altruistic. They brought humanity new technologies and the solutions to many of our problems, as well as information about the galactic community that stood ready to welcome us.

But unfortunately, these aliens were natural shape-shifters.

Basically humanoid in shape and size, dubbed "Facedancers" after such a race in an old science fiction novel, they could alter their appearance at will to resemble anyone.

This protean gift was apparent from the first. The Facedancers did not dissemble. When the doors of their ship, parked in the middle of New York City's First Avenue in front of the UN, opened up, a parade of dead celebrities emerged: Marilyn Monroe, Gandhi, Nelson Mandela, Benjamin Franklin, Michael Jackson. The Facedancers—appointed by the galactics to make First Contact with Earth specifically because of their talents for mimicry—believed that such a display of idols would put humanity at ease, and to some extent the tactic worked.

But as the Facedancers established embassies around the world, their very existence sowed unease and paranoia.

How could anyone be certain of the identity of anyone else? Even a trusted person of long intimacy could be a Facedancer, acting out of obscure and secret motives of impersonation. Likewise, any person could now disavow any offense. "That wasn't me, it was a Facedancer disguised as me!"

Civilization, based on security of identity and on trust between known individuals, started to creak and exhibit fault lines.

When the king of England suffered a car crash, was rushed to the hospital, died, and reverted to Facedancer appearance—the baseline state of the aliens was green and with a complexly structured epidermis—the final straw on civilization's back had been dropped. None of the protestations by the royal family and the British government that they had been cooperating with this deception (to conceal the real king's abdication with a Las Vegas showgirl) had any effect. Neighbor turned against neighbor, parent against child, in a bloody pogrom of Facedancer accusations and slayings.

All the real Facedancers rushed back to their ship and left the planet in haste.

But they assured us as they left that our entrance to the galactic community, although delayed for a few centuries until our civilization recovered from this apocalypse, was still guaranteed.

VI

The perfection of cloaking garments that rendered their wearers invisible seemed to offer freedom from many types of public surveillance. Although one's electronic communications could still be tapped, once out in public, unmediated by the Internet, the invisible man was king.

The special fabric worked by bending light rays around itself, to convey vistas and images, real-time action and sights that would normally have been occluded by the presence of a person. Tiny pinhole camera lenses were the only break in the seamless clothing. These unnoticeable input devices wirelessly fed exterior sights to the special electronic goggles worn by the invisible person under their cloak, allowing the wearer to navigate through the world. At first, moving too rapidly while cloaked produced uncanny shimmering of the surrounding environment in the eyes of those looking toward the invisible person, as the smart fabric sought to refresh its display. But even this hallucinatory defect vanished with subsequent generations of the technology.

Invisibility was the perfect solution for those who were morally opposed to having their innocent activities unnecessarily monitored, and the technology was hailed as empowering all good citizens. But it fostered many bad behaviors as well. Voyeurism soared, as did gropings. An assassins' guild materialized: they favored knives and poisoned needles over guns, allowing for quick escapes while confusion reigned over what exactly was ailing the hapless victim with no one around. Soon no politician dared appear in public. Robberies proliferated: any stolen item brought under the cloak became invisible as well. As with so many counterespionage technologies, this one actually fostered a new kind of easy eavesdropping.

Vigilante action proved the only suitable response. In the beginning, people employed cans of spray paint, unleashing jets of aerosol color toward any suspected lurker. But after many lawsuits from innocent bystanders who got accidentally sprayed, the proactive citizens switched to more accurate and less staining paintball guns and, later, special bulbs of nanopowder that would cling harmlessly but blatantly to the cloaks, revealing their outlines.

Ultimately, the development of highly sensitive and portable carbon dioxide detectors put an end to the invisibility craze.

At least for humans. Invisible drones are all around us still.

VII

When the entire atmosphere of the planet was seeded with ineradicable, military-grade, self-replicating smart dust, the war against surveillance was finally lost.

The dust penetrated everywhere, even into the securest environments, hiding in the nasal passages and other intimate crannies of otherwise disinfected individuals, and broadcast whatever it saw and heard on publicly accessible channels.

The Totally Transparent Society was born, willy-nilly.

Like any birth, the process was traumatic and painful. Chaos reigned for several years. But, like any infant, the TTS did not remain the same as when it first emerged.

The people who survived the interregnum began to curate the billions of feeds from the dust: human and animal, vegetable and mineral.

Most importantly, every living person became the star of their own reality show channel, shaped by themselves or others.

All forms of fictional entertainment went extinct in the face of being able to share the candid lives of one's fellow citizens. So did all nature shows, as audiences became privy to the most intimate moments of wildlife, like watching old-fashioned urban hawk-cams ramped up by several orders of magnitude.

Surprisingly, no lynch mobs or finger-wagging shaming conditions obtained when inevitable feedback ensued. Stones could be thrown only when one's own sins remained hidden, and that state of being was impossible.

Nonetheless, for some strange reason, even without public censure, individual behavior—and, consequently, corporate and government communal behaviors—began to grow more ethical. Experts puzzled over the reasons for such improvements, and then decided that brand maintenance was the answer. Having become, even if only informally, publicly traded commodities with audiences and market shares, each person was focused on not alienating their fans with egregious misbehaviors.

Except, of course, if one's persona was that of a "bad boy" or "bad girl."

Then, of course, it was a race to the bottom.

VIII

The wearing of uniform Guy Fawkes masks by protestors worldwide, intended to stymie identification and indicate a commonality of purpose, reached an inevitable conclusion when nano-based flesh-sculpting was finally perfected. The eventuality that came about in real life had been partially foreseen by a twentieth-century science fiction writer named John Varley, who predicted a cult in which all members subjected themselves to an androgynous full-body makeover to encourage solidarity.

But in the world of 2054, no such blandness prevailed.

Instead, a thousand cliques and bands of rebels sprouted, each of whose members chose to share a certain somatotype. Quite often, the artificial appearance did not relate in any way to the original gender, race, or ethnicity of the adopter.

One group might be composed entirely of Robespierres. Another might be all Margaret Sangers. There were legions of Edward Snowdens and Chelsea Mannings, Chairman Maos and Rasputins, Malcolm Xs and Dr. Kings. Some groups took a more blithe and playful approach, molding themselves into hordes of identical celebrities. Others chose to mirror the faces of the very politicians they were castigating.

The identicalness of each set of activists among themselves did indeed prove effective at confusing law-enforcement and national security experts. But the authorities always held out the ultimate option of doing DNA tests on any arrestees and finding their true identities.

But the first DNA tests revealed an unanticipated glitch in the process.

The nano-sculpting extended inadvertently down to the cellular level. Each Gloria Steinem now exhibited the same genome as any other. And the changes were ineradicable, irreversible. Each person was stuck for their lifetime with the adopted somatotype.

After a wave of suicides, people adapted to their less-than-ideal looks. But the real unfortunate fallout came in the next generation, when the children of the protestors arrived.

You really don't want to see what the offspring of Abe Lincoln and Betty Friedan look like.

IX

As always, my flock of tiny personal drones surrounded me in a whirring, buzzing cocoon of perfect safety, privacy, and inviolability. Each drone was the size of a housefly, and there were thousands and thousands of them, forming a mutable, responsive, intelligent shell around me at a distance of some three inches from my skin. They relayed sensory telemetry to my contact lenses and earbuds, and continually refreshed the air within the multiparticulate eggshell they formed around me, while maintaining the perfect ambient temperature in all circumstances.

I couldn't consider living without my swarm of drones. How did our ancestors ever interface directly with the environment? What a brutish state of existence! My drones kept all my actions secluded, all my expressions opaque, all my vulnerabilities concealed. They could mass together to dispense sonic or laser or chemical assaults against my enemies. When I lifted my legs to walk, or my arms to hoist, the drones configured closer to my epidermis and assisted as exo-musculature. When I stood or sat or reclined, they adjusted accordingly between me and whatever surface I was interfacing with.

All of Earth's two billion inhabitants were now solitary sovereign states, secure within their portable drone castles.

I must admit, though, that the important and necessary business of mating was rendered somewhat more complex and difficult by our invaluable and indispensable drone carapaces.

Personal appearances could no longer be relied on when seeking to render esthetic judgments upon possible mates. Every individual looked identical: a shimmering, humming humanoid blob. One had to choose to accept telemetry from strangers, feeds that ostensibly showed their true faces as recorded by the inner sensors of the drone shells. These sendings could, of course, be faked.

But, assuming one found a likely mating partner, based on telemetry that included a sufficient amount of introductory conversation, one still faced the trouble of merging drone shells. In order to come skin to skin to enact the ancient biological imperatives, two (or more!) drone swarms had to temporarily blend into a single entity.

But the drones, possessing artificial intelligence geared toward protecting the wearer, sometimes didn't agree with the wearer's choices or decisions. Sensing danger or incompatibility, drones would fight a merger or, if forced, descend into chaotic states, leaving the individuals helplessly naked to the world.

But, assuming all went well, sex could still happen as of yore, with the chosen instances of pregnancy. Then, with the drones assisting at the birth, the newborns would emerge and be instantly encapsulated in their own drone shells hived off from the mother's mass.

I think there are few things more beautiful than a little infant sporting its first flickering cladding of drones, which, around its lips, merge with the drones at the mother's nipple, as the nutritive milk of life is pumped by the little palpating mechanical assistants from her buzzing breast.

X

In the grocery store, I was immediately beset by animated advertising holograms from the products on the shelves. Thank goodness they were tightbeamed to my ears and eyes only, because some of them were quite personal.

"Ms. Leakey, we know you and your family enjoyed your last box of Cheerios. You finished it in only six days from the time of purchase. Little Charles Leakey had the last bowl, of course, and wished for more the next day. But there were no more boxes in the house. Don't you think you should buy two boxes this time?"

"Ms. Leakey, your daughter Amanda had a most embarrassing and awkward incident during co-ed gym class yesterday. Her current brand of tampons failed to handle her menstrual flow and conceal that she was experiencing her period, resulting in a spotting incident that caused her male peers to mock her. Shouldn't you switch from Tampax to the higher-rated Playtex now?"

"Ms. Leakey, your husband Roy has been a little tired during the performance of his marital duties lately. We recommend some ginseng from our vitamin aisle. And oysters are on sale today."

I managed to ignore these solicitations—I had a mind of my own, after all—until there came one I couldn't resist.

"Ms. Leakey, we can tell from your vital signs and brain waves that you are utterly tired of shopping and sick of running your household, as well as fed up with your children and spouse. Out in the parking lot you will find a black Corvette in which sits a man whom we have selected as the ideal candidate to enliven your life with a short-term love affair. If you consent to this purchase, just swipe your store loyalty card on the card reader secured to his stick shift. If not completely satisfied, you may apply for a refund."

I left my shopping cart blocking the frozen foods aisle and was in Las Vegas before nightfall.

I hope more specials like this show up in weeks to come.

XI

Ultimately, USA authorities realized that the most effective and cost-cutting form of surveillance was self-surveillance. If the target of spying could be induced to spy and report on himself, then no outside agents would be necessary. Incomplete or erratic information would be obviated. No one could compile a more complete dossier on an individual than the individual himself.

This revelation occurred to a lowly GS-3 clerk in the Secret Service named Wilbert Punsal, who happened to receive by accident from Netflix the disc of *A Scanner Darkly* when he thought he had requested Agatha Christie's spooky murder mystery *In a Glass Darkly*. Viewing the Philip K. Dick film, he saw the real-life potential of its twisted scenario.

Punsal was rewarded by being the first person to undergo the enforced self-spying modification. To put a point on the procedure, he was chemically induced to develop a secondary personality which would keep track of everything his baseline personality did, and which would file reports when Wilbert Punsal the Original was sleeping.

Upon satisfaction with their new technique, various government agencies in collaboration infiltrated the nation's water supply with a drug that produced Directed Dissociative Identity Disorder. In weeks, three hundred million citizens, more or less, were spying on themselves.

Other nations quickly followed suit.

All went well, until the secondary personalities began to develop wills and motivations of their own. At this point, tertiary personalities had to be introduced to spy on the secondaries.

Naturally, the regress was infinite. Or would have been, if the computational capacity of the human brain had not been reached with Personality Number Ten. After that point, complete hebephrenia and catatonia set in, leaving a planet populated with drooling idiots who quickly died off in hecatombs. The globe's resources were duly apportioned among the few remaining unmodified humans—basically, a single tribe of Pacific islanders, some Inuits, a few Scandinavian elk herders, and a handful of Amazonian primitives—who had failed to encounter the DDID drugs.

XII

The more far-out physicists had long contended that the entire universe was composed of information. Not atoms, but bits. Since information was the stock-in-trade of spies and governments, many top-secret attempts were made to prove or disprove this theory. Eventually, one black-budget project succeeded in proving the postulate: all of creation was simply a quantum computer. And, with this verification of the nature of reality, it was not long before the tools to access the flow of information were perfected.

Physical spying was no longer necessary. It was enough to probe the various "registers" and "buffers" of the universe to learn anything one wished to know.

Terrorists were astounded—in the milliseconds before their deaths—to be blown up in their most secure hideouts. Embezzlers were caught before they could spend the first penny of their ill-gotten gains. Murderers were halted before their fingers reached the triggers.

Amazingly, abuse of the secret omniscience was kept to a minimum. The political plans of opposition parties were not leaked. The sexual peccadillos of celebrities were not made into headlines. The plots of movies-in-progress were not spoiled. The people in charge of probing the quantum computer exhibited extreme moral fiber.

But then someone discovered the universe was not read-only, but could be overwritten.

The temptation was too much. Reality began to shift on a minute-by-minute basis, as those in charge of the quantum computer access began to tinker to achieve their personal preferences. Entire countries disappeared. New genders arose. Multiple moons swam through the skies. The fabric of reality began to unravel.

But then someone must have hit "reboot," for the universe winked out of existence, and then restarted, but this time with access to the cosmic software denied.

Life goes on now as of old. But people are spotted and tentacled and possess many, many eyes.

XIII

A secure information utopia had at long last been attained.

There was no more surveillance upon the planet. Spying had been rendered physically impossible by a number of clever stratagems and technologies, buttressed by strictly enforced laws and legislation.

Privacy was ultimate and complete. Humans could no longer intrude on the sacred sphere of nondisclosure surrounding each individual.

But then the Sparrowfall movement was born.

A certain radical, self-ordained preacher began lambasting God as the ultimate snoop.

"Does He not see each sparrow fall? Has He not numbered the hairs upon our heads and our days upon the earth? His omniscience is the unsurpassable affront to the integrity of our lives! All our mortal privacy protections are as naught before His prying eyes!"

Something about the incredible diatribe and accusations made them go viral. The preacher graduated from YouTube videos with very few views to filled stadiums. People began to panic at the thought of God piercing their otherwise inviolable barriers of privacy. A population that had forgotten the old notion of the Creator peering into their souls no longer possessed the mental immunity against such a shattering concept.

Because, of course, there were no scientific or technological impediments against God, the clamoring supplicants turned to all sorts of magic. Charlatans and scammers proliferated, offering curses, charms, and talismans that would cloak the sinner from God's inspection. But such individual gestures failed to satisfy a populace growing more and more alarmed over surveillance by the Big Spook, that deific NSA in the sky.

At last the governments of the planet had no choice but to respond.

And so the construction of an orbital magic curtain around the entire globe began.

The project, still only partially finished after two decades, currently usurps half the combined GDP of all the world's economies. But the majority feel that fencing themselves off from God's view is well worth the bankrupting costs.

No one has yet raised the prospect that God is already inside the curtain, rather than outside it.

About the Contributors

DAVID ABRAMS is the author of *Fobbit* (Grove/Atlantic, 2012), a comedy about the Iraq War, which *Publishers Weekly* called "an instant classic" and named a Top 10 Pick for Literary Fiction in fall 2012. It was also a *New York Times* Notable Book of 2012, an Indie Next pick, a Barnes & Noble Discover Great New Writers selection, a Montana Honor Book, and a finalist for the *LA Times'* Art Seidenbaum Award for First Fiction. His essays, reviews, and short stories have appeared in *Esquire, Narrative, Salon, Salamander, Connecticut Review, The Greensboro Review, Consequence, Fire and Forget* (Da Capo Press, 2013), *Home of the Brave: Somewhere in the Sand* (Press 53), and many other publications. He lives in Butte, Montana, with his wife. His blog, The Quivering Pen, can be found at: www.davidabramsbooks.blogspot.com. Visit his website at: www.davidabramsbooks.com.

AIMEE BENDER is the author of five books; the most recent, *The Color Master*, was a *New York Times* Notable Book of 2013. Her short fiction has been published in *Granta, Harper's, The Paris Review*, and more, as well as heard on *This American Life*. She lives in Los Angeles, and teaches creative writing at USC.

CHANELLE BENZ's fiction has been published in *The O. Henry Prize Stories 2014, Granta, The American Reader, Fence*, and others. Her work has also been selected as one of the Top Ten Longreads of 2012. She has an MFA in creative writing from Syracuse University and a BFA in acting from Boston University. She teaches at the University of Houston.

SEAN BERNARD is the author of two books, the story collection *Desert sonorous* (2015), which received the 2014 Juniper Prize, and the novel *Studies in the Hereafter* (2015).

T. CORAGHESSAN BOYLE is the author of twenty-five books of fiction, including, most recently, *When the Killing's Done* (2011), *San Miguel* (2012), *T.C. Boyle Stories II* (2013), and *The Harder They Come* (2015). His next novel, *The Terranauts*, will be published by Ecco in 2016. Boyle's work has been translated into more than two dozen foreign languages, and his stories have appeared in most of the major American magazines, including *The New Yorker*, *Harper's*, *Esquire*, *The Atlantic Monthly*, *Playboy*, *The Paris Review*, *GQ*, *Antaeus*, *Granta*, and *McSweeney's*. He has been the recipient of a number of literary awards, including the PEN/Faulkner Award for best novel of the year (*World's End*, 1988); the PEN/Malamud Prize in the short story (*T.C. Boyle Stories*, 1999); and the Prix Médicis Étranger for best foreign novel in France (*The Tortilla Curtain*, 1997). He currently lives near Santa Barbara with his wife and three children.

MARK CHIUSANO is the author of *Marine Park*, which received an honorable mention for the PEN/Hemingway Award. His stories and essays have appeared in *Guernica*, *Narrative Magazine*, *Harvard Review*, *The Atlantic*, and *The Paris Review Daily*. He writes for *Newsday* and was born and raised in Brooklyn.

ROBERT COOVER has published fourteen novels, three short story collections, and a collection of plays since *The Origin of the Brunists* received the William Faulkner Foundation First Novel Award in 1966. At Brown University, where he has taught for over thirty years, he established the International Writers Project, a program that provides an annual fellowship and safe haven to endangered international writers who face harassment, imprisonment, and suppression of their work in their home countries. In 1990–91, he launched the world's first hypertext fiction workshop; he was one of the founders in 1999 of the Electronic Literature Organization, and in 2002 created CaveWriting, the first writing workshop in immersive virtual reality. His most recent novel is *The Brunist Day of Wrath*.

LUCY CORIN is the author of the short story collections *One Hundred Apocalypses and Other Apocalypses* (McSweeney's Books) and *The Entire Predicament* (Tin House Books), and the novel *Everyday Psychokillers: A History for Girls* (FC2). She spent 2012–13 at the American Academy in Rome as the John Guare Fellow in Literature.

PAUL DI FILIPPO sold his first story in 1977, and since then has published over thirty books of short fiction, novels, and nonfiction, including *Ribofunk* and *The Steampunk Trilogy* (just reissued by Open Road Media). He lives in Providence, Rhode Island, with his partner of some forty years, Deborah Newton. He suspects he is being watched.

CORY DOCTOROW (craphound.com) is a science fiction author, activist, journalist, and blogger—the co-editor of Boing Boing (boingboing.net) and the author of the YA graphic novel *In Real Life*, the nonfiction business book *Information Doesn't Want to Be Free*, and young adult novels like *Homeland*, *Pirate Cinema*, and *Little Brother* and novels for adults like *Rapture of the Nerds* and *Makers*. He is the former European director of the Electronic Frontier Foundation and cofounded the UK Open Rights Group. Born in Toronto, Canada, he now lives in Los Angeles.

STEVEN HAYWARD is a novelist and short story writer born in Toronto, Canada. He is the author of the Canadian national best-seller *Don't Be Afraid*. A critical and commercial success, *Don't Be Afraid* was a Globe and Mail Best Book for 2012 and was also named one of the top ten novels of the year by Toronto's *Now Magazine*. His most recent book is a collection of short fiction, *To Dance the Beginning of the World*. He lives in Colorado and teaches creative writing at Colorado College.

BRYAN HURT is the author of *Everyone Wants to Be Ambassador to France*, winner of the Starcherone Prize for Innovative Fiction. His work has appeared in *The American Reader*, *The Kenyon Review*, the *Los Angeles Review of Books*, *Recommended Reading*, *Tin House*, *TriQuarterly*, among many others. He teaches creative writing at St. Lawrence University.

MARK IRWIN's seventh collection of poetry, *Large White House Speaking*, appeared from New Issues in spring of 2013, and his *American Urn: New & Selected Poems* (1987–2014) will be published in 2015. Recognition for his work includes *Discovery/The Nation Award*, two Colorado Book Awards, four Pushcart Prizes, and fellowships from the Fulbright, Lilly, NEA, and Wurlitzer Foundations. He teaches in the PhD in Creative Writing & Literature Program at the University of Southern California and he lives in Los Angeles and Colorado.

RANDA JARRAR's novel, *A Map of Home*, was published in half a dozen languages and won a Hopwood Award and an Arab-American Book Award and was named one of the best novels of 2008 by the *Barnes and Noble Review*. Her work has appeared in *The New York Times Magazine*, *Utne Reader*, *Salon*, *Guernica*,

The Rumpus, *Oxford American*, *Ploughshares*, *Five Chapters*, and others. She has received fellowships from the Civitella Ranieri Foundation, Hedgebrook, Caravansarai, and Eastern Frontier, and in 2010 was named one of the most gifted writers of Arab origin under the age of forty.

DANA JOHNSON is the author of *Elsewhere, California* and *Break Any Woman Down*, which won the Flannery O'Connor Award for Short Fiction and was a finalist for the Hurston/Wright Legacy Award. Her work has appeared in *Slake*, *Callaloo*, and *The Iowa Review*, among many others. Born and raised in and around Los Angeles, California, she is an associate professor of English at the University of Southern California where she teaches literature and creative writing. She lives in downtown Los Angeles.

MIRACLE JONES is a Sagittarius. He is a very private person from Texas.

KATHERINE KARLIN's fiction has appeared in the Pushcart Prize anthology, *New Stories from the South*, and journals including *One Story, TriQuarterly, Alaska Quarterly Review, [PANK]*, and many others. Her 2011 collection, *Send Me Work*, was published by Northwestern University Press and won the Balcones Fiction Prize. She lives in Manhattan, Kansas, and teaches at Kansas State University.

Born in Tel Aviv in 1967, ETGAR KERET is a winner of the French Chevalier des Arts et des Lettres, a lecturer at Ben-Gurion University of the Negev, and the author, most recently, of the memoir *The Seven Good Years*. His work has appeared in *The New Yorker*, *The Paris Review*, and *The New York Times Magazine*, and on *This American Life*.

MILES KLEE is an editor for the web culture site the Daily Dot as well as author of *Ivyland* (OR Books, 2012) and the story collection *True False* (OR Books, 2015). His essays, reportage, fiction, and satire have appeared in *Vanity Fair*, *Lapham's Quarterly*, *The Awl*, *Guernica*, *The Collagist*, and elsewhere.

ALEXIS LANDAU studied at Vassar College and received an MFA from Emerson College and a PhD from the University of Southern California in English literature and creative writing. Her first novel, *The Empire of the Senses*, was published by Pantheon Books in the spring of 2015. She lives with her husband and two children in Los Angeles.

KEN LIU (http://kenliu.name) is an author and translator of speculative fiction, as well as a lawyer and programmer. A winner of the Nebula, Hugo, and World Fantasy Awards, he has been published in *The Magazine of Fantasy & Science Fiction*, *Asimov's*, *Analog*, *Clarkesworld*, *Lightspeed*, and *Strange Horizons*, among other places. He also translated the Hugo-winning novel, *The Three-Body Problem*, by Liu Cixin, which is the first translated novel to win that award. Ken's debut novel, *The Grace of Kings*, the first in a silkpunk epic fantasy series, was published by Saga Press in April 2015. Saga also published a collection of his short stories, *The Paper Menagerie and Other Stories*, in March 2016. He lives with his family near Boston, Massachusetts.

KELLY LUCE's story collection, *Three Scenarios in Which Hana Sasaki Grows a Tail* (A Strange Object), won the 2013 *Foreword Review*'s Editors Choice Prize in Fiction. Her work has appeared in *O: The Oprah Magazine*, the *Chicago Tribune*, *Salon*, *Crazyhorse*, *The Southern Review*, and other publications. Her debut novel, *Pull Me Under*, will be published by Farrar, Straus and Giroux in 2016. A

Contributing Editor for Electric Literature, she hails from Illinois and lives in Santa Cruz, California.

CARMEN MARIA MACHADO is a fiction writer, critic, and essayist whose work has appeared in *The New Yorker*, *Granta*, *The Paris Review*, *AGNI*, *NPR*, *The American Reader*, *Los Angeles Review of Books*, *VICE*, and elsewhere. Her stories have been reprinted in several anthologies, including *Best American Science Fiction & Fantasy* 2015 and *Year's Best Weird Fiction*. She has been the recipient of the Richard Yates Short Story Prize, a Millay Colony for the Arts residency, the CINTAS Foundation Fellowship in Creative Writing, and a Michener-Copernicus Fellowship, and nominated for a Nebula Award and the Shirley Jackson Award. She is a graduate of the Iowa Writers' Workshop and the Clarion Science Fiction & Fantasy Writers' Workshop, and lives in Philadelphia with her partner.

LINCOLN MICHEL is the Editor-in-Chief of electricliterature.com and the Co-Editor of *Gigantic* magazine. He is also the Co-Editor *Gigantic Worlds*, an anthology of science flash fiction. His own work has appeared in *Granta*, *Tin House*, *NOON*, *The Believer*, *American Short Fiction*, *Pushcart Prize XXXIX*, and elsewhere. His debut collection, *Upright Beasts*, was published by Coffee House Press in 2015. You can find him online at lincolnmichel.com and @thelincoln.

ANNIE MCDERMOTT studied literature in Oxford and London before spending a year in Mexico City, working as a teacher, editor, and translator. Her translations of the short fiction of the Mexican writer Juan Pablo Villalobos have appeared in the magazines *World Literature Today* and *The Coffin Factory*, and she has also translated the Argentinian poet Karina Macció for the magazine *Palabras*

Errantes. She also reviews fiction and poetry for *The Literateur* and *Modern Poetry in Translation*.

BONNIE NADZAM's work has appeared in *Harper's Magazine*, *The Iowa Review*, *Epoch*, *Tweed's*, *Granta*, and many other journals. Her first novel, *Lamb*, was the recipient of the Center for Fiction's Flaherty-Dunnan First Novel Prize in 2011 and was long-listed for the Women's Prize for Fiction in the UK in 2013. She is co-author with Environmental Philosopher Dale Jamieson on *Love in the Anthropocene* (OR Books, September 2015) and her second novel, *Lions*, is forthcoming from Grove Press in 2016.

ALISSA NUTTING is author of the novel *Tampa* and the short story collection *Unclean Jobs for Women and Girls*. Her fiction has appeared in publications such as *The Norton Introduction to Literature*, *Tin House*, *Bomb*, and *Conduit*; her essays have appeared in *Fence*, *The New York Times*, *O: The Oprah Magazine*, and other venues. She is an assistant professor of creative writing at John Carroll University.

DEJI BRYCE OLUKOTUN graduated with an MA in creative writing from the University of Cape Town. He also holds degrees from Yale College and Stanford Law School. His novel *Nigerians in Space*, a thriller about brain drain from Africa, was published by Unnamed Press in 2014. Olukotun's work has been featured in *Slate*, *Guernica*, *The New York Times*, the *LA Times*, the *Los Angeles Review of Books*, *The Millions*, *Joyland*, *Words without Borders*, *World Literature Today*, and other publications. He founded the digital freedom program at PEN American Center, which focuses on online free expression and surveillance.

DALE PECK's twelfth book, *Visions and Revisions*, a memoir, was published in April 2015 by Soho Press, which will also be reprinting his first five novels throughout the year. He lives in New York City with his husband.

JIM SHEPARD is the author of seven novels, including *The Book of Aron*, and four story collections, including *Like You'd Understand, Anyway*, which was a finalist for the National Book Award and won the Story Prize. His short fiction has appeared in, among other magazines, *Harper's*, *McSweeney's*, *The Paris Review*, *The Atlantic Monthly*, *Esquire*, *DoubleTake*, *The New Yorker*, *Granta*, *Zoetrope: All-Story*, and *Playboy*. He's won a Guggenheim Fellowship, five of his stories have been chosen for the Best American Short Stories, two for the PEN/O. Henry Prize Stories, and one for a Pushcart Prize. He teaches creative writing and film at Williams College, and lives in Williamstown with his wife Karen, his three children, and three beagles.

MIRIAM SHLESINGER held an honorary doctorate from the Copenhagen Business School (2001), the 2010 Danica Seleskovitch Prize, and the Lifetime Achievement Award of the Israel Translators Association. She was co-editor (with Franz Pöchhacker) of the *Interpreting Studies Reader* (Routledge, 2002), and since 2006 was co-editor of *Interpreting: International Journal of Research and Practice in Interpreting* (John Benjamins) as well as associate editor of *Benjamins Translation Library*. She taught translation and interpretation (both theory and practice) at Bar Ilan University, Israel. She passed away in 2012.

CHIKA UNIGWE was born in Enugu, Enugu State. She has degrees from the University of Nigeria and the KU Leuven. She holds a PhD from the Leiden University in Holland. She is the author of three novels, including *On Black Sisters Street* and *Night Dancer*. She has won the 2012 Nigeria Prize for Literature, a BBC Short Story

Competition, a Commonwealth Short Story award, and was short-listed for the Caine Prize for African Writing. Her other writing awards include a Rockefeller Foundation award, a UNESCO-Aschberg Fellowship, a Ledig House Fellowship, and a 2013 Cove Park Fellowship. She is the most recent winner of the Nigeria Literature Award, and a 2014 Sylt Fellowship for African writers. Her works have been translated into several languages including German, Hebrew, Italian, Hungarian, Spanish, and Dutch.

JUAN PABLO VILLALOBOS is the author of *Down the Rabbit Hole* and *Quesadillas* (both FSG). His work has been translated into fifteen languages. He was born in Mexico and currently lives in Barcelona.

CARMEN YILING YAN was born in China and raised in the United States. Since starting out as a fan translator, her translations of Chinese science fiction have appeared in *Lightspeed*, *Clarkesworld*, and *Galaxy's Edge*. Her writing has been published in *Daily Science Fiction*. She currently attends UCLA.

CHARLES YU is the author of the novel *How to Live Safely in a Science Fictional Universe* and the short story collections *Third Class Superhero* and *Sorry Please Thank You*. His fiction has appeared in a number of magazines and journals, including *Oxford American*, *The Gettysburg Review*, *Harvard Review*, *Mid-American Review*, *Mississippi Review*, and *Alaska Quarterly Review*.

Born in 1981, ZHANG RAN graduated from Beijing Jiaotong University in 2004 with a degree in computer science. After a stint in the IT industry, Zhang became a reporter and news analyst with *Economic Daily* and *China Economic Net*, during which time his news commentary won a China News Award. In 2011, Zhang quit his job and moved to southern China to become an independent writer. He began publishing science fiction in 2012, with his debut story, "Ether," winning the Yinhe (Galaxy) Award as well as the Xingyun (Nebula) Award. His novella, *Rising Wind City*, won the Yinhe Award and a Silver Xingyun Award.

Acknowledgments

MY THANKS

To Kate Johnson: super agent, who believed in this book long before it was a book and without whose wisdom, support, and guidance this book would not exist.

To John Oakes: publisher extraordinaire, generous, enthusiastic, and patient even as our cell phone calls were dropped as I was driving up into the mountains.

To Andy Hunter, Jennifer Abel Kovitz, Julie Buntin, and everyone else at Catapult.

To Aimee Bender, T. C. Boyle, Etgar Keret, and Jim Shepard for your early support of this project.

To Sean Bernard, Steven Hayward, Mark Irwin, Dana Johnson, Katherine Karlin, Alexis Landau, and Bonnie Nadzam for your friendship.

To all of my contributors: it's been an honor, deeply moving, and deeply satisfying to work with so many of my heroes.

To my parents, Jeanne and John Hurt, and to my sister, Emily Hurt, for your unconditional love and support.

Most of all to Marielle and Ezra: for everything.

Credits

"The Entire Predicament," from *The Entire Predicament: Stories* by Lucy Corin. Reprinted by permission of the author.

"Thirteen Ways of Being Looked at by a Blackbird SR-71," by Paul Di Filippo. Printed by permission of the author.

"Scroogled," by Cory Doctorow. First appeared in *Radar Online*. Reprinted by permission of the author.

"Strava," by Steven Hayward. Printed by permission of the author.

"Moonless," by Bryan Hurt. Printed by permission of the author.

"The Gift," by Mark Irwin. Printed by permission of the author.

"Testimony of Malik, Israeli Agent, Prisoner #287690," by Randa Jarrar. Printed by permission of the author.

"Buildings Talk," by Dana Johnson. Printed by permission of the author.

"Ladykiller," by Miracle Jones. Printed by permission of the author.

"Sleeping Where Jean Seberg Slept," by Katherine Karlin. Printed by permission of the author.

"Second Chance," copyright © Etgar Keret. Published by arrangement with the Institute of the Translation of Hebrew Literature.

"Drone," by Miles Klee. First appeared in *3:AM Magazine*. Reprinted by permission of the author.

"What He Was Like," by Alexis Landau. First appeared in *Amor Fati*. Reprinted by permission of the author.

"Dinosaurs Went Extinct around the Time of the First Flower," by Kelly Luce. Printed by permission of the author.

"Transcription of an Eye," by Carmen Maria Machado. Printed by permission of the author.

"Our New Neighborhood," by Lincoln Michel. Printed by permission of the author.

"The Witness and the Passenger Train" by Bonnie Nadzam. Copyright © 2014 by Bonnie Nadzam. Reprinted by permission of Georges Borchardt, Inc., on behalf of the author.

"The Transparency Project," by Alissa Nutting. Printed by permission of the author.

"We Are the Olfanauts," by Deji Bryce Olukotun. Printed by permission of the author.

"Making Book," by Dale Peck. First appeared in *Zoetrope: All-Story*. Reprinted by permission of the author.

"Ether," by Zhang Ran. First published in Chinese in *Science Fiction World*; translated by Ken Liu and Carmen Yiling Yan. Reprinted by permission of the author.

"Safety Tips for Living Alone," by Jim Shepard. First appeared in *The Canary Press*. Reprinted by permission of the author.

"Prof," by Chika Unigwe. Printed by permission of the author.

"Terro(tour)istas," by Juan Pablo Villalobos. First published in Portuguese in *Estadão*; translated by Annie McDermott. Reprinted by permission of the author.

"Coyote," by Charles Yu. Printed by permission of the author.